SYSTEMS

A NOVEL

Saleena Karim

Libredux Publishing

SYSTEMS: A Novel

ISBN: 978-0-9571416-0-5

Published by Libredux Publishing, Nottingham
http://www.libredux.com

To My Mother

Part 1

POSSESSIONS

CHAPTER ONE

Since Yesterday

January 2014, Hadescape, New York

The last thing she saw was a tree appearing out of nowhere. She steered furiously to turn the car, but it was too late.

She screamed.

Everything went blank.

When Joanna came to, she had no idea where she was. She could see very little, except for something glowing in the darkness right in front of her face. It looked like a dial. An icy draught hit the back of her neck, sending the cold down her spine and through her entire body. Her face was resting on something very hard and uncomfortable, and her head was pounding.

Joanna groaned and lifted her head. She heard hissing. Slowly she turned her eyes upward, and saw the steering wheel, broken glass, mangled metal, the glowing dials on the dashboard – and then a tree trunk.

'Oh no,' she murmured in dismay, as she remembered what had happened to her.

She wondered how long she'd been unconscious.

Joanna tried to sit up, and a sharp pain tore through her thigh. She sucked in through her teeth and looked down. Her right leg was trapped between the dashboard and her seat. She tried to move it, but it was too painful.

She had to get out.

Joanna took hold of her trapped leg with both hands. She took a deep breath and clamped her teeth shut. Then she pulled as hard as she possibly could.

She cried out. Her leg felt as though the flesh had virtually ripped from the bone, but she got it free. Blood poured from the pulsing gash. She had nothing to tie round the wound.

Joanna leaned against the inner door arm rest with her left palm, placing her right hand flat against the steering wheel to support her weight, and carefully eased herself back up enough to sit upright. She turned her head and looked out of the cracked glass of her window. A full moon slipped in and out of the clouds, but the dense woods all around blocked out much of the light.

She opened the door and tumbled out onto the grass. A few yards in front of her she saw the road. It coursed through the middle of the woods and steel guardrails ran along it. The railing broke at semi-regular intervals. Her car had skidded off the road at precisely one of these intervals, and it had flown straight through the gap and into the tree. A combination of high speed and black ice had done it.

Her pursuers were maybe a couple of miles behind her. She'd lost them by getting off the main road and taking a number of side roads, heading backward long enough to suggest that she was heading to the city centre, and had then turned back toward Wheeler Park. But they would soon work out what she'd done, if they hadn't done already.

Joanna checked her leg again. The bleeding had slowed, but she doubted it could support her weight. Her last resort was to drag herself along the ground using her three working limbs. Sludgy mud, twigs and stones started sticking to the leg. Burning soon surpassed the throbbing. Her fingers numbed, making it difficult for her to feel her way around. She advanced at a measured pace, moving between trees and shrubs as quietly as possible.

Somewhere a car pulled up and two doors slammed shut. She heard voices. They'd found her car.

Joanna crawled behind a shrub.

'Oh Joanna, where are you?'

Listening carefully, she soon heard the crunching of leaves as Adam stalked around somewhere nearby. A short distance away she could also hear the hissing from the car engine.

'Come out, come out, wherever you are,' Adam sang.

Shivering uncontrollably with cold and nerves, she wondered if she should take a chance and move further. She worried about the trail of blood from her leg that could lead him right to her.

'Joanna!' Adam hollered. 'You can't hide forever!'

She stayed absolutely still, praying he wouldn't see her. She waited until she was sure he'd moved away, and then edged onward. Eventually she reached a small clearing where there was no more shelter. Now she was exposed.

'Joanna!'

He was close. In her condition she couldn't get to the safety of the woodland before he reached the clearing. She looked helplessly around for more undergrowth, a log, a rock, anything behind which she could hide. There was none.

Joanna stopped and listened again, conscious of the fact that Adam was no longer shouting. It was too quiet. Panic surged inside her. She hastily moved forward again.

A beam of light suddenly flashed along the ground.

Her blood ran cold.

Adam stepped round and stood in front of her. She looked up at her prospective brother-in-law standing over her, gun in hand. Though the moon shone into the clearing, his features were barely visible. It was just as well, for it would have devastated her to see them. He looked almost identical to the man she loved.

Adam shone the handgun's tactical light in her face.

'Hello … what have we here? Ah, it's you,' he said in a mocking tone. 'I was just thinking to myself, why am I driving myself crazy trying to find her, when she'll probably come *crawling* back to me all by herself? And bam! There you were!'

'Adam, listen to me! I don't have it! I –'

'Shut up!'

He crouched and pinned her left shoulder blade with his knee whilst he rummaged through her coat and trouser pockets.

'Okay, we've established you don't have it,' he said, once he'd searched her. 'So let's talk about your plans. Where were you going after your little rendezvous?'

She pressed her lips together and gazed at the ground.

Adam grabbed her by the chin and put the gun to her head. 'My dear, you really ought to be more cooperative. You see, it's very straightforward. You just give me the information I need, and I grant you your freedom. It's a fair exchange, don't you agree?'

Her fear turned into anger. 'Go to hell!'

'Wrong answer!' he snarled, digging the gun into her temple. 'If you don't talk, I'll …'

Joanna smiled despite the pain. 'You'll what? Kill me?' she said. 'I don't think you will, because if I die, you'll never find out!'

He hesitated. But then he exploded.

'Tell me! Now!'

'No.'

'Then you'll die! And so will David!'

Hearing her fiancé's name from his lips was too much for her. In her mind she could see him curled up on the ground with a bullet in his abdomen; a bullet that Adam had put there.

'He's already dead!' she yelled. 'You killed him, Adam! You killed your own brother! You goddamn murderer!'

Suddenly Adam was silent. He loosened his grip.

Joanna waited for what felt like an eternity. Nothing happened. A cloud shrouded the moon, leaving the gun as the only source of light. His breath quivered as he battled with his feelings. Which would take precedence – the life of an old friend or his mission? She winced, unable to stand the waiting.

'Adam, what happened to you?' she asked in a whisper.

Adam was no longer listening. He stepped back behind her. She heard him shuffle, adjusting his position. He swung the gun. The beam flashed sideways and out of her field of vision.

All in front of her became dark.

'I'm sorry,' he said.

Tears rolled down her face.

'Goodnight Jo,' he said flatly, and pulled the trigger.

Wednesday, 17 September 2042, Alterham, Britain

Elise gasped and sat upright.

Then she breathed a sigh of relief, as she realised that she was safe and sound in the passenger seat of the CID car, outside Wingdale Police Station. She and Detective Sergeant Michael Scott had been about to set off to the scene of an incident when suddenly her mind had entered another time zone. For a short while she'd become Joanna Sinclair. And she'd died.

But she wasn't worried about that.

Mike had been chatting to her when it had happened. He hadn't even switched on the engine. He was frowning now.

'Elise,' he said slowly. 'What did I just say?'

'Er …' She hoped she hadn't missed too much. 'You still don't know what to get Stella for your wedding anniversary?'

'Nope! That was five minutes ago. Right, now tell me honestly – what just happened?'

The fact that she'd just entered a trance in the middle of a conversation wasn't abnormal for her. The officers at Wingdale Police Station were quite used to their detective constable / psychic aide having visions at unexpected moments, and thought nothing of her occasionally odd behaviour. It was part of her work. But the incident she was investigating had only been reported in the last hour, and she hadn't even been to the scene of the crime yet.

Elise couldn't think of a good response. This particular *vision* wasn't connected to any of her cases.

Mike was onto her. 'It wasn't a *vision* vision, was it? … Elise?'

She admitted defeat. 'Oh, all right, it wasn't a *vision* vision. It was a random one!'

'I thought so. That's the second one this week.'

'Mm-hmm …'

It was actually the fourth. Fortunately for her, only two of them had occurred at work. She'd embarrassed herself once in public so far, but she had it covered. People in her neighbourhood thought she suffered from narcolepsy, an uncontrollable sleep disorder. It was the standard explanation for anyone outside police circles.

Another had occurred in her house, where she had no potential witnesses to worry about.

'Of course, those are just the ones I know about,' Mike added, as though he'd read her mind. 'Are you feeling okay? The Hornets inquiry isn't getting –'

'No! Don't you dare start! I'm fine to handle the case. And I'm not telling Johnson anything. I don't need any time off.'

'Are you sure about that? You have a habit of conking out at the worst possible moment.'

'Yes, I know. You don't have to remind me. But they'll stop eventually. They always do.'

Mike rolled his eyes. 'I should've known you'd be like this! But Johnson's bound to notice sooner or later.'

Elise changed the subject. 'Yeah, well … forget about that now. Aren't we supposed to be going somewhere?' she said, looking indicatively at the car clock.

It read 9:02 a.m. Mike's eyes widened.

'Is that the time? We'd better get a move on.'

* * * * * * * * *

It should have taken Michael and Elise under ten minutes to reach the scene of the incident, but traffic diversions on the outskirts of Alterham delayed them by a quarter of an hour. Michael was relieved when they finally got onto the A72.

The A72 was normally a busy country road which led out of Alterham towards the city of Varborough. Traffic Police had blocked off both its lanes following the incident as well as a flyover intersecting it. The flyover itself formed part of a main road leading back into the city. No one had seen what had happened at the flyover itself, though there were several witnesses from below.

Michael and Elise were scheduled to arrive from above. At the point where the Traffic Police had cordoned off the main road stood an officer. Michael showed him his warrant card and the policeman let them pass.

They parked a short distance from the scene. At around seven in the morning a man had apparently leapt off the flyover, eight metres above the ground, and fallen into the path of an oncoming people carrier. The driver hadn't even had the time to react. He'd slammed on the brakes, right after he'd run straight over the man; and subsequently a second car had crashed into the first from behind, trapping the body between the two vehicles. Messy, but that at least was the limit of the damage. Had it happened during the rush hour it could have been much worse.

Miraculously, the man had lived long enough to give his name before he passed out in the ambulance. But he'd died before he could tell the police what had happened to him.

Running a check on his ID card at Wingdale Station, the police had learned that the man was a known drug addict. Interestingly, the man's dealer also happened to be a member of the Hornets, the gang that Wingdale CID was currently investigating. Thereafter the control room had called Detective Inspector Jeremy Paige, just in case the man's death turned out to be suspicious. Michael and Elise were part of the CID callout. The scenes of crime officers, who would have to collect the evidence, hadn't arrived yet, and Detective Chief Inspector Johnson, the senior investigating officer for the Hornets inquiry, was due to arrive later.

One of the uniformed officers had already cordoned off the immediate area with police tape. DI Paige had instructed Traffic to cordon off more of the area than necessary since they didn't want anyone getting close enough to see their psychic aide doing her work. Outside of Alterham Police Force and one or two academic bodies, Elise's psychic abilities were not known to the public.

An ambulance had already taken the two drivers involved to hospital, so only the police remained at the scene. Other than the uniforms, Michael spotted Detective Constable Martin Francis, who'd arrived in a separate CID car with the DI. Martin didn't even need to be there but as an enthusiastic new CID officer he'd come along for the ride.

Michael nudged Elise and grinned. 'I told you Martin would be here. I wish I'd put some money on it now. It was a dead cert.'

'Of course it was,' she mumbled irritably.

'Oh, well. I wouldn't want you to go flat broke.'

She gave him a fake smile.

The DI was busy talking to a uniformed sergeant a short distance away. He looked at Michael and Elise and nodded in the general direction of the spot where the man had jumped off, indicating that he wanted Elise to go ahead. Clearly he wasn't worried about disturbing the scene, which meant that he suspected either accidental death or suicide. Of course the scenes of crime officers would be unhappy if it turned out to be anything else. At least Elise was wearing gloves. She could conduct a psychometric check even with them on.

'What do you reckon?' Michael asked her.

'I'm not sure. What about you?'

'I think Paige might be right.'

Not that he was going to bet on it. That would be in bad taste.

The pair turned to Martin, who pointed to the precise spot where the man had jumped off the flyover onto the A72. Michael stayed with the other officers a short distance from the spot whilst Elise went on ahead.

She slowed down with each step, and looked up and around her. Michael knew she was looking at the aura of the area. She'd described crime scene auras many times as a shadowy depression. This particular cloud was probably still vivid to her, since the incident had only occurred in the past few hours.

Elise reached the flyover railing at the point where the man had jumped off. She took a few slow breaths and placed both hands on it. She turned her head in their direction, but looked straight through them. She frowned. Her steel-grey eyes glazed over and closed. The tension in her brow eased. She was clearing her mind for a procedure Michael had seen countless times.

For the uniformed constable standing with them however, it was a fascinating first. 'What's she doing?'

'She's establishing a psychometric connection,' replied Martin in a low voice, like a wildlife documentary narrator. 'It means she's seeing the crime through the eyes of the offender.'

The uniform was confused. 'But I thought you said that she can't read people's minds.'

'She can't.'

'So how –'

'Trust me – she's not a mind reader.'

Michael didn't contribute, though he could have explained the facts a lot better.

As Elise established the connection they saw a distinct change in her posture. Her limbs slackened, and her head dropped to the side. Her face had the expression of someone sound asleep. Her whole body relaxed to the point that she might collapse at any moment, but she remained standing. Then her brow furrowed. She muttered incoherently and shook her head. She grunted as if in a fever, then suddenly grasped the rail and pulled back.

'My God! She's going to jump!' said the constable, and he stepped towards her.

Michael stopped him.

'No, she's not.'

True to his words, she let go of the rail. She opened her eyes.

The three officers looked at her expectantly.

She gave them a small smile. 'You're right,' she said, apparently unaffected. 'It was suicide.'

* * * * * * * *

Four weeks earlier: Location unknown

Gregory Marshall Kingswell was one of the first to enter the assembly hall. He quickly squeezed his large frame into the seat to avoid drawing attention to himself, and watched apprehensively as ninety members of the clandestine Elite Triumvirate Committee arrived one by one and seated themselves in their designated places. Soon it was only the front stage that remained empty.

The Secretary-General of the MWA had arranged the meeting, but he hadn't named the speaker. The speaker for each meeting was always different, depending on which Committee sector it concerned. It could be a country leader, a corporate CEO, or even a prominent cleric. They represented three very different groups, and their unwitting lower factions often had conflicting interests. In the public eye Gregory sometimes had to act against them, but everything that he did benefited the whole Committee in the end.

Gregory was normally perfectly at home in assembly and board meetings, whether they were on his turf – the Global Agency for Intelligence and Law Enforcement headquarters in Washington – or for any general Mutual World Alliance conference, wherever it happened to be held. But then this was not a GAILE or MWA meeting. The men and women in attendance only came together in one place when there was something very important to discuss; and it was rare indeed to have representatives from all three sectors of the Committee present at once.

They'd not had a meeting of this size in thirty years. Not since the beginning of the twenty-first century, when it had come up against the advent of the information age and its lethal side effect: The global village mentality. Physical borders no longer impeded the flow of information and ideas between peoples; nationalist ideology was no hindrance to the discovery of common values and aspirations. The villagers wanted an end to dictatorships, corporatism, environmental destruction and poverty. People demanded universal democracy, fair trade and green energy for all. They pressured the United Nations to make changes, but it wouldn't do their bidding. They failed to see that this was as it was meant to be. In their infant wisdom they deemed the UN incompetent and corrupt, having too many despotic and undemocratic nations among its members. Countries in the Middle East and Africa experienced civil uprisings. Western countries witnessed mass protests and even riots. People called it the beginning of a global democratic revolution.

The Mutual World Alliance was conceived of the villagers. Unlike the UN, it admitted only bona fide democracies as members. Its member nations pledged that they would develop alternative energy sources, reduce their dependency on oil, and favour one another in international commerce. Their goal was to encourage all remaining nations to also clean up their acts and become proper democracies.

Committee sentinels planted in the MWA did everything to slow its growth and keep the UN alive, with little success. But just when it seemed all was lost, the finest minds of the Committee chanced upon a new power source, and with it came the opportunity to take back control. Today the citizens of the MWA had what they wanted, of sorts; and the Committee was stronger and more prosperous than ever before. For the first time in history they seemed to have permanently warded off the rebellious few who had always fought against them.

That is, until someone put everything in jeopardy.

Gregory was surprised when he saw the speaker for this particular meeting. He'd expected to see the Chairperson of either the Socioeconomic Commission or the Science and Technology Resources Organisation of the MWA.

Instead he got the President of Egypt, Shafiq Al Badri.

Gregory couldn't immediately see why it was Shafiq, but he wouldn't have to wait too long to find out. Unlike its counterparts in the public eye, the Committee never had time for introductory speeches or other diplomatic niceties.

As the president walked onto the stage, his gaze swept across the audience, and he nodded at them in greeting. He made eye contact with no one in particular, least of all Gregory.

Shafiq headed toward the arc shaped oak desk on the front stage and sat down. He looked straight at Gregory and smiled. His expression, though courteous, was only that. Gregory shifted uncomfortably in his seat.

As soon as Shafiq spoke, the reason he was acting as speaker became perfectly clear.

'Gregory,' he said, in a tone that immediately indicated who was on trial and why, 'I hope you're about to assure us that the problem has nothing to do with our old friend Hanif Omar.'

CHAPTER TWO
Evasion

Joanna was thunderstruck. The people in the restaurant were all looking at her, smiling, waiting for her to respond.

With the number of things they were already celebrating, a marriage proposal was definitely something she hadn't expected this particular night. They were celebrating David's new job – his dream job, in fact – as Systems Analyst for the MWA's newly established research body, the Science and Technology Resources Organisation. Joanna had recently landed a job with the MWA herself, at another new body; SECOM, the Socio-Economics Committee. She was one of its first social scientists.

So many times she'd wondered when he'd ask her officially, and how he would do it. There'd never been any question of *if*. Over the past couple of years he'd innocently begun so many sentences with the words 'When we're married ...', or 'Our kids ...' They'd both assumed it was inevitable. She and David had been together for so long that for everyone who knew them it was practically a foregone conclusion.

She gazed tenderly at her suitor now. He'd chosen the old fashioned way: Take the girl to a fancy restaurant, get down on one knee and just ask her. His dark eyes gazed intently, albeit a little nervously, into hers. That warm gentle smile – the one she'd fallen in love with when they were still in university – was on his face. In his right hand he held out a sparkling diamond ring.

She smiled back at him and opened her mouth to speak, but struggled to find her voice. She blushed.

'Yes,' she whispered. It was the best she could do.

Their audience however seemed to have missed it, for they were still watching in anticipation.

David looked around at them, and leaned toward her. 'You'll have to speak a little louder,' he said in her ear. 'It doesn't count if they don't hear you in the back.'

She laughed, and tried again.

'I'm sorry! I don't know why I'm getting all ... oh, it's so silly! ... Yes. Yes, of course I'll marry you!'

The other diners cheered and burst into applause.

With that, David slid the ring onto her finger.

'I thought you were going to run out on me, it took you so long to answer!' he said.

She laughed again. 'As if I'd do that!'

'As if you'd do what, Archer?'

Elise was still in the moment, but she soon stopped laughing. Lots of faces stared at her, but why were they all so familiar? And what were Mike and Martin doing here?

Suddenly she became alert. She was in the incident room, in the middle of a briefing. That meant –

Oh, no.

The voice that had just addressed her belonged to DCI Johnson. The officers were in the middle of a brief on the day's targets for the Hornets inquiry. She had no idea when she'd lost track, but all eyes were on her now. Had the DCI not been in the room, the other officers might have been making fun of her; but since he was, they were all deadpan, and silent.

Elise turned her eyes slowly towards Johnson's desk. He sat tall, stiff as a board in his brown suit, his stocky arms folded, with a stern expression beneath his coarse grey beard.

She was barely able to look his way. 'Sorry sir?'

Johnson sighed and got out of his chair.

'Can I have a quick word with you outside please, Archer?'

He never addressed anyone by their first name.

Elise glanced at Mike, who shrugged helplessly. The other officers in the room politely turned their collective attention to their computer screens, even though they weren't using them.

Reluctantly she followed the DCI out of the room. He closed the door behind him and led her a few steps down the corridor so no one might hear him from the other side.

He looked her straight in the eye. 'Now then,' he said in an admonishing tone, 'I'm assuming that what happened in there was *not* a post-connection?'

That was stating the obvious. The man she'd connected to at the flyover the previous morning was dead. She could only retain a psychic *post-connection* with someone who was alive.

'No sir,' she admitted.

Johnson's next words were almost an exact echo of Mike's from the week before. 'That makes it the seventh random vision in two weeks. You know what that means.'

'Yes sir,' she said, but it was actually the twelfth; and that was just counting the ones that Mike knew about. Still, a tally of seven was more than enough to warrant concern.

'If there is one more, Archer – and I do mean even *one* more any time soon – you will take mandatory leave. Is that clear?'

'Yes sir.'

It was clear all right. He was giving her a minimal grace period so she wouldn't be able to bargain with him later. They both knew she'd probably have another vision long before the week was out.

In fact, it was a dead cert.

'You do realise,' said Stella that evening, 'that if you actually bothered to take some time out and decorate like I keep telling you to, you might lower your stress levels.'

Stella was the only person in the world who knew about Joanna Sinclair. She'd been watching Elise go through flashback floods for nineteen odd years, since the time that they'd lived together in a children's home. The floods tended to occur when Elise was feeling stressed or overworked. On this occasion however, she didn't know the reason for it. Not that knowing would have made any difference, because there was nothing she could do to stop it. The flashbacks would fizzle out in their own time, either in a few days, or at worst, a few weeks.

Her friend looked around the living room with a wrinkled nose.

'I'm surprised at you, Elise,' she said, fiddling with an amethyst talisman around her neck. 'You're in the best possible position to understand what I'm talking about. Your house should be a sanctuary of free-flowing energy. But what do you have? A feng shui nightmare, that's what!'

Stella should really have been the psychic. She was much more enthusiastic about all things paranormal; auras, chakras, astral projection, reincarnation, extrasensory perception, the lot. A qualified Reiki healer and acupuncturist, she'd been running a complementary medicine health centre for years, and it was very successful, thank you very much. More recently Stella had also expanded her services to include feng shui consultancy; interior design with a spiritual twist.

She was looking for victims to practice on.

'You're not touching my house.'

'Honestly! You're worse than Mike. He kicked up such a fuss when I wanted to redecorate our house! "I don't want to live in a temple," he said! But is our house overrun with candles and incense sticks? No. What are you looking at me like that for? He hasn't once complained about my choice of décor.'

'He wouldn't dare.'

Stella ignored her. 'Just you wait! One of these days when you're not looking I'm going to sort this place out!' Then she became a little more serious. 'Of course if you really don't want to decorate, you could always tell CID the truth – about the flashbacks, I mean.'

Here we go, thought Elise. 'Stella –!'

'Then you wouldn't have to keep up this daft pretence about psychic stress and random visions and you probably wouldn't be sent home so often. And who knows? CID might even help you find out what happened to Joanna.'

Stella had never approved of Elise's decision to keep the flashbacks a secret. She'd long had a theory that Joanna's final experiences and the emotions they'd evoked had transferred to Elise, resulting in psychological trauma. The flashbacks were occurring because Elise's subconscious was trying to remember something about Joanna's murder, something that she'd forgotten in her present life. If she took the trouble to find out what it was and dealt with it, the flashbacks would probably stop. To be fair it wasn't a bad theory, and in fact unbeknown to her friend, Elise had tested it a few years earlier. But she hadn't liked what she'd found. These days Elise kept her secrets entirely to herself.

'That's assuming they'd even believe me.'

'They know you're a psychic. Why shouldn't they believe you have a past life too?'

Impeccable logic.

Elise sighed. 'How many times have we talked about this? It was hard enough just to convince the force that I was psychic. Had I added the flashbacks to the mix they would have written me off as someone with serious issues: "Oh, poor thing, she's attention-seeking! She still can't handle the fact that she was abandoned as a baby!" Besides, even if they did believe me,' she added for good measure, 'it'd make no difference. They'd still send me home every time the flashbacks started.'

Stella went quiet. Her hazel eyes were staring upward. Elise knew what she was thinking.

'Don't say it.'

'What?' said Stella innocently.

'You know what! You're going to tell me I'm in denial.'

'Did I say anything?'

'You didn't have to.'

Stella reverted to a safer subject.

'Oh, for crying out loud! You haven't even changed the wallpaper since you moved in!'

'I don't have the time.'

'You will, once the DCI puts you on mandatory leave,' retorted Stella, with a smirk.

* * * * * * * * *

Gregory stood on the podium and forced a smile.

Ten or more microphones were crammed onto the lectern under his nose. He looked down at the hundred or so men and women on the floor, many with mikes, and lots of cameramen, causing a hubbub as they talked among themselves, waiting for him to start.

Riffraff.

He nodded at the press officer to indicate he was ready. The press officer called for quiet. Gregory cleared his throat and began the speech he'd rehearsed and memorised during his ritual morning workout at the gym.

'Good afternoon, ladies and gentlemen. For the past few weeks GAILE's Intelligence Office has been investigating claims that the late Doctor William Palmerton was once involved in an illegal research programme to develop and test methods of interrogation using nanotechnology.

'These were serious claims, especially as the man accused of this crime was one of the founding members of the MWA's Science and Technology Resources Organisation. As you know, these allegations were made by an anonymous person who tipped off the press. This person claimed to have proof to support the allegations, but neither did he or she tell the press who it was Doctor Palmerton supposedly worked for, nor did he or she come forward with the proof. Nevertheless we took the claims seriously and investigated them; and we can now confirm that they are false. The press have cooperated with us but we have not been able to find the person responsible for the claims.

'Since there is insufficient evidence we have decided not to continue with this investigation. Now we ask that the press leave a dead man in peace, and to respect the privacy of his family and friends, all of whom have always maintained his innocence.'

The ladies and gentlemen of the press were watching him expectantly, waiting for him to open the floor to questions.

'That is all. Thank you,' he said, and stepped off the lectern.

Realising he was trying to make a sharp exit, they all began shuffling forward with a barrage of questions.

'Mr Kingswell, do you intend to keep searching for the person who tipped off the press?'

'Is it true that you suspect a GAILE operative was responsible for making the allegations?'

'Can you confirm sir whether you have detained one of Doctor Palmerton's former assistants?'

'Why do you think anyone would want to make defamatory claims against a deceased scientist?'

'Mr Kingswell, would you like to comment on recent claims that the STRO has in the past funded a number of research projects that are deemed unlawful under the terms of the International Human Rights Convention?'

The press officer waved a shooing hand at the crowd. 'The director of GAILE is not taking any questions today,' he said, and he quickly ushered Gregory off the podium and out through a large door situated behind the stage.

* * * * * * * * *

It was seven minutes past one in the morning when the staffs' pagers sounded.

None of the three nurses in the room – except one – had expected the call. All of the nurses moaned about the graveyard shifts, but in fact they were generally uneventful. The patients slept soundly most nights without making a disturbance, and the staff spent their time gossiping in the coffee room.

The three checked their pagers.

'Oh no, it's Timothy,' said one nurse, the senior.

Timothy had given them a fair amount of trouble lately, but he couldn't help it. He was in one of his delusional phases.

This time he was also suicidal.

'He's refused to eat for, what? Two days?' said the second nurse. 'Maybe he's finally given up.'

The senior sighed and got up. 'I doubt it. Shall I go?'

The third nurse had been very quiet tonight, but he spoke now. 'No,' he said with a cracked voice. 'I – I'll go.'

The senior smiled and he sat back down. 'Aw, thanks Ben. Listen – why don't you take up some leftovers from the kitchen just in case, save you a trip?

Ben nodded and left the room. He walked straight past the kitchen and made an unscheduled detour to the staff toilet. He relieved himself and at the sink he washed his sweaty face with cold water. He looked at his chubby double in the mirror.

'You're in deep, Ben,' he muttered. He knew what he was supposed to do next. He'd been through it mentally dozens of times. He'd had it down to a fine art. But now that the time had come for real, he wasn't sure that he could go through with it. If he got caught, he would no doubt be sacked and probably banned from working in a hospital again.

But it had to be done. He owed it to his friend.

Now was his best chance. He was one of only three nurses on duty. The others were in the coffee room, taking it easy. No one else was around except for a couple of security guards.

Ben exhaled resolutely and left the toilet. He headed towards the lift past reception and took a security card from his left trouser pocket. He glanced up at a closed-circuit camera positioned adjacent to the lift. It watched him swipe his security card next to the lift and enter. He put the card in his right pocket and pressed a button for the third floor, the furthest it would go.

He tapped his right trouser pocket nervously. Aside from the security card, there was a different card inside this pocket, one that shouldn't even have been in his possession. Now he was going to hand it over to someone who was never supposed to possess it under any circumstances.

On the third floor he walked down the corridor as calmly as he could, not wanting to rouse suspicion on the tape they would surely examine later on. At the end outside the common room door, a security guard sat on a plastic chair reading a newspaper.

'Hello Ben,' he said when he saw the nurse. 'Timothy being a nuisance again, is he?'

Ben smiled vaguely and went past him. He quickly made his way through the common room. The door at the back end offered the only access point – barring the fire exit – to the fifth floor. It was permanently locked to all except staff. Ben swiped his card at the door and went through to the lift on the other side.

The lift had only one button, since it only went one way. Ben pushed it and arrived a few seconds later at the fifth floor. This ward had three rooms and only one patient. The doors to the rooms were made of solid steel. The only way to see inside the rooms was via a security monitor. Ben switched on the small monitor next to the middle door. It showed that the patient was curled up on the floor in the dark, next to his bedside table where the distress alarm button was. His back faced the camera.

Ben switched on the light from the outside and knocked on the door three times. The patient didn't move.

The nurse slowly reached for a panel next to the door and pressed the intercom button.

'Timothy,' he said, in a flat tone. 'Are you all right?'

Still the man didn't move.

'Timothy?'

Ben pressed a different intercom button.

'Er … Ben here,' he said, trying to sound normal. 'I think we might have a problem. Brooks seems to have collapsed.'

'*I'll be right up,*' was the reply.

Ben was following security protocol to the letter.

He immediately pressed the room's intercom button again. This time he called out the patient's preferred name.

'Peter?'

The camera recorded that the patient was unresponsive.

Everything was going like clockwork.

Sweat began forming again on Ben's brow. It was his turn to be still this time, as he waited for another nurse to join him.

It was the senior nurse who eventually came through the door. In one hand he had a medicine bag, inside which was a syringe containing a sedative drug just in case. During his delusional phases the patient had a tendency to lash out.

He glanced at the monitor. 'You sure he's unconscious?'

'I think so,' said Ben.

The senior nurse pressed the intercom button. 'Timothy?'

The patient moved slightly.

'All right, I think he's just weakened from not eating.' Then he looked at Ben. 'Weren't you supposed to bring him some food?'

'Couldn't find any leftovers,' he mumbled.

The senior sighed. 'Go on then, open the door.'

Ben slid his security card through a scanner at the door. The door unlocked with a loud curt bleep.

He slid the card inside his right pocket to join the other. The setup was complete.

He pushed the door open and the nurses stepped inside cautiously. Ben was wary of the security camera in the corner of the room capturing their every action. He didn't dare look up.

They stood over the patient. His eyes were closed.

'I'll check on him,' said Ben.

The senior nodded.

Ben swallowed hard and knelt down beside Peter.

'Timothy? Can you hear me?' he said, his heart thumping so hard he thought the senior would hear it.

The patient didn't stir.

Ben braced himself. He leaned down and pressed his fingers against the patient's neck.

The pulse was good and strong.

The patient sprang to life. He grabbed Ben's arm and threw him off. Ben made no effort to resist the push, and landed on his back.

Before Ben could even sit up, Peter was on his feet.

Startled, the senior dropped the bag and hastily reached for the pager on his belt.

Peter snatched the pager from him and threw it out of the door into the corridor.

Ben sat upright. He noticed the medicine bag on the floor.

So did Peter.

'Ben!' shouted the senior.

Ben reached for the medicine bag. Peter kicked it. The bag shot across the floor and under the bed, out of reach.

The senior tried to tackle the patient, but Peter shook him off easily. Ben watched helplessly as Peter delivered a powerful blow to the man's gut, seized his face with one hand and slammed his skull back against the wall.

The senior crumpled to the floor.

Before Ben knew it, Peter had leapt on top of him and taken hold of his throat with both hands. But his ice blue eyes were mild, unthreatening. His grip on Ben's throat was equally mild.

'Don't hurt me,' said Ben, although he knew he was in no danger of getting hurt.

'I never harm the innocent,' replied Peter.

The camera was recording him from behind. It didn't catch the grateful look he gave Ben.

Then without warning, Peter let go of Ben's throat and punched his jaw hard, setting his head in a spin.

'Argh!'

Ben hadn't anticipated this particular move.

Peter took the opportunity to search Ben's right-hand pocket. The camera recorded that he took the nurse's security card.

He got up and left.

Still dazed, Ben slowly sat upright again, holding his jaw. The senior nurse sat propped up against the wall, head to one side like a marionette, mumbling incoherently.

Somewhere out of his sight, he heard someone yell in surprise at the sight of his friend. Sounds of a scuffle followed. Then the security alarm began ringing.

A few moments later, a security guard rushed into the room to see to him and the senior.

CHAPTER THREE
Painting the Walls

Elise gazed over the living room on Monday morning and clicked her tongue in annoyance. Another flashback on Friday afternoon had sealed her fate, just as she'd known it would, and this time Johnson had sent her home for a whole week. If Elise hadn't protested so much he would have made it two.

She was supposed to be forgetting about work and decorating the living room. She'd been living in the house for two years, but she'd never quite put her personal mark on it. The living room walls still had pale blue wallpaper, there from the day she'd moved in, and she was happy to let them stay that way. She simply wasn't a house-proud person, and she'd found herself becoming bored just trying to decide what colour to paint the walls. She hated to think that she was wasting time at home when she should be out doing her job. Unfortunately there was an obstacle – in the form of a bet – preventing her from cutting her holiday short. The bet was between her and Mike, but she had a feeling that his other half was behind it. Stella could be very devious when she wanted to be.

Still, she secretly wished she could get Stella's help. The conditions were that she had to work alone, and she had to get it done in a week. She couldn't even ring Mike to check up on what was happening with the Hornets case. He would only ask her about the decorating if she rang him; and besides, DCI Johnson had already warned her not to bother calling in no matter what happened whilst she was off. Now she had to make do with gleaning little bits of information from whatever they released for the public on news channels and in the newspapers. It was no substitute for being at Wingdale CID. The press didn't account for every little thing that happened on the streets of Alterham, and they weren't reporting on the Hornets case, which was after all a long-term covert police investigation. The press would get the full details only when the police had finally succeeded in bringing down one of the city's biggest gangs.

That reminded her; she wanted to read the paper. She sat down on a sofa covered in an old bed sheet, picked up Monday's newspaper lying on the armrest and checked the headlines.

Undetected Fraud Estimates at Highest Rate in Ten Years

'Not my department.'

City Councillors Eating Lobster at Our Expense

'Are we really surprised?'
Finding nothing of interest on the front page, Elise took a quick look through the next couple of pages.

More Cuts in Education Funding

'Boredom' a Leading Cause of Suicide

Finally, beneath that headline were a couple of stories that were more interesting.

Body Found

She read through the first few lines.

A body found in Plumbwood has been identified as that of a man who was a member of a local gang. He cannot be named for legal reasons.

Elise's stomach fluttered. It was a psychic indication that there was something important about the story. Could the victim be a member of the Hornets? *Unlikely*, she thought. Plumbwood was on the outskirts of the city. The Hornets operated in the city centre and surrounding estates, within Wingdale's area of jurisdiction.

He died of a single stab wound. A spokesperson for Jaythorpe Police has said that the man died sometime between ...

The rest of the article was about the problem of gangs in and around Alterham. It mentioned nothing about the suspects in the case, which meant that they were probably members of a rival gang. This also explained the placement of the story on the fourth page. No one really cared about the death of a criminal.

She moved on.

Psychiatric Patient Still Missing
Concern is growing for the safety of a mentally ill patient who escaped from Roseleigh Psychiatric Hospital in Jaythorpe in the early hours of Sunday. The man, who cannot be named for legal reasons, is thought to suffer from schizophrenia and could be dangerous. Police have asked the public not to approach the man, as he has a history of violence. He has been described as ...

Her stomach fluttered a second time. She doubted that the missing patient or the gang killing was causing the feeling. In all honesty she was probably just looking for an excuse to get away from the decorating. Whether or not the killing had a link with the Hornets gang, the body had turned up in the wrong area. Plumbwood happened to be in Jaythorpe Station's division, so it was their inquiry. Come to think of it, so was the missing patient.

Elise sighed and put down the paper. At least she didn't seem to be missing too much at Wingdale. She stared at the wall for a minute, and tried half-heartedly to imagine it in different colours. However she lacked the domestic creativity, and moreover she lacked the patience.

Time for some fresh air, she thought. She went to the hallway, got her coat from the closet under the stairs, and left for a run.

Elise enjoyed watching the world go by whenever she had the chance. The reason was something only she and perhaps a few individuals could appreciate – being able to feel the pulsing energy of people around her. It was a unique experience; an ample reminder that life is precious. Sometimes she detected the energy of thousands of people, even from inside their homes if she chose, though she always avoided lingering upon it for fear of psychic overload. She could also see that energy – better known as the aura – as a very faint light, but only if she focused on it. She was aware of the notion that aura colours indicated personality types, but in her experience most auras were similar from person to person; and in her specialised line of work, black and red were the main two colours she saw on a regular basis.

Cars whizzed by on the main road. Present day electric motors were much quieter than their petrol-fuelled predecessors, though the excessive white noise – electromagnetic radiation – coming from their engines made her head feel fuzzy.

On the hills to the east she saw the line of windmills that supplied the town's electricity via both wind and solar power. Eight of the nine turbines consisted of the typical tall white pole with three blades; and the blades were covered in shiny black photovoltaic cells. The central windmill was much older than the others, being an old paper-making mill from the sixteenth century. Alterham County Council had granted its conversion into a wind turbine early in the twenty-first century, mainly in order to appease a public that considered wind turbines an eyesore. The other eight turbines had appeared much later, after the public had become more environment-conscious, to establish a wind farm. The old mill however still had its traditional brick tower structure as well as its original white sails – after which Wingdale was said to have been named – for posterity. It housed its photovoltaic cells on the dome cap.

Seeing the soft aura of the natural surrounding hills every day, Elise had often wondered how petrol-fuelled pollution must have affected it. As things stood now, global oil dependency was at an all-time low. Crude oil reserves were limited for partial use in aircraft and for some areas of the chemical industry. The world was presently tackling its energy demands with diverse green alternatives, including biofuels, solar and wind energy sources, and, most controversially, nuclear energy, although the STRO was exploring new pollutant-free fusion options involving plasma.

She reached the end of the road and turned round, but she didn't go back home the whole afternoon. By the time she'd finished her run, had lunch at the local coffee shop, popped over to the grocers, and been to see how her elderly neighbour was after her recent heart operation, there wasn't enough time left in the day to resume the decorating.

What a shame.

* * * * * * * * *

The director of GAILE sat back in his chair and switched on the datafile on his desk. It was a few inches wide and tall, and as thick as a greetings card. With considerably lower data storage capacity and functionality than an average ebook reader, it was more like a memory stick with a screen and inbuilt scanner. The datafile was used in offices and wherever it was more convenient to have copies of documents or photographs on something other than a computer or paper.

Shafiq's words kept echoing in Gregory's mind.

You know that this problem is threatening the balance, don't you?

Of course he knew. Gregory hadn't appreciated Shafiq's tone, though he understood the man's concerns. After all, the Egyptian Prime Minister had not only been speaking for his own sector. The crisis affected the whole Committee.

Presently the members of the Committee knew only that there was a traitor in their midst. It was obvious that it was someone from GAILE, because he – Gregory assumed it was a he – had taken classified information directly from GAILE's files and forwarded parts of it virtually word-for-word to the press. In doing so, the traitor had placed a deceased scientist at the centre of a serious crime – a scientist who was also an ex-MWA employee. It had caused a public outcry, forcing GAILE to investigate.

More than a month had passed since then, and whilst GAILE had assured the public that the rumours were unfounded, the Committee was still on the hunt for the traitor. Though the traitor hadn't directly implicated either GAILE or the MWA, not even as the source of his information, he'd demonstrated that he could do a lot of damage. Gregory had yet to determine why the traitor had opted for a strategy that so blatantly alerted GAILE to his existence. Either he was very stupid, or he had an ulterior motive. Gregory doubted it was the former.

The Committee blamed Gregory for the whole affair because it had revealed two major oversights on GAILE's part. Although Gregory had not even been a GAILE officer at the time of the first oversight, it was today's GAILE – the one under his authority – that was responsible for the second, namely a failure to spot the existence of the traitor prior to the leak. The Committee might not have been so concerned about the traitor had the first oversight not come to light; and that too would never have surfaced if it hadn't been for the investigation into the source of the leak. In fact the traitor's actions and the first oversight had no obvious connection, except for the name Doctor William Palmerton.

The intercom buzzed.

'Come in.'

Gregory studied the agent as he delivered his latest status report. Admittedly he'd had his doubts about the Canadian import. Not quite twenty-eight years old, he was rather young and inexperienced by Intelligence standards, and Gregory had doubted his suitability for a leading role in this investigation. But Lloyd had come highly recommended by former SECOM chairperson Robert Benedict. Gregory was beginning to see why. Within a matter of a few weeks he'd not only uncovered the fact that the Project subjects were still alive, but he'd also compiled a list of individuals fitting their criteria across the States, positively identified one of them as a surviving Project subject and had brought him in for questioning. He'd even detained one of Palmerton's former assistants. Agent Aaron Lloyd had an air of quiet confidence and had demonstrated the command and competence of a seasoned operative. All that remained was for him to achieve the most important objective, which was to identify the person or persons who had leaked Palmerton's past activities to the press.

'We had to let him go,' said the agent, referring to the Project subject they'd had in custody on and off for the past week. 'But we're keeping him under surveillance. We'll try talking to him again when we've found the others.'

'How is the search coming along?' asked Gregory.

'We're still looking. We might find them more quickly if Ms Weston would tell us where the other surrogates are.'

Now Gregory asked the question which was foremost on his mind, and to which he already knew the answer.

'Are you any closer to finding the informant?'

'No sir. Agent Kash is working through our remaining suspects. No one is entirely ruled out as yet.'

Gregory looked at him indifferently. 'Come and see me as soon as there are any developments.'

'I'll have Kash report to you directly,' said Lloyd.

The agent left and Gregory glanced again at the datafile in his hand. Lloyd had given it to him in the first week of the investigation. It contained a list of individuals from various positions of authority in government, law enforcement and research institutions. Most of them were Palmerton's former colleagues and associates. Every single one of them also happened to be members of the Committee.

He chuckled. For all his fine qualities, the young operative had failed to produce a single credible suspect.

Gregory switched off the datafile and threw it into his desk drawer, amongst such important items as his stationary.

CHAPTER FOUR
Catharsis

Perched at the top of the scaffolding with his legs crossed, he focused his thoughts on emptiness. This was the only way he could distance himself from the droning energy of the people.

His eyes were closed, and his body perfectly at rest. His pale blue T-shirt and black jeans dripped constantly as the rain pelted down. Yet he was oblivious to the cold and the wet. His mind simply sought the peace.

Most would find it difficult to believe that a man of such quiet composure could at the next moment be possessed with wild, irrepressible energy. However it was as natural to him as the weather. The red ribbon that he wore permanently round his head symbolised that he was different. His self-appointed title, the Peace Man, was a testament to his mission. No one knew it but him.

Doctor Hargreaves believed that his patient's sociophobia was just a part of his illness, but the Peace Man knew better. He felt utter contempt for the state of the human race. He'd been free for just three days, but in the world of the so-called sane he'd found only what he'd known all along. Hell was earth. The people had vacuous minds, empty souls. They weren't even *alive*. They merely existed from the cradle to the coffin. They were not human beings, but androids tagged with serial numbers, whose sole purpose was to work and make never-ending payments for the things they would never own. And in all their mindless running around, they had no time to stop and think; certainly not before their bodies wore out and forced them into the death before death. The have-nots of the modern world were not the unemployed; they were the unenlightened. They knew nothing of their potential, their immortality. Of course it wasn't entirely their fault. They were victims of the ultimate ruse.

The Peace Man vowed to eradicate the real culprits – those parasitic elitists. They readily betrayed humanity to indulge their own interests. They could serve no purpose in a peaceful world. For millennia they had divided the people into classes of every kind, economic, political and religious. In the past century or so they'd taken the game to the global level, setting up entire nations of haves versus nations of have-nots. They had set up their looting expeditions on the back of wars against people of the wrong nationality, or ideology, or faith. But in recent decades, for reasons that were not clear to him, they'd changed the rules. Most nations of the world were presently united under the banner of the Mutual World Alliance – the body of so-called democratic nations formed during the World Democratic Revolution. He still remembered when the MWA was little more than a monument to the times, its future undecided. Since then it had supplanted the United Nations. Resources from the old have-not nations were no longer controlled by soldiers fighting contrived wars, but by bureaucrats imposing ambiguous international regulations. *They* claimed it was a better world. And to ninety-nine point nine percent of the people, it no doubt seemed that way. But it was all an illusion.

The Peace Man knew, for he felt it everywhere.

From somewhere inside his head he began to hear a soft whistle; a high pitch sound, a bit like ringing in his ears. He heard it every night as he went to sleep, and each time he meditated. It was the sound of his intuitive radar. The whistle eventually faded from his conscious awareness, as he became habituated to it.

Peter remained meditating for almost an hour, by which time it had stopped raining. He opened his eyes and gazed into the distance. He saw nothing before him but buildings, layer after layer of concrete stretching as far as he could see and beyond. He inhaled deeply, and felt the cacophonic energy of the people inside those buildings, all carrying on with their pointless little lives. He resented their ignorance. Part of him pitied them, but the resentment was stronger. Things might change if the world knew the truth, but that depended on whether he could find his old comrades. Without them he would have to do it the hard way. He would have to kill them all.

He stood up, balancing on the narrow scaffolding beam easily as he didn't fear the height. With his arms outstretched he hung his head low, allowing his long brown curly hair to drop in front of his face and hide his taut expression. Suddenly he thrust his head back to reveal the brilliant red stripe across his forehead, and he stared at the evening sky, in communion with the heavens.

Once he returned to the ground, the Peace Man retreated to a derelict residential estate and took refuge next to a large skip near a row of flats. He waited awhile for the excess water in his clothes to drain away. Then he closed his eyes and began to concentrate, probing the energy fields in the surrounding area for a sign of a mind belonging to a criminal. It wasn't difficult as he was in an area of the city that had a high crime rate. He soon felt the hairs on the back of his neck stand on end, in response to an energy field – or rather, a field with an absence of energy. He looked out from behind the bin. All was yellow and orange under the streetlamps. A man came down the street in his direction.

Peter got up and headed towards the man. The man had a rough face with telling lines on his forehead. His life force was devoid of light, typical of a corrupted soul. Peter hunched his shoulders slightly to make himself look vulnerable, and walked straight in his path, just as he was about to pass an alley. He held out his bony hand.

'Have you any change, friend?' he asked meekly.

The man scowled. 'Get lost!'

He tried to barge past. The Peace Man slid behind him, grabbed his left arm and forced it round his back.

The man grunted in both surprise and pain.

Bloody images of baseball bats and smashed skulls flashed inside Peter's head. He ignored them.

'You have lived a worthless life, friend,' he said in the man's ear, 'but you will die for a good cause.'

He dragged the man into the alley and pushed him over. Taking a large dagger from his back pocket, he strode towards him. Without a moment's hesitation he jumped forward in a motion to fall on top of the man, holding the dagger high with both hands.

'No!'

The man tried to get out of the way. The Peace Man brought the dagger down with all his strength and plunged it into his heart.

The look of sheer terror remained on the man's face. He had himself been a murderer, having battered another man to death for reasons unknown. Whether or not he'd evaded the judicial system, it didn't matter. The Peace Man had punished him for his crime.

Peter wiped his hands on the man's coat. The dagger that he'd used – taken from his first mark – was very sharp and it had sunk in deep, making a relatively clean wound in the man's chest, but some blood had splattered onto Peter's hands. After cleaning it off he searched the man's clothing and found his wallet.

He noticed the man's ID card inside and paused. As a man living in isolation his entire life, Peter had never possessed his ID card, but most other people had theirs from birth. The cards held not only details such as date of birth and residence, but also information on medical records and work history, and even criminal records. An officer of the law could arrest anyone who failed to produce a valid card when asked.

Peter tossed the card aside. It was useless to him. He needed a normal credit card, or preferably cash. He found some of the latter inside the man's wallet. As he took it, he noticed the man wore an expensive looking watch. He took it off and put it for the time being on his own wrist. Finally he removed the dagger from the body. He wiped the blade and slid it back into his pocket.

He reached into another pocket and took out a small notepad, damp round the edges, tore off the top page and scrunched it up.

He put the paper ball inside the man's gaping mouth before he turned and walked away.

Two down, two to go. Bloodshed wouldn't be necessary after that. Soon enough, he would have *their* attention too.

He decided to return to the construction site, where plans to build an expensive new playhouse were already underway. He had enjoyed the tranquillity he had found up on the scaffolding, and it was there that he would spend the rest of the night.

* * * * * * * * *

'Goodnight Jo,' said Adam flatly, and pulled the trigger.

Elise gasped and sat upright.

For a moment she was disorientated. Then she recognised the partly stripped walls of her living room.

She'd been taking a short break from the decorating that morning, sitting on the sofa and watching the news, when suddenly her mind had returned to that cold winter night in Hadescape, where Joanna had died. She'd lost count of the number of times it had happened in the past week.

'Damn it!' she said, realising that she'd missed the report she'd been looking out for.

Why Elise kept having these flashbacks was a mystery, and frankly she didn't want to know. For years she'd had mixed feelings about her past life. On the one hand she'd been curious to know why Joanna was in the car that night, what it was that Adam wanted from her, and why he killed the poor woman. On the other, an inexplicable dread always filled her whenever she tried to remember anything. For most of her life the dread had overruled the curiosity, and she'd listened to her instinctual feelings not to pursue the matter. Then a few years earlier during a particularly bad flashback flood, she'd had the silly notion that Stella was right; she should do some research into Joanna's life, learn about her death, and perhaps finally lay her ghost to rest. She regretted it. Having encountered a special security seal preventing her access to Joanna's personal files, Elise discovered that contrary to her blatantly biased assumptions, her previous incarnation was not the innocent victim she'd always seemed to be. Realising her mistake, she'd decided then and there to leave the past well alone, and never speak of it to anyone, not even Stella. If she could have her own way now, she would have Joanna's existence wiped from her memory altogether.

Elise pointed the remote control at the TV screen hanging on the wall and hit the live rewind button. She was anxious to know about the psychiatric patient whom she'd read about on Monday.

Apparently he was a suspect for two murders in the city. The first murder had occurred on Monday night in Plumbwood, but since the victim had belonged to a gang, the press had assumed it was down to gang rivalry. The case of the missing psychiatric patient had not taken priority until Tuesday morning, when the press had reported the second murder, this time in an estate around four miles east of her own house. At this point, the police had said they were looking for him in connection with both incidents, and that they were following up on some leads.

The police were not providing all the details to the press as it might hinder their investigation. But this was definitely a major inquiry. Elise had been watching the morning news when one of the blasted flashbacks had interrupted her.

She finally found the right story and played it back.

Police have launched a serial murder inquiry after it emerged that a string of murders across Alterham may be linked. The first body was discovered on Monday morning and so far two more have been recovered.

It was official. Alterham had a serial killer, one who was committing his crimes at the frightening rate of one person a night.

The latest victim's body was found in Bolton in the early hours of this morning. None of the victims have been named for legal reasons.

She raised her brow. Bolton was a suburb right next to Wingdale, and part of its policing division. With the bodies turning up all over the city, every division in Alterham had to be involved by now.

Police are continuing their search for a man they want to question in connection with these incidents. Timothy Brooks hasn't been seen since the weekend when he escaped from Roseleigh Psychiatric Hospital in Jaythorpe. The police are appealing for any information ...

Elise had been tempted to phone Wingdale several times since Wednesday. The only thing stopping her so far, other than her bet with Mike and Johnson's order, was a minor technicality: Neither of the first two bodies had turned up in Wingdale's division.

Now the situation was different. In terms of crime scenes, the inquiry had just entered her territory. Wingdale would have set up an inquiry team to support Jaythorpe after Tuesday night's murder. If she'd still been at work, she would have been part of it.

Elise suspected Johnson didn't want to involve her because of the suspect's psychological profile. She had dealt with serious crimes involving mentally ill individuals before, and she'd found it difficult to establish a stable psychometric connection with them. Johnson probably thought that it would be better to leave her out of the case rather than risk aggravating her psychic stress.

She looked miserably at the walls. In five days – including the weekend – she'd managed only to strip two of them and partially pull out a ceiling light. She'd brought home two small cans of paint for testing along with some brushes, but she still couldn't decide on the wall colour. Green or yellow: Who cared? She certainly didn't. All week she'd spent as much time as possible away from the house, despite the flashbacks, itching for the holiday to end. One or two of her neighbours had been round to ask her how she was coping with her narcolepsy; otherwise she'd had no decent company, since both of her closest friends were off limits. This was the longest, most tedious week of her life, and it was only Wednesday. She couldn't believe there were still four days to go.

Four whole days!

She sighed at how much her next action was going to hurt her pride – as well as her pocket – and went to the phone in the hallway. She consoled herself with the thought that she couldn't really get the decorating done on her own in four days anyway and dialled the number for Wingdale police station.

DCI Hugh Johnson was not, as far as she could tell, especially surprised to hear her voice at the other end of the line. Elise explained that she'd seen the news reports on the serial murders, and that she had little to do in the house so she might as well return to duty. He asked her whether she was well enough, and she lied and told him she was much better. At best she'd hoped to convince him to let her come back the next day, but to her surprise he asked her to come in that afternoon for a briefing. It wasn't often that a constable got to attend a meeting in the DCI's office. She had a sneaking suspicion about the reason.

Elise hung up and looked at her watch. It was almost half past twelve. There was enough time to grab some lunch and coffee. She shot the TV with the remote to switch it off, and stepped over the paint cans and brushes on the floor. She hesitated at the door and took a last look at the partly stripped walls and the furniture covered in old bed sheets. The decorating would have to wait.

Elise left her small suburban house in Hayfield wearing taupe grey trousers, a white blouse and a light grey wool jacket, as there were no uniform requirements in the Criminal Investigations Department, and her black hair tied in a ponytail. She got into her car and drove off to Wingdale Police Station.

She arrived just before two o'clock, and headed straight to the second floor of the station. As she hurried along the corridor towards DCI Johnson's office she heard a voice behind her.

'Elise!'

She stopped and turned to face Martin coming out of the CID office. Wearing a light grey suit, tie and shiny black shoes, he had the classic appearance of a keen and squeaky clean officer. He'd always wanted to join the CID, and even as a PC he'd tried to get himself into as many inquiries as possible as a CID aide.

'Oh, hi Martin,' she said with a guilty smile.

'I thought you were having some time off,' he said.

'Johnson called me back in.'

'Really?' There was a hint of the knowing in his tone. 'Don't worry,' he said, touching the side of his nose. 'If the sarge asks, I never saw you.'

Evidently he knew about her bet with Mike.

'Thanks,' she said evenly.

Martin meant well, but he tried too hard. Mike had been her partner in (tackling) crime for years, but since his promotion to sergeant, Martin had been trying to replace him as her DC buddy. Five months on, she still wasn't used to the idea.

'Look out,' said Martin suddenly.

Mike had just arrived in the corridor. 'Oh Elise, I knew you'd crack!' he said with a grin.

'No,' she began, 'you've got it –'

'Don't even think of trying to wriggle out of this one! Unless you've decorated your living room?'

'No, but –'

'Then it's time to pay up!'

'But I'm only back because Johnson called me!'

Mike's eyes gleamed. 'Not according to my sources.'

She saw him glance at Martin.

The DC went red. 'I was dropping some messages off at the DCI's office when you rang,' he said sheepishly.

'He heard everything,' added Mike.

She gave Martin a cold stare.

'And you blabbed. Thanks a lot, Martin.'

'Sorry, it slipped out,' he mumbled, and hurried away.

'Now that was just cruel, Elise,' said Mike. 'I think you just broke his heart.'

She was sure he was stifling a grin.

'Oh, shut up.'

'I'm telling you Elise, he likes you.'

'Then someone ought to tell him I don't date anyone from work,' she replied tetchily.

Or anyone outside work either. But at least Mike was kind enough not to remind her.

She hastily changed the subject.

'So, what's been happening with the inquiry?'

Mike combed his fingers through his dark curls. 'We've got a definite suspect, but it's a weird one. You'll see what I mean when we get to Bolton. We've been there most of the morning. I just had my lunch break and was on my way back there now, when the DCI told me to wait for you. He wants you to join us as soon as you're done here. And I believe you owe me twenty?'

She groaned and handed him the money.

A minute later she was knocking at Johnson's office door.

'Come through.'

She entered, greeted him, closed the door and seated herself opposite him at his desk.

He peered at her through round spectacles. 'Before we start Archer, are you sure your psychic stress is under control?'

It was as she'd suspected.

'I'm getting there, sir.'

He sighed. 'You do realise I had no intention of calling you, don't you? I'd much rather that you stay at home and rest. But we really need you on this one. Even so, for the duration of this inquiry I'm restricting you to your psychic aide post – part time.'

This was his way of telling her that she could only act as a civilian officer, and that she couldn't work with any of the inquiry teams unless he specified otherwise. He'd taken this course of action once before, the last time she'd resisted taking a mandatory holiday. He'd called it a demotion *pro tem*. She wasn't about to argue with him. At least this way she wouldn't be paired up with Martin. In all likelihood Headquarters had already approved Johnson's decision anyway.

'Understood, sir.'

He nodded. 'Jaythorpe has opened a major incident room and Superintendent Bailey is the senior investigating officer, but since the inquiry has crossed over into other areas, including ours, a team from our side is also assisting them. Our suspect's name is Timothy Brooks, alias Peter Manner. He escaped from Roseleigh Hospital in the early hours of Sunday, and he began his murder spree less than twenty-four hours later. He has killed one man every night – three so far – using a sharp weapon, probably a dagger, and has taken their money and their valuables. All of the victims are male, and are all convicted criminals.'

Male victims were highly unusual in serial murder cases.

'Enemies of his?' she asked, with a frown.

'Unlikely. He doesn't know anyone in the outside world. He was abandoned as a baby' – *What a coincidence*, she thought – 'and he has no family. He has lived in psychiatric institutes for most of his adult life. His psychiatrist tells us that he never had any visitors, and he never wrote any letters to anyone.'

'Then how is he selecting his victims?'

'We don't know yet. We'd like you to try and find out.'

Her stomach fluttered as it had been doing at home all week.

'Are there any other suspects?' she asked, though she knew the answer already from having spoken to Mike.

Johnson leaned back in his chair. 'No, we're sure it's him. He's been ringing Jaythorpe's incident room every day from public phone boxes to tell them where to find each body. He's also been leaving handwritten notes with the bodies. On each note he's listed the names of a few people.'

The DCI opened his desk drawer and took out a datafile. 'These are the pictures of the notes that the scenes of crime photographer took. The crime lab made a comparison between the notes and a sample of his handwriting from the hospital, and found a positive match.' Then he took out a plastic envelope containing a small sheet of paper. 'I also had the crime lab send back the note from the first crime scene for you to look at.'

He handed both the file and envelope to her.

As soon as Elise touched the envelope, she felt a cold rush that almost overwhelmed her.

She gasped. Both items fell out of her hand onto the desk.

'What is it?'

'I ... I don't know.'

Elise lied. Deep down she knew exactly what was wrong.

Johnson picked up the datafile and handed it back to her. 'Look at just the file photos. You won't have to handle the evidence directly that way.'

Somewhat shakily Elise accessed the file and started to scroll through. As soon as she saw the photos of the notes, she froze.

'Archer, we did a background check ...' He stopped briefly, as if to read her expression before finishing. '... And apparently, the people on this list have been dead for nearly thirty years.'

He was right. The cold rush she'd felt when she touched the file was remnant of an emotion she knew only too well. It was the fear of impending death.

Elise recognised every name on that list – Leon Morton, David Cohen, and Hanif Omar. Another name on the list was hers – or least it had been many years ago.

It was Joanna Sinclair.

CHAPTER FIVE
Making the Connection

'What's wrong?' asked the DCI.

Psychic stress. She reckoned it was what he was thinking, even if he wasn't saying so.

'Oh, I was caught off guard, sir. It's the – the connection was just a bit strong, that's all. It was, er, – death. You know, the murder victims,' she said falteringly, and only semi-truthfully.

'Right,' he said doubtfully.

'So who are these people?' she asked before he could say any more about it, though she had a fair idea of the answer.

'We're not entirely sure. We couldn't access their identity records as they're classified under GAILE jurisdiction. They must have belonged to an organised crime syndicate or terrorist group.'

Elise nodded. That was what she'd concluded too.

When she'd searched for Joanna on her own a few years earlier, she'd searched for information on the net, taking advantage of the police computer to get into global databases. When the search returned nothing, she tried Hadescape census archives instead. A couple of other names floated around in her memory … David, and an Arabic sounding name … *Salaam*, or something like that. She hardly remembered anything about them at all, but she entered the two full names she could recall – Joanna Sinclair and David Cohen – into the archive's search engine. She found them eventually, but their identity records were inaccessible to her under GAILE jurisdiction.

GAILE. Seeing the name there had startled her. The Global Agency of Intelligence and Law Enforcement was the world's first truly international police organisation. As the name implied, it was a perfect blend of intelligence gathering and law enforcement to protect the nations it served from high-level organised and international crime. GAILE was one of several organisations created along with the Mutual World Alliance.

A GAILE stamp would not typically have appeared on a public census record. Had Joanna simply been the victim of a murder, her name would have appeared in the public death records. But GAILE had sealed the records of both Joanna and David, a privilege normally reserved for Intelligence reports on high-level criminal investigations. It meant that Joanna was a criminal, and not an ordinary one at that.

Elise's rational side finally began to take over. She glanced again at the photo images of the notes. All of them were the same. Manner had listed the names, then the name of a city – *Hadescape* – and then the year they *disappeared*, as he wrote it, around 2014. He'd added a cryptic message: *The innocent will be avenged. You thought you were rid of them, but their legacy endures. This time I will complete the mission and fulfil my promise.* He'd signed each note with his initials: *PM.* He'd left the police enough information that they could easily look it up.

'Where did he get these names from?' she asked.

'We don't know. His psychiatrist thought he'd invented them, but we decided to check up on them since he supplied some specific details. I'll tell you this – it took us a while to find them. Manner must have read about them somewhere, but no one here or at Jaythorpe has been able to confirm where. We've asked the hospital, and they say that he's been obsessed with those names for years. He's also an avid reader, but any relevant magazine he might have read would have been thrown away years ago. And with the case still being classified, I don't see how any magazine could have produced an article about them. We've asked if he's good with computers, in case he found the information somewhere on the web. They've said he has no internet access.'

Elise was mulling over the notes. *The innocent will be avenged ...* Was Manner talking about the people who killed Joanna and her friends? And what did he mean by *their legacy*?

'What's he after?' she said quietly.

The DCI however was inclined to stick to detecting the crime. 'Let's leave the psychological profiling to the experts. You can read the forensic psychologist's report in your own time. I've put it in with Manner's personal file for your information. Right now I'm more interested in learning how he's been selecting his victims. If we can work that out, we might be able to track him down and put a stop to these murders. I've asked DS Scott to pick you up. Go with him to Bolton and do a psychometric check. Paige is expecting you.'

Bolton was a quiet, seemingly unassuming middle-class residential area. Dainty houses with neat fresh green lawns lined the streets. Nice looking area, except that drug use and theft was rife.

The murder had occurred sometime on Wednesday night at an underpass. It had gone unnoticed until around half past six the following morning, when a local man and his dog had found the body lying conspicuously under the arch, with a scrunched up piece of paper sticking out of his mouth.

The blue and white police tape cordoning off the underpass and surrounding zone was still up, and a uniformed officer was guarding the boundary point. Behind him on the other side of the tape a couple of scenes of crime officers were collecting evidence. One was putting a swab into a nylon bag, and the other was taking photographs. They'd already removed the body.

Twenty metres away from the underpass, Elise saw the gloomy miasma hanging over the area. It was a typical crime scene aura. The blues and greens of the natural environment were gone, burned away in the heat of the destructive act done by human hands. Streaks of red, grey and black were suspended in the air like sporiferous clouds, whilst the officers worked in the thick of it, blissfully unaware of what was sapping at their auras.

Ordinary people passing through the place with their normal healthy auras would overwrite the imprint, eventually. Had this been a better area, like Wingdale, it would be sooner. But in Bolton the gloom was almost perennial. Elise had noticed that people living in areas like this were generally more stressed, tired, and pessimistic. She was sure the negative imprints harmed them at a level that science couldn't yet measure.

DI Paige, the tie-wearing giant, beckoned them over.

'Won't be long Elise – the SOCOs are nearly done for now, so we'll get you some protective clothing in a minute. The uniforms are making house-to-house enquiries, but I don't expect we'll have any positive witnesses for this one either.'

He had a quick word with the forensic liaison officer and soon Elise was kitted out in a protective white scene suit, overshoes and gloves. The forensic liaison officer led her to the entrance of the arch and pointed to a patch of blood indicating where the body had lain. Then she left Elise alone.

Even in the day the underpass was poorly lit. Elise passed tentatively under the arch and looked round. The victim's death had been quick but a residue from his final frantic emotions remained, charring the ether as fire does wood. Following her instinct, she moved a metre or so past the stain and crouched down. Placing her right palm flat on the ground, she closed her eyes. She breathed more slowly and deliberately, and waited.

The energy imprints that people left in space and time were generally too faint for her to establish a psychometric connection, which was just as well, or she'd probably have a breakdown from psychic overload. She connected only if an event contained strong emotional energy. Even this had its limits. Litmus paper could show whether a substance was acid or base, but not what it was composed of. Similarly, a psychometric connection could tell Elise what had happened at a crime scene, but not necessarily who the people at the scene were, and certainly not what they thought or felt. From direct physical contact however she sometimes picked up on the most significant moments from their lives, the ones that had stirred up enough emotion to leave a permanent mark.

Elise began to hear a familiar soft hum, a sound she always became aware of whenever she cleared her mind. It was a high pitch sound, a bit like ringing in her ears, but more resonant. It was the flow of her psychic energy. She would stop hearing it as soon as she fully connected.

Finally, an image began to form in her mind.

Through his eyes she peered out from the underpass into the night, scanning the entrance and the public footpath leading to it. Everything within ten metres of the entrance was amber beneath the streetlamps. The hairs on the back of her neck stood on end. Her heart beat hard. Her ears were ringing. Her knees were sore from kneeling on the concrete. Her wet clothes clung to her, and the cold cut to her bones.

A short distance away she watched a man walking towards the underpass entrance. He was in his late thirties, and wore an expensive-looking sheepskin coat. But more than anything else, she saw a dark vapour surrounding him.

Her brow became tense.

As the man approached the underpass, her shoulder muscles also stiffened up. She came out of the underpass and onto his path.

A mellow male voice came from her mouth. 'Excuse me friend, have you got the time?'

The man shrugged. 'Haven't got a watch,' he said dismissively, and tried to walk past.

She stepped to his side and grabbed his arm.

Vile energy oozed from every part of the man's body, spiralling around her in a cankerous vortex, and scraping against her skin like a wire brush.

Suddenly the underpass vanished, and she found herself face to face with a young woman. Elise had her hands wrapped tight round the woman's tiny neck, squeezing the life out of her. All she saw was her face, skin turning blue, eyes bulging, veins on the eyeballs about to burst. The woman clawed desperately at her, but the hands only squeezed harder.

Elise recoiled and tipped over backwards, landing clumsily on her rear. She caught her breath.

'What was that?' she murmured.

This connection was unlike any she'd ever experienced. Not only had she seen, heard and felt everything from the suspect's perspective, but she'd also seen the victim's aura. And as if that wasn't strange enough, somehow she'd established a brief psychometric connection with the victim as well, taking her back to yet another violent crime. The shift had come so suddenly that she'd lost the original connection.

She glanced at the SOCOs working outside. Thankfully no one had seen or heard her. She decided not to try connecting again, in case it was too much for her psyche to cope with. She'd simply come back later if necessary. She got up and came out of the dusky arch, and back into the tepid autumn sunlight.

'Get anything useful?' asked DI Paige.

Elise barely heard him. Her mind was still buzzing.

Could she actually establish a psychometric connection *from within* a psychometric connection? Never had this happened before. She'd only ever experienced an event from the perspective of the victim or the criminal. Sight, sound, smell, touch, and taste; that was the range of sensory information they gave her. She'd never seen auras from their perspective, simply because they couldn't see them. Most people had five senses. She was the only one with a sixth. *Unless ...*

'The victim, sir – he had a criminal record, didn't he?' she said. 'What was he convicted for?'

'Officially,' said the DI, 'it was manslaughter. The man had an anger-management problem. He *accidentally* strangled his wife during a row, served six years. He'd only just come out of jail when Manner got to him.'

That confirmed it.

Mike was looking at her curiously. 'Why do you ask?'

Elise hesitated, uncertain of how to explain the fantastic theory in her head. She scarcely believed it herself.

'It's the way Manner was talking to the victim,' she replied, 'like he was punishing him for something. He ...' she checked herself.

Paige didn't notice. 'Yes, it does look as though Manner is on some sort of twisted moral crusade. What his notes say about *avenging the innocent* and his choice of victims fit together. All our victims were violent men.'

'Yeah, they were all nasty types,' said Mike. 'The first one was implicated in a gang shooting a few years ago, never convicted. The second beat his cousin to death for stealing his girlfriend. Our man certainly knows how to pick 'em.'

'It's clearly not a coincidence,' remarked Paige. 'He's deliberately targeting known criminals. The question is, how? Did you get any clues Elise?'

She decided to spare them the bad news, at least until she had a chance to check things out more thoroughly.

'No sir.'

The three became silent for a moment.

Paige sighed. 'Right then Elise, if you've picked up nothing here we'll try the other scenes. I'll take you. Michael, can you attend the PM on today's victim?'

Mike nodded stoically.

No matter how long they worked in the force, few officers were completely comfortable at a postmortem.

* * * * * * * *

Elise spent the next couple of hours visiting the sites where Manner had killed each of his victims. The SOCOs had spent more time at these scenes and their presence had gradually been overwriting Manner's imprint. With all the care the SOCOs took to not disturb crime scenes, it was a pity that they didn't have the equivalent of a scene suit to prevent aura contamination.

Nevertheless Elise established a connection at both scenes. To her dismay, the connections only reaffirmed her experience from the first location. Manner waited for his victims in the shadows. He ambushed and killed them with a single strike to the heart. At all three scenes she saw the victims' auras; and at all three she made a secondary connection and witnessed the crimes that they'd committed at an even earlier time. It all pointed to only one conclusion, but she couldn't bring herself to accept it.

Back at Wingdale, Elise filled three Psychometric Evaluation forms, scanned them to a datafile for her own use, and handed in the originals at the DI's office. For every action the police took in their enquiries, there was an action form; and similarly, for every psychometric check she carried out Elise had to fill in a PME form. The details she provided on the PME forms never reached the courts. Their main purpose was to help CID look in the right places for hard evidence to link their suspects to the crimes. The police could never acknowledge their psychic aide's work in public, though behind the scenes they gave her all due credit.

Elise remained in the CID office for the next few hours and compiled a detailed report of her visions. She spoke to no one, and no one disturbed her. She typed away diligently, describing everything she had observed during each connection: What the victims wore, what the suspect wore (the same blue T-shirt, black jeans and leather boots), what instrument he used to kill (a large dagger, always the same one), the exact spot and position from which he launched his attack, and more.

When it came to reviewing the sensory information, she hesitated. It had already occurred to her that much of the sensory information from the scenes was identical. She looked through the copies of the PME forms on her datafile to review the data again.

Increased heart rate: Okay, so that was probably down to an adrenaline rush in anticipation of the kill. *Muscle tension*: It was almost certainly an emotional reaction. He'd become increasingly tense as each victim had approached him, almost as though their very presence had irked him. *Goose pimples*: Again, it could reflect Manner's feelings of nervousness, or excitement, or simply a response to the cold. *Ringing in the ears*: Now that one was strange. Why had she noticed it not just the once, but all three times? It could be an ear infection, she supposed, but somehow that wasn't a convincing explanation. It had been a continuous sound, humming away in the background; a soft, high pitch. Come to think of it, she'd heard it before – many times, in fact. She knew the sound very well.

Suddenly it hit her. It had been there the whole time, but she'd overlooked it because of its familiarity.

That humming sounded like the flow of psychic energy.

She looked again at the PME forms. The rest of the sensory data also corroborated what she suspected. Eventually someone would take a look at them and notice their consistency. The senior officers would expect her to mention it in her report, and provide possible explanations. Elise didn't want to pursue it. She was afraid of confirming her theory.

What were the odds that two individuals could be from the same town, both abandoned as babies, and both have knowledge of the same names listed on classified GAILE files?

And *how* did Manner know about those names in the first place?

Elise shuddered. The theory for that bordered on the bizarre.

She left a blank space in the report to fill in later. There simply *had* to be a rational explanation for the sensory correlation.

Elise was an agnostic, but she prayed.

Please don't let him be psychic.

CHAPTER SIX
Will-o'-the-Wisp

The Peace Man took a notepad out of his back pocket, tore off the top page and crumpled it up. Crouching down next to the body of mark number four, he stuck the note unceremoniously in its mouth. He got up again, leaving the dagger lodged inside the mark's chest, as he couldn't take it with him. He'd get himself a replacement later on.

Peter should have left immediately in case anyone saw him, but he was distracted. He took a few steps backward and gazed in awe at the glittering expanse in front of him. He'd never beheld anything so beautiful: Water, the source of life, vessel of the Creator's throne, with energy as pure as that of a *tabula rasa* newborn. A soft bluish white radiance hovered in the moonlight over the river. The water force drifted slowly from the river like fine mist and spread out along the riverbank. He closed his eyes, held out his arms and absorbed the fresh unbroken energy as it flowed over him. Rain with its energy dispersed in droplets, like waning faith, offered little solace; but here in its coalesced form, it was as holy water. It neutralised his pain, washed away his fury, and brought to his scarred mind a stillness that he couldn't hope to find anywhere else. He would be happy to die in a place like this.

He almost forgot the ghastly mess that he'd left at the riverbank; but not completely. The negativity was still sizzling away in the background, though it was abating. It wouldn't be long before the water force engulfed it completely.

After a while Peter reluctantly opened his eyes. He wished he could stay a while longer, but it was time to go. He'd received a poignant reminder of the fact earlier that evening, whilst dozing in a bus shelter. In a strange and vivid dream he'd revisited the sites where he'd brought down his marks, and had looked upon the scorched hole in the earth's aura that he'd left in his wake. Though a harrowing sight, it was nothing compared to what *they* were doing every minute.

The dream was really a subconscious warning that he mustn't lose focus of the important target. Peter knew what needed to be done. It would be a difficult feat to achieve on his own, but at least he could rely on his old comrades to help. They were out there somewhere. Of that he was certain.

When he listened carefully he could still hear the voice, calling out his unspoken name, as it had on that fateful day, the day of his deliverance. Up until that day he'd always doubted his memories, his knowledge, and, God forbid, even his convictions. Even after that ECT session, when he'd recouped more memories, he'd had reservations. He'd believed them when they told him he was ill. That was why he'd never confided in them, and had expressed his innermost thoughts only in writing, the civilised way to scream.

But the voice had changed everything. It had confirmed that he wasn't deluded after all; that everything he'd always known about the Original Conspiracy was real, and not a product of his paranoia. It had reaffirmed his conviction in all that was possible.

And it was calling him home.

* * * * * * * *

Upon returning home Elise tried to forget the case for the night. If she entered deep sleep as she half-hoped she would, then her psychic sense would switch itself off, and nothing would disturb her. However the knowledge that Manner would likely continue his murder pattern prevented her from doing so. She awoke once every ten to fifteen minutes, waiting in angst for the connection.

Sure enough, at around half past one in the morning Elise sat up with a jolt, her heart beating fast. She'd seen a man with a knife in his chest, lying near water.

Still only half awake, as she reached for the bedside lamp she noticed something out of the corner of her eye. A tall shadowy figure stood at the foot of her bed. She couldn't see his face, but he was looking right at her.

She let out a sharp scream, slammed her hand on the lamp switch and jumped out of bed.

But when she looked again, the figure had vanished.

Now fully awake, she realised it was a hallucination. The post-psychometric connection with Manner was, as expected, unstable. Still, she felt unnerved. For a moment she'd been convinced he was in the room with her.

Elise got out of bed and went downstairs to phone the incident room. She reported that there was a new body out there. She hadn't recognised the location, but thought it might be a canal that ran through part of Alterham city centre. Manner might have also left the weapon at the scene. Afterwards Elise returned to bed and spent a few fitful hours tossing and turning, succeeding only in dozing on and off until daylight.

She rose early. She would have gone straight to work, except that she was on civilian part-time duty, so she had to wait either until the afternoon or the police found the body, whichever came first. Elise couldn't help locate the body for two reasons. One, as she'd explained so many times to Martin, finding a body would require a divining ability. Divining and psychometry were two different things, and she only possessed a talent for the latter. For some reason he couldn't comprehend that being psychic didn't automatically mean she had a broad ability ranging from telepathy to predicting the future. Two, water had a neutralising effect on energy signatures. It rendered her senses virtually useless.

After getting dressed and having breakfast – two slices of toast and a mug of milky coffee – Elise went into the DIY crime scene that had once been her living room, and sat down to watch the news. A bulletin covered the continuing search for Manner, but there were no reports of a new body. The search teams were still at the canal. It wouldn't be easy for them to find anything, certainly not without clues. She wondered if Manner had phoned Wingdale yet to let them know where to look.

Elise switched on the datafile containing Manner's personal profile. Johnson always gave her the personal profiles of suspects to help her make sense of ambiguous psychometric information. She resolved to put her psychic feelings aside whilst she read the file. She left the TV on in the background and began to read. Some of the details regarding the murders were missing pending post-mortem and other forensic examinations, but she didn't need to see them. She was perfectly aware of how deftly Manner inflicted mortal wounds with a dagger. He'd killed all of the men over the last few days with a single strike, straight to the heart.

Manner's past bore an uncanny resemblance to hers. He was 27 years old, her age exactly. He had no family, just like her. His mother had abandoned him outside a hospital soon after he was born; again, just like her. He'd been named Timothy Brooks after a doctor who took care of him. Similarly, Elise's mother had left her at a hospital only a week after giving birth. Elise had legally acquired her full name based on the false details her mother had given the doctors about herself.

The authorities had assumed Brooks was the child of someone not listed on the UK's National Identification Database, which identified every citizen of a country under MWA legislation. People not on the list included homeless people, illegal immigrants and some wanderer travellers. Subsequently Brooks had ended up in foster care, as Elise had.

As he'd grown older he'd become so withdrawn that he'd never remained in a single home for long. Elise knew what that was like. She too had been a frustrated and difficult child, and no one had ever wanted to adopt her. No one realised she was actually a young psychic struggling to cope with the energies coming from every person that she met. For most of her early childhood Elise assumed that everyone saw the world in the same way she did.

She couldn't understand why others didn't care that she was afraid of all the energies around her. It was only when she grew a little older that Elise came across the term extrasensory perception. Suddenly she realised that people were not extraordinarily callous. She was extraordinarily sensitive. Once she'd understood that, her anger had diminished.

If Brooks was indeed a psychic too, then Elise could relate to his childhood difficulties, but in adulthood she and he had taken very different paths. Today Brooks liked to call himself Peter Manner. He had a condition similar to Dissociative Identity Disorder – more commonly known as multiple personality disorder. In one mode he was a quiet, intelligent man; in the other he was hostile. He exhibited signs of obsessive-compulsive disorder, being fixated with numbers and their symmetry. He also suffered from paranoia and frequently entered delusional phases and experienced powerful hallucinations. These, she thought, had to be flashback floods. His personal profile made no mention of his psychic abilities – assuming that he really was a psychic. This meant that somehow he had kept it secret. Elise wondered how he could have kept such a secret to himself for so long.

Manner had been physically violent on two occasions, once in the past six months. Soon after the second attack, the Forensic Psychiatric Service had become involved in assessing his care needs. A forensic psychiatrist concluded that Manner's extreme reaction against people he considered bad reflected his very black and white view of right and wrong, and possibly connected to a compulsive need to restore balance after perceived injustice. He cited both instances of Manner's violent behaviour to prove his point. The first was an apparently unprovoked near-fatal assault against a new doctor who, Manner believed, had been physically abusing his patients (later it had emerged that Manner was right). The second was Manner's tussle with a drunken outpatient who tried to attack a nurse with a broken bottle.

The forensic psychiatrist recommended that Manner be moved to a higher security hospital. But Roseleigh Hospital's managerial board seemed to have ignored the recommendation. All they'd done was move him to a higher security ward until they could evaluate his condition at his next routine mental health review tribunal due in early October. Elise wondered whether they'd have him back in time.

Next she glanced through a couple of photos of Manner's room. CID had been analysing the writing on the walls in an attempt to find a pattern in his movements, but had been unable to establish anything from the gibberish. For the most part Manner had written incoherent phrases that sounded quasi-religious, such as: *The gravest Evil lies closest to Truth*; *Peace Man*; *Return to Liberty*; *The Original Conspiracy*; *The Truth has no name*. Nothing made any sense. Some of the words weren't even English.

Returning to the section of the file containing copies of Manner's handwritten notes, Elise reviewed the names: Joanna, her fiancé David, Adam, David's brother, and Leon, a friend. All of them were familiar yet they were strangers to her. She knew that both David and Joanna worked for the MWA, only because of a single memory of the night in which Joanna celebrated their new jobs and their engagement. Otherwise she couldn't recall a single thing about her work, her social life, or even her family, although she'd picked up some of Joanna's minor personality traits, such as her dedication to fitness, and her love of coffee. Nor did she know what either Leon or Adam did for a living.

What did these people do to end up on GAILE's files, and what compelled Adam to want to kill his friends and even his own brother? Elise could still see David curled up on the ground, dying, but recalled nothing of what happened immediately before or afterwards, except for the car crash. Whatever had happened, it all had something to do with the one person on the list about whom she knew nothing.

Hanif Omar.

Elise could visualise his face, but that was all. Joanna may not have known him very well. Though she recognised the name, she wondered why the name *Salaam* was in her head where *Omar* should be. Maybe it was a code name. The word Salaam was a greeting among Muslims, a bit like Shalom among Jews. Well, Omar was a Muslim name she'd heard before.

She pored over the photographs of the walls to see if Manner had written the word anywhere. The first photo contained nothing, but eventually, on the bottom corner of the second she saw something. She magnified the picture and found that it was what she'd been looking for. But it was actually in the form of two words: *Abdul Salaam*. Now she knew the word Salaam wasn't just a phantom memory, but to her disappointment, seeing the words together didn't elicit anything in her brain. So was it a code name? It was possible, but she had no way of finding out. Or did she?

Elise glanced again at Manner's file photo, and wondered just what it was that he knew.

* * * * * * * * *

'Nathalie Weston has escaped,' said Kash.

Gregory frowned at the two young agents. This would not do. The previous evening he'd assured the Committee that everything was under control. Weston had admitted to her part in saving the Project subjects, and she'd agreed not to name anyone in court, Gregory having ensured that she knew the alternative. He'd even let her return home – albeit under house arrest. She ought to have known better than to run away.

Stupid woman.

'How did she get out?' he asked Lloyd.

'I don't know.'

'Pathetic. How quickly can you get her back?'

'Soon. The search team has a couple of leads.'

'And the other assistants?'

'No, sir.'

'Have you at least got something on our informant?' Gregory addressed Kash, as he'd been assigned to go through the suspects.

'We haven't identified any more suspects,' said Kash, with an oblique glance at Lloyd, and then added, 'yet.'

Gregory eyed them both. 'Then I suggest you try harder.'

CHAPTER SEVEN
Vision at Roseleigh

A nervous Elise went to see DI Paige in the incident room at one o'clock. Mike arrived at the same time, having just returned from the canal to report on the latest. He began with the news that despite checking the whole perimeter, the search team on the ground had not yet recovered a body. They'd dispatched the Underwater Unit to look inside the canal as well.

'He definitely left the body near water,' said Elise.

'Are you sure it was the canal?' asked Paige.

'Not completely. It was dark, and I couldn't see much beyond the water's edge. I thought I saw a concrete wall lining the other side of the waterfront, and made a guess based on that.'

'Let's see if the underwater search team comes up with anything. We've also got a couple of teams checking out the city reservoir and the River Northrop. I'm surprised something hasn't turned up already. Manner normally leaves the corpses in conspicuous places.'

'He hasn't rung in yet either,' said Mike.

'And I think he might have left the weapon at the scene this time,' added Elise. 'It's a change of MO.'

As any officer knew, a change of *modus operandi* was a bad sign.

'We shouldn't assume anything. He might still pick up the phone,' said Paige. 'In the meantime we need you to visit his psychiatric hospital and do a psychometric check on his room. The doctor knows who you are so there'll be no need to clear the zone.'

Normally the police had to divert all unauthorised people away from a crime scene to allow Elise to perform the psychometric check undisturbed. It was easy enough most of the time. Police tape was often all they needed to prevent public access to the scenes she wanted to check. Manner's room might have posed a problem, had it not been for the fact that he was a psychiatric patient. Other than the police force itself, specialists from a variety of fields, including criminology, psychology, psychiatry and parapsychology, had all heard of the psychic marvel Elise Archer; hence the reason that Doctor Hargreaves, Manner's psychiatrist and head of the hospital, had heard of her too.

Officers from Jaythorpe CID had met the doctor once before and had taken preliminary statements from him and the other staff. Wingdale had copies of the statements but now they wanted to make an inquiry of a different kind. According to Dr. Hargreaves Manner had spent most of his time in his room. Since his escape the scenes of crime officers had been inside the room to take forensic evidence, but no one had entered it since then. Elise believed she would easily pick up Manner's signature.

After the briefing Elise and Mike left the station, got into a CID car and headed west. Paige couldn't accompany them since he needed to stay back in the incident room.

At around half past two in the afternoon, they arrived at the gates of Roseleigh Psychiatric Hospital. A white chateau style building surrounded by vast lawns and pretty conifers, it looked more like an exclusive country club than a hospital. The main foyer was small and quiet, with a large reception desk in the centre. The receptionist looked askance at them, like a librarian.

'How may I help you?' she said.

Mike showed her his warranty card. 'I'm DS Scott, and this is my colleague, DC Archer,' he said. 'We're here to see Doctor Hargreaves with regards to the disappearance of a patient.'

'Just a moment.'

The receptionist picked up a phone at her desk and spoke quietly into it. A few minutes later, a gangly man in his early sixties wearing a dark grey suit emerged from a lift at the far end of the foyer. He beamed as he walked up to them.

'Good afternoon Sergeant,' he said enthusiastically, as he shook hands with Mike. Then he took Elise's hand, and his smile grew bigger, revealing large, bright white teeth. 'Miss Elise Archer, I presume? It's a privilege to meet you.'

He looked at her like a starstruck fan, and continued to hold her hand. Mike rolled his eyes.

'Thank you,' Elise replied politely, and gently pulled her hand away. 'So, you are Mr Manner's psychiatrist?'

'Yes – and his name is actually Timothy Brooks,' he said. 'We've never encouraged him to use the name "Peter Manner", as this only affirms his fantasies.'

'We know, Doctor,' said Mike. 'But we've been referring to him by his alias name.'

'Whatever suits you, I suppose.'

He led them through reception and to the lift from which he had arrived. He pushed a button to take them to the third floor of five. On this floor the corridors were cold and sterile, with bare white walls and a plain grey-blue carpet covering the floor. The floorboards squeaked as they walked along the corridor.

They reached the end and went through a pair of swinging doors with the words *Common Room* written above them. Even before they entered, Elise sensed the dull energies of people on the other side of the door. Inside, the room was big and largely empty, with drab decor. It smelled a bit like dirty laundry. The patients sat in armchairs that were dotted about the room.

'This is where our patients come to relax and socialise,' explained the doctor.

Elise looked at the patients sitting in their chairs. One or two were reading, one was doing a jigsaw puzzle, and a couple were playing cards. Others were simply staring into space. One patient was watching an old television – which was switched off.

'Sorry to bring you this way,' said the doctor, 'but there's no direct lift to Timothy's room. It's security.'

They followed him to the door on the opposite end of the room. On the other side was another lift. They took it and arrived on the top floor. Elise felt a chill around her.

'It's lonely up here,' she said.

The doctor's expression told her he was impressed. 'So it is. Timothy was the only patient staying on this floor.'

In front of them were three large heavy doors labelled with ward numbers. The doctor took a security card out of his pocket and slid it through the reader next to the middle door to unlock it.

The room was a tiny cube, and was furnished with just a set of drawers and a small bed that stood against the back wall. A door adjacent to the bed presumably led to the bathroom.

They turned to the writing scrawled so generously all over the walls. Mike seemed intrigued, and as he walked slowly across the room he temporarily forgot his professional tone. 'Wow!' he remarked. 'The man must have been pretty damned bored!'

'How long has he been staying in this room?' asked Elise.

'About six months,' the doctor replied, 'but for the most part he's been happy here. Timothy has always been uncomfortable around other people and prefers being alone.'

'Did you ask him what he was writing about?'

'Many times, but he didn't want to tell me. He just said he had some things in his head that he had to get out. We provided him with writing materials, but he always seemed to prefer the walls.'

Elise could feel something of Manner's presence even though he hadn't been in the room for several days. 'Gentlemen,' she said, 'can I be alone for a few minutes?'

Mike understood and nodded. 'Doctor, we need to get out of the way so she can do her work. Shall we leave her to it?'

'I was hoping I might –'

'Sorry Doctor,' she said, 'but your energies might interfere if you stay here.'

'Oh, right,' he replied disappointedly.

He followed Mike out of the door and shut it behind him. The security system reset itself with a bleep.

Elise moved slowly towards one of the walls and perused the writing. Much of it made no sense, and much more was totally illegible. Amongst the masses of words, she noticed some of special significance – the names of Joanna and her friends.

She began to breathe slowly in a meditative manner, gently placed her fingers on the cool white surface and closed her eyes.

The impressions came slowly at first. To begin with she saw the face of a man whom she recognised to be Adam Cohen, standing with a gun pointed straight ahead. It was the middle of the night, he stood in front of a fountain, and was about to pull the trigger. She was right in the line of fire, but she didn't move. Now she felt the sensation of being shoved aside. She heard a scream, and saw David fall to the ground. A woman with long blonde hair – Joanna Sinclair – knelt next to him and shouted his name over and over, her eyes streaming.

The same images played again in random order, mixed with the images of other faces, some of which were familiar, whilst others were not. Then she saw Adam about to pull the trigger again.

Suddenly she was lying on a bed, immobilised, staring upwards. A bright ceiling lamp dazzled her. Unable even to move her head, she turned her eyes away from the light and saw a man in a white lab coat coming towards her, holding what looked like a pair of electrodes.

The room melted away, and she saw David Cohen, younger, maybe around twenty years old, on a bright sunny day. An older Adam took his place, and day turned instantly into night. He raised his weapon to shoot, but a hand holding a gun appeared in front of her and fired. Joanna screamed but there was no sound from her. A gun fired simultaneously. This time Adam fell to the ground. The hand in front of her started to shake, and then it dropped the gun.

The images and sounds came faster and faster, flashing relentlessly through her mind. Elise was unaware that the intensity of the impressions had brought her to her knees.

She saw David fall to the ground again, before she saw another familiar face – that of Hanif Omar. Other faces appeared and disappeared in an instant, the images bombarding her. She heard voices talking, laughing, crying and screaming at the same time. Yet again she saw David – or was it Adam? The hand reappeared in front of her and shot him down.

This time she noticed something about the shaking hand in front of her. Though it was under the moonlight, it clearly had dark skin. As the hand dropped the gun, she suddenly realised that she was seeing everything through the eyes of its *owner*.

'Elise!'

'What ...? Oh ...' Elise groaned, holding her spinning head as she tried to find her bearings.

Mike helped her to her feet.

'Are you okay?'

'Yeah ... I think so,' she replied wearily.

'What happened?'

'The images were a little overpowering, that's all.' She noticed the doctor staring at her in awe. 'Doctor, I need to ask you a couple of questions.'

'Elise,' Mike began, 'what did you – '

'I'll explain later. Let's just get back to the doctor's office. I really need some coffee.'

CHAPTER EIGHT
Past Fixation

Doctor Hargreaves' office was compact and neat, with clinical furnishing. A silver filing cabinet stood in one corner of the room. His qualification certificates hung on one wall. A black desk faced the door, complete with a rotating black leather chair.

'What is it you'd like to know?' asked the doctor, as he handed Elise some coffee in a plastic cup.

'Mr Manner has been your patient for a while?' said Elise.

'For around nine years.'

'And he recently requested a transfer to a general ward?'

'With hindsight,' he said, 'I think he was trying to make it easier for him to escape.'

'Has he ever tried to escape before?'

'No.'

Elise sipped her coffee. 'In your statement to Jaythorpe CID, you said that he talked to you about some people – Leon Morton, David Cohen, and so on.'

'He has talked about them in the past, but not of late.'

'As you know,' she said, 'he's written these names on the notes that he's been leaving with his victims. As I understand it, you thought that these people were a figment of his imagination. But we've since learned that they really did once exist.'

'I know, and I must admit I was surprised to hear it myself. I hadn't realised they were real people – though he couldn't really have known them, of course.'

Don't be so sure, thought Elise, and put down her mug.

'Even so,' she said, 'I'd like to find out why he listed their names on his notes. What did he tell you about them?'

'Aside from what I've already told you, not very much, I'm afraid. The DCI at Jaythorpe tells me they were involved in organised crime?'

'Any idea why he was so interested in them?' she asked.

'I have never established the reason for his fixation with them,' said the doctor, 'but I suspect something he read about them may have initiated it. By inventing this kind of relationship, he gets to have friends and avoid real social interaction at the same time. Unfortunately his delusions only serve to make the relationship seem more real to him.'

Elise took out a jotter and pen from her jacket pocket and began to write some notes.

'When you say delusions – what do you mean, exactly?'

'He hallucinates, he has nightmares, he screams, he cries. He mourns the loss of his friends. He says that they died and he couldn't save them. But he won't tell me what happened to them. He also talks about finding his parents. He was abandoned soon after birth, you see.'

'How have you treated the delusions?' asked Mike.

'He has such a complex and severe psychosis that treating him has been almost impossible. We've tried a variety of treatments, including drug and even electroconvulsive therapy. Nothing seems to work anymore.'

Elise realised Manner's ECT treatment was one of the images she had seen in his room. But for some reason he was conscious during the treatment. As far as she knew, ECT patients were supposed to be given general anaesthetic.

'How many times have you administered ECT?' she asked.

'Twice. The first time was five years ago. At the time, the treatment had some effect. He didn't talk about his friends again for a long time. His delusions and nightmares also stopped for a while.' He checked a diary on his desk. 'Then a couple of weeks ago his condition deteriorated again, and we had to resort to ECT for a second time. We administered a typical number of treatments – six over a three week period.'

His flashback flood had occurred at around the same time as hers. Elise wondered whether the ECT was the catalyst for his decision to break out.

'So his treatment had only just ended when he escaped?'

'Yes. Initially we thought it had worked. He stopped talking about his delusions and in fact his overall mood appeared to improve, but then ... you know the rest.'

Elise wrote down the times for later reference.

'Just out of curiosity, what are the side effects of ECT?'

'Most of them are minor. Some patients report muscle pain, headaches, and nausea. Occasionally they report short-term memory loss as well, but they return to normal within a few hours, or sometimes a few days. There's also a small risk of permanent long-term memory loss,' he added, 'but that's rare.'

'What about hallucinations ... or flashbacks?'

'... Not hallucinations. ECT is used to *treat* this symptom and delusions, and also extreme depression. And I've never heard of ECT causing flashbacks.'

'Okay ...' she murmured, taking more notes.

So ECT had not likely caused the flashbacks. But it still might have given Manner an influx of old memories.

Doctor Hargreaves was watching her warily. 'Do you think that Timothy's recent ECT contributed to his decision to leave the hospital?' he asked.

'You're better qualified to answer that than I am, Doctor.'

'I'd say it's unlikely,' he replied slowly. 'If you don't mind my asking, what was it you saw in Timothy's room?'

'I'm sorry, Doctor. I can't really discuss it with you at this time. You know how it is – police business, and all that.'

There was a pause. Mike exchanged looks with Elise, indicating it was time to go. The doctor was becoming a little too curious.

'I think we've covered everything here,' Mike said, and rose from his seat. 'Thank you again for your assistance, Doctor. We will be in touch.'

They all stood now, and shook hands.

Elise lightened the mood. 'You can scrub the writing off the walls now, Doctor! It's been a pleasure meeting you.'

His teeth came back on show. 'Oh no, the pleasure was all mine,' he insisted. 'We won't be scrubbing those walls though. There'd be no point. When Timothy returns he'll only start writing on them again.' He took her hand once more. 'Miss Archer, I hope to see you again sometime in the future.'

Elise smiled sweetly. 'I should know if we will!' she quipped.

'What? Oh!' said the doctor with a giggle. 'Very good!'

Mike rolled his eyes.

Elise was glad to be outside again. The evening, arriving early, had brought a fog that wrapped itself around the hospital's exterior. The place looked much more sinister now, like a haunted house. She almost expected it to disappear when she looked behind her one more time; but it didn't.

They headed back towards the station. In the car Elise said nothing. She was preoccupied with what she'd seen.

'Elise, you're pretty quiet,' said Mike suddenly. 'Don't tell me you fell for the doctor's charms! Tell me, was it his smile?' he said teasingly, baring his teeth in imitation of the doctor.

Elise gazed at him from her seat. 'Michael...'

'Uh-oh – she's calling me "Michael" – it's serious, isn't it? You've got a thing for men with dentures!'

She smiled half-heartedly. 'Listen, I need to tell you something, but you can't tell anyone else. Not yet, anyway.'

Mike watched the road but sensed the tension in her words. 'It's Manner, isn't it? What did you see in that room?'

'Let's pull over so we can talk properly – no, no – don't go to self-drive. Can we just stop for a bit?'

'Just a sec,' he said and turned the car into a side street. He parked the car at the end and switched off the engine.

He turned to face her. 'What's going on?'

She wasn't sure where to start.

'Well … I think there's something big with this inquiry. As a matter of fact, it has a lot to do with me.'

'In what way?'

'I'm – I – I mean Manner and I are … I mean – damn it!'

'All right, now breathe,' he said. 'You're talking to me. Just tell me what's wrong.'

She collected her thoughts.

'You know those names on Manner's notes? It's going to sound crazy, but I know almost as much about them as Manner does – and I knew about them before he even escaped from the psychiatric hospital.'

'How?'

'Remember what the doctor said back there about Manner thinking they were his friends?'

He hesitated. 'Yeah?'

'Manner was telling the truth.'

'… You mean he *thought* he was.'

'No, he *really* was. When I touched that wall, most of what I saw wasn't from Manner's point of view. It was all from the viewpoint of another man.'

'Elise, you're making no sense.'

'Okay, let me put it another way. Manner is a reincarnation of one of the terrorists. He used to be Leon Morton. When I connected to Manner, I actually connected to Leon Morton's memories.'

'What? Are you –' he began. Then he smiled. 'Ah, hang on, hang on, this is a joke, right?'

He looked at her for a moment, waiting for her to also crack a smile, and tell him yes, it was a joke. But she didn't.

His own smile soon turned into a worried frown.

'You're serious, aren't you?'

'Afraid so.'

'… Bloody hell! Elise … you *can't* be serious! It's – you're right! It sounds completely crazy!'

'You haven't even heard the best bit yet. I don't think Manner is alone in all of this. I think there are others out there – reincarnated people from the same group, I mean. No, wait – I *know* they are.'

Mike raised his brow. 'What? How?'

'Promise me you won't get excited.'

'Why do I get the feeling I'm not going to like this?'

'I know, because I'm one of them. I used to be Joanna Sinclair.'

He stared at her, totally astonished. There was a silence for a while, broken only by the crackling of the car's comms system.

'I don't believe what I'm hearing,' he said eventually. 'Why didn't you tell me this before?'

'Because I always had the feeling that something weird was going on – and now I have the proof. Think about it, Mike. Manner and I have very similar backgrounds. Neither us knows anything about our real families, and we're reincarnated individuals from the same time period and the same circle of friends! It's got to be more than just a coincidence!'

Mike combed his fingers through his hair. 'I really don't –'

'There's something else. We're both psychic.'

'You're both *what?!*' he exclaimed, jumping in his seat.

His eyes almost popped out of his sockets.

'I didn't want to say anything in front of Doctor Hargreaves, but yes, we're both psychic. That's how he's been targeting his victims. I don't think the doctor knows anything about it though. Manner has kept his abilities a secret.' She looked at him apologetically. 'And that … brings me to something else.'

Mike threw himself back against his seat. 'Oh, Elise! I'm not sure I can take much more of this.'

She touched his arm. 'Listen. It's just that Stella knows about my reincarnation. She's always known.'

'… Oh.'

'But that's only because we grew up together, you know?' she added quickly, eager to explain herself. 'We were just kids when I told her, and even then it was *only* her. I haven't told anyone else since. She's been bugging me to tell you for ages –'

'Come on Elise, you don't have to explain. I understand. Really.'

Another long silence followed. When he finally spoke again, Mike's tone was grave.

'You sure Manner is psychic?'

She nodded.

'Is there any chance he's also connected to you from the link – that it's a two-way thing, I mean?'

'I don't know. I've never connected to a psychic before. But I don't think he's ever taken control of his abilities. Being around even one person makes him extremely tense. Out there amongst the public, he might fail to detect me through their noise.'

'I do hope you're right. But you have to tell Johnson about this. We'll only find out what Manner is up to once we know a bit more about that old case. Johnson's bound to have a contact in GAILE somewhere with the number of years he's been on the force.'

GAILE?! She had to talk him out of that.

'But that case is classified,' she said. 'They won't talk to him.'

'They might do, once he mentions your memories.'

A bleep from the comms system interrupted their conversation.

'*One-eight-seven, one-eight-seven, this is Control,*' a female voice said through the speaker.

'They're looking for us,' said Mike, and pressed a button on the dashboard. 'This is one-eight-seven. Go ahead.'

'*Please report back to the station as soon as possible. Over.*'

'Control, we're on the way. Will be back in ten minutes. Over.'

'*Received, thank you. Out.*'

A sharp click followed.

Mike turned back to Elise. 'What did they do, anyway?'

'Who?'

'The people from your past life.'

'I don't remember. My memories are all over the place.'

'Then talk to Johnson. If somehow Manner becomes aware of you, there's no knowing what'll happen.'

As much as she hated to admit it, she knew he was right.

CHAPTER NINE
Dread and the Grave

'What took you so long?' asked Johnson in a huff as soon as they entered his office. 'I've just had the chief superintendent from Varborough Constabulary asking me if we've got any leads on Manner. They've got a body fitting his MO by the River Northrop, and just as you said, he left the weapon behind. Now we know why we couldn't find the body. It was twenty miles away!'

Elise raised her eyebrows. 'Varborough?'

Mike had other things on his mind. He pulled a face at her.

'Go on then. Tell him.'

'Huh? Oh ... er ...'

Johnson frowned. 'All right you two, what's going on?'

Elise took a deep breath.

As she explained everything, Johnson remained impassive. She suspected a more heated emotion was rippling beneath the calm, but she managed to tell him the whole story without faltering. He waited for her to finish recounting the details.

'So let me get this straight,' he said. His tone rose with each word. 'You have memories of Joanna Sinclair's life?'

She gulped. 'Y-yes sir, and I was thinking ... I mean I was wondering if you might have some contacts in GAILE, you might be able to find out –'

'I don't think so!' he said gruffly. 'Do you realise how ludicrous that sounds? How do you expect me to go to anyone with a story like that, let alone GAILE?'

Mike came to her aid. 'But sir, there's no logical explanation for how Manner knows about those people. Their records are classified, and there's no public information on them anywhere. If nothing else, GAILE would have to acknowledge that. And if Elise is right about Manner's psychic ability, then he could be even more dangerous than we previously thought.'

Johnson scratched his beard as he considered Mike's reasoning.

'All right,' he said eventually, 'as implausible as your story sounds, I believe you. Frankly, if you were anyone else, I wouldn't. And I will contact GAILE for you. Obviously I'll have to inform HQ first. Lord knows how I'm going to explain it to them, but I will do it. Nevertheless Archer, as from now you're off the case.'

'What? But – but sir– '

'You know the rules. No officer can work on an inquiry that affects him or her personally.'

She wasn't about to give up that easily.

'What about my connection to Manner?'

'Ever heard of conventional policing? We value your input, but that doesn't mean we can't make do without it.'

'But I'll keep having those visions whether I'm working on the case or not. I might as well stay on.'

'Hmm … we can't do anything about that. I suppose you can continue to provide us with information as psychic aide until you lose your connection. But you definitely won't be attending any more murder scenes.'

'Please, won't you –'

'Don't push me, Archer! You've brought this all on yourself. I may well have considered making an exception for you, if you'd only told me about your past the very minute you saw the link – which was when I first handed you that envelope.' He looked at her closely. 'I saw how you reacted, Archer. Why didn't you say something right away?'

She looked down. 'I was … I wasn't thinking,' she mumbled.

'That much I agree with. You were driven by your personal feelings. That's why I can't let you stay on the investigation. You of all people should be able to understand that.'

'Yes sir. I'm sorry.'

Johnson's tone softened. 'In future don't keep anything like this from me again.' He was quiet for a minute, still reflecting. 'It might be prudent not to let too many people know about this,' he said. 'Paige will need to know, but otherwise neither of you are to speak to anyone else about what you have told me today.'

The pair nodded.

January 2014, Coppice Gate, Hadescape

Joanna turned right onto Hegel Boulevard and stopped just short of the grounds of St Mary's Cathedral. The Gothic structure was partially covered in what seemed to be permanent scaffolding. She'd read somewhere that repairing its main dome would take at least three more years – and it was already well over its budget.

Through the windshield she saw the empty road ahead of her, lined with sycamore trees. Finger-like twigs reached into the black sky as if to try and touch the stars, whilst under the streetlights the sidewalks were ashen with frost.

Joanna checked her wristwatch. It was exactly 1 a.m. From the rearview mirror she saw a hatchback pull up behind her. Leon got out of his car wearing a woolly coat and scarf, and came up to the passenger door. Joanna rolled down the window.

'He should be here any minute,' he said.

'I think I see him,' said Joanna. 'Look.'

A man in a long coat was on the opposite side of the street. He came toward them.

'That's David all right,' said Leon, and waved at him.

David returned the wave and advanced more quickly. He crossed the street and reached the cathedral grounds. Joanna quickly unfastened her seat belt and got out. She and Leon caught up with David in front of the arched alcove over the central portal.

A big illuminated fountain ten or so metres before the portal dimly lit up the area, and two tall bronze statues at its centre conveniently obstructed the view, thereby providing seclusion for the three friends meeting there in secret.

'David!' said Joanna, wrapping her arms around her fiancé's neck. 'Thank God you're all right! I've been so worried …'

'You only saw me yesterday,' David said lightly.

'You know what I mean! Even though I was expecting that message from you at any time, I was still terrified when I got it.'

'I'm sorry,' said David. 'I should never have involved you – either of you.'

She hit him in the arm. 'How can you say such a thing? You had to involve us. You couldn't keep the biggie of all time to yourself!'

They laughed nervously, except for Leon, who looked at his old friend in concern.

'When did Omar get in touch?' he asked.

'This afternoon,' replied David. I couldn't get out right away, so I carried on as normal and left work at the usual time. No one suspected anything. Then I went straight home and downloaded the most recent – Leon! Look out!' he shouted suddenly.

Joanna turned and looked behind her. Near the entrance of the grounds, four men came running toward them. They carried guns. One stopped a short distance from the side of the fountain and took aim at a bewildered Leon.

She looked again at the man, and knew who it was.

'Adam!'

'No!' cried David.

He pushed Leon out of the way just in time.

Adam fired.

David grunted and fell down.

The shock took her like a tidal wave.

'David!' she shrieked. 'David!'

Forgetting the commotion around her, she knelt next to him, eyes filling with tears. He was curled up on the ground, holding his stomach, and she couldn't see the wound.

'David?!'

He was still conscious.

'G-get out of here!' he said deliriously. 'Now!'

Elise sat up abruptly in bed in a cold sweat and met the darkness. It took her a few seconds to realise that she'd been dreaming. She turned and looked at the glowing green digits on her alarm clock. It was 2:58 a.m.

She'd been expecting a post-psychometric connection to wake her at some point during the night, and she was supposed to ring the station the minute it happened. Instead her connection to Manner had induced a new flashback. Her brain was dealing with the data from her experience at the hospital, trying to correlate it with her own memories.

Elise switched on her bedside lamp and took her jotter and pen from the bedside drawer. She always kept them handy for psychometric visions in the middle of the night. Then she sat on the edge of her bed to think.

This was the first time she'd explicitly remembered what had happened to David. From what she could tell, Joanna and Leon had gone to meet him at a secret rendezvous in the middle of the night. What was it David had started to say when Adam's arrival had interrupted him? It was something about a *download*.

She quickly jotted it down, and along with it the other thing Joanna had mentioned: The *biggie*. That certainly had something to do with the download. She wished she could go back and ask Joanna what it meant. Everything made perfect sense whilst she was reliving the moment; but as soon as she left it, the greater part of the memory remained behind in that world and time, and the rest receded into something without substance.

At least some of the images she'd seen at Roseleigh Hospital were making sense now. But she still didn't know what had happened immediately after Adam shot David, and how Leon had ended up shooting Adam. It must have occurred soon after Joanna and her friends had become separated, and after Adam had killed her in the forest.

Elise held her head in her hands and stared into space. Her mind returned to the moment Adam fired that gun. He'd known exactly what he was doing, comfortable with firearms, purposeful, professional ... soldier-like.

Seeing Adam had rattled her, but it was more than plain fear. This was the dread she'd felt all her life, running deep within her, trying to warn her about *something*. Elise still had no idea what it was, but she was certain that it had nothing whatsoever to do with psychological trauma.

* * * * * * * *

Friday, GAILE Coordination Center, Washington, D.C.

The agent entered Gregory's office and stood before him.

'Report,' said Gregory, without looking up from his computer.

'Yes sir,' he said.

Finding he wasn't saying anything more, Gregory looked up at Kash. He noticed a slither of a smile on the agent's face.

'Well? What is it?'

'We've located the grave.'

The enthusiasm in Kash's voice, though restrained, was unmistakable. He reminded Gregory of himself in his younger days, when he was still overawed by everything he was learning from the Committee, and eager to prove himself. Kash – full name Darian Kashif – was the American born and bred son of an Iranian diplomat, another Committee member. He also happened to be President Shafiq Al Badri's nephew.

Gregory smiled internally. Membership often continued through blood lines, but the young man also inherently possessed the qualities that Gregory deemed essential for the Committee; unwavering patriotism, an acceptance of the inevitability and necessity of war, and most importantly of all, the ability to make tough decisions for the best of the self, and only ever the self. The first two were absolute prerequisites. It was possible for the third, as a byproduct of the first two, to pre-exist in principle, but it always had to be honed. Every Committee member had to learn and fully comprehend what was meant by the *self*.

As an old hand Gregory understood the inner workings of the Committee very well. Its ideals made much more sense than simple patriotism. Long before he'd ever heard of the Committee, Gregory had been a devout patriot, attending military school so he could make a smooth transition into the Army as soon as he was old enough. At the time he was emulating the late General Frank Kingswell – his father. Quite wrongly Gregory surmised that the old general's distinguished career was a mark of his dedication to his country, and so he believed that the greatest tribute he could pay his father was to follow in his footsteps. Gregory chose his eighteenth birthday to surprise him with the announcement of his intentions, completely unprepared for the much bigger surprise that his father had for him on the same day.

It had taken some time for Gregory to fully appreciate the value of his father's legacy, but once he'd learned everything there was to know about the Committee, he'd thrown himself into his responsibilities with great enthusiasm. Instead of joining the Army, he'd gone to college and then applied for a position as a GAILE agent. The ideals that the director of GAILE served were technically the same as before, except that now he was better informed about their underlying functions.

Kash was currently going through a similar learning process. At thirty years old he was still a relative newcomer, but shaping up well. Gregory liked to think that he would have raised his own children to a similar standard, had he ever had any.

'Where is it?' he asked Kash now.

'Pakistan.'

'How soon can we get it identified?'

'A few days. The grave is in a remote village in the northern frontier, close to Khyber Pass. The team is standing by. We have no DNA to check against, but we still have some dental records from the STRO. They'll need just the skull for analysis.'

It was the best news Gregory had heard in weeks.

'We'll head out tomorrow,' he said coolly, and turned back again to his computer.

'Yes sir,' said Kash deferentially, and left.

CHAPTER TEN
Homeward Bound

In the morning Elise got up feeling agitated. After the flashback she'd barely slept at all, fully expecting a post-psychometric vision to come in the early hours of the morning, but nothing had happened. No murder, no body. Technically that was a good thing, but Wingdale were dealing with a serial killer. Manner had been true to form for the first four nights, but the fifth night had passed quietly. He'd definitely changed his MO.

She arrived at the station for the morning shift and went straight to the DCI's office to deliver the ominous no-news.

'Nothing at all?' said the DCI, his brow furrowed. 'You're positive?'

Elise nodded.

He grunted. 'That's not in line with his MO. Maybe your connection is unstable, on account of his psychological state.'

'Yes sir,' she said, but they both knew it wasn't that.

All that remained was for him to send her away. Her report was nothing but a formality, and in a couple of days even her post-psychometric connection would die, leaving her with no more excuses to continue her part in the inquiry.

But he didn't dismiss her right away. 'I've spoken to HQ about your situation,' he said, 'and it didn't exactly go down well with them. They wouldn't authorise me to contact GAILE.'

Technically that was bad news, but then she hadn't exactly been ecstatic about involving GAILE in the first place.

'I suppose it's understandable, sir,' she said.

Johnson hadn't finished. 'But –' *No! No buts!* '– I reminded them about their misgivings when you first applied to the force, and how you proved that your abilities were genuine,' he said, to her dismay. 'I convinced them to hear you out. The superintendent will come and see you later today.'

He dismissed her. Dejected, she returned to the incident room for the Horn inquiry where a sergeant allocated her to the computer team for the day. She sat down and resigned herself to a dreary morning of receiving and relaying public calls and messages to officers on the beat.

After a while she glanced at the door, which was slightly ajar. A number of officers came past. Among them were DI Paige, Mike and Martin. She knew they were on their way to a briefing at Jaythorpe. The DCI followed a few minutes later.

It was a quiet morning. Two other officers were in the room with her, but they were busy on their workstations. With no one to talk to, she got on with her work.

A couple of hours passed. After half past ten she kept her eye on the door, expecting the officers to return from the briefing. But no one came by.

At around 11 a.m. the sergeant left the room for a couple of minutes. To her annoyance he closed the door behind him on his return. After that she had no idea who might be walking past.

She bided her time until lunch hour, and at the first available moment she headed back to the CID office, where she saw just a couple of DCs.

'Anyone back from Jaythorpe?' she asked.

'Don't know.'

She hurried back downstairs and to the canteen. There she found Mike, sitting at a table with a cup of tea and a roll.

'What's happening?' she said. 'And where is everyone else? I'm supposed to be seeing the superintendent.'

A mouthful of roll delayed his reply.

'The seniors are still at Jaythorpe nick,' he said. 'You'll never believe what's happened!'

'Do tell.'

'Halfway through the briefing we got a message from the reception officer saying that Ben Ward had just handed himself in.'

'Ben Ward?' She had to think for a second. 'You mean the nurse from Roseleigh? Why?'

'Apparently, he's confessed to aiding and abetting.'

Her jaw dropped. 'He helped Manner escape? What on earth possessed him to –'

'You've read the forensic psychologist's report on Manner? And the incident in which Manner took on an alcoholic outpatient to defend one of the nurses?'

'Yeah?'

'Guess who the nurse was?'

* * * * * * * * *

'Ben Ward,' said the nurse, for the tape recorder.

It was a pointless name for the machine. The tape recorder didn't even have a tape inside. It recorded on hard disk.

The nurse confirmed his name and address in the presence of Superintendent Stanley Bailey, a uniformed chief inspector, Hugh and a uniformed sergeant, plus a solicitor. It was a sizeable party crammed into an interview room that was a fair bit smaller than either of the ones at Wingdale. Jaythorpe Station covered the outer area of the city, and it had fewer citizens to cater for. Ordinarily only a couple of officers would have sufficed, but then this wasn't an ordinary interview.

Hugh wasn't sure what to expect from the nurse. He couldn't imagine why anyone in their right mind would willingly help someone like Peter Manner escape from Roseleigh Hospital, especially a psychiatric nurse who knew his violent history. But then what had started like a typical absconder incident had quickly turned into a major inquiry. As such psychiatric patients went missing from hospitals all the time, a fact rarely advertised in the press. Normally the police would have absconders back within a day or two, no real harm done. Almost never did such a situation develop into something as serious as a murder investigation, yet here they were dealing with a serial monster. As if that wasn't enough to deal with, DC Archer's extraordinary confession meant that Alterham might soon have to involve the international law enforcement bureau, GAILE. Understandably HQ found the proposition a little excessive, and a highly sceptical chief constable had instructed Johnson to keep it to himself for the time being. Superintendent Bailey was the only other person in the room who knew anything about it. He too had made it perfectly clear that he wasn't willing to believe anything until he'd seen some proper proof, or at least until he'd met Archer.

Hugh sized up the man sitting despondently opposite them. Never mind the saying that you can't judge a book by its cover. Police officers did it all the time, and did it well. The nurse was dressed in a cheap zip-up jacket over a green jersey and worn out corduroy trousers. He was overweight, and other than looking pale and tired, he looked like an honest bloke. Hugh had half expected him to be what most in his profession would term shifty.

The superintendent began with the all-important question. 'Why did you help Timothy Brooks to escape from Roseleigh Psychiatric Hospital?' he asked.

'Because he saved my life,' Ward replied. 'I owed him.'

'Is that what he said to you? That you owed him?'

'No. I just ... *did*, is all.'

'Because he saved you from the outpatient who attacked you?'

Ward nodded.

'Mr Ward has nodded,' said the sergeant, for the tape.

'But you must have known the risks of letting him loose in the community,' said Hugh.

Ward sighed. 'You wouldn't understand.'

'You do need to give us an explanation, one way or another.'

Ward gazed at the door. 'Well, soon after the business with that patient, Doctor Hargreaves decided that Peter –'

'That's Timothy?'

'Yes, but he prefers Peter. Doctor Hargreaves decided that Peter needed ECT. Actually the outpatient had fractured ribs, and his family filed a complaint. Doctor Hargreaves prescribed it partly because of that.' He shook his head disapprovingly. 'But it wasn't right – I mean it wasn't even Peter's fault. That patient was the one with the broken bottle in his hand. If Peter hadn't stopped him he might have killed someone.' Ward picked at one of his thumbs. 'Anyway, after the ECT sessions Peter went quiet. He wouldn't even talk to the doctor. The managerial board had him moved to the top floor. I went and gave him his food every day. I talked to him, though at first he ignored me. He just kept writing on the walls. I'd ramble on, practically talking to myself, because he wouldn't answer me, being busy with his writing. Then one day, I made a comment about it – something silly, like it reminded me of a teacher's blackboard, covered in formulas – and he must have liked what I said, because after that he started talking to me. He told me that he was writing out his thoughts in shorthand.'

'What was he writing about?' asked the superintendent.

'Philosophy and religion, mainly. Deep stuff. He was well-read too, which is odd because all that the patients get to read in the hospital are magazines and newspapers. I asked him how come he knew so much. He said he'd become interested in these things when he was at university.' He glanced up sheepishly. 'Not that I believed him. I know he's been institutionalised for most of his life. But you know, he really was smart. I mean, he was talking like some sort of professor. And the more I got to know him, the more I realised he wasn't crazy – not in *that* sense, anyway. So ...' Ward trailed off, and he turned his gaze to the floor.

The chief inspector folded his arms. 'So ... what? Just because he's smart, you decided he was fit to leave the hospital? That was your professional opinion, was it?'

'You don't have to answer that,' said the solicitor.

'It's fine, I'll answer. It wasn't as simple as that. There was something about him ... I don't know, he has a sort of presence. If you met him you'd know what I mean. I can't explain it.'

Hugh and the superintendent exchanged looks.

'How did he talk you into abetting his escape?' asked Hugh.

'I started getting him some proper books from a library. And he loved it. He said he'd always liked reading books and that he missed his old collection of books at home. I knew he lived in foster homes before he was admitted to Roseleigh, so I thought he was talking about his childhood. But one day, I happened to ask him where he lived before.' He paused. 'And he said that he used to live in Hadescape.'

Bailey raised his brow. 'Hadescape – as in New York?'

'He was an economics lecturer at Hadescape University,' he replied, his eyes glued to the floor.

The chief inspector scoffed. 'Was he now? And what made the good professor move to humble Alterham?'

'Actually … he didn't move here.' The nurse cleared his throat and dared to look him in the eye. 'He died.'

There was silence all round.

'Come again?' said the chief inspector.

'See, he lived in Hadescape … in his past life.'

Bailey shot a worried glance at Hugh. The chief inspector and the solicitor looked bemused.

'Oh, brother,' mumbled the sergeant.

Ward scowled. 'I know how it sounds, mate, but I haven't lost the plot, okay?'

'Never mind how it sounds,' said Bailey. 'What else did he say?'

The solicitor butted in. 'Before we go on, can I have a few minutes with my client?'

'I want to carry on,' said Ward.

'I really think –'

'No.'

The solicitor reluctantly backed down. 'It's up to you,' he said.

Ward went back to picking at his thumb. 'Where was I? Oh yeah … he said he died in Hadescape. He wouldn't tell me any more than that. At first, I was like you – thought it was nonsense, he's making it up. But the more he talked, the more I began to wonder. I mean, it was the little details. Like that cathedral – you know, Saint Mary's. He told me that when he was last alive it was covered in scaffolding. They were restoring one of its domes. Took seventeen years to finish, on and off.'

'He could have read that anywhere,' said the sergeant.

'Oh yeah? What about the description of his old neighbourhood, the streets, the shops? And he told me so much about Hadescape University – his colleagues, his students, the department he worked in, the books he wrote, and how his favourite café was five minutes away from his department building. He said it served the best sundaes in Hadescape. So I checked some of it out. I got hold of the university campus guide from their website and looked for the department building he'd mentioned. And there it was, just as he'd said. So I emailed the university, asked them about an economics lecturer named –'

'Peter Manner?' interrupted the sergeant, who clearly hadn't paid proper attention to the list of names on Manner's room wall.

'No. Leon Morton.'

'Oh.'

'I told them I was doing a local history study. They gave me a retired professor's number. I called him and asked what he knew about a Leon Morton who worked in the Social Sciences Department thirty years ago. I even asked about the café. He told me that Leon Morton used to teach there, but he'd died. He also said there used to be a small café just five minutes from his department. The professor even mentioned that Leon used to order sundaes there. I hadn't said *anything* to him about that. I tell you, I was spooked. There was no obvious explanation. I tried to think of one, really I did. But in the end I had to accept that Peter was telling the truth.' He blinked slowly. 'And ... and that was when I decided to help him get out.'

'Even though you knew he was dangerous?' said Hugh.

The words stung him. He looked up sharply, the colour rising rapidly in his cheeks.

'Dangerous?! He wasn't *dangerous*! He'd never attack anyone unless he was provoked!'

'What about the four men he's killed since he got out?'

Ward hung his head. The red rush of indignation faded.

'I didn't think he was capable of that,' he said after a while, his voice subdued. 'I wouldn't have helped him if I had. I – I'm still having trouble believing it, to tell you the truth.'

The superintendent looked at him reproachfully. 'I'm sorry,' he said, 'but that *is* why you came in today, isn't it? Because deep down you know that he did it – and, I daresay, because you feel at least partly responsible?'

'This interview is not about the murders,' said the solicitor. 'My client will not answer the –'

'I *do* feel responsible,' said Ward. 'But I never knew he was killing those men. When I heard he was a suspect, I didn't believe it. Not at first.' He gave a melancholy sigh. 'See, I just kept thinking it must be a mistake. I mean – there wasn't any evidence, not really. Just a coincidence with the timing of his escape.'

'You know he's been leaving a handwritten note at every murder scene?' said the chief inspector.

'I didn't know about that most of the week, because I was off from work. I only found out yesterday, when I got back.'

'A couple of our officers interviewed you at home on Tuesday, didn't they?' said the chief inspector. 'They would have told you that we had some evidence to link Mr Brooks to the crime.'

'They did,' he acknowledged, 'but they never mentioned the notes. So I still didn't believe it.'

'You didn't want to hand yourself in, more like,' said Bailey.

Ward's face flushed again.

'No! It wasn't like that! … But okay, yeah, I was scared as well, all right? Not for me, but for my family. I have a wife, a two year old son, another baby on the way. If I went inside, what would happen to them?'

Hugh watched a drop of sweat trickle down Ward's temple.

'So why are you here now?'

Ben's gaze returned to the floor. 'Well,' he said slowly, 'Peter worked on his escape plan for weeks. He came up with the perfect way to make it look like he was acting alone, to get the police off his back. To pull it off he said he'd do two things once he got out. First, he said he would post a suicide note to the hospital in a few days, to put you off the scent. See, if you thought he was dead –'

'– We'd wind down our search. I get it,' said Hugh. 'This explains the whole shebang; the sudden lapse into depression, the hunger strike, the suicide talk. It was all an act to convince us he was capable of killing himself.'

'It wasn't *all* an act,' said Ward. 'Okay, so Peter was never suicidal. But he was very unhappy at Roseleigh. The energy of the place drove him mad. He said anyone who stayed at the hospital long enough would go mad.' He chuckled faintly. 'Even the staff, he said. Maybe he was right.'

'So the suicide note – it never turned up?'

'Mr Ward has nodded,' said the sergeant, for the tape.

'But I was still thinking, maybe the note got lost in the post,' said Ward, 'or maybe he forgot to send it. Then I went back to work and heard about those notes with the bodies, and … and …'

'And …?'

'It got me thinking about the second part of the plan. See, he wasn't supposed to stay in Alterham. He …' Ward stopped again.

'He … what?'

'You've got to believe me. I honestly didn't think he could ever hurt anyone. I just …'

He looked at the ceiling with watery eyes.

Hugh was unmoved. 'He *what?*' he repeated.

Ward looked at him remorsefully. 'H-home!' he blurted out at last. 'He wanted to go home!'

The chief inspector didn't immediately follow. 'Home? But he doesn't … oh, no. Don't tell me you mean Hadescape!'

He gawped at them like a frightened child, and answered with a miniscule movement of his head.

'… Mr Ward has, er, nodded,' said the sergeant, for the tape.

Hugh leaned towards the nurse. 'But he can't leave the country, can he? Not without ID. You didn't arrange ID for him, did you?'

Ward gulped. 'Y-yes …'

Bailey threw his head back. 'Good God, man! Do you realise what you've done?'

'But it's okay! He hasn't left! I'm sure of it!' said the nurse hastily. 'He hasn't used his bank account, see? So he couldn't –'

'All right, slow down,' Hugh interjected calmly. 'And go back a bit. What bank account?'

Ward dried his forehead with his sleeve. 'Peter wanted to make sure that nothing would lead back to me. If ever the police became suspicious that he'd had help, like financially, they'd probably check certain people's bank account statements, including mine, and Doctor Hargreaves'. And anyway, if Peter tried to leave the country using my credit card, the airline would want written authorisation from me. So Fred –'

'Who's Fred?'

'He's the one who arranged the fake ID. I met him through a friend of a friend. I don't think Fred was his real name, though.'

'You don't say.'

'Fred set up a fake ID and bank account for him. I borrowed money from a friend and gave it to Fred to put in the account – enough to cover the ticket, food and anything else he might need for a couple of weeks. When Peter got out, all he'd have to do was go to the airport. The night he escaped I just had to make sure I had three cards in my right-hand trouser pocket: The hospital security card, the ID card, and the credit card to his new account.'

'Clever,' said Bailey.

'He said he'd post the suicide note once he got out, so there'd be a postmark on the envelope showing he was still in Alterham. But the note never turned up. And when I heard the police had evidence to link him to the murders, I didn't know what to think – until I remembered the bank account. So I logged into the account at the bank's website and found out he hadn't withdrawn any money. Then I knew for sure he was still in the country ... and that he was probably behind the murders.'

Ward sighed and said no more. Bailey nodded at the sergeant.

'Interview terminated at fifteen-o-four,' said the sergeant, and stopped the machine.

'What happens now?' asked Ward glumly.

'You'll be charged as an accessory to the escape, obviously,' said the chief inspector, 'and your friend Fred too, once we catch up with him. But before that we need to freeze the account. That'll stop Brooks from accessing the funds. And if you give us the name on his ID card, we can issue an alert to the relevant authorities.'

Ward sniffed. 'That's that, then.' He wiped his eyes with the back of his hand. 'Not that it makes much difference. I mean, what I've told you – it won't undo the murders, will it? I just hope you'll find him before he decides to leave the country after all.'

It was an innocent remark, but the impact was monumental.

Every police officer arrived at the same thought at the same time. It was a matter of basic maths. Manner had killed one man every night for four nights. He'd gone out of his way to tell the police where the bodies were, and he'd also left them a note at every crime scene, listing the names of *four* individuals. But on the fourth night, he'd suddenly changed MO; he'd killed a man in another town, he'd left the weapon at the scene, and he hadn't rung in. Now it was day five, and there were no signs at all of a new murder. With everything Ward had just told them, it could only mean one thing.

They all inhaled at once.

'Oh, my God!' said the chief inspector, looking wide-eyed at Bailey. 'Do you think we're too late?'

Hugh turned back to Ward. 'When did you check that account?' he asked with urgency. 'When?'

'… Last night.'

'What time?'

'It was pretty late – I went online after midnight, after the missus had gone to bed.'

Hugh's eyes narrowed. 'Then we might still get him.' He got up. 'Have Control issue an alert to every airport!' he ordered the sergeant. 'Peter Manner is on his way out of the country!'

* * * * * * * *

Peter stood in the queue and anxiously awaited his turn. He wore a short tweed jacket and a cream shirt that he'd bought specially for the day. He'd even temporarily removed his red ribbon and used it to tie back his hair. He carried a single kitbag over his shoulder. It contained his regular clothes and a few other personal possessions that he'd added for the sake of appearing like any other traveller. Countless people passed through the terminal, their droning energy closing in and suffocating him. He fought to block it out.

Eventually it was Peter's turn at the self-service kiosk. He checked for the next available flight to New York State. There was one to New York City scheduled to take off in half an hour, and there were still a couple of seats left in economy class. He booked himself a one way ticket and paid by credit card. The card didn't belong to him. It was just on loan, courtesy of a man named Fred.

The kiosk processed the payment and printed out a boarding pass. He couldn't help feeling it was too easy. Things had changed since Leon's day. He remembered a time when travellers had to arrive up to three hours ahead of their journey, and go through several queues' worth of tedious airport procedures. And that was with a pre-booked ticket. MWA interstate flights however were so straightforward that he could go from England to Australia and it'd be not much more complicated than getting a train from Alterham to London. Besides that, it would take only three hours or so to get to New York, as commercial supersonic flight had become available again since 2021. Leon had witnessed only the demise of the previous generation of supersonic commercial aircraft, with the decommissioning of the Concorde in 2003.

Peter put the credit card in his pocket. He'd dispose of it later. He couldn't use it again even if he wanted to. He'd already taken out as much money as he could from the account that morning, leaving only enough to cover the cost of the ticket.

He passed his kitbag through security. Since it was only hand luggage, and didn't need to go in the cargo hold, he took it with him to the check-in area. Peter wished there was a self-service kiosk for this part. But flight regulations required that airport staff check passenger ID in person, even for MWA interstate flights.

Standing in a new queue of around twenty people, he looked anxiously around him. A security guard wandered around nearby. Peter was sure he could take him on if he had to, but he hoped that it wouldn't come to that.

He reached the front.

The woman behind the desk was all smiles. 'Good afternoon sir,' she said cheerfully.

He nodded in acknowledgment and casually handed over his travel documents and ID card. She checked the travel documents. They were legitimate; no surprises there.

Next was the vital test.

The woman typed his booking number into her computer and waited a few seconds. Peter resisted the urge to stare as she scanned his ID card.

The machine whirred.

Then it bleeped, coarsely.

She tried again. The same thing happened.

The woman glanced at a message on her workstation. Peter couldn't see what it said.

Her expression was unreadable.

'Excuse me for a moment sir,' she said politely.

She took the card and went somewhere behind the desk area to speak with her superior.

Manner strained to listen in.

He definitely heard the word *rejected*.

The card had failed on the scanner.

Out of the corner of his eye he saw the security guard looking in his direction. No doubt he'd heard the machine bleeping. Peter couldn't afford to wait for him to move off. The woman would be back any second. It was no good. He'd have to fight.

Adrenaline rushed to his limbs.

He'd taken a step backward when the woman returned with the superior. Both appeared calm. So he waited.

The superior addressed the queue. 'Ladies and gentlemen,' he said, 'I'm sorry, but we seem to be experiencing a problem with one of our computers.'

He directed the disgruntled passengers to a new line. Peter started to follow, but the woman stopped him.

'It's all right sir,' she said, all smiles again. She turned to another computer. 'If you just bear with me I can see to you here. That scanner's been on the blink all day.'

Within a few minutes Peter was safely through to the departures lounge.

Part 2

LIFE

CHAPTER ELEVEN
Leon's Promise

The fifty or so attendees in the small lecture room had listened to the professor with rapt attention for half an hour.

'In short, capitalist democracy focuses on freedom, at the cost of stability; and communism focuses on stability, at the cost of freedom. Since justice and liberty originate from the same source, we should expect to find that where one is present, so is the other. Yet instead we find in the long term that capitalist "liberty" creates inequity, and communist "justice" translates to oppression. Does this mean that the two ideals are incompatible? No. Justice and liberty are actually interdependent. The absence of one means the absence of the other. Therefore we can only conclude that there is neither true liberty nor true justice in either system. We need to set the foundations that will simultaneously allow for both. Obviously before we can do this, we must learn to differentiate between justice and stagnation, and between liberty and chaos. Then we can choose justice and return to liberty.'

Soon the professor got to the heart of his proposal.

'In view of the practical difficulties in setting up the original social experiment,' he said, 'I propose an alternative that eliminates the need for physical territory entirely, and in fact provides scope for a more reliable and thorough test.'

What he described next was most interesting indeed.

Leon turned to his right. 'What do you think?' he whispered.

'He's either mad, or a genius,' said David.

Leon smiled. 'Told you this would be one to remember.'

Unlike David, Leon had heard of the infamous professor before. Hanif Omar had a doctorate in linguistics but his real interests revolved around religion, ethics and metaphysics. He was candid about his beliefs, an idealist to the core, and incapable of thinking inside the box. These traits had landed him in trouble in his native Egypt. Academics shunned him, orthodox clerics accused him of heresy, and he'd been in court charged with writing dissenting and inflammatory literature. Most critics called his work madness. But what fantastic madness it was.

Professor Omar was currently causing a storm with a theorem. Had it been a mathematical or physical theorem, any interest in it would have been purely academic, and any objections grounded in logic. But since it concerned ethics, the interest and objections were anything but. Omar believed that justice and liberty are the only universal ideals; all other ethical principles are either derivatives or aspects of these ideals. But justice and liberty are themselves interconnected because they come, just like the physical universe and every law of nature, from a single source. He called this universal relationship *cohesive ethics*. On its own, the Cohesive Ethics Theorem was benign; but its premise was highly controversial. Omar claimed he was inspired by principles enshrined in various holy texts, and wasn't shy about attributing his theorem to God.

To preemptively foil the critics, he'd come up with a way to test the theorem. The idea was to set up a small community that would be totally independent for two years. This community would live in a social system with no fixed rules, except for one binding principle which could not be broken under any circumstances. This binding principle represented the Cohesive Ethics Theorem in action, and it would be the only distinctive feature of the system. In 2008 he'd presented the idea to the Egyptian government, asking for permission to be temporarily allotted some land in order to set up the experiment, and recommending that at least a thousand people take part. If the community prospered, it would prove that the theorem worked. Unsurprisingly, the Egyptian government had dismissed the idea out of hand.

Now Omar was presenting a new version of his proposal at Hadescape University, before representatives of the MWA's two main research institutes, the Socioeconomic Commission and the Science and Technology Resources Organisation. Leon and David were attending as representatives of their fields.

'Some would say that what I have suggested is utopian, and moreover impossible,' said the professor. 'This is not so. As I see it, humanity cannot realise its true potential until we accept that an ideal society is not only possible, but absolutely mandatory.'

Leon didn't really understand what the professor meant by that closing remark. But the theorem – and the proposal to test it – had left him and David positively intrigued.

Apparently they weren't the only ones, for a week later SECOM and the STRO gave the go-ahead to fund the experiment.

The Systems Experiment cost 1.2 billion dollars, requiring a supercomputer to run the complex simulation and the most qualified personnel from the STRO and SECOM to put it all together. Leon and David both had the privilege of working on the project. David, a brilliant systems analyst at the International Computer Science Institute, a subsidiary body of the STRO, was the obvious choice as head of the programming team. Leon, an economist by profession, was one of a number of consultants brought in from a variety of disciplines in social science, to help construct the human element of the simulation.

Of the five socioeconomic systems to be put to the test, two were known historical failures, and so together they acted as the control. The next two were presently being tried in history. The fifth represented Omar's theorem in action, and it was the only one without a name. Omar wasn't keen on giving the model a formal designation. To his mind it created the false impression that his model was offering a fixed system, when in fact dynamism was its driving force. Nevertheless for the sake of the experiment he gave his model a descriptive name:

Libredux.

14 January 2014, Crescent Bay East

The professor entered the coffeehouse in an anorak and rubber boots, his dark wavy hair windswept. Leon and David stood to greet him as he came to their table, and Leon leaned over to shake hands with him. Omar however was preoccupied with his umbrella, which was dripping all over the floor. He propped it against an empty chair before perfunctorily shaking hands with the pair, and sat down.

Three years had passed since work had begun on the Systems Experiment, and Omar was finally looking to be vindicated. The experiment had run for ten weeks, simulating a time frame of two hundred and fifty years, and the computer had produced data on the five different political systems almost continually. Though the closing results had yet to come through, it was an open secret that the theorem was proven. The implications were enormous. Some were speculating that the theorem had the potential to influence policymaking in individual countries, and thereby affect the character of the Mutual World Alliance as well. The MWA, a body of democratic states, was only a few years old and still finding its feet. No analyst could yet make a long term forecast of its future. Its destiny was waiting to be written.

The MWA research bodies had conducted the experiment privately, but everyone expected the results to become public knowledge soon. Leon could hardly wait. For days he'd been walking around in an almost constant reverie, elated at the prospect of being part of such a momentous time in history. Omar however had a more self-effacing attitude towards his achievements, and he'd credited the success of the experiment primarily to David. In his typically offbeat style Omar had humorously dubbed him Abdul Salaam, or Servant of the Peace, for bringing about a bloodless "virtual revolution", one that had incurred not a single human casualty.

As these thoughts passed through his mind, Leon hadn't been fully cognisant of the anxious look in the professor's tawny eyes. Omar combed his short neat moustache with his fingernail nervously, lowered his head and with a quiet voice he uttered the most awful words Leon would ever hear in his life.

'They're shutting it down.'

Leon frowned. 'Sorry, what –?' He looked at David, and saw the consternation on his face. Then he realised what Omar meant, and his heart sank. 'The experiment?'

David looked sharply at Omar. 'Where did you hear that?'

His indignation was justified. David was an integral member of the team and he'd written much of the main program himself. If anyone was pulling the plug, then he'd expect to be amongst the first to hear about it.

'I have a friend on the inside,' said Omar. 'I can't tell you his name, but I trust him. He called me to warn me of their plans.'

Leon looked at Omar in alarm. He knew the professor had received numerous threats throughout his career. Officially they'd come from religious fanatics, but according to Omar they answered to a higher authority of evil.

'Y-you don't mean –?'

'It's *them*. My friend has heard that the STRO executive board is about to hold a meeting. It'll happen sometime in the next forty-eight hours, maybe less.'

'They can't do that!' said Leon.

'They can, and they will,' said Omar, 'because they don't want the truth to get out.'

David was still on the defensive. 'But then why did they let the experiment run in the first place?'

'Because they always have to be the ones pulling all the strings,' replied the professor with a wry smile. 'They knew I wouldn't give up until I found someone to test the theorem. It was to their advantage to let me run the experiment where they could keep an eye on me, and terminate everything at the first sign of trouble.' He sighed. 'I was aware of this possibility, but I had to take the risk. Now they want to get rid of me, because they know I won't go quietly. And, I'm sorry to say, you're in danger too. My friend says they've had all of us under surveillance, and they've identified three people as my *accomplices*. That's both of you, and Joanna.'

'Joanna?' said Leon. 'She isn't even working on the experiment.'

'But she knows too much. She applied for a consultancy position at the same time you did.'

'But she didn't even get the job,' said David.

'That doesn't matter. Due to her relationship to you they've assumed that she is involved. Now we need to get away before they come for us. My friend has a safe house and I'm going there tonight. No one should notice my absence right away. David, you're the only one with direct access to the data. I need you to get it to me before they destroy it. Will you do it?'

David responded with a blank look. Leon had the feeling he was struggling more with accepting the situation than the request.

'Are you sure your friend's information is reliable?' asked Leon.

'Absolutely sure. He has many connections. He even knows who supplied them with their information on us.' He looked at David intently. 'It's someone you know.'

'Who?'

'Adam.'

Leon was appalled. He'd known Adam since university, and had always known that unlike his twin, he could be arrogant, brash and selfish. But Leon would never have thought that Adam was capable of anything like this. He glanced at David, imagining that he felt much worse. David however appeared strangely calm, as though he'd known it all along and had only been waiting for a confirmation. His eyes were sad.

'I'm sorry,' said Omar.

David shook his head. 'Don't be. If truth be told, it explains a few things. Adam's been asking me all sorts of odd questions lately. Most of them have been about you.'

Omar nodded, almost knowingly. 'Oh, yes?'

'Last week he was even asking me what Abdul Salaam meant. It really seemed to bother him. I told him that it was just a nickname but I don't think he believed me. Instead he advised me not to associate with you. He said –' He looked at Omar somewhat guiltily, and then smiled faintly. 'Never mind. With hindsight, I suppose I should have realised what was going on.'

'Your brother is just misguided,' said Omar. 'In his mind he's doing the right thing. They have invented many lies against me.'

'That's very kind of you to say, but he changed some time ago. I don't know my own brother anymore.' David closed his eyes momentarily, as if to offer a silent prayer. Then he looked at Omar. 'Right, let's do it.'

Omar smiled appreciatively. 'And you, Leon?'

Leon needed no persuading. 'Count me in.'

16 January 2014, St Mary's Cathedral

'G-get out of here!'

Leon scrambled to his feet. He turned to David lying a few feet away from him, in front of the central arch, grimacing in pain and holding his abdomen. David had taken the bullet intended for him. Joanna was kneeling by her fiancé's side, sobbing hysterically.

'Now!' yelled David.

Another bullet flew past with a sharp crack, and hit one of the stone columns supporting the arch behind them.

The sound jolted Joanna. She tore herself away from David with a futile cry and ran as fast as she could to her car, parked some fifty metres away. She had to pass the fountain to get to it. Adam got a clean view of her, and took aim.

Gasping in panic, Leon remembered the pistol he'd brought along with him for protection and took it out of his inner coat pocket. Hastily he aimed at Adam and fired. The gun gave out a thunderous report and the recoil jerked his arm. He missed by a couple of metres. Adam flinched, and then grinned.

Leon's attempt however had granted Joanna a few valuable seconds, and she reached her car. Adam aimed at her again and fired. The bullet bounced off the roof of the car, missing her by a mere few inches. She screamed and quickly got in.

Adam stepped backwards and waved two men forward as he and a partner headed back to his own vehicle.

'Take care of them!' he ordered as he got in.

Joanna had already set off down the road. She was fifteen or twenty seconds ahead by the time he gave chase.

More bullets came at Leon and David from behind the fountain. The shooters used the statues in the centre as cover. Leon shot a couple of rounds randomly in their direction, and then ran to David and helped him up. Together they hobbled up three or four steps and into the relative safety of the colonnade.

Still clutching his abdomen, David put his back against one of the pillars and slid to the ground, breathing heavily.

'Drop your weapons and surrender!' shouted one of the men.

'Never!' bellowed an enraged Leon.

He poked his head out from behind the pillar and took another shot. They returned fire, and he pulled back in.

'Leon!' said David, his voice strained and desperate. 'You go! Leave ... me here!'

Leon stared wildly at him. 'I won't! You're coming with me!'

'You ... h ... have to save Jo! And the data ...' He took a DVD case out of his pocket and pressed it into Leon's hand. 'I didn't give it to her. I-it's up to you now.'

David's expression said it all. The plan was coming apart, but giving up wasn't an option. Tears came to Leon's eyes and he put the box in his pocket.

'I promise I'll protect the data,' he said, choking with emotion, 'whatever it takes.'

'You'd ... better! I'll c-cover you,' said David with a tense frown, moving his bloodied hand from his stomach. He took hold of the pillar with both arms and hauled himself upright. 'Now go!'

Leon ducked his head and sprinted past the fountain, giving it a wide berth, as more bullets whooshed around him. As he reached the car, he heard a couple of piercing gunshots from a weapon without a silencer. David had opened fire. Leon turned and saw one of the men sprawled out on the ground next to the fountain. He turned his face away from the scene and got into the car. He started up, flicked on the headlights and raced down the street.

Leon was too far behind Adam to see his car, but he quickly worked out the direction Joanna must have gone. In accordance with their plan, she would be aiming to get to the city exit. Hegel Boulevard was the main road out of Coppice Gate and at the end was an intersection. If he went on from there, he would go directly toward Cape's End at the east coast. If he took a right turn, he would end up at Penrose Fjord, a small sea inlet which was little more than a fishing village. The left turn was the likely one Joanna would have taken. The road wound back into Soren Forest in Wheeler Park, technically remaining in Coppice Gate district, and then westward all the way through the forest, back to Rock Moor. From there she could get to the city exit.

He reached the intersection and steered left. As he approached Wheeler Park, he left the lights of the main road behind and moved onto a lane without any streetlights. A line of Catseyes were all he saw for the next two or three miles.

Suddenly he spotted the rear reflectors of Adam's car. The vehicle was parked off the road. Leon slowed down to get a better look and soon saw why Adam had stopped there. Rammed up against a tree a few feet away, hood smashed, was Joanna's car.

He quickly pulled up and got out. The moon had just come out from behind the clouds. He went up to Adam's vehicle and noticed that the car was unattended. Leon looked into the dense black woodland and wondered which way Joanna might have gone. It was too dark to see anything properly. He crept in cautiously, holding his handgun tightly in front of him, eyes wide as he peered into the darkness, listening for movement, and praying that his feet, which seemed to have a knack for snapping every twig on the ground, wouldn't give him away.

After a few minutes he reached a clearing. Moonlight broke through the trees and cast its milky light over the rough vegetation. It revealed a human form in grey lying on the ground. It was Joanna. Another person in a suit and tie stood over her, holding a gun with a mounted light in one hand, and what looked like a syringe in the other. It was Adam.

The two laid eyes on each other at exactly the same time.

Adam dropped the syringe and automatically raised his weapon, as did Leon.

The tactical light flashed in Leon's eyes. He yelled and blindly fired straight into the beam.

Whether Adam had succeeded in firing his gun, Leon didn't know. At any rate the marksman collapsed at the knees, and slumped sideways.

Leon was the victor.

He almost wished he wasn't.

He remained rooted to the spot for some time, holding the gun tightly, quaking, and he stared at Adam's lifeless body. The man used to be his best friend. How had it come to this?

Leon's eyes turned slowly to his hand in front of him. His fingers relaxed, and he dropped the gun.

Now he remembered Joanna. She lay lifeless.

'Jo!'

He began moving toward her, when he glimpsed the movement of a flashlight in the woodland beyond the clearing.

It shone onto him, and he gasped.

A man came running out, his rifle pointed at him.

'Freeze!'

Leon looked woefully at Joanna. He could do nothing for her. He turned and fled, going back the way he'd come. His pursuer came after him, but didn't catch up. Leon got back into his car and escaped into the night.

He wept as he sped down the forest highway, thinking about his friends, hating himself for taking Adam's life, and terrified that he wouldn't make it on his own. The three friends were supposed to have gone their separate ways at any rate, to make it harder for anyone to catch them all. But David was dead now, and so was Joanna. He was the only one left. *If only there was someplace else to …*

He suddenly realised there was one place he could go: His parents' house. To date his family knew nothing about the work he'd been doing. Considering that he and his friends had all been under surveillance, Leon was glad that he hadn't discussed it with them. Still, if he turned up there at this ungodly hour he would have to explain himself. What was he going to tell them? He had little time, and anyway, the less they knew the better. But should something happen to him later, not knowing why would destroy them. He couldn't bear to put them through that.

The horror of that potential eventuality provided the impetus for his decision. As he crossed the small bridge over Silver River, which cut its course through the forest, Leon decided he had to see his parents one more time. If nothing else, at least they would have the chance to say goodbye. And he would have the best possible chance of saving the data.

Leon emerged out of Soren Forest and entered Verity Square, where he dumped his car and took a taxi to his parents' house.

It was around one o'clock in the morning when he arrived, and the lights were all out. Leon rang the doorbell and waited. He had to try a couple of times before the landing lights finally came on.

His father came downstairs and peeped through the eyehole in the door.

'Leon?'

'Dad!'

His father opened the door in his nightgown and slippers, with a mixed expression of puzzlement and apprehension.

'What are you doing here at this time, son?' he asked. 'Is everything all right?'

After leaving his parents' house Leon took another taxi straight to Hadescape Airport. It didn't matter which flight he took, as long as he got away from Hadescape. He carried just a rucksack with some clothes and the disc inside.

Leon was taking David's place in delivering the data to Omar. He had to do it in person. If they'd had more time David would have uploaded it to the internet. But it would have taken several hours, and he couldn't have risked being in one place for so long.

Even at that time of night the airport bustled with people. Leon felt almost safe in the crowd as he walked toward the entrance of the terminal. But he never reached it. Two men in suits appeared in front of him and blocked his path. Leon stopped and about-turned; but two more men stood behind him.

'Don't cause a scene, Leon,' said one of the men in front. 'There's nowhere to run.'

They led him to a black panel van parked in a lonely area of the enormous lot, and ordered him at gunpoint to get into the back. Three of them went in with him, and the fourth went to the front. The van had no side or back windows at the rear, so no one could see inside even though the interior light was on.

Two men pinned Leon down while the leader went through his pockets. He found nothing until he searched Leon's rucksack. He found the disc and pocketed it. Then he nodded at his men, who proceeded to roll up Leon's left sleeve. The leader produced a plastic case containing a syringe from his breast pocket.

Leon shouted and struggled, to no avail. The leader injected him, and as soon as the deed was done he told the driver to get going. The driver set off to an unknown destination.

The men let go of Leon and left him to succumb to the drug. The tiredness came over him within minutes. The rocking of the vehicle on the road soon became a floating sensation, and the sound of the engine a distant drone. He drifted away into unconsciousness.

When Leon next opened his eyes, he found himself on a bed. The upper mattress was raised so he was partly sitting up. A bright white light above dazzled him, forcing him to shut his eyes again. He tried to move his arms and legs, but couldn't even feel them, let alone move them. He felt no sensation at all in his body.

Bleeping sounds came from a monitor, and he smelt the sweet scent of disinfectant. Leon assumed he was in some sort of clinic or hospital. He tried opening his eyes slightly and the light was still intolerable. He couldn't move his head, so he turned his eyes from the lamp; and then he noticed a trolley with monitoring equipment all over it. A man wearing a white lab coat, latex gloves and a surgeon's mask, possibly an anaesthetist, stood behind the trolley. Leon now became aware that someone else was behind his bed, as a pair of hands placed something on his head. He was terrified as he contemplated what they might be doing back there.

'Electrodes are in place,' he heard.

The anaesthetist inserted a tube in Leon's mouth. The man either didn't notice or care that Leon was wide awake.

He heard another indistinct voice elsewhere in the room. After that someone must have flicked a switch. Every muscle and every sinew in Leon's body contracted to breaking point. His back arched involuntarily. His teeth clamped down on the tube. He could scarcely breathe. There was no real pain, but a powerful electric wave passed through his body and shook his every atom. The shock forced his brain into shutdown again; but as he blacked out, for reasons that he would never have the chance to ponder, his mind latched onto a single, simplified, skeleton of a thought.

Man .... of ... Peace ...
Man ... of ...
Peace ... Man ...

CHAPTER TWELVE
Agenda

Friday: Long Island

At Roseleigh Hospital, in the weeks before his escape, the Peace Man had formulated a plan of action. It entailed travelling halfway across the world in order to resume another much older plan. Most would call it an impossible task, but he knew it could still be done. He'd already proved to himself that he was capable. Against all odds, he'd arrived at John F. Kennedy International Airport that morning, marking the completion of the most difficult phase.

A waitress placed a cup of tea by his side, and he nodded in thanks. Before sitting at the table, he'd had to order something as well as pay a small fee. Ten or fifteen other customers were in the café, some with friends, and others by themselves, surfing the net, eating, drinking and socialising. Their energy patterns however were soft and quiet. He'd noticed the difference the moment he'd entered the café, like walking in from a storm. Outside the city was swarming. It wasn't simply that the people were comfortable and relaxed here. The electromagnetic field from the computers masked their energy, with the result that for once, he was almost as oblivious to it as they were.

As far as his radar was concerned he was as good as alone. Feeling safe for the first time since he'd left the hospital back in England, he allowed himself some time to drink some tea.

Then he turned to the computer.

Peter found the online telephone directory for the State of New York and went to the search page for Hadescape. In the search box he typed in the surname *Morton* and hit the *enter* key. A couple of seconds later, the results page revealed that from a population of 3.5 million people living in Hadescape, 173 addresses appeared under the name *Morton*. That was too many.

Next he narrowed the search by first name. He tried Laurence J. Morton, Leon's father. There were four listings for *Morton, L*, one listing for *Morton, L. R.* and one listing for *L. M.* There were no instances of. *L. J.* The latter two would not need checking, at least not until he'd exhausted the rest of the addresses.

He took a pencil and a piece of paper from his pocket and began writing them all down, and as he did so it occurred to him that he also ought to check for Yvonne. He didn't accept the very real possibility that they were both dead, for if they were, his mission would be doomed. He could search for either of Leon's sisters, but if they were married they would almost certainly have changed their surnames. Everything hinged on finding at least one of his parents alive; and this was the one thing utterly out of his control. But with all he had worked so hard to calculate and accomplish, he refused to make allowances for the random variable called fate.

He finished writing out the addresses and then ran the search again for just *Y. Morton*, assuming that she would be on the list, still alive, and not remarried. This time, under the more unusual letter *Y*, the search yielded only three addresses. He'd begun writing them down when he noticed that the second *Morton* was in Ashby. He realised that he might be saved the trouble of having to visit any of the others. Nevertheless he added all three addresses to his list as a precaution.

Peter folded the paper and put it back in his pocket, and then ordered himself a late lunch. He planned to stay another hour or so to do some more research, in order to deal with the issue of where to go to rest at night. By now he was at home almost anywhere when he had to sleep, but after tonight he would need something more permanent, not just for shelter but also for storage space.

Saturday: Long Island

Peter walked slowly around the vehicle, scrutinising the paintwork for blemishes. It was the final test for the orange camper van. It had passed with flying colours in the engine and interior check.

'What's this?' he asked, running his index finger along the bottom edge of the driver's door.

'Oh, the rusting is minimal,' the man replied, slowly chewing a dirty matchstick. Only the lower half of his stubbly face showed from beneath his baseball cap. 'It won't cost much to sort it out, but I'll give you another forty off. Can't be fairer than that, man.'

Peter had contacted the man that morning in answer to a private advertisement on the net. The man, also named Peter, was a camper van enthusiast. He was selling some of the vehicles from his auto repairs shop. Seven assorted vans stood neatly in a row, glistening in the sunshine. Peter had selected the orange van after asking the enthusiast which was the most fashionably common colour on the roads.

The Peace Man was by now satisfied with his choice, and for the first time he took his eyes off it to look directly at the enthusiast.

'I'll take it.'

Peter the enthusiast nodded and led him into the shop. They passed a woman at the counter and went into the back, where they sat down at a desk. The Peace Man took a wad of brand new notes from his pocket. The cash comprised much of the money he'd brought with him from the UK, exchanged into US Dollars. He hadn't yet pawned the items he'd obtained from his marks. That would last him a few more days, maybe a week, but to meet his needs beyond that, he'd have to improvise.

He laid the money down on the table. The enthusiast lifted his cap and his whole face came into view. He had a friendly smile.

He picked up the cash and counted it.

'Thanks, man,' he said, and pulled open a drawer on his side of the desk. He took out the keys and documentation. 'Here you are. Take good care of this one,' he said. 'It's the first camper I ever owned. We've been to many places together. I hate to see it go.'

The Peace Man nodded. 'I will,' he said solemnly.

'So, you planning a trip?'

'… Yes.'

'Ah, you're a traveller, aren't you? I was something of a nomad too once – wandered America for fifteen years. I practically missed the Democratic Revolution! I got so used to living in camper vans that I couldn't bear to be apart from them after I settled down. So I started collecting them.'

The two Peters headed outside.

The enthusiast put out his hand. 'Nice doing business with a fellow traveller. Have a good trip.'

The Peace Man shook his hand. 'Peace,' he replied.

The enthusiast smiled and returned to his shop.

Peter climbed into the van, inhaled deeply, and turned the key. The engine hummed, possessing present day technology. The van complied with present energy consumption regulations, having a hydrogen fuel cell engine. The dark sunroof consisted of tiny photovoltaic cells that charged the car battery. Standard modern technology also enhanced the interior – satellite navigation, diagnostic facilities, and self-drive – but otherwise the van stood in its original glory. And for a traveller's vehicle, it was basic. Other than seats that could open out into a bed, it contained no cooking or other appliances.

But it was suitable for his needs.

He glanced at the self-drive button. It was there for convenience, and for safety on long tiring journeys; and in his case, since he hadn't driven a vehicle in almost thirty years, the safety aspect was a must. Nevertheless he decided to risk it on manual. He put his foot gently on the accelerator, and the van rolled forward. He got off the premises and pulled carefully onto the side road. All things considered, the attempt went quite smoothly.

Pleased with his investment, and feeling confident, the Peace Man turned onto the main road and drove away. He had found himself a mobile home.

Sunday: Hadescape

At a quarter past ten in the morning a woman came out of number 41 Preston Avenue with a bag of rubbish. She wore a long elegant skirt and cardigan, and a blue bandana over her long grey braids.

Charlotte put the bag in the bin, and as she was about to head back inside she looked around, and her gaze moved in the direction of the van. Peter shrunk away from the back window. By the time he ventured to look out again, she was gone.

The Mortons were still living in the same house after forty years. He'd recognised the address when he'd seen it in the internet café at Long Island, and now he'd verified it.

Originally a married couple and their three children lived here. His senses told him that now only two people were resident. He'd seen one of them – Charlotte, Leon's younger sister – a couple of times, but he had yet to set eyes on the other.

He wondered whether their decision to remain in the same house had anything to do with Leon. Any other family that had experienced a tragedy such as theirs might have moved away many years ago. Perhaps they were still clinging to the last words he'd said to them.

Peter had been to the house twice in the past fifteen hours; first the previous evening, just before sundown; and now in the morning, keeping his van parked well away from the property and that too for just an hour at a time, so as not to rouse suspicion. He limited his stakeout to daylight hours. He didn't stick around at night, for he wanted to make his move during the day, when there was a greater chance that Charlotte would be out.

Peter got back into the front and headed into the next street. He parked his van in front of a house which stood back-to-back with the Morton residence. He was closer to the house now than he had been whilst on Preston Avenue.

Once again he went to the back and drew the curtains. Then he opened out the back bed seat and closed his eyes. He hadn't slept for more than a few hours a night since his return to America, but he was as close to relaxed as he could get.

Even as he dozed, his radar was on the alert. If there was any change at the house, he'd know about it immediately.

* * * * * * * * *

Saturday: Federally Administered Tribal Areas, Pakistan

The cemetery was a clean three miles away from the village, so the team could infiltrate the zone without any of the locals ever knowing. A military helicopter dropped them off around five miles east of the site, where they met a local man who was their hired guide. As far as he knew, he was aiding a classified US government investigation.

The four men wore dark combat gear and night vision goggles. They carried tools including trowels and spades in their backpacks. Of the three Americans, two were soldiers belonging to a unit with a special code name. They answered to the Elite Triumvirate Committee. The third was the team leader. He was known in public as the Director of GAILE.

Gregory hadn't undertaken any work in the field in ten years, and trekking through harsh mountainous terrain in the middle of the night was demanding even for a young operative, let alone a man of forty-eight years. It was a good thing he was fighting fit. They were headed to the top of a mountain accessible only by foot. The mountain pass was three kilometres long, surrounded in part by steep cliffs. At their present altitude the air was thin and the temperature close to freezing, but they climbed up reasonably quickly and reached their location by 1 a.m. Here the land was relatively flat, and the burial ground covered an area of a couple of acres. The navigator took them past ten or twelve rows of tombstones and when he got to the right row he went along it to the very end.

He pointed at the last headstone, which had a couple of lines on it written in Urdu script.

'This is it,' he said.

Gregory knew from an earlier briefing that the deceased would have not have been laid to rest in a coffin but directly into the ground, in a specially dug body-sized chamber. In accordance with local religious tradition the gravediggers would have dug a wide trench with a smaller cavity at the bottom, just large enough to place the body inside. They would have sealed the cavity with a stone slab and filled the trench to a few inches above ground level.

With time the mound had sunk. The grave was nondescript, indistinguishable from any other in the cemetery, and long forgotten. Gregory had made it his business to be there when they dug up the corpse, to see with his own eyes its final resting place. And having now looked upon this pitiful spectacle, he felt more than a little smug.

Gregory lifted his spade and struck the first dint.

* * * * * * * * *

Sunday: Iowa

The sun was low in the sky, only an hour from setting, when the little red car got off the highway and entered a country lane. The lane was only a couple of miles long, and about halfway along it was a left-hand turn marked with a signpost for a farm. The car took the turn, slowed at the end of the pike, and then wobbled along the dirt track to the back entrance of the country house.

Nathalie got out of her car, wrapped in a shawl. She heard not a sound except for the birds and the wind in the trees. Though she'd been told it was safe here, she was acutely aware of her physical limitations, especially at her age. To even up the odds against any potential trouble, she carried a pistol.

She passed beneath an elder tree and made her way round the side of the house. A black sedan with tinted windows was parked at the front. Someone was home.

That much she'd expected. But when she got up to the front door, she found it ajar.

Nathalie went no further. She was smart enough not to knock or to call out. She took the pistol from her purse, its weight giving her some reassurance, and tiptoed away, hoping against hope that whoever else was on the property hadn't heard her arrive.

She trod softly to the back of the house, and was relieved to find no one about. Nathalie hastened to her car and was taking out her keys when she heard:

'Going somewhere?'

She froze. Her pistol was in her left hand, but she knew that the person behind her was probably armed, and she couldn't possibly outshoot him. She turned her head to see a man in a charcoal suit, with a handgun pointed at her.

'Drop your weapon,' he said coolly.

She knew his face from the time she'd been in GAILE custody. Of all the agents who had interrogated her, he'd been the most polite, kind even.

But it didn't change the fact that he worked for *them*.

'I said, drop your weapon.'

She complied. The pistol landed in front of her.

'How did you know I was here?' she asked.

'Let's just say I got a tip-off,' he replied, 'from a mutual friend.'

CHAPTER THIRTEEN
Reassignment

'We've identified both of the other Project subjects,' said Agent Lloyd on Monday morning, as he handed Gregory a datafile.

Gregory might have received the news sooner, if he hadn't been on his way back from his excursion on Sunday.

'Both of them?'

The agent nodded.

'About time,' said Gregory, switching on the datafile. He began skimming through. 'Where did you find them?'

'Both of them were in the UK.'

Gregory stopped and looked up. 'You never said you'd extended the search outside the United States.'

'That's because we hadn't, sir. They came to us.'

'Is that so?' He went back to the file to read the details for himself. 'A police officer who recalls a past life as Joanna Sinclair ... works as a *psychic aide* as part of her job. How quaint. And a serial killer – from the same town, I see.'

'The local police were investigating and she was on the case. When she saw the connection between herself and the killer, she reported it to her superiors, who contacted us.'

'That means two of the surrogates delivered at the same place. I want them found and dealt with. I assume you've made arrangements to visit our subjects?'

'Yes sir – except there's an added complication with Mr Manner. He has left the UK with the intention of returning to Hadescape.'

Gregory frowned. He could think of only one reason why a Project subject would want to go to Hadescape.

'He must be looking for the data.'

The agent looked puzzled. 'The data? I thought it was found on Leon Morton's person, and that all other evidence was destroyed at David Cohen's home.'

'It was, but Manner doesn't necessarily know that, does he?'

'Well, he is mentally ill,' said Lloyd thoughtfully. 'We have no idea of what he remembers – or thinks he remembers.'

'Exactly. He's unpredictable. That makes him a threat to MWA security.' ... *And much more besides*, he thought, but didn't say so out loud. Lloyd wasn't privy to that kind of information. 'Just make sure you find him before he starts making trouble. You've seen what Mr Katayama tried to do, and he didn't even know what he was looking for.'

'We have a team on it, sir. Agent Kash is arranging surveillance outside the Morton house and at Hadescape University. It should be in place before tonight. We'll also get the local police department to put out an APB on him.'

'Very well.' Gregory switched off the file. 'Now get the third subject in for psychological assessment as soon as possible. She might have approached us voluntarily, but we must treat her as a potential security threat as well.'

* * * * * * * *

Elise sat in the CID office late on Monday afternoon and sipped her coffee, lost in thought. She was in the middle of her shift, and was supposed to be finishing a report on a Hornets gang member whom they'd charged with armed robbery. Anyone who saw the shark swimming slowly across the computer screen however, would have known that the last thing on her mind was doing her work. She took no notice of the police officers rushing in and out, someone grumbling about the paperwork, and other staff filling in forms and filing reports.

They'd had no news on Manner in the last couple of days. On Friday evening East Midlands Airport staff had confirmed that he'd flown out several hours before the police contacted them; and since a flight to New York took only three hours, Manner had vanished after entry. Now he might be in Hadescape, or another city in New York, or anywhere in the USA. Wingdale Police had issued a warning to Hadescape Police Department, but no one expected to find him.

On Saturday the chief inspector at Jaythorpe nick had called to inform Johnson that a new note from Manner had arrived at their main station, this time by post. It read: *By the time you get this, I'll be back in the Land of the Dead.* If Elise hadn't been on the force, and if Ben Ward hadn't already confessed to his part, no one would have read between the lines of this supposed suicide note, or realised the significance of the wordplay.

Over the weekend Elise had post-connected to Manner twice, and both times she'd been inundated with excessive sensory information. She saw overcrowded city streets through his eyes, and felt the scorching energy of an entire metropolitan population searing through his veins. He had no control over it. Years of social isolation had made him hypersensitive. That information was not particularly useful to her colleagues, whose only concern was finding him. Unfortunately she couldn't be more specific about Manner's location; and even if she could, they couldn't do much except to try and warn the relevant local authorities.

Her hands hovered over the keyboard ready to type, but she couldn't focus. She let them drop to the desk and sighed. She was desperate to know what had happened with GAILE. Alterham Police HQ had finally given DCI Johnson the go-ahead to contact them back on Friday, but she hadn't had an opportunity to talk to the DCI herself again since then. He seemed to be living in the incident room despite the lack of new developments; and the one time she'd gone in to try and speak to him privately he'd been busy talking with the Chief Super.

Mike's voice disrupted her thoughts.

'I thought you liked white coffee,' he said, peering into her cup.

'I just fancied a change.'

'You mean you needed something to stay awake! You look shattered, Elise.'

'I'm just having a little trouble sleeping at night, that's all.'

Mike smiled sympathetically. 'Hang on in there. I'm sure we'll get to the bottom of this eventually.'

'That's what I'm afraid of.'

DI Paige arrived at her desk. 'Ah, there you are. The DCI has called an impromptu briefing on the Manner inquiry. I think,' he said, lowering his voice, 'he's heard back from GAILE.'

Four or five other officers including Superintendent Bailey and Martin were already in the incident room. Johnson stood at his desk. He glanced her way before he started.

'I'll get straight to the point,' he said. 'You're all off the case. In fact, it's out of our hands. GAILE is taking over.'

There was a baffled hush in the office.

'A Police Liaison Bureau officer called HQ this morning,' continued the DCI. The Police Liaison Bureau was an intermediary GAILE unit that exchanged information with local police forces. 'He told me that Manner has been phoning GAILE's Hadescape office and making threats. They checked up on him and learned about our inquiry. They want to deal with the matter themselves.'

It was a terribly thin story, but no one seemed to notice. They were just gawping at the DCI.

'Archer,' he continued, 'I've recommended that you assist them in tracking him down, on account of your psychometric connection to him. Two GAILE officers are coming here tomorrow morning to take you to Hadescape.'

Elise was stunned. He made it sound like normal procedure.

'Hadescape?!'

Johnson ignored her. 'Our task now is to allay public fears about the murders,' he said. 'The Chief Super will hold a press conference and tell them that we believe Manner may have committed suicide. After that, unless HQ informs us otherwise, this inquiry is winding down. Is that clear?'

His firm tone conveyed the message. They all nodded.

'Dismissed. Archer, before you go I'd like a quick word.'

The others left. Mike winked at Elise on his way out, though she knew he was just as anxious as she was.

'I apologise for taking so long to get back to you,' said Johnson. 'I was trying to get in contact with anyone who had access to the information we need. I finally got through to GAILE's deputy director today, and asked him about the people listed on Manner's notes. As it turns out, they have recently reopened their case.'

And there was that dreaded feeling again.

'Really? Why?'

'He said he'd discuss it with you.'

She grimaced. 'To be honest sir, I'm not comfortable with –'

'I know it's sudden, and a little ... irregular,' said Johnson, always ready to use euphemisms for the sake of averting a melodrama. For senior officers who dealt with the hysteria-hungry press on a regular basis, it was all part of the job. 'But this is a serious situation.'

She knew as well as he did that there was no other way of getting Manner back.

'Yes sir.'

'Have you any questions?'

Only about a million.

'No, I don't think so.'

'Then report to my office at eight-thirty a.m. tomorrow. And forget about your other assignments. But I still expect to see that report on Friedman first thing in the morning. Have the rest of the day off, and finish it at home.'

'Thank you sir.'

Elise coolly left the office, waiting until she was alone in the corridor before she leaned against the wall and took a few breaths. Then she headed towards the CID office, passing Paige as he came from the opposite side. He looked at her concernedly.

'Elise, are you all right?' he asked.

She regained her self-control.

'Oh, yes sir,' she replied. 'I guess it just took me by surprise. Working with GAILE, I mean.'

Paige smiled. 'I've just been in the CID office, and already Martin has been spreading the news. I think you'll be the subject of much gossip over the coming days!'

'I suppose I can't blame them.'

He laughed. 'Good luck Elise – and try not to be too nervous. Think of this as an opportunity to work with one of the finest police organisations in the world. I've always wanted to see how they operate. I really envy you.'

* * * * * * * *

Gregory arrived home from work that evening in a good mood. He'd had a productive day. The house was quiet. Some would call it empty, but he liked it that way. He'd lived alone for ten years, having given up on marriage altogether after the third attempt.

He asked his housekeeper to have the spa ready for him so he could have a soak after dinner. He went upstairs to get out of his stuffy suit, and came down in a jersey and slippers. In one hand he carried one of his favourite books on military history. In the other he had a cellphone taken from his bedroom. He didn't use this particular unit very often.

He went to the dining room and the housekeeper served some lamb stew. Once she'd left, Gregory picked up the phone and dialled a special number.

The Egyptian President answered in person. '*Yes?*'

Gregory quoted the two words he'd received in a text message back at his office.

'It's him.'

CHAPTER FOURTEEN
Transference

Shortly after midnight Peter walked past the Harper Building, the huge central building in GAILE's Office Complex in Hadescape. It stood – quite deliberately, he thought – at the east end of Verity Square district. Dense forest enclosed the complex at the rear.

He looked up at the national flags that hung in honour of each of the one hundred and ninety-three members of the Mutual World Alliance. He read the large engraved plaque hanging over the entrance gate with some incredulity: *Defending democracy, justice and liberty for all*.

Peter sensed a few people roaming around inside. Two guards were posted outside the building, but otherwise it was largely empty. Only a short driveway and a single security checkpoint separated him from the main entrance. From where he stood he could see the glass front door, reinforced though it probably was. At any rate he wasn't interested in entering the building. None of *their* kind would be in there, at least not now. He'd already visited a far more secure and prominent building – the MWA Headquarters in New York, formerly the old United Nations HQ – and had found nothing remarkable there either.

Being merely Hadescape's GAILE HQ, the Harper Building was not their real stronghold. It was just one of numerous administrative buildings where civilian worker ants and intelligence soldiers all played their part in maintaining the status quo. The GAILE Coordination Center – the grandiose title for their high command – was in Washington; and it was here that a few witting minions working in Intelligence reported directly to their hidden masters. They worked in an ultra classified unit with a secret name. Almost no one even knew they existed.

Peter was confident he would complete the mission. As Leon's father had always said, the people crazy enough to believe that they can change the world usually do.

Wrapping his overcoat around him, he returned to his van parked a couple of blocks away, settled down in the back with the curtains drawn, and slept.

* * * * * * * * *

'Pleased to meet you, Mr Taylor,' said DCI Johnson.

The deputy director of GAILE looked much younger than DCI Johnson, thought Aaron, though they were about the same age. Taylor had few noticeable wrinkles, he hadn't gained much weight over the years, and the wisps of silver throughout his dark hair gave him a distinguished look.

'Where is Miss Archer?' Taylor enquired, taking a seat.

Aaron remained standing.

'She should be on her –' A knock on the door cut Johnson short. 'Oh, she's here. Come through.'

A young woman entered the room. Aaron's eyes flickered, though he was careful to maintain his poise. Their psychic officer looked like a sorceress out of a fairytale; slender figure, olive skin, ebony hair, and pellucid grey eyes.

Wait a minute! Those eyes were looking right at him. He had to keep his thoughts in check. GAILE had yet to establish the full extent of her psychic ability. She might easily read his mind, despite their precautions. He couldn't afford to slip – not now.

He turned his eyes away in an instant, and he could feel hers looking him up and down. He was sure she was trying to read him. Glancing sideways, he caught a bemused expression on her face as she failed to do so.

Johnson began the introductions. 'DC Elise Archer, this is Deputy Director Brent Taylor, and Agent Aaron Lloyd – from GAILE Intelligence,' he said, with mild emphasis.

Aaron knew that Alterham CID must have been surprised to learn which office he represented. He and Taylor were from two separate branches of GAILE. Taylor was Deputy Director of GAILE by title. In practice he headed the Law Enforcement Office – nicknamed the Civil Office – which directly tackled criminal activity within the MWA nations. Aaron worked for the Intelligence Office, which gathered information on anything from gangsters to politicians and passed it onto both the Civil Office and the MWA's policymakers as necessary. Civil Office activities were better known in the public domain, whilst Intelligence was more clandestine, being the right arm of the MWA's Security Council, and was under the sole charge of the Director of GAILE. Intelligence routinely withheld information from even the Civil Office to protect the MWA's key interests and personnel. In a world of open communication, it was the only remaining body of secrecy. It was the Intelligence Office that decided what counted as classified; and the only time that GAILE ever classified its information was to safeguard MWA security.

For a GAILE Intelligence officer to walk into a regular police station (especially overtly) was practically unheard of. Curiosity and perhaps apprehension on the part of its staff was therefore only natural. But Aaron was only interested in what the woman was thinking. It depended, he supposed, on how much she remembered about Joanna Sinclair. Her eyes had widened at hearing who he was, but that on its own didn't mean much.

'Lets get straight down to business, shall we?' said Taylor. 'Elise, I understand that you possess the memories of a deceased person – Joanna Sinclair?'

'Yes.'

'You also know of another individual who also has similar memories – Timothy Brooks, alias Peter Manner – is that correct?'

She nodded.

'How much do you recall about your past?'

'Not much, but I've remembered a bit more since I established a psychometric connection to Mr Manner.'

'Do you think you might remember more once you're in Hadescape, whether consequentially, or psychically, so to speak?'

'Consequentially, I don't know. But I doubt I'd get anything from establishing a psychometric connection there. The imprints associated with events fade with time and I can't detect them after just a few days. Here we're talking about twenty-eight years.'

'I see. We'll discuss this properly later,' said Taylor. 'We're interested in knowing how much you recall, but we also need you in Hadescape for other reasons. I assume you've already packed?'

'Yes. I just have to go home and pick up my bags.'

'And how far away is your home?'

'About ten minutes.'

'Good. I need to take Mr Johnson through some of our procedures and sign a few forms. Aaron, go with Elise to her home and wait for me there. I'll be another twenty minutes.'

'Archer, I'll see you when you get back,' Johnson said as Aaron and Elise moved towards the door.

She gave a small smile.

'Don't worry about your officer, Mr Johnson. We'll take good care of her,' they heard Taylor say as they left the office.

* * * * * * * *

The pair headed out of the building in silence and went to Elise's car. The GAILE agent had a vacant expression, and didn't look her way. His pristine charcoal suit and shining black briefcase denoted a man of maturity as well as of authority, though from his face she guessed he was in his late twenties, perhaps around her age. To most people he would have appeared as an ambitious career-minded man on a decent salary, somewhat standoffish, but nothing out of the ordinary. To Elise however, he was downright unnerving, and his being a GAILE Intelligence officer wasn't the only reason. The fact was she couldn't even tell if he was alive.

Elise took her ability to see auras for granted. Most of the time they were background noise and she barely even noticed them. She hadn't so much as blinked at the faint shimmering hues surrounding the DCI and the GAILE deputy director. But the Intelligence agent's aura was as blank as his face. He was either dead – and evidently he wasn't – or he was shielding himself somehow. The shield was probably meant to guard against psychic intrusion, though she was sure that DCI Johnson must have explained the limits of her abilities to Mr Taylor. Or maybe, she thought wryly, GAILE had been consulting Martin.

She got into the driver's seat and braced herself for an uncomfortable, quiet half hour. The Intelligence officer didn't seem the type for small talk. She was wrong.

Once they were in the car, the agent's demeanour became more relaxed. It began with the appearance of a smile that spread across his face and lit his eyes. Elise didn't notice the change at first. She focused on driving, and made no effort to make conversation.

Next he loosened his tie. He threw his head back and sighed. Still Elise kept her eyes on the road, hoping to get through the ride without having to speak to him.

They'd been on the road for a few minutes when all of a sudden he said: 'So, you've lived round here all your life?'

Elise turned to look at the breathing mannequin, only to be startled as she encountered his smiling face. She quickly turned her gaze forward again.

'Yes,' she said slowly, intending to leave it at that.

The agent had other ideas.

'Why did you decide to become a cop?' he asked, after a pause.

'I thought it was a good career option.'

'And a good use of your ability?'

She knew he was trying to gain her confidence. She'd done the same with suspects countless times. But his attempt was completely transparent.

'I suppose.'

Admittedly she was curt, but it worked. He said nothing for several awkward minutes.

Then without warning he carried on. 'Must be rewarding work.'
She nodded in reply, eyes on the road.

He was quiet again. Elise thought that was the end of it, until –

'So aren't you going to tell me a bit about it?'

'Nothing to tell really,' she said as politely as she could manage, wondering why he couldn't just shut up.

Thankfully he didn't speak again until they reached her house.

'I hope you have coffee,' he said as they got out of the car.

'Yeah, I do.'

He looked pleased. 'Ah, there's nothing like a cup of coffee to wake you up in the morning. You could certainly do with it.'

She raised her brow. 'Why do you say that?'

'Because you seem a little … grouchy.'

'I beg your pardon?'

'Sorry, that came out wrong. What I meant to say was you seem tired. Had a bad night?'

'Not at all.'

'Oh,' he said, not sounding very assured.

She frowned and headed to the front door.

* * * * * * * * *

Aaron stepped gingerly into Elise's living room. The place was a shambles. Three of the walls had wallpaper strips hanging off them, and daubs of paint in a variety of shades of yellow and green remained on them as evidence of thorough colour testing. Old bed sheets concealed most of the furniture and carpet, with the exception of the TV, which hung on the one untouched wall. All manner of items littered the floor; wallpaper strips, DIY tools, an empty mug – he yelped as he almost trod on a dinner plate.

'Halfway through a revamp, are we?' he asked, as he glanced in quiet horror at the ceiling.

The uneven, zigzagged path taken by the paint roller was plain to see. An ancient lamp dangled from a cord with wires sticking out around the base, where cracks showed in the paintwork.

The girl needs help, he thought.

Elise stood near the living room door with folded arms.

'You know, Mr Lloyd,' she said, 'I can see most people's auras. For some reason I can't see yours, but something tells me you know that already. So would you care to explain?'

'Let's not talk about work. We have to go through all that at Hadescape as it is. Right now I'm parched.'

She glared at him for a second and then asked grimly, 'How do you like your coffee?'

'Black with one sugar, thanks.'

With that she turned and went to the kitchen. Aaron followed.

'I thought I'd give you a hand,' he said. 'There's nowhere to sit in your lounge.'

She looked up despairingly, reached for the coffee jar and handed it to him.

'Here you are,' she said. 'The mugs are in that cupboard. You can see the kettle and the fridge – help yourself.' She headed towards the kitchen door. 'By the way – I take milk but no sugar.'

'Where are you going?'

'To get my bags,' she said, with her back to him.

'Take your time. And while you're at it, why don't you freshen up a little?'

Elise spun back round, smiling incredulously. 'Mr Lloyd,' she said, 'you're unbelievable.'

'Thank you,' he replied with a grin. 'And please call me Aaron.'

* * * * * * * *

The forty minute drive to East Midlands Airport was quiet. Lloyd had reverted to his former state as soon as the deputy had arrived to pick them up. The three of them sat in the back of the black cab, and neither GAILE officer spoke to her at all on the way. Once at the airport they boarded the 11:30 a.m. flight and within three hours they reached Hadescape Airport, on the outskirts of the city, local time 10:30 a.m.

A black saloon picked them up. They came in from higher ground at the northwest side, enabling Elise to see a web of roads flowing to the hub from all directions. Hadescape was located south of New York City, and at approximately 207 square miles, it was around two thirds its size. The main city was at the heart of a peninsula that jutted out eastward into the Atlantic Ocean. It bordered with New Jersey at the west, the only side connected directly to the mainland; and that too via a short strip of land just a mile wide and three miles long. Elise had learned in school that logically Hadescape ought to have been part of New Jersey; but in the 19th century a long running territorial dispute had ended with its rival New York winning the prize, earning Hadescape its nickname, the *Prized Peninsula*.

The limousine passed through Murdock, a small industrial area, and Rock Moor, Hadescape's largest district which was also sparsely populated. The local authorities had allowed for the conservation of wildlife and beautiful scenery. Rock Moor was adjacent to the Pine Hills, a highland range that completely lined the north coast and was the source of Hadescape's two rivers. At Cape's End, just off the northeast shore, was the internationally renowned Creux Island, an artificial island named by its French designer for its hollow inner structure. It housed the main energy production plants for the city, and was also the site of an international meteorology research centre.

Further into the city, the view turned increasingly urban. Parks and streams gave way to playgrounds and streets, and the tallest trees to skyscrapers. Soaring effortlessly into the sky, and decorated with stripes of solar panels, the high-rises sparkled in the morning sun as heralds of present-day prosperity. The streets teemed with traffic and people, minus most of the dirt, litter and noise from the petroleum-fuelled twentieth century. Hadescape felt familiar, but Elise couldn't decide whether this was based on a recollection of having once lived here, or whether it was because she'd seen it so many times on television.

The limousine went through the city centre, continuing east over Dean Bridge, a suspension bridge built over Mustang River.

The southbound river marked the border of Verity Square, an exclusive district partly surrounded by forest and comprising mainly government and financial institutions. It was best known for a particular landmark, and, as she soon discovered, it was where they were headed now. At its main gate the limousine turned onto a short drive and went through a security checkpoint before they finally reached the group of buildings known as the GAILE Office Complex.

The T-shaped Harper Building was the main office. It was twelve storeys high, and much wider than tall. The tail of the T forming the front entrance was a relatively short length, whilst the arms spanned almost the full width of the site. The flags of the MWA nations lined the roof perimeter along each arm of the T. They stopped at the bottom of a short flight of steps leading to the front entrance. They got out of the car and the officers led the way.

As she followed them up the stairs, Elise suddenly became aware of the energy inside the slate grey edifice. There were perhaps a thousand personnel inside, no more than she would expect to find in a building of that size. She certainly sensed far more every day on the streets. Yet it made her feel anxious.

Elise ignored it and continued. With each step the feeling only intensified. She couldn't understand it. It wasn't like her to become so conscious of human energy; yet at that moment the collective life force in the building – and in fact all around her – made the hairs on her neck stand on end.

And she had no idea why.

* * * * * * * * *

Peter sprung forward with a growl, fists clenched, ready to take a defensive swing.

'Get away from me!' he yelled.

But there was no one there.

Peter looked round. His eyes confirmed what his intuitive radar was already telling him. He was on a side street in Rock Moor, still outside the computer shop where he'd just made a query. Other than one or two people inside the shop, there was not a soul nearby. His van was parked right in front of him.

He was nowhere near Verity Square – let alone the Harper Building. So why, for that brief moment, had he just found himself outside its entrance?

He jumped into his van and drove off to find out.

CHAPTER FIFTEEN
Disclosure

Elise made it to the top of the stairs, and her awareness of the energy suddenly waned. She gave no more thought to it.

At the door a security guard checked their ID cards and ran a portable retina scanner in front of their eyes. They passed through the massive glass doors and entered a huge foyer which was empty apart from the reception desk at its centre. On the far left wall she saw the instantly recognisable MWA flag: Navy blue with a bold yellow trim. The silver MWA logo at its centre consisted of a large capital letter *A*, with a smaller capital *M* inside its upper frame, and a matching capital *W* inside the lower frame.

The party took a lift to the top floor and emerged in an office suite. Taylor showed Elise and Lloyd to a small reception area where they waited a couple of minutes while he talked to his secretary, and then he took them into his spacious office. Taylor's desk faced a large tinted window, through which was a beautiful view of the city. As they all sat down, Elise noticed the name plaque on his desk:

Brent Patrick Taylor
GAILE Deputy Director

She glanced at a photograph next to Taylor's name plaque. It was at an angle, and she could just about see the people in the picture. A woman in her late forties had her arms around two young men in their late teens. Presumably they were Taylor's wife and children.

'We were surprised when your DCI contacted us,' said the deputy director. His voice had a coarse quality, like that of a raven. 'GAILE Intelligence had just reopened the case of Joanna Sinclair's disappearance after thirty years. We're hoping you might help us with a few details from the last hours of her life. I know you've said that you don't remember all that much, but we'll work with what you can recall, and help you fill in any gaps – as far as we can allow, anyway.'

'Meaning?'

'Meaning that the case is classified, and protocol limits how much we can tell you.'

She appreciated his frankness, and so she returned the favour.

'And Mr Lloyd is shielding his mind also because of protocol?'

Taylor smiled. 'Ah, you've noticed.'

'It was hard to miss.'

'Much of Lloyd's knowledge about this case is classified information. We can't run the risk of you or anyone else getting into his mind, so he has an implant in his cranium to protect it.'

Lloyd remained silent. Thanks to his shield she detected barely any sign of life from him at all. Conversely she could easily see the colours in Taylor's aura.

'Why don't you have an implant?' she asked him.

'I don't need to,' he replied simply. 'Lloyd knows more about the details of this case than I do. The Intelligence Office is in charge of this investigation. The Civil Office doesn't have full security clearance, and is merely providing assistance. Even I only know what is necessary for me to aid the Intelligence Office effectively.'

She turned to the younger officer. 'Intelligence wasted its time giving you that implant,' she said. 'I couldn't get into your head like that, even if I wanted to. I'm not telepathic or even empathic.'

'It's still a reasonable precaution,' Lloyd replied.

'But that doesn't mean we won't help you make sense of your memories,' said Taylor. 'In fact, it's important that you know your background, as you are a key witness in our investigation.'

He nodded at his younger colleague.

Lloyd took over. 'Let's begin with Joanna's death. Do you remember how she died?'

'I remember that Adam Cohen killed her and also his brother.'

'Do you know why she was killed?'

'I think Adam wanted some sort of data.'

Lloyd and Taylor looked at one another.

'What do you recall about that data?' asked Lloyd.

'Nothing really. David mentioned something about a download shortly before he was shot down. That's all I know.'

'Then let's start at the beginning,' said Lloyd. 'That data consisted of highly sensitive information belonging to the MWA. David Cohen stole it and copied it to disc. He was going to pass it onto Hanif Omar, an Islamist fanatic, who in turn intended to use it to blackmail the MWA.'

He paused, allowing his words to impact her fully – and impact her they did. A few moments passed before she next spoke.

'… I see,' she said eventually. 'So we were terrorists?'

'Yes.'

'How did they get involved with Omar?'

It was an irrelevant question, but she couldn't help herself.

'That information is classified.'

And there was the first *classified* barrier. Still, she couldn't complain. They hadn't kept too much from her so far.

Her mind still on Omar, she suddenly had a thought.

'Omar's group … was it called Abdul Salaam?'

'Abdul Salaam?' said the deputy director, looking puzzled.

Lloyd didn't react.

'It's always been in my head,' she said. 'I didn't even remember the name Omar until I saw Manner's notes to Jaythorpe CID. Omar's name is familiar, and I think I remember what he looked like too – but for some reason … it may sound odd, but I always thought that his name was something like *Salaam*. I got the full version from some writing on a wall in Manner's old room.'

'You're almost right,' said Lloyd. 'It was the group's name. It means: *Servant of the Peace*. Does that sound familiar?'

'A little … I don't know.'

Lloyd explained that Omar tried to secure the release of some of his cohorts who were in prison in the USA, and the data was the means to that end. The plan was to take the data and upload it to the net unless his men were released. At that time the MWA still had enemies in a number of rogue states, and couldn't afford to let such sensitive information become so readily accessible.

The sophisticated nature of the attack convinced GAILE Intelligence that Omar had insider help; and David Cohen was the primary suspect. He was the chief systems analyst for the International Computer Science Institute, the body responsible for implementing the MWA's computer networks. He was familiar with most of the critical aspects of the network and was an expert on its strengths and weaknesses. He also had access to the decryption key, without which it would have taken up to ten years to crack the stolen file.

'After further checks,' said Lloyd, 'Intelligence became certain they had identified the right person.'

Up until that moment Elise had been trying to picture the events as he described them. Whilst bits and pieces were familiar, like the term *Abdul Salaam* and the data, the story connecting them felt totally alien. But she was totally unprepared for what Lloyd was about to say next.

'The only problem,' he said monotonously, 'was that David Cohen was the twin brother of one of the investigating officers.'

It took her a couple of seconds to register his words; and when she did, she was wrenched out of the fuzzy world of imagining, and hurled into the vivid world of flashback memory.

She was at the grounds of St Mary's Cathedral. Adam was beside the fountain, wearing that sharp suit, poised with gun in hand, ready to fire without a second thought.

Her feeling of dread returned: A fear of Adam, and of what he represented. The truth simultaneously materialised in her mind.

Adam was a GAILE officer.

CHAPTER SIXTEEN
Discovery

Elise was hit so hard that she reacted impulsively.

'GAILE?! GAILE ordered Adam to kill his own brother?'

'Of course not,' replied Lloyd. 'GAILE issued no such order. He was on an information-gathering assignment and it just happened that one of the suspects turned out to be his brother David. Intelligence immediately reassigned him, but Adam failed to report to his unit, and a search team was sent to find him. The next day GAILE received reports of a crashed car in Wheeler Park. It belonged to Joanna Sinclair but there was no sign of her. She and the entire group had disappeared along with the disc. Adam's body turned up later in the woods, not far from the wreckage. Someone had shot and killed him.'

'Leon,' she said.

'Yes.'

'But he did it in self-defence. So what was Adam doing there?'

'We believe that he acted on the instructions of a third party,' replied the agent.

'Who?'

'That information is classified. But I can tell you that he was instructed to bring in the group members for interrogation.'

She shook her head. 'No, that can't be right. Adam killed Joanna. She definitely died in Wheeler Park. And I'm pretty sure he killed David too.'

'Did you see him shoot her?' asked Lloyd.

'... Not as such. It was dark, and he stood behind her.'

'Then he probably just knocked her out, possibly with a drug – or Joanna fainted out of shock, or she succumbed to her injuries.'

Elise recalled how much blood Joanna had lost that night, and her emotional state. The explanation was plausible, even if she had trouble either believing or remembering it.

'How do you know we were interrogated?' she asked.

'Because we know who carried out the interrogation. It was Doctor William Palmerton.'

Her stomach lurched.

'You mean *the* William Palmerton?'

The agent nodded.

William Palmerton was a household name. He was renowned for his pioneering efforts in nanosurgery, and his research for the Science and Technology Resources Organisation. His work had won him some coveted awards. In the last couple of months someone had anonymously accused him of experimenting on human beings without their consent. The scandal had been all over the news. But hadn't GAILE cleared his name?

'He interrogated them using experimental technology,' said Lloyd. 'He'd developed something called *electroencephalic transmission*, or, in plain English, a mind reading device.'

Her eyes widened. 'A *mind reading* –?'

'Suffice it to say that the device was an untested prototype and Joanna and her friends were guinea pigs. It caused irreparable brain damage and killed them. But Palmerton devised yet another way to retrieve the information. And that's where you come in. You must have wondered why you remember Joanna Sinclair's life, and why Manner remembers Leon Morton's.'

'Of course I have.'

'As you've probably gathered by now, you're not really *reincarnated*,' he said. 'You're the surviving subjects of a memory transplant experiment. Palmerton transplanted the brain tissue of the dead terrorists into you at the foetal stage.'

He put it rather bluntly.

Elise felt sick. 'Oh, God.'

'We learned of the experiment during our investigations into the allegations against Palmerton,' he continued. 'We uncovered a hidden lab in Arizona, and when we examined the site we found some lab computers containing data that hadn't been erased properly, and human brain tissue samples in storage.'

Unsettling questions came to her. Where had they acquired the foetuses? Did the biological parents know? Who was her mother?

But she let him continue.

'We might never have identified the samples, but we got a lucky break when we brought in one of Palmerton's oldest assistants, Nathalie Weston, for questioning. She told us that the lab was the site of an experiment called the Phoenix Project, and that the samples belonged to the American members of a terror group.'

It didn't take a genius to work out why they'd called it *Phoenix*. It was either the objective or geography; perhaps both.

'And Omar?'

'Omar was not among the subjects,' said Taylor. 'No one knows his whereabouts to this day. He's probably dead by now.'

It seemed Lloyd had nothing to add on Omar. He resumed with the Phoenix Project.

'Palmerton's team genetically altered your brain physiology,' he said, 'so you would withstand the effects of the mind reading device when they tried it on you. An unforeseen result of that is your psychic ability.'

Elise stared at him briefly, and then snorted in disbelief.

'But what was so important that they went to all that trouble?' she asked. 'I mean they got the disc when they captured us. What else did they want?'

She waited for another *classified* barrier.

'We hoped you might shed some light on it,' said Lloyd.

'Oh.' She hadn't expected that. 'Sorry, I don't remember anything after the forest.'

'That's a pity. Palmerton was the only other person who could have told us, but he's dead.'

'What about Ms Weston?'

'She doesn't know either.'

Rather convenient for her, thought Elise. Or perhaps the agent was holding back for classified reasons. She decided to drop it.

'What happened to us?' she asked instead. 'How did Manner and I end up in England?'

'When Palmerton tried the mind reading device on the newborns, it failed again. Thereafter he was ordered to terminate the Project and dispose of all the evidence, including the subjects. Palmerton put Ms Weston in charge of getting rid of the infants, but neither she nor the surrogate mothers could go through with it. So she helped them take the infants away, and let Palmerton think they'd been killed.'

'Where are the surrogates now?'

'We don't know.'

'Who were they?'

'Volunteers from amongst Palmerton's staff.'

Elise became quiet. As a child she'd often wondered who her parents were and where they might be, or whether they were even alive. As a teen, she'd stopped daydreaming and had become bitter instead, waiting for the day when she might confront them. As an adult, she'd stopped waiting even for that. But now, she didn't know what to think.

Taylor at least was sympathetic. 'I understand that this is a lot to take in,' he said, 'but we really need you to think about what we've told you. This investigation began with the Palmerton allegations, and we're bringing his case to court. The preliminary hearing is in Washington next week.'

So regardless of what GAILE had said publicly, the allegations against Palmerton were in fact true. Intelligence had merely adopted a security blanket policy in the interests of the case. As an officer herself, Elise knew that law enforcement authorities sometimes withheld sensitive information from the public in order to protect their investigations.

'Due to the classified nature of the case the proceedings will be held in secret,' said the deputy director. 'We'd like you to testify for the prosecution as a Project subject.'

'I'm willing to testify, but what if I can't remember anything?'

'We're not expecting you to remember everything,' said Taylor. 'We just need you to testify that you're a Project subject. Our prosecution will show the court how this has affected you. In a day or two we'll perform a physical examination for some relevant evidence. In the meantime we must find Manner. We've put both Leon Morton's old home and workplace under twenty-four hour surveillance in case Manner turns up at either location.'

'We must also establish why he's decided to come to Hadescape now, just as we've reopened the case,' added Lloyd.

Elise nodded slowly. With everything else that had happened in the past week, it hadn't occurred to her that the timing of the investigation and Manner's escape were rather coincidental.

'Actually, we wondered if you knew anything,' said Taylor. 'Has your psychic connection to him revealed anything about his motives? For that matter, did you have any prior knowledge, no matter how vague, of our investigation here?'

'I have no precognitive ability, so no, I didn't. And I doubt that Manner could have known about your investigation either.'

There was a pause.

'There's still Hitoshi,' said Lloyd suddenly.

'Who?'

'The third Project subject – David Cohen's counterpart.'

Elise couldn't conceal her surprise, and an unexpected feeling of excitement. 'Oh! You – you've found David? – Er, David Cohen?'

'We found him three weeks ago,' said Lloyd, 'but for some reason he isn't talking. We suspect he remembers much more than he's letting on. He might also know something about Manner.'

Considering her own long-standing feelings about GAILE, Elise could understand why the man might be reluctant to engage with them. Not that she was about to explain this to the agent.

'Where is he?' she asked.

'He's originally from Brooklyn, but as luck would have it he lives right here in Hadescape,' said the deputy with a touch of sarcasm. 'He likes to hang around in those wretched nightclubs in Glensville. I'd like you to go and meet him tonight. Perhaps you might persuade him to talk to us, if nothing else. Ideally we'd like him to testify too, but if not, we'll have to rely on just your testimony. He never wanders too far – circumstances won't allow it – you'll see what I mean for yourself. That reminds me …'

Taylor went over to a filing cabinet and took out a small item from the top drawer. It looked like a watch.

'What's that?' she asked.

'An ES tag.'

The electro-security tag was an advanced version of a device designed to keep track of criminals on probation. Tampering with the tag or moving beyond the boundary of a set limit caused it to administer a painful electric shock, as well as alert the police.

Elise raised her brow. 'You've got to be joking,' she said.

From the look on his face, he wasn't.

She noticed for the first time that Taylor already wore an observer strap, which allowed him to monitor an ES tag's activity. It too looked like a watch, albeit one with a man-sized display screen; and up until that moment she had thought it was nothing more. Glancing at Lloyd, she saw that he also wore one.

'I'm sorry to do this,' Taylor said as he attached the strap to her wrist. 'But it's security protocol – for your own protection as well as ours. Whilst I have no doubt that you're a law abiding citizen, we must take precautions. The other Project subjects are behaving in a way to suggest that their memories are influencing them.'

'*Both* of them?'

He nodded. 'I'll give you Hitoshi's profile for your information.'

Taylor and his colleague calibrated their observer straps.

'Is this really necessary?' she said.

'We either do this, or you and Lloyd go everywhere together.'

'Everywhere?'

'Even the bathroom.'

Elise glanced at the Intelligence agent.

'In that case,' she said, 'I'll take the tag.'

* * * * * * * *

Peter parked a couple of blocks from the Harper Building and went the rest of the way on foot. He wasn't worried about security. He could stay well away from the building and get all the information he needed with just his psyche.

He sat and watched from a nearby bench as executives and subordinates alike went in and out of the building. As a guard checked their ID cards on entry and ran a retina scan with a portable device, Peter took the opportunity to run a scan of his own. Their auras all contained the typical muddy shades: Greens, reds and browns of worldly ambition, yellows of slavish and selfish intellect, blues of stress and worry. He couldn't guess what colours might be in the aura of the one he sought, but he would identify that person by a single characteristic.

Peter kept his senses focused on the building and refused to budge. His patience paid dividends. At almost one o'clock three people came out of the main entrance. As soon as they were out of the door, a certain whistling sound got his attention.

He took a closer look. He recognised the two men in suits, having seen them already in his earlier psychic vision. One of them had an extremely weak signal, as if he was at death's door. But Peter was more interested in the third person, a woman dressed in a grey jacket and trousers. There was nothing special about her earthy brown, blue and green hues. In fact her aura was outrageously ordinary. But the sound was definitely coming from her. It signified an exceptional awareness of life energy, the kind that he'd only ever observed before in himself. She was definitely a *psychic*. And that convinced him that she also *had* to be ...

* * * * * * * * *

Elise came to a halt. 'What was that?'

'What's the matter?' asked Lloyd.

Elise looked round. 'I – I hear ...'

'Hear what?'

'I could have sworn ... but now ... I must have imagined it.'

'Did you sense something?' Taylor asked concernedly.

'I thought it was –'

'Manner?' Lloyd said, reaching towards the holster hidden beneath his jacket and looking round.

'I don't know. … It's gone now.'

Lloyd and Taylor exchanged glances.

'Just to be sure we'll have the guards check things out,' said Lloyd, and he nodded at a security guard.

The guard hurried off, talking quickly into his two-way radio.

'You go and get settled in your apartment, Elise,' said Taylor. 'Aaron will accompany you.'

A black car was waiting for them at the bottom of the steps. As they got in, Elise took one last look behind her. She just knew she'd picked up on a psychic signature. She wondered if her feelings outside the Harper Building a couple of hours earlier had been indicative of him too.

* * * * * * * * *

Peter had moved away as soon as he'd realised that she was onto him, long before the GAILE agents had even alerted the guards. He got back to his van and headed back to Ashby. At last he'd found one of his comrades. He would have to find out later which one she was. It was only a matter of time before she led him to the others. He couldn't imagine how he'd established a connection with her at all. He doubted that she was the *caller*, since the caller's voice had sounded distinctly male … and American. But if she was not the caller, then perhaps she, like himself, had been *called* back to Hadescape. That would explain her presence in the city. He thought it extremely unlikely that she just happened to live here.

The Peace Man had already worked out that he and his old comrades were not naturally reincarnated. Evidently they were borne of a process of *unnatural* resurrection. He assumed that *they* were responsible for it. How and why was immaterial. In time they would regret everything they had done. He would see to that.

Only one question troubled him. Could he trust this woman? He would know only after he'd ascertained what she was doing with those GAILE officers. Finding her again wouldn't be too difficult, assuming she remained within a few miles of his reach.

What he needed now was a way to contact her.

* * * * * * * *

The doorbell rang.

'Charlotte!' said Yvonne loudly from the lounge. 'Charlotte!'

'It's all right, Mom, I'll get it!' shouted Charlotte.

She hurried from the kitchen where she was peeling the vegetables. Looking through the peephole she saw a cop in uniform. She opened the door.

'Sorry to bother you, ma'am,' he said politely, holding up his badge. 'I'm Lieutenant Kash, from the Police Department. We're looking for someone and we think he might be somewhere in this neighbourhood. Have you seen him?'

He handed her a small photograph of a white man with long curly brown hair, a goatee and a red ribbon round his head.

'No, I haven't,' she said, and handed the photo back to him. 'Should we be worried?'

'Well ma'am, he's mentally ill, and he's absconded from care. He's unlikely to hurt anyone, but obviously we need to find him for his own safety. Is there anyone else at home whom I might show this photograph?'

'Only my mother,' she replied. 'But she won't have seen him. She's not well and she stays indoors most of the time.'

'I see.' He gave her a card. 'If you do see him, please don't approach him. And just as a precaution, please also beware of strangers. If someone resembling him comes here, don't answer the door. Just call us on this number.'

* * * * * * * *

As he walked away he picked up the radio hanging on his belt.

'Kash here,' he said. 'I've checked the premises. No sign of him. Is everything set at your end?'

A reply came from the unmarked surveillance vehicle parked two hundred yards or so down the street behind him.

'We've got the whole block covered. If he so much as puts a foot into this zone we'll know.'

'I'll join you once I've questioned the neighbours. Kash out.'

CHAPTER SEVENTEEN
Smoke

The black car took Elise to an apartment that was only a mile from the Harper Building. Lloyd instructed her to unpack and then go shopping for some suitable clothes for the evening assignment. He expected to find Katayama in one of Glensville's numerous nightclubs, where his small-time rock group performed frequently.

Elise bought a dress and shoes from a local boutique that afternoon. In light of the fact that Manner seemed to have become aware of her, Lloyd insisted that another GAILE officer go with her, for her own safety. Thankfully it was a female officer from the Civil Office who accompanied her.

A couple of hours later Elise was back in her temporary home, reading Hitoshi's Katayama's file. She flicked through the first few pages. His profile matched that of a Project subject quite neatly: Abandoned in Brooklyn as an infant; parents unknown; a former pickpocket, with the street name *Shaman*; suffered bouts of delusions; assessed for schizophrenia but not positively diagnosed. Significantly, he'd moved to Hadescape some years ago.

Katayama's criminal record also offered compelling evidence for his connection to David Cohen. According to IRS records, he was earning a meagre wage as a lyricist for a struggling rock band. Another statistic foiled. Katayama's main source of income, for which he certainly paid no taxes at all, really came from the seven computers and drawers full of software in his bedroom. He had no formal qualifications, but his computer skills were second to none. He'd been hacking professionally for years, mostly for companies spying on each other for trade secrets, and sometimes for even seedier purposes. He'd been a suspect in some computer crime investigations and convicted in some cases, going in and out of jail for a few months each time.

In the past year he'd tried breaking into the MWA network, twice. He'd covered his tracks so well that security analysts could only trace the attacks to Hadescape, but not directly to him. His reputation preceded him, and that had made him their prime suspect. But a lack of evidence meant he'd eluded prosecution both times, and so neither incident showed on his criminal record.

The last few pages of the datafile described GAILE's attempt to contact Katayama, and his refusal to cooperate. Having identified Katayama as a Project subject, Intelligence had finally established his likely motive for the attack on the MWA network, and so had arrested him. But he'd remained defiant; and since all they really had was circumstantial evidence, they'd had no choice but to release him, pending further investigation.

And now Elise understood why she was wearing an ES tag.

The intercom buzzed. Once Lloyd reached her floor she opened the door; and both of them stopped in surprise. The agent was unrecognisable in jeans and a midnight blue shirt. With a short black suede jacket slung over one shoulder, and his tousled hair, he looked like a young rogue. She wore a short white fleece coat over an ivory flowing frock cut at the knee, and pearl shoes. Hummingbirds made of light hovered at her earlobes. They had blurred wings like the real thing. Holographic jewellery was at the height of fashion. She had left her hair untied.

They both stood stock-still for a moment, each looking the other up and down. Then as their eyes met, Lloyd grinned.

'Now that's more like it!' he said, leaning on the doorframe. 'But I thought we were supposed to be dressing *inconspicuously!*'

Elise looked at him reproachfully.

Lloyd had only to consult his observer strap to locate Katayama's current position. As Taylor had rightly assumed, Katayama was currently at one of his regular haunts in Glensville, the entertainment centre of Hadescape. Lying to the southwest of Verity Square, its streets were lined with clubs, bars, restaurants and shops. It was as busy by night as it was by day.

By the time Elise and Lloyd arrived at The Chase at 9:40 p.m., there was a long queue of people waiting to enter. The nightclub was relatively small and had no visible windows, but a large flashing neon sign lit it up. Stepping past the bouncers at the door Elise saw that the place was already crammed with people. Scores of excited energy patterns surrounded her in close vicinity. Some people drank at the bar or at the tables surrounding the dance floor, whilst others danced under strobe lighting. The air was hot, reeking of smoke and alcohol. Up on the stage, a group of musicians clad in black supplied the entertainment. The music was very loud, but that was the least of it. Nightclubs were definitely not her scene. She wondered how any psychic could happily enter such a place at all, let alone on a regular basis.

Lloyd nudged her. 'See the band on stage? Hitoshi writes for them. They're called The Glitch.'

Three Japanese-American men and one woman were on stage. The music was soft at first, and harsher chords came in towards the latter end of the verse. The lead singer swayed side to side slowly, his hair falling over his sweating face, and he sang with his microphone close to his lips.

'Cause in the silence I hear
'This is my fate'
Conflicted voices in my ear
Tell me, tell me, 'this is my fate'

'They're pretty good, huh?'

Elise turned to Lloyd. He was grinning, having made his remark after noticing Elise looking aghast at the band.

'If you like that sort of thing,' she replied above the noise.

'You want to dance?'

'I don't see how you can dance to this kind of music. Besides, aren't we here on an assignment?'

He laughed. 'How about a drink, then?'

She nodded.

A hell of a choice
Like a double-headed coin so
I lose the game
Either way

They weaved through the dance crowd and made their way to the bar, where they each ordered a glass of orange juice.

Elise looked to the stage again. The shrieking guitars and heavy bass were deafening.

Like a loaded die
And only I know
Just what is at stake
How much is at stake, oh-oh-oh

They found a small round table in a dark corner. 'It'll be difficult to find him,' said Elise, sitting down.

'I don't see him – too many people in the way.'

'My problem exactly. There are too many energy patterns here.' She looked at the clubbers drinking at the tables. 'I almost wish I could have something stronger – calm my nerves,' she said. 'But I don't drink anyway.'

'Oh?'

'I lose control of my senses if I do, and with my flashbacks being a liability anyway, I can't.'

'Me neither – I don't, I mean.'

She wondered whether he had a cultural reason for not drinking or if it was just a lifestyle thing, but didn't ask.

Is this my fate?

The final guitar chord rang out and the crowd stopped dancing and applauded. The nightclub manager walked onto the stage.

'Ladies and gentlemen, let's give a warm hand to The Glitch!' he said into the stage mike.

The crowd applauded and cheered again more loudly.

'They're going on a break,' he continued, 'but don't you go nowhere, 'cause they'll be right back!'

The manager and the band left the stage. The music started again, this time from a stereo system, but it was not quite as loud as the live band.

Lloyd motioned with a movement of his head. 'Keep an eye on the lead singer, Kenzo Nagano,' he said. 'Wherever he's headed, you can be sure –'

'I'm already on it,' Elise interrupted with a frown.

She'd just detected an unusual energy. She'd missed it so far because the ambience was so distracting, but now the music had died down, she could hear it clearly – and it was close by.

She turned her eyes to the other end of the bar, towards the source of the sound.

'Forget him,' she said. 'I think I've found our man already.'

CHAPTER EIGHTEEN
Fire

He sat on a stool hunched over the bar with his back to them. The collar of his black leisure jacket was high enough that she couldn't quite see the back of his head.

Hitoshi Katayama suddenly raised his head, as he too had become aware of something. He sat up straight and turned round to see where the energy was coming from. He had a thick mop of bleached hair, longer at the front and cropped shorter at the back. Strands of his long flaxen fringe fell in front of his face, and against the deep red shirt he was wearing they looked like flames. A thin tie the same shade as his hair hung loosely around his neck.

Lloyd craned his neck to look through the crowd.

'Yeah, that's him,' he said.

Katayama saw Elise and froze. After a long pause, he slowly lifted the cigarette that he held in his hand and put it to his lips. He nodded at her and rose from his stool.

'I think he's coming our way,' said Elise, turning to Lloyd.

'I think not,' Lloyd replied.

Elise looked back at the bar. The stool was empty.

'Where did he –?'

'Let's go.'

Hurriedly they pushed their way through the crowd, and caught a glimpse of Katayama as he escaped through the back exit.

'We'll have to catch him from the other side,' said Lloyd, and they quickly made their way to the front entrance.

They rushed round the building to the rear car park. Other than a few cars and recycling bins, they saw nothing. Lloyd was on the verge of checking his observer strap but Elise stopped him. She could hear humming again.

'Wait,' she said.

She pointed at the nightclub's rear wall. In a pitch-black corner under the shadow of a skip was a small orange dot of light. It appeared to dance on its own in the air, glowing fiercely, and then quickly became dim. She smelled cigarette smoke.

Then from the same corner they heard a deep voice.

'Hi.'

As her eyes grew accustomed to the darkness she saw the rough silhouette of a figure. Katayama stepped out of the shadow into view with a gliding movement, his black and white brogue shoes barely touching the ground. He took the cigarette from his mouth.

'So we meet,' he said. His eyes turned to Lloyd. 'Again.'

'I told you I'd be back with proof,' said the agent. 'Here she is.'

'Good for you.' Hitoshi's eyes turned to Elise and shifted downward. 'Nice chronometer.'

'Huh? Oh.' He was referring to her ES tag. 'Snap,' she said, noticing the same model on his left wrist.

The silence that followed had little to do with not knowing what to say. For Elise, meeting David, or the man who used to be David, had triggered a sensation much like déjà vu.

Lloyd coughed deliberately. 'Sorry to interrupt the reunion,' he said. 'Hitoshi, we need to talk.'

'What about? I told you before. I don't know anything.'

'And I suppose you don't know who she is?'

'Should I?'

'I'm the same as you,' said Elise. 'A psychic.'

'I know. I got your vibe.'

'And also –'

'We might be the same in some ways,' he said, 'but I'm not who you think I am.'

'Really?' said Lloyd. 'Can you remind me what you did to end up with that fetching *chronometer*?'

Katayama waved dismissively. 'Yeah, yeah.'

'We don't hand those things out to just anyone, you know.'

'And what did *she* do, Agent? Rob a bank?'

Elise suppressed a smile. 'Mr Katayama,' she said, we'd like to talk to you about the case.'

'I have nothing to say on that. Especially to *him*.' He turned and began to walk away.

'Hitoshi!' Lloyd shouted after him. 'Come back here!'

'Wait!' said Elise.

Katayama ignored them. He sailed towards the back entrance of the nightclub where a bouncer stood guard to only allow authorised people through, and disappeared through the door.

Lloyd checked his observer strap. 'He's just gone backstage.'

They returned to the bar, and saw another bouncer standing by a door near the stage.

'You go on ahead,' said Lloyd. 'He won't talk to me anyway. It should be easy for you to get in. Just tell the bouncer you're a fan. I'll wait for you at the bar. And be warned – he'll do his best to avoid answering your questions.'

Elise nodded and headed towards the door. She slowed her pace as she approached the bouncer, not entirely sure how to handle the situation.

'Hey little lady. Dance floor's *that* way,' he said, pointing in a direction over her shoulder.

Elise smiled pertly. 'Actually, I'm looking for someone,' she said. 'Do you know where I might find Hitoshi Katayama?'

'Why? Who's asking?'

'Backstage, is he?'

'You a friend of his?'

'... Yeah.'

He folded his arms. 'I can't let you past.'

She tried Lloyd's suggestion. 'I just want his autograph,' she said. What harm would it do?'

'*His* autograph?'

Okay, she thought, so maybe that didn't sound convincing. She made another stab.

'The Glitch might sing the songs, but he writes them. His lyrics are amazing. … But I won't complain if I get to meet the band too.'

The bouncer clicked his tongue thoughtfully a few times, and she gazed at him as though she'd be heartbroken if he denied her the chance to meet her idols.

It worked.

'They're in the second room on the right.'

He stepped aside and Elise entered a corridor. She reached the room he'd indicated, and heard chattering voices and hooting laughter behind the door.

Before she even knocked the noise suddenly stopped, as though someone had signalled the others in the room to be quiet.

'Who's there?' asked a woman from the other side.

'My name's Elise Archer. I'd like to speak to Hitoshi Katayama.'

'He's not here.'

'I *know* you're there, Mr Katayama. We're the same, remember?'

Voices whispered among themselves. And then –

'Let her in,' said Katayama.

A band member unlocked and opened the door for her. A dressing table was on her left, with makeup and toiletries lying all over it, and a mirror with lights along the top. Wisps of cigarette smoke wafted through the air.

The members of the band had positioned themselves wherever they could fit into the small space. Katayama stood leaning against the dressing table at the back end of the room, and a woman with purple hair sat on a stool near him, with an electric guitar in her lap. The lead singer, Nagano, sat on another stool opposite them, cigarette in one hand, and beer bottle in the other, beside the drummer who sat on the floor. They all stared at her.

'Who is she?' asked Nagano. 'An ex-girlfriend?'

'She doesn't seem his type,' remarked the woman, chewing gum. 'Hitoshi, aren't you going to introduce us?'

'I would, but I only met her five minutes ago myself – in this lifetime, anyway.'

All heads turned to look at him.

'Mr Katayama,' said Elise, 'We didn't finish what we started.'

'We didn't start anything.'

'Look,' she said a little impatiently, 'even if you don't care about the case, I do – so please, just give me five minutes. That's all I ask.'

He looked down briefly in thought.

'Leave us alone,' he said to Nagano.

His friends got up and shuffled to the door.

'We've got to get back on stage in a bit anyway,' said Nagano, patting Katayama's arm on his way out. 'We'll be at the bar.'

'Sure.'

Nagano walked out after the band. The woman however lagged behind, hovering at the door.

'Go, Tami,' Katayama said firmly, heading towards her. 'Now.'

Reluctantly she turned away, and he immediately closed the door on her. He took Nagano's stool, and Elise took Tami's.

Katayama took a silver lighter from the breast pocket of his jacket and lit a fresh cigarette. He regarded her closely, his eyes so intense she couldn't look away. She almost felt his mental energy behind them, and wondered if he was trying to read her aura. With nothing said between them for those few moments, she had the opportunity to see his as well; not that it was of any use to her. Mustard yellow was the main colour she saw, but she had no idea what that said about him. Stella had given her a book on auras years ago, and she'd never read it.

'Jo?' he said, after exhaling.

'That's right.'

He looked her up and down. 'Thank God. If you were Leon … well, that'd just be *wrong*.'

She couldn't stop herself from smiling. 'Mr Katayama,' she said self-consciously, 'I –'

'It's Hitoshi. Where's Lloyd?'

'In the bar. He thought you might prefer to speak to me alone.'

'How considerate of him.' He took a puff from his cigarette. 'So, how did they find you?'

'Actually, I contacted them.'

His eyes widened. 'Why the hell did you do that?'

'It's a long story, but I didn't have much choice.'

'Then give me the abridged version.'

She gave him a brief explanation of who she was and how the Manner case had brought her to Hadescape. 'It was only after I arrived here that they briefed me about the Palmerton investigation,' she said finally. 'I found out they'd reopened the case just before Manner escaped. Quite a coincidence, huh?'

She waited for a comment. He betrayed no emotion on his handsome feline features.

'Have you agreed to testify?' he asked.

'Yes.'

Hitoshi took another puff.

'Good luck.'

She looked at him, puzzled. 'Is that all you have to say?'

'What do you want me to say?'

He had her there.

'I don't know. I thought you might tell me why you've refused.'

'So they've been talking to you about me.' He leaned forward to flick some ash into an ashtray lying on the dressing table, his eyes never leaving hers. 'How much do you remember, Elise?'

'Not much.'

'Figures. If you remembered anything at all, you'd stay well away from them too.'

'So you *do* remember something?'

'I never said I didn't.'

'Not to me. But you've been telling GAILE you don't know anything – that they have the wrong man.'

He gave her a wicked smile. 'So I lied. But I had no choice. They wanted to pin that hacking charge on me.'

'I don't think so. Admitting you have David's memories doesn't prove that you hacked that network. At best it supplies a motive. That isn't enough to secure a conviction.'

He didn't answer.

'Or is there some other reason you won't talk to GAILE?'

He remained quiet. She made a guess.

'Is it because of Adam?'

His expression darkened. 'You remember what he did?'

'You mean what he did to his brother?'

'He worked for *them*.'

It was as she'd suspected.

'Yes, he was a GAILE officer,' she said. 'And I know what you're thinking, because I thought it too. But GAILE didn't order Adam to kill us. He took his orders from someone else.'

His brow twitched. 'What?'

'They explained it to me today. He worked for a third party – some people who wanted to take the data off Omar.'

'... A third party? That's what they said?'

She nodded.

He was quiet for a moment, and then he burst into laughter.

'What's so funny?'

'You really don't remember a thing, do you?' He paused to get over his private joke and take another puff from his cigarette. 'But you know what? You're better off. God, I wish I could forget. Just thinking about it gives me the creeps. Haven't you ever felt it, Elise, that there's something amiss about this whole thing?'

She frowned. *The dread!* Had he really felt it too?

Her hesitation had given him his answer.

'You have, haven't you?' he said. 'Then listen to your gut. Trust me. It's on the money.'

Whether he was sincere or avoiding her questions, Elise would worry about it later. For now she had to stick to her objective.

'Normally I would, believe me,' she said. 'But I've thought about it a lot, and I've come to realise that these negative feelings I've had all these years are only natural, seeing as GAILE tried to bring us – I mean, the Abdul Salaam members, to –'

'Abdul Salaam?'

'The terrorist group.'

'The –? Oh, right,' he said slowly. 'They told you about that too.'

'My point is that since they were fugitives, we still remember their fear of getting caught – their fear of GAILE. Adam's actions would have only added to that fear, don't you think?'

'... I guess.'

'So, will you reconsider?'

'Not a chance.'

'Give me one good reason why not.'

His reply was instantaneous. 'I can give you two. This for one,' he said, pointing at his ES tag. 'I can just about understand them giving me one of these, but why have they tagged *you*, copper?' he said derisively, switching from his Brooklyn broad to a London accent at the final word.

She gave him a fake smile, and shot back just as rapidly. 'Ah, but you see, that's down to you and Manner. You hacked a sensitive network for goodness knows what reason –'

'– They never proved it was me.'

'Whatever – and Manner has returned here just as GAILE started their investigation.' His expression changed subtly just then, and she knew she had his attention. 'See how it looks? Your memories have influenced your actions. Manner can be excused since he's ill – but you can't. So they're making me wear a tag too, just in case I follow suit. So, what's your second reason?'

'Agent Numbskull out there,' he said, nodding at the wall. 'That shield of his doesn't exactly fill me with confidence.'

She sighed. It was hard to argue with him when on the inside she knew his assertions were valid.

'There are some aspects of the case that are classified,' she found herself saying. 'They're only taking security measures.'

He looked at her incredulously. 'Wow. For someone who's lived twice, you're pretty naïve.' He flicked more ash. 'Like I said, I don't trust them and I won't have anything to do with them. And if you had any sense, neither would you.'

Elise looked at him. She'd sensed something in his tone, and now she saw it in his eyes as they stared shamelessly back at her.

'That's the second time you've tried to warn me off,' she said.

His eyes never moved, but they glazed slightly. 'You know, I always wanted to be a cop. But they'd never let me in.'

'Don't change the subject. If there's something I should know, then tell me. Please.'

His gaze shifted sideways, and he took another puff of his cigarette with drawn in cheeks. When he looked back at her again, she saw it on his face: Fear, desperation … *dread*. He took a short breath, as if he was about to tell her something. But whatever was on his mind, he couldn't bring himself to say it. He turned away from her altogether.

'I think you should go,' he said abruptly. 'Tell the agent, nice try but I'm exercising my right to remain silent.'

She thought it best not to push him any further for now.

'Okay, look, you don't have to tell me. Just answer me this: Shouldn't the people who did this to us be called to account?'

'Even though GAILE won't tell us who they are?' he replied, his face still turned away.

He must have tackled them about it before.

'Yeah, I was angry about that too,' she said. 'But the important thing is to bring the perpetrators to justice. Won't you at least just think about it? They just want to ask you a few questions. And you'd really be helping me out. I want to know more about these memories in my head. The problem is that they're too sketchy for me to work with on my own. To be frank, I need your input.'

'You mean they do,' he said, nodding again at the wall.

'Yes, they do too,' she conceded. 'But this way you wouldn't have to testify in court. Taylor has already told me they only really need one of us for that, and I've agreed to it. One statement and that'd be it for you. They'd leave you alone after that. I'm sure of it. So will you talk to them? You don't even have to answer me right away. Just tell me you'll think about it.'

At last he turned back to her. 'Okay, let's say I decided to talk. What would I get out of it?'

'You'd help to put those people away.'

'Is that all?'

'It's better than nothing,' she said, thinking quickly. 'We'd also get to find out what happened to us, and who we are. Maybe we'd even find out about our biological parents. And you and I would have the chance to compare our memories, exchange notes. We'd both benefit from that.'

Another moment of telling silence passed. Hitoshi didn't even come close to resembling the man whom she remembered as

Joanna's lover, but there was fire in those dark flirtatious eyes, and only she could see it.

He caught her off-guard with a devilish smile. 'You might have a point there. I wouldn't mind getting to know you a little better – or perhaps I should say, reacquainted.'

Elise blushed, and chided herself inside.

'Does that mean you'll join us?' she hastened to say.

'Maybe …' He tossed the cigarette butt to the floor and put it out with a twist of his foot. 'I'll think about it – but no promises.'

She smiled. 'Then we'll come to your place tomorrow morning.'

She got up, and he hopped off his stool to open the door for her.

'And, Lise?'

'Hmm?'

Hitoshi came in close, though he didn't touch her. His voice purred in her ear.

'I look forward to reminiscing about the good old days.'

Elise and Lloyd left the nightclub and got into the agent's car.

'How did it go?' asked Lloyd as they pulled onto the road.

'He's still refusing to testify,' she said, 'but he agreed to consider giving you a statement. I've arranged for us to see him again tomorrow morning.'

'Really? He's been impossible with us. Well done.'

Elise smiled to herself. 'I'm not saying it was easy, but as far as I can tell, his only real problem is with GAILE. He took issue with your policy of classifying the details of the case.'

He scoffed. 'Is that what he said?'

'Not in so many words. But then I suppose his frustration is perfectly understandable.'

'Oh yeah, perfectly understandable,' he repeated, in a tone that fell short of sincerity. 'Did you ask him about Manner?'

Elise realised that at the beginning of their conversation she'd headed that way, but had subsequently lost the thread.

'Oh. I never quite got round to it,' she said guiltily.

'Not to worry. We'll get it out of him tomorrow.'

CHAPTER NINETEEN
Satan's Whisper

'Report,' said Gregory, speaking to Lloyd via a laptop in his Washington office.

'Miss Archer remembers nothing,' said Lloyd.

'Is that the actual state of her memory, or is she just feigning ignorance, like Mr Katayama?'

'She's given us no reason to doubt her. However we'll know for certain after the tests.'

'When will that be?' asked Gregory.

'The final tests on the nanospheres are almost complete. Dr Fischer tells me they'll be ready for us by Thursday or Friday. We'll have the biological data back before the end of the week.'

If the results corroborated Archer's statement, the Committee would likely strike her off their threat list.

'Has she agreed to testify?'

'Yes sir.'

Then she really must not remember anything, thought Gregory.

'How did she fare with Katayama?' he asked.

'She convinced him to reconsider. We're meeting him again in the morning to discuss it further.'

Gregory drummed his fingers on the desk thoughtfully. Katayama had given them the runaround from the start. If he was consistent in anything, it was in being inconsistent. That they could live with, but what if Katayama was to make a definite decision and it was not the desirable one?

'If he keeps his mouth shut, all the better for him,' said Gregory.

'And if he doesn't?' said Lloyd.

'We'll see how things progress first. Always keep casualties to a minimum,' he said, repeating a favourite phrase of the old general. 'Of course we may have to dispose of Mr Manner. Fortunately for us, no one will miss him.'

* * * * * * * *

Elise had gone to sleep thinking about her encounter with Hitoshi Katayama, and it was the first thing that entered her mind when she awoke. She'd never remembered much about David Cohen except for how deeply Joanna felt about him. She knew even less about the man who possessed his memories now, and yet she couldn't deny that she was drawn to him. From the way he'd looked at her she knew he felt it too.

Despite the connection between them, Hitoshi had been extremely cagey. Taylor was probably right in suspecting that he could recall as much as Manner. That being the case, she had to seriously think about what he'd said, and even more seriously about what he hadn't. She'd only recently accepted the logical theory that her feelings of dread were irrational, based on some echo of Joanna's own hatred of GAILE and of Adam Cohen. Now she had cause to think again.

At the Harper Building she told Taylor and Lloyd about Hitoshi's stated reasons for refusing to testify. She skirted round the issue of his unspoken reasons.

'He was evasive, as you said,' she told them. 'He wasn't willing to talk to me about anything.'

'At least he's thinking about giving us a statement,' said the deputy director. 'You've managed to get more from him in ten minutes than we did in two weeks.'

'But he could be up to something,' said Lloyd.

'True. You should go and catch Hitoshi now, before he decides to leave his apartment,' said Taylor, looking at his observer strap. 'We don't want to have to chase him around all day. That boy moves pretty fast.'

Hitoshi lived with band members Kenzo and Tami in an apartment in Rock Moor, at the south side bordering Glensville. Elise looked up as she approached the high-rise building. Metal grating covered many of the smashed windows on the lower floors. Music blasted from one of the higher floors. A number of youths lurked around with nothing to do. Elise felt their eyes on her and Lloyd as they headed up the concrete steps to the ground floor entrance.

Lloyd pressed the intercom button for apartment 22.

'*Yes?*' came a woman's voice.

'This is Agent Lloyd from GAILE Intelligence and Elise Archer. We're here to see Hitoshi.'

'*Come on up.*'

The front door released and they went into the lobby, getting away from the biting chill of the morning air. They took a lift to Hitoshi's floor and reached the apartment. Tami opened the door. She was in a bathrobe and had a towel round her head. The look on her face could hardly be described as welcoming.

Elise and Lloyd stepped into a studio flat comprising a merged living room and kitchen area.

'He's getting dressed,' she said.

As she didn't offer them a seat, they remained standing. Tami took her place on a bright blue sofa. She rested her left foot on the rim of the small coffee table in front of her and carefully painted her toenails purple.

'Nice place you have here,' Elise remarked in an attempt to break the ice.

Tami ignored her. But Elise meant what she said. The interior was nothing like she'd expected, being much roomier than she had thought it would be. The décor was well coordinated in lilac and blue. It was clean and tidy, almost immaculate, and there was not a cigarette or ashtray in sight. The only scent in the studio was that of the nail varnish.

A stereo system sat silently on the floor next to the sofa. The place would have been perfectly still had it not been for the bass sound booming from somewhere on the floor above.

On the left wall next to the kitchen area a single oil painting caught her eye. Two winged figures flew in a stormy sky, reaching out towards each other, ready to collide in battle. They were identical apart from their colouration and their wings. The black one with feathered wings was an angel; the other was white, with bat-like wings – it was a devil.

Elise looked at a bedroom door to her right. From the humming sound she heard, she knew Hitoshi was in there.

Suddenly he entered, wearing a T-shirt and jogging pants, his hair wet and ruffled, and a mug in his hand. He took a swig, and without so much as a glance at them he moved towards the kitchen area and shook the kettle. It was empty.

'Coffee, anyone?' he asked as though he'd greeted them already.

'I'll have one,' Elise replied, and she joined him at the sink. 'I take milk and no sugar.'

Hitoshi filled the kettle and took a mug from a cupboard.

'You're early,' he said.

'We weren't sure you'd still be here if we were late,' said Lloyd.

'I'm sure you would've caught up with me eventually,' Hitoshi retorted, tapping his ES tag, 'if you really wanted to.'

There was an awkward silence as Hitoshi made the coffee. He handed Elise her mug and they returned to the living room area.

Hitoshi looked indicatively at Tami. She got up sulkily.

'Okay, I can take a hint! I've got to be at the computer anyway. We need to confirm our booking for Saturday's gig.'

With a dirty look at Elise, she went into Hitoshi's bedroom and closed the door.

'Where's Kenzo?' asked Lloyd.

'Still asleep, I imagine,' he said, and took an armchair. 'He won't be up for a while. Grab a seat.'

Elise sat next to Lloyd on a sofa opposite Hitoshi.

'I'm glad you finally agreed to talk to us,' Lloyd began. 'We –'

'I haven't agreed to anything yet. We need to negotiate terms.'

The agent leaned forward in his seat. 'We're not here to negotiate,' he said curtly. 'We just want your answer. Are you testifying or not?'

'Sure … once we've settled on the terms.'

'The only term you should be concerned about is the one you'll spend behind bars if you don't cooperate.'

'You don't have a basis for arrest.'

'Really? How does obstructing a GAILE investigation sound?'

'I'm not obstructing anything. I just want to talk terms.'

Lloyd glowered like a father at an unruly child. Hitoshi calmly finished off his coffee and took his mug to the sink.

So far Elise had stayed out of their verbal fisticuffs. Now she took the opportunity to intervene.

'Lloyd,' she said in a low voice, 'why don't you hear him out?'

He looked indignant. 'I'm not making any deals with him!'

She raised a brow. 'Is that GAILE's official stance, or just yours?'

He sighed irritably. 'You don't know him, Elise. He's been playing games with us from the start.'

Elise glanced at Hitoshi. He was busy with the washing up.

'That may well be,' she said, her voice still low, 'but the fact is he hasn't refused to talk outright this time. Give him a chance. What will you tell your superiors otherwise – that Hitoshi might have cooperated but you let your personal feelings get in the way?'

Lloyd looked up in despair. 'Fine. … Fine! Just tell us what you want!' he said loudly.

Hitoshi dried his hands and returned to his seat.

'I'm glad you finally agreed to talk,' he said, impersonating Lloyd with an insolent grin.

The agent snorted.

'Here's the deal,' said Hitoshi. 'I'll tell you what I know, and maybe even testify in court, as long as, one, you grant me blanket immunity, and two, you expunge my record. And I mean *all* of it. I want my freedom back. I want to be able to leave town, start over – do whatever the hell I please. Get the picture?'

Elise looked at Hitoshi in dismay. The bid was preposterous.

Lloyd chuckled in disbelief. 'Expunge your record? You know full well we won't do that!'

Hitoshi lowered his head slightly, allowing his damp fringe to come in front of his eyes, as if to conceal their plot.

'But I could give you just the information you need.' He paused before he dropped the bait. 'Mind you, you're a smart guy. Maybe you can stop Manner on time. But then again …'

'What are you talking about?'

Hitoshi smirked in reply.

'If you know what Manner's doing here, you tell me now!'

'Sorry, Agent. No terms, no statement.'

Lloyd had a wolfish countenance. 'Hey! He's already found her!' he snapped, pointing in Elise's direction with his thumb. 'Will you let her remain in danger, just to spite us?'

'Oh, please. She's not in any danger. Not from him.'

'He's murdered four people! Who knows what he's capable of?'

Hitoshi sneered. 'Like you give a damn about her, or anyone but yourselves!' Just then he looked Elise's way, and restrained himself. 'It makes no difference what I tell you,' he said. 'It's not like I know where he is.'

Lloyd smiled contemptuously. 'Of course you don't – *right now*. No one does. But you know where he's headed, don't you?'

'No.'

'You just implied that you did.'

'I don't know where he is, and that's the truth.'

'Then what *do* you know?'

'Do we have a deal?' said Hitoshi, without missing a beat.

Lloyd became quiet. He placed his elbow on the sofa armrest and rubbed his temple with his thumb as though he had a headache. He had a look of suspicion in his eyes, trying to decide if Hitoshi really had some important information to give them, or he was just stringing them along; and Hitoshi was brazenfaced, daring the agent to take a guess.

Eventually Lloyd made the logical decision, albeit grudgingly.

'I don't have the authority to give you what you want.'

'I know you don't, Agent,' replied Hitoshi with a crooked smile. 'But the deputy does.'

Taylor was not impressed when he heard the news.

'Trust the conniving little rat to pull a fast one,' he said.

'Can't you offer a compromise?' asked Elise.

'He's not after a compromise,' said Lloyd briskly. 'He's just messing us around – again. I say we charge him with obstructing the investigation. He might rethink his attitude if we lock him up.'

'No,' said the deputy. 'We don't have time to waste throwing him in jail and hoping he'll talk – not with Manner still on the loose.' He rubbed his palms together slowly and gave the matter some thought. 'All right, bring him in.'

Lloyd headed out of the office and returned with Hitoshi.

Taylor put on a pleasant smile. 'Please sit down, Hitoshi. I'm sure we can do this in a way that works best for everyone.'

'No,' he said, staying on his feet. 'It's my way or nothing.'

'Don't be so hasty. I believe we can offer a fair compromise. Aren't you even prepared to hear what it is?'

Hitoshi cocked his head to one side. Something about Taylor's tone seemed to make him curious, and he sat down.

The deputy put forward a tantalising proposition. Whilst expunging Hitoshi's record was totally out of the question, GAILE would concede to his secondary demand and grant him blanket immunity. This meant that they couldn't later use anything he said in or out of court to prosecute him for any other crime, even if they found incriminating hard evidence. In addition they would give him a commendation note as a rehabilitated hacker who had assisted in protecting the MWA. It was far better than anything else on paper that could certify him as a reformed citizen.

'So,' said Taylor, 'what do you say?'

Hitoshi pulled a face. 'That's only half of what I asked for. And the smaller half at that.'

'What you asked for is legally impossible,' said the deputy. 'If you consult your attorney –'

'I don't need an attorney. He'll only tell me to be a good boy, and not aim so high. So thanks for the offer,' said Hitoshi, getting up again. 'But no thanks.'

Taylor's smile withered.

Lloyd moved to intercept.

'No Aaron, let him go,' said Taylor. 'Hitoshi, I'll give you forty-eight hours to think about it. But if you don't cooperate after that –'

'Yeah, yeah, you'll throw me in the pen.' He looked at Elise. 'See you around, Lise. You're on your own.'

His tone was resolved and final. She opened her mouth to speak, but didn't know what to say.

Hitoshi turned and left the interview room.

'He'll come back,' said the deputy, sounding completely unconvinced of his own words. 'He won't risk jail again.'

But Elise knew, just as he did, that Hitoshi was never going to join the investigation.

CHAPTER TWENTY
The Old Guard

Though he couldn't show it in front of Taylor and Elise, Aaron was actually relieved to see Hitoshi leave. Over the past three weeks he'd been as patient as possible, but had gradually grown tired of the hacker's capriciousness. And regrettable though it was, Hitoshi had left of his own accord.

Now Aaron could stop worrying about him and focus on Elise. He'd known her for just two days, but he already had much more confidence in her than in he'd ever had in Hitoshi; and after today's exhibition, it wouldn't take much to convince her that the dubious Shaman was best left out of the equation.

Aaron went to a small office allocated to him on the sixth floor of the Harper Building. He switched on the desktop computer and as it booted up he checked his observer strap. Elise was just a block from her apartment. He could in theory head over and talk to her right after his report to the director, but wondered if it might be better to wait until after dark.

He connected to the director's office at the GAILE Coordination Center, and Kingswell's image appeared on the monitor. He welcomed Aaron's report, but with caution.

'I'm glad you've given Katayama time to think it over,' said the director. 'If he knows anything about Manner's motives, then he'll be back to renegotiate.'

'I doubt it,' replied Aaron.

Kingswell frowned. 'You seem quite sure of yourself.'

'He made totally unrealistic demands in exchange for the information, knowing that we wouldn't submit to them, and he was totally disinterested in our compromise. He was bluffing.'

The director drummed his fingers on his desk. 'Perhaps. We'll wait and see if your theory bears out.'

* * * * * * * *

Alone in the apartment that afternoon, pacing up and down the lounge area with a mug of coffee in her hand, Elise was brooding. Taylor had given her a file on the upcoming court case and she'd just finished reading it, only to find there was nothing in there that GAILE hadn't told her already.

Why had Hitoshi hinted that he knew something of Manner's motives, if he'd had no intention of telling them? Was it all just a perverse prank, as Lloyd believed it was, or was it really more complicated than that?

Of course it made no difference to her now. Hitoshi had opted out despite the threat of jail. And in any case GAILE seemed disinterested in following through with the threat. They'd accepted that they would have to rely on Elise's sole testimony, even though she knew that she was probably their worst witness. Coming to Hadescape hadn't helped her remember anything new at all. Of course she couldn't have established any sort of psychometric connection here after thirty years; but just being back ought to have given her *something*.

The other Project subjects didn't seem to have the same problem. She knew that Manner's memory had probably returned after receiving ECT; but what about Hitoshi? He'd moved to Hadescape in his early twenties, and his past life probably influenced his decision. He may even have come to Hadescape expressly to try and jog his memory.

Assuming she was right, how had he achieved the desired result? Perhaps his memories had gradually resurfaced with long term exposure. No, it wasn't that. Then perhaps he'd visited specific and significant places that she hadn't yet been to.

She stopped pacing and sipped her coffee. That was feasible.

Now it was just a case of figuring out where he might have gone. That was easy. The most obvious place for him to go would be the place where David died: Coppice Gate, at the east end of the peninsula. Joanna had died in the same district but a couple of miles away, in Wheeler Park.

Was it worth going up there? It wasn't too far, being around eight or nine miles from Verity Square. She looked at her watch and her gaze fell on the ES tag. They'd advised her not to go anywhere alone; and they were probably monitoring her movements. So what? She wasn't doing anything illegal. And they'd made no mention of having set a boundary on the tag.

She put down her mug on the table near the apartment door.

Forget them, she thought, and headed straight out.

* * * * * * * * *

After finishing his report Aaron went down to the ground floor, rubbing his temple with his thumb. Pain was gnawing at both sides of his head, behind his eyeballs, and he wanted to get back to his apartment for a painkiller before it got any worse. He was halfway across the entrance hall when his observer strap beeped.

'What's he doing this time?' he grumbled to himself, pressing the left-hand button on the strap a couple of times to get feedback. He was surprised to find that it was Elise, not Hitoshi, who had triggered the alarm. He'd checked the strap only a few minutes earlier and she'd still been in the apartment. Now she was out and heading west at around twenty-five miles per hour.

Aaron guessed she was doing some investigating of her own. Perhaps he could catch her alone and have a word.

His strap beeped again, in a slightly lower tone. Kash was contacting him on the communications frequency – a facility missing on the ES tag.

'*I'm within range of Archer's signal. I can follow.*'

Aaron frowned. The Harper Building was much closer than either the Morton house or Hadescape University.

'Aren't you on stakeout?' he said.

'*I was, but I just came off my watch. I'm at home.*'

Kash's apartment was situated at the Silver River waterfront in Coppice Gate, so right now he was closer to Elise's position. Aaron couldn't really argue with that.

'Okay, go ahead. Lloyd out.'

Aaron stood in the middle of the entrance hall and sighed. The perfect chance to speak to her was lost. He contemplated returning to his apartment and waiting until Kash had escorted Elise back to her place. He could give it another hour and then head over.

But just then his cell rang.

It was an officer from the Police Liaison Bureau. The Hadescape branch was on site at the GAILE Office Complex.

The liaison officer told him that police had just picked up a man at Rock Moor for shoplifting. She was unable to confirm his accent, but he had no ID card, suggesting he was a vagrant, and his physical description seemed to match that of Peter Manner.

Aaron was obliged to go down and check it out. Had Kash not already gone after Elise, Aaron could have asked him to do it, but never mind. If anything, the present distractions only proved that he really was better off waiting until nightfall.

* * * * * * * * *

Soren Forest stretched as far west as Verity Square and east almost to the peninsula tip; and much of it lay within Wheeler Park's territory. The cab driver told Elise that the only place he could stop was at a camping area partway through the forest in the west side, just a few miles from Verity Square. But Elise wanted to get closer to where she believed Joanna crashed her car. In the end he took her to the southwest entrance of the park and told her she could reach the woodland on foot if she took one of the nature trails.

Elise stepped out of the cab and walked through the entrance gate. With its gentle grass slopes and wooded zones, Wheeler Park was one of the most popular green spaces in Hadescape. Tourist attractions were scattered throughout – a museum, a bird sanctuary, bridleways, nature trails, and lakes. Though it was a weekday there were some people about. Again it felt only faintly familiar. In the daylight the park was picturesque; starkly different to the black frosty terrain Joanna crawled through in her final moments. As determined as Elise had been when she'd left the apartment, nerves and uncertainty caught up with her now. But turning back after having come so far would be a waste of time, and she might not have the chance to go out alone like this again.

Elise summoned up her courage and went over to the nearest signpost. It had a small map and a list of the places within walking distance of her current position. She took the pathway signposted: *Soren Forest – 7 min.*

She reached the woods and began looking for the main road that ran through it. She could hear traffic, so the road wasn't far from where she was. Elise looked round at the half shed trees, trying to recapture the essence of the area. Then she sat down on the red and golden leaves, placed her hands on the ground and closed her eyes. She thought that if she immersed herself in the energy of the forest, it might unlock something hidden in her unconscious memory.

Elise waited for several minutes, picturing the forest as she saw it in her mind.

Unsurprisingly, nothing happened.

She got up and moved further into the woodland, found a spot to sit down and tried again.

Again, absolutely nothing.

Maybe she was trying too hard. For her final attempt she took the uphill path towards the sound of the traffic. Near the top she saw the road, and spotted steel guardrails running along the side, similar to the ones Joanna had seen just after the car crash. She moved towards them, so absorbed in her thoughts that she didn't hear the footsteps coming up behind her.

'Elise?'

She gasped and turned to see two men in suits. She'd never met them before, but since neither had a detectable aura, it wasn't difficult to work out who they were.

'Let me guess,' she said. 'GAILE Intelligence?'

One of them showed her his ID card.

'Agent Kash, ma'am,' he said. 'Sorry to scare you, but you really shouldn't be out here on your own.'

* * * * * * * * *

Peter had been parked on Preston Avenue for about half an hour, reading a newspaper in the back of the van, when he sensed movement at the house. He put the paper aside and looked out of the rear window just as Charlotte came out of the front door. She wore a coat and carried a handbag, so he assumed that she'd be gone for a while. She closed the front gate and walked away.

He'd found no opportunity to get to the house the day before. Charlotte had left the house once, but only after a young woman, presumably her daughter, had come and taken her place for a few hours. Today however it seemed the young woman was not available. This was probably his only chance and he couldn't pass it up. Ben must have buckled under pressure long ago and told the police everything he knew; and by now the message had probably reached *them* too. Time was short.

He readied himself and looked out of the window. The street was empty, as most people had already gone to work. He opened the driver's door and got out.

There was one energy pattern inside the house, and he was certain that he knew whose it was. Peter headed over and entered the front gate quickly, not wanting anyone to come by and see him. He got to the door, and as he was about to press the doorbell he suddenly stopped. Nervous feelings were building up inside his chest, and he wasn't sure why. He closed his eyes and forced himself to press it.

'Charlotte!' shouted an elderly woman's voice. 'Charlotte!'

She was answered with silence.

Peter rang the bell again.

'Charlotte!'

The old woman eventually came to the door herself. It took her almost a full minute to reach it.

'Wait, I'm coming,' she said, and opened the door. 'Yes?'

Peter was awestruck. She was shrunken and frail, noticeably shorter than the proud, strong silver-haired woman he remembered. Her hair was as copious as it had always been, but now it was cotton white.

The sun was behind Peter and it shone in her eyes. She squinted, and the wrinkles gathered in her brow.

'Laurence? Is that you?'

Laurence?

Peter was sure that Laurence was dead, for not once had he sensed his energy in the house. Laurence had been a deeply committed man and would never have left his family for any earthly reason, at least not for long. Perhaps, thought Peter, she was referring to someone else in the family who had the same name. But he was about to be proven wrong.

'Laurence John Morton!' said Yvonne reproachfully. 'Where have you been? You were supposed to pick up the girls from school –' Suddenly she checked herself and frowned. 'Wait, you're not Laurence! Who are you?'

Alarmed, Peter looked closely at her aura and noticed how weak it was. The pale colours were not necessarily a sign of advanced age. He'd seen similar grey and sickly yellow auras at Roseleigh many times. She was battle worn, tired of life's cruelties, and the only way to cope with her loss was to deny it.

He was the cause of her suffering. A promise that had been forcibly broken, the insurmountable barrier that had separated him from his family for almost three decades, bringing them untold anguish, and made worse by the fact that he'd never explained why he had to leave. The nervous feelings that had been building up inside him suddenly mixed with immense grief, and they culminated in a compulsion to speak. Numerous thoughts rushed to the fore; he wanted to tell her he was back; he was going to get revenge; he was going to expose the ones who had tried to destroy them; Leon's memories were preserved in him; he hadn't forgotten his promise, or his duty; and he could prove who he was by repeating Leon's last words to his parents.

Instead his eyes misted, and a single word came from his lips.

'Ma?'

His quivering voice sounded alien to him. But it evoked quite a different reaction from Yvonne. She looked searchingly into his eyes, shielding her own from the sun with a cupped hand.

'L-Leon?'

Her frown melted away, and she smiled. She seemed younger just then, revitalised.

'Leon!' she whispered, touching his face. 'You've come home! Oh, my sweet child!'

The contact provoked a fleeting connection and suddenly he was transported into her mind. He saw what she saw: A clean-shaven, fresh-faced young man with smartly trimmed black hair and large deep brown eyes; her son, standing before her. As soon as she moved her hand away, the connection was severed.

She brought him inside and into the living room.

'Let me take a look at you! My word! When did you last have something to eat? You just sit yourself down, and let your mama make you some –'

'I'm not hungry. Do you remember what I told you that night?'

She nodded. 'We rang the police forty-eight hours after you left and told them you were missing, just as you asked us to. We told them we hadn't seen you for days. Oh, they said some awful things about you, Leon! But I know you'd never do the things they say! I told them, my son is a God-fearing Christian! He wouldn't associate with terrorists! And your father, he – where is your father?' she said, looking round. 'Laurence?'

'Ma, I gave you something for safekeeping?'

'But Laurence, I – I can't –' she began, and then saw Peter and seemed to refocus. 'Oh, yes son. Don't worry – I know where it is!'

She left and was gone for several minutes. Peter took in the layout of the room while he waited. To him it was a stranger's abode, lacking the atmosphere of his home and his time. The only familiar thing was the old fireplace. He looked at the photographs on the mantelpiece, recognising Leon's two sisters Charlotte and Claire even in the recent pictures. They were with their husbands and children, and also their grandchildren. Laurence wasn't in any of them. He must have died many years ago. In the centre was a much older picture of the original family unit: Laurence, Yvonne, Claire, Charlotte, and Leon. They were younger, in happier times, clueless as to what was coming in their future. The picture had been taken around the time Leon had started work as a lecturer in economics at Hadescape University, long before he'd met the man who would change everything.

Yvonne returned at that moment, carrying a small plastic box of the kind for keeping small items of jewellery. Peter's eyes flashed. He held out his hand and she handed it to him. He opened it. Inside was a small flat disc around 8 cm across, known as a mini DVD, or digital video disc. By present-day technological standards it was an ancient relic, outmoded, and ultimately worthless. Peter however knew its real value, the timeless legacy it contained. If his enemies knew it was here, they would do everything in their power to destroy it.

He closed the lid and put the box in his jeans pocket.

Yvonne sighed happily. 'I knew you'd come back, Leon! I knew, because you swore to me, you said –'

'On my life, I'll come home,' he finished for her in a quiet voice, recalling Leon's words, 'no matter how long it takes.' Then, in the stark remembrance of just how long it had been, he looked at her intently. 'Did you ever take a look at what was on this disc?'

'Your father did, but he said it was all numbers. We didn't show anyone else. It was our secret, your father's and mine. Then he said he was going to look for you. Where is he? Someone should tell him you're here.'

Peter glanced again at the photos on the mantelpiece. Just how long had Yvonne been carrying her burden alone?

He looked at her. She was smiling at her son.

'Leon,' she said, 'you should eat something.'

Peter shook his head. 'I must go,' he said.

Her eyes widened. 'But you've only just come back.'

'I haven't fulfilled my promise.'

The colour in her cheeks drained away again. Whether she was reliving the night she last saw her son, or whether she could no longer differentiate between the past and the present, she seemed to resign herself to the fact that he was leaving. Her eyes brimming with tears, she nodded slowly and went out of the room for a second time. When she returned, she had a purse in her hand. She produced some notes.

'Here, son,' she said. 'Take this. Make sure you eat properly.'

He was hesitant, but she pressed the money into his hands.

'When will you be back?' she asked hoarsely.

His throat became dry. Unable to tell her the truth, and unwilling to lie, he turned and headed out of the room.

'Leon?' she said from behind him. 'Leon, you will come home soon, won't you? You must come back. Promise me, you hear? Promise me, on your life! ... On *my* life!'

He went to the front door. Yvonne trailed feebly after him.

'No! No, no, no! Leon! Promise me!' she pleaded. 'Please! Or I won't let you go! You must –'

He opened the front door just as she emerged in the hallway, struggling hopelessly to catch up. Her distraught expression was the last he saw of her through the gap of the door as he swung it shut. He stared at it, transfixed.

'LEON!'

Like a startled animal he jumped back, and then darted down the front path.

Her desperate cries continued inside the house.

'Leon! Leon!'

Peter flew through the front gate and to his van. He got in and started the engine; and as he did so, he saw a small boy of maybe ten years approaching the residence. He'd just come round the corner, and was looking at the house with a puzzled expression, apparently having heard the commotion. Peter glanced at the gate, and realised that in his haste he hadn't closed the gate properly. He put his foot down on the accelerator.

The boy had by now reached the gate. He turned and saw the van as it sped past the house. Peter turned his face away and hoped that the boy wouldn't remember him for long.

He drove nonstop for fifteen or twenty minutes, and in that time his emotions began to cool. He drove up through Rock Moor, remaining roughly parallel to Mustang River, and then turned onto the route into Pine Hills. He went west through the highland for a couple of miles, before he finally got off the road and stopped the van on unspoilt soil, in a secluded spot under some trees. He got out of the van, and detecting no signs of human life, he sat beneath a cedar with his legs crossed, and meditated.

An hour passed before Peter opened his eyes. When he did, he reached into his pocket and pulled out the precious box Yvonne had given him.

For the next part of his plan, the Peace Man was going to need some old technology, and help from an old expert.

CHAPTER TWENTY-ONE
The Call

Elise had just made herself some coffee and curled up on the sofa, her fingers wrapped snugly around the mug, when Manner invaded her mind.

* * * * * * * * *

'Old friend ... whoever you are, I'm in Crescent Bay West.'

His heart was beating fast, and his ears were ringing. He was on a quiet street, watching a young man on the other side approach a cash machine outside a bank. The man's energy was characteristic of youth, light and fresh. There was no instability in the aura, no black, grey or red to indicate trauma, violence or any other corruption. The man was emotionally healthy.

He didn't have the energy pattern of a criminal.

'Crescent Bay West,' muttered Peter once more.

He crossed the road. The mark had just put the card into the machine and was keying in his pin number on the touchpad when Peter came up behind him. He grabbed his left arm and twisted it round his back.

'Ugh!'

Peter touched the man's lower spine with the tip of his dagger.

'Don't make a sound, friend,' he said. 'I'm not going to hurt you. I just want your money.'

'Okay, okay,' the man said hastily, 'whatever you say.'

The man had been about to select the amount to withdraw from a list of options on the touch screen. The highest amount he could choose was 1000 dollars.

'Take out a hundred,' Peter ordered him.

The mark did so without protest, using his free hand to select *100* on the touch screen. A few seconds later a small pile of banknotes emerged from a large slot beneath the screen, and the card reappeared from a smaller slot next to the touchpad.

The man reached out to take the money. Peter pulled him back.

'Leave it there.'

Retaining a tight grip on the man's left arm, he rotated until the man faced the road and Peter had his back to the cash machine.

'Thank you,' said Peter. 'Now go, and don't look back.'

He released the man with a push to the right, showing him the direction he wanted him to go. The mark walked away, consciously pacing himself until he was close to the end of the block, and then he ran the rest of the way.

Peter watched him to make sure he didn't look back. Only when the man went round the corner did Peter take the card and the money from the machine. He entered an alleyway in the opposite direction, passing a café sign and a telephone box on the way in.

* * * * * * * * *

Elise came to. Out of the corner of her eye she thought she saw a tall dark figure at the apartment door, looking right at her. In fright she half got up, and as she did so she accidentally tilted the mug, spilling hot coffee onto her fingers.

'Yeow!' she exclaimed.

* * * * * * * * *

Peter felt the heat and breathed in sharply.

He examined his fingers, which felt as though someone had poured hot water on them. They were in fact cold from exposure to the night air. He nodded slowly to himself. He didn't understand what exactly had happened, but he was sure of what it meant.

She'd got the message.

* * * * * * * *

Elise went to her bedroom, took the jotter she'd left on top of the bedside drawer for such an occasion, and scribbled down all she could remember from the scene. The only notable thing she'd noticed was a blue neon sign that Manner had passed on his way into the alley. It had read: *Buzz Café*.

Back in the living room she called Lloyd on her mobile and informed him of the post-connection.

'He seemed to know I was reincarnated like him,' she told the agent anxiously, 'because he called me "old friend". He said he was in Crescent Bay West.'

'I'll be right over.'

Lloyd arrived within five minutes in casual wear. It occurred to her that she still didn't know where his apartment was.

'It's funny,' he said. 'This afternoon I was called to a police station in Rock Moor. They had a man in custody who closely matched Manner's physical profile. But it wasn't him.'

So that was where he'd been. Elise had been wondering why Lloyd wasn't among the agents who followed her to Soren Forest. But he must have heard about the incident. Elise thought he might mention it now. He didn't.

'Anyway, I can confirm there is a Buzz Café in Crescent Bay West,' he said, being focused on present matters. 'I've sent a team of plain clothes officers ahead of us to see if he's still in the area. 'They have shielding implants to avoid detection.'

Just then she noticed that he was squinting, as if in pain.

'Are you all right?' she asked. 'You look a bit off-colour.'

'I've just got a headache,' he replied. 'Do you think he's trying to meet you?'

'I doubt it. When he first connected to me, he saw us together at the Harper Building. He wouldn't trust me enough after that to risk meeting me. But I'm thinking … what if he's left a message? That's what he did in England. He left a note with each body.'

'It's possible, I guess. Where would he have left it?'

'I'm not sure,' she said. 'I saw him enter an alleyway. We should probably take a look around there.'

* * * * * * * * *

Peter had stopped at the end of the alley, still close to the cash machine where he had targeted his bait, and now he held his position. If her abilities were like his, then her connection to him would have lasted only as long as his emotions and energies were heightened. He assumed it was broken now, but he waited a short while to be sure. Then he about-faced, came back through the alley and out onto the main street.

He turned left and returned to his van, parked almost a quarter of a mile up the road. As it ran uphill it provided a good view of the café whilst allowing him to stay at a safe distance. He'd wilfully picked a parking spot in an area which was busy even at that time of night. He was within two miles of Hadescape University, which had a large student population going out to clubs, bars and cinemas every night of the week.

This had complicated the preliminary setup. He'd had to be vigilant, taking pains not to let the mark see his face, whilst working quickly before anyone else saw him. But now the complication was to become his advantage. The noise of the people masked Peter's own energy signature; and his orange van, parked inconspicuously behind a battered old pick-up truck, was right at home. He took a pair of binoculars from the glove compartment and watched from the rear window. People on the street passed the phone box outside the café once or twice every five minutes. At that distance their energy patterns were dim blips in the rest of the background noise.

About ten minutes later he saw a car pull up. A man and a woman got out and went to the café. Peter zoomed in with his binoculars. He barely detected the woman's regular signature, let alone the unique psychic hum that set her apart from most people; and the man's signature didn't even register on his radar.

Peter was convinced now that she must have come to the city for a purpose. Surely she'd heard the voice too. He'd hoped that she would bring a certain someone with her, perhaps even *two* certain people. Why had she brought one of *them* instead? The obvious answer was that she didn't remember enough, and they were manipulating her with their lies; and in that case, speaking to her candidly might endanger him and her both.

Fortunately he'd prepared a contingency plan.

* * * * * * * * *

The pair arrived in Crescent Bay West, a couple of miles from the coast, just after half past eleven, and walked towards the café, which was closed for the night. Aaron noticed that Elise was looking up and around at something invisible in the air.

They soon spotted the neon Buzz Café sign.

'That's the sign I saw,' said Elise. 'Manner entered the alley at this end. I lost the connection after that.'

Aaron repeated the information to his colleagues in the search team via his observer strap. Then they headed to the alley. It was darker than the main street, but partway down the alley was a side door, most likely the café's kitchen entrance, with a small halogen lamp above it supplying limited light.

'I don't see anything,' said Elise.

'Nor me. Perhaps you could –'

The sudden sound of a phone ringing startled them both. It came from a phone booth adjacent to the café.

'Manner,' said Elise. 'It must be.'

They dashed to the glass cubicle outside the café. Aaron nodded at her and she answered it, holding the phone away from her ear so he could hear both sides of the conversation.

'Hello?'

'*What's your name?*' said a male voice.

'Elise Archer,' she replied.

There was no answer.

'Hello?'

Manner repeated the question more slowly. '*What is your name?*'

'… Oh! Joanna. Joanna Sinclair.'

'*Who is the man with you?*'

The pair exchanged looks.

She put her hand over the mouthpiece. 'He's watching us,' she muttered, hardly moving her lips, and looking obliquely around her. Then she answered Manner's question. 'He's a GAILE officer,' she said frankly, to Aaron's surprise.

'*Come without them next time – and that includes their spies – because I will know, and you won't hear from me again. Understand?*'

She looked to Aaron. He nodded.

'Yes, I understand.'

'*Where is Omar?*'

The pair exchanged looks for a second time.

'He wasn't brought back like we were,' said Elise.

There was a pause.

'*Was David brought back?*'

'David? Ah, well, he …' she began, but faltered.

'*Have you found him?*'

She evaded the question with a counter. 'What if I haven't?'

'*Then there'd be no point in our meeting.*'

'Ask him what he wants with Hitoshi,' whispered Aaron.

Elise repeated the question unthinkingly. 'What do you want with Hit – er, David?'

She cringed and shook her head in self-reproach.

Sure enough, he'd heard her slip. '*Then you* have *found him?*'

Elise shrugged helplessly at Aaron. 'Y-yes, but –'

'*Tell him I have it.*'

She frowned. 'You have what?'

'... *He knows. Bring him with you next time,*' said Manner, and replaced the receiver.

Aaron immediately pressed a button on his observer strap.

'Do you see him?'

'*Negative,*' came the reply.

'He's around here somewhere,' he said, quickly assessing the situation as he'd been trained, 'probably within visual range. There's no other phone booth around here so we can assume he's obtained a cellphone. We'll trace the number from the phone company. I'm noting the time: Phone call made and concluded at twenty-three forty-one. Keep looking. Lloyd out.' He turned to Elise. 'I wonder how he knew about our search team?'

Elise had put the receiver back on the cradle, but she still had her hand on it. She seemed a little put out.

'He couldn't have picked up on them psychically,' she replied, not quite immediately. 'I think he had us in visual range, as you said, and he saw you communicating with your officers.'

'Oh yeah,' he said discontentedly. 'Had we known what he was going to do beforehand I would have been more discreet.' They stepped out of the phone booth. 'Do you sense him now?'

'I haven't picked up on him since we arrived,' she said. She looked at the booth. 'What was all that about, anyway?'

'You heard the man. *David* knows.'

'Why did Manner assume that Hitoshi would know what he was talking about, and that I wouldn't?'

'At a guess, it was something between Leon and David, and it didn't involve Joanna.'

'But what was it?' Then Elise ventured a theory that he suspected had occupied her mind for the past few moments. 'Could he have been talking about the disc?'

'I don't think so.'

He answered truthfully, though to be fair, even he couldn't imagine what else it could be.

'But even you've said that you don't know what happened to it. Could Leon have hidden it or something?'

Her persistence was admirable, but she was wide off the mark. GAILE Intelligence may have given her the impression that they'd lost the disc, but that was a lie. They'd actually destroyed it themselves. Elise probably thought that a missing disc was a possible motive for the Phoenix Project. She didn't realise that the real motive behind the Phoenix Project had little directly to do with the disc, missing or not.

'Manner must have been talking about something else,' he replied. We've had surveillance outside both Leon's home and at the university for days. If he'd been to either location we would've caught him already. He couldn't have slipped past us.'

'Unless he beat you to it beforehand,' she remarked with a thin smile. 'It wouldn't be the first time he's outwitted the authorities.'

'Our people went to the university and the house earlier in the week and made enquiries. No one has seen him.'

'Well, he got past you somehow. So what do we do now?'

Aaron glanced to the east. 'We'll think about it later,' he said, but he already knew what needed to be done.

And he wasn't happy about it.

* * * * * * * *

Peter had lain on the van floor for the duration of the phone call. Having seen the man talking into some type of comms device, he'd quickly ducked down and waited a few moments before making the phone call. No doubt the whole area was crawling with their foot soldiers. They were probably still looking for him now.

He had a pay-as-you-go mobile which wasn't registered. But he knew that once they obtained his number they would be able to track him within a couple of days, maybe sooner. He'd already bought a second phone from a different store for that reason.

Peter took a chance and again put his binoculars to the rear window. Elise and the agent had come out of the phone box and they were talking. They were probably about to join the foot soldiers in their search.

He slid back into the driver's seat and pulled out onto the road. No one noticed him as he drove away in the opposite direction.

* * * * * * * *

'Tell me the path he took,' said Aaron.

'He came from across the road,' said Elise. 'After the mugging he came this way to the alley, and then probably to the next block.'

'But you're not absolutely certain?'

'I suppose not.'

'Then while we're here, why don't you try making a connection in the alleyway?'

'It doesn't work like that,' she said. 'I'll only see the mugging.'

'But that happened at the ATM machine, not in the alley.'

'I understand what you're saying, but believe me, I'll connect to the event that has left the strongest imprint in the local area. That would be the mugging itself, not Manner's escape.' Then she must have seen something in his expression, because she added, 'Look, I haven't made a direct connection to one of his crime scenes in a week. So I'll do a check now, just to refresh my link to him. But don't expect me to get any extra information.'

He smiled. She didn't return it.

They returned to the alley and stopped at the entrance.

'Stay here Mr Lloyd, or your energy will interfere,' said Elise.

'Aaron. My name is –'

His words were unheard. She'd gone down the alley as far as the side entrance to the café to begin her psychometric evaluation. He stood by as instructed, and watched.

Her sorcery involved little ritual but it captivated him. She simply knelt down on one knee and placed her hand on the ground, with her delicate tapered fingers closed together. She stared in his direction, but not at him. Her quicksilver eyes had a dreamy look in them; after a few seconds they closed, and she had a tranquil air about her. The night breeze gently lifted her hair from her face, almost as though she had induced it by a spell.

As much as Aaron was attracted to her, he was well aware that it wasn't professionally appropriate, and at any rate she didn't trust him, much less like him. He couldn't blame her, considering that he was a GAILE officer and it was his job to stop her from either learning or remembering too much. If only she knew how badly he wanted to tell her the truth about everything.

Her eyes opened just then. She gave him a frosty look.

'What are you gawking at?'

Aaron scratched his head and smiled guiltily. 'Me?' he said. 'I was just watching.'

Elise rolled her eyes and got up. 'I told you, didn't I?' she said, dusting off her trousers. 'I lost the connection as soon as he entered this alley. If you like I can go back and write up my observations. But I don't have anything particularly useful to give you.'

'Oh, there's no –'

Just then Aaron's observer strap beeped.

'*No sign of him. How do you want us to proceed?*'

Elise shook her head at him.

Aaron pressed a button on his observer strap and told them to stop the search. Manner had said he would call again. They would be better prepared to handle it next time.

CHAPTER TWENTY-TWO
The Confession

Aaron reported to the director of GAILE at 9:15 a.m. via his laptop in his Verity Square apartment, just three blocks from Elise's place. He was dressed in his suit, ready for a meeting at the Harper Building in the next hour.

'Last night Manner told us that he has obtained something and that Katayama is in the know about it,' he said. 'I suspect that Morton and Cohen planned something thirty years ago, and respectively Manner and Katayama both remember what it was.'

Kingswell's image was being transmitted from his office in Washington. He was calm and composed.

'Now we know Mr Katayama wasn't bluffing,' he said. 'Bring him in for further questioning.'

'We're already arranging it sir,' said Aaron. 'I'll report back again before the end of the day.'

He logged off, closed the laptop, and groaned. He placed his elbows on the kitchen table and massaged his temples with his palms. The headaches were almost constant now, and the cranial implant shielding his mind was to blame. It was less than half a millimetre long, and inserted beneath the skin behind his ear. GAILE's Security Tech Lab had manufactured it soon after Intelligence had learned of Hitoshi's alleged psychic abilities, and had fitted it mainly as a precautionary measure. At that time no one had determined the full extent of the Project subjects' abilities.

The implant produced an electromagnetic field at a similar frequency to delta waves, which the brain produces when a person is in deep sleep, in a coma, or brain damaged. Apparently the Lab had chosen this wave for the implant because psychics were unable to read the minds of comatose or brain damaged individuals. How the doctors knew this, Aaron had never asked. They'd simply told him that the implant would probably make his mind completely impenetrable but that the constant radiation from the implant might cause headaches. What an understatement. Right now he felt as though someone was twisting a corkscrew into his temples. Thankfully he'd only have to tolerate the implant for a few more days at most and he would no longer need it.

Had it not been for Manner's rude interruption last night, Elise might already know the truth. In fact Aaron had been about to go to her apartment. It would have been an opportune time to talk to her, with everything else being in place, and by a stroke of luck, Hitoshi also being out of the picture. But Manner had inadvertently scuppered his plans, and now Intelligence wanted to see Hitoshi again.

Contrary to his better judgment, Aaron also felt that he ought to give Hitoshi one more chance to clarify his position. Though the hacker was quite right to be wary of GAILE, Aaron couldn't understand why he was prepared to bargain with his information. Of course, it was possible that Hitoshi simply didn't remember very much at all. Otherwise he would have to give an exceptional reason for his reckless behaviour; and if he failed to do that, Aaron would finally be able to write him off with a clear conscience.

He filled a glass of water at the sink and took a painkiller. Next he took a tea towel from a drawer, wrapped it round a pack of ice cubes from the freezer, held it to his temple and sat at the kitchen table again. Aaron had already sent a couple of officers ahead to Hitoshi's apartment, so he had time to rest for a while. Just as well, he thought, because it was going to be a long day.

* * * * * * * *

When Elise awoke, she didn't bother to look at the alarm clock. She was too relaxed to want to know if it was time to get up. Instead she looked at the golden ray of sunlight coming through the gap in the curtains. The dust sparkled as it drifted desultorily through the beam. People were a bit like that, she thought; particles of energy scattered about, always on the move, not necessarily knowing where they were going.

Her sleepy brain was beginning to wander into more serene random nonsense when she realised the curtains shouldn't be there. There should be a door.

This isn't my house!

Suddenly she was alert. She was in Hadescape, not Alterham. The events of last night came back to her with a bump, along with her feelings of apprehension. Was Intelligence going to drag Hitoshi in for questioning?

Elise glanced at the clock, which read 7:26 a.m., preemptively switched off the alarm and got out of bed. She was scheduled to spend the morning at the Harper Building, preparing her testimony for the court case, before undergoing a physical examination in the afternoon – specifically, a brain scan. Lloyd had told her that the prosecution wanted to use the results of the scan at the trial against Palmerton. They were going to show that foreign memories had been implanted in her brain.

Elise had a quick mug of coffee and then headed out of the apartment in her tracksuit. Before she went anywhere she was going for a run.

* * * * * * * * *

When Elise arrived at Taylor's office suite just before 10 a.m., Aaron was the one to tell her that the meeting was postponed. From her expression he inferred that she might have been expecting the change of schedule.

Though Hitoshi was already in the Harper Building, neither Taylor nor Aaron had seen him yet. Together with Elise they went to a spare office where they found him sitting on one of the desks. He rose as soon as he saw them.

Hitoshi looked as though he'd been in a fight. He had dark circles around his eyes like a raccoon, and dishevelled hair. His lemon leisure suit was crumpled, his black shirt stuck out of his trousers, and his red tie was undone. He stank of stale cigarette smoke. This was the man Aaron knew best, the ruffian he'd met three weeks ago in much the same state; a despicable sight.

'Hey Lise,' said Hitoshi, without so much as glancing at her.

He had his sights on Aaron, and his cheeks were drawn in, as if he was about to spit.

'Had a late night?' asked Aaron innocently.

'None of your damned business!' he said churlishly. 'Why the hell did you send your goons round to get me? I thought I had forty-eight hours. It hasn't even been a full day.'

'Manner contacted Elise last night,' said Aaron, 'by phone. Details aren't important. He had a message for you.'

Hitoshi's anger subsided all of a sudden. 'For me?'

'His exact words were: "Tell him I have it." Does that mean anything to you?'

Aaron watched carefully. The hacker had stopped to think. This was unusual for him.

Hitoshi's brow twitched ever so slightly. '… Maybe.'

Aaron looked at him scornfully. '*Maybe?*'

'Come on, Hitoshi,' said Taylor, his voice a little coarser than normal. 'You can't keep this up forever. Tell us what you know or we'll have to detain you.'

Hitoshi's gaze shifted sideways.

'Your offer from yesterday … it still stands?'

'I suppose so,' replied the deputy, somewhat wearily.

'Which is more than you deserve,' said Aaron. 'Now sit down.'

They seated themselves around a desk whilst Taylor went and fetched the relevant paperwork. It had been prepared the day before – just in case – and rushed through both the offices of the attorney general and the director of GAILE.

Taylor returned and handed Hitoshi the documents and a pen.

'Are you sure you don't want an attorney?' he asked dutifully.

Hitoshi gave him a sly smile. 'As I understand it Deputy, I'm just a witness, not a defendant. And once I've signed this, it'll be official.' He skimmed through the document first, and though he'd not once consulted a lawyer, he seemed to know his legalese. 'I the undersigned, agree ... without prejudice ... blah, blah, withdraw the charges ... Yeah, looks good to me.'

He signed the undertaking with a flourish.

Aaron took a small slim device resembling a pen – a tape recorder – from his jacket pocket, waved it at him, and switched it on. He placed it on the centre of the desk.

'You can start by telling us what Manner was on about,' he said.

Hitoshi's eyes darted in Elise's direction. 'Didn't he tell you?'

'He said you'd know.'

'Do you?' asked Aaron.

Hitoshi looked at the agent with lacklustre eyes. 'Yeah,' he said. 'I think he has the disc.'

'I knew it!' murmured Elise.

Of course that was the only thing Manner could have been talking about, but it was still a shock for Aaron, for whom the notion was technically impossible.

Hitoshi had assumed a posture of relative indifference. 'I know what you're thinking, Agent,' he went on. 'You're wondering how Manner could have gotten the disc, when to the best of your knowledge it vanished with the terrorists. Am I right?'

Aaron looked fixedly at the hacker. '... You're exactly right. So what really happened?'

'David made two copies of the data.'

Three pairs of eyebrows rose at once.

Aaron realised right away what had transpired. Oh, but it was so simple! Why hadn't he thought of it?

'– And one survived! But how?'

'They must have put one away somewhere before the meeting at Saint Mary's,' said Taylor.

'Actually, he brought both discs to the cathedral,' said the hacker. 'David and Leon were supposed to take one each and split up. They thought they'd double their chances of holding onto the data that way. But Adam ambushed them and shot David down. David told Jo to get away, but in the confusion –'

'– In the confusion she forgot to take his disc and took off in her car,' Elise finished for him. 'And Adam followed her. I remember it now. He chased her into the forest.'

'Yeah. So David gave both discs to Leon and told him to go and save his fiancée. I don't know what happened after that, but Leon must have hidden one of them.'

'And Manner's come back for it?' said Aaron.

'Yeah. And I think it might be my fault.'

The agents and Elise looked at one another in puzzlement.

'What do you mean?' asked Aaron.

Hitoshi sighed loudly. 'I *called* him here. With my mind.'

They were all astounded, but for different reasons.

'Why?' asked Aaron.

'How?' asked Elise at the same time, in an impassioned tone.

'I didn't set out to do it. It was an accident … sort of.'

Aaron eyed him sceptically. 'Come off it.'

'I didn't set out to do it,' he insisted. 'At that point I wasn't even thinking about the discs. I thought they were both gone.'

'But *why* did you do it?'

'I don't know. Just trying to reach out, I guess.' He nodded indicatively at Elise. 'She'll understand. I've grown up remembering these people who died: Jo, and Leon. And I died with them – only I came back. On my own,' he said, gazing hopefully at her. But as she was still awaiting his explanation, she didn't reciprocate. 'When I found out about the Phoenix Project,' he went on, 'I was ecstatic. And I really wanted to meet the other Project subjects. But I was already on GAILE's watch list because of that hacking charge from last year. I knew if I admitted to being a Project subject, you'd use it to convict me. So I had to deny it. The stress really got to me. One night I went out partying with friends to take my mind off it. But I made the mistake of having too many tequilas. I don't know about you,' he added, addressing Elise, 'but alcohol really messes with my head.'

'You mean your psychic sense?' she said.

'Yeah. It goes hyper.'

She nodded knowingly. 'Mine too.' She turned to the two GAILE officers. 'You know how alcohol affects brain functions? Psychic ability – being a brain function – is affected too. Our brains have a kind of safety mechanism which filters excess energies from objects and people around us, and prevents us from being inundated with sensory information. When we're intoxicated, the brain has less control over that mechanism, and we get psychic overload. It's quite frightening.'

'You can say that again,' said Hitoshi, evidently grateful that she empathised. 'Now normally I can hold my drink. But that night I got wasted. I felt like I was connected to everyone in the world. It got so bad I thought my head would explode. And in the middle of it all I had this crazy idea. I thought: What if I made a call on this worldwide neural network? What if I could contact Jo and Leon? So I left my friends at the bar and got a cab to Verity Square. Then I wandered over to the Harper Building. I looked up at the stars, and hollered your names as loud as I could.'

Taylor frowned. 'Both Joanna and Leon?'

'Yep – until some cops came by and arrested me for being drunk and disorderly. The next day, I figured there was no way I'd reached either of them. I'm no telepath, right? But when I met you,' he said to Elise, 'and you told me about Manner, I realised that he'd probably come here because he *heard* me.'

Taylor turned to Elise. 'How come you didn't?'

'Manner's much more sensitive than I am,' she said. 'What he has in terms of sensitivity borders on telepathy. I've suspected it ever since I first connected to him. It has a lot to do with the environment he grew up in.'

'Has Manner attempted to contact you telepathically since then?' asked Aaron.

'If he has, I don't know anything about it,' said the hacker.

Both GAILE officers looked at him suspiciously.

'I think he's telling the truth,' said Elise. 'Manner may well have tried to contact him and failed.'

'But Manner's contacted you,' said Taylor.

'That's different. Manner doesn't have a true psychometric connection to Hitoshi. He's properly connected only to me. He must have realised that, and so he exploited it.'

'All right, I'll accept that you've had no other contact with Manner,' said Aaron to Hitoshi. 'But how do you know that he's back for the second disc?'

'Because of something she said at the club.'

Elise frowned. 'Me?'

'You mentioned Manner's obsession with some old *promise*. You didn't know what it meant, but it struck a chord with me. I remembered a promise that Leon made to David. He swore to protect the data at all costs. But for Manner to make good on that promise now, the data would have had to survive. I suspected then that the second copy must still be out there.'

Hitoshi was totally at ease now, sitting back in his chair with his legs to the side. Aaron watched him, partly enraged, partly mystified. In the whole time he'd known the Shaman, not once had Aaron been able to work out what went on in his inscrutable mind. But it had been clear from the outset that Hitoshi remembered much more than Elise; and now it was also clear why he'd lied about his memories for almost a month until circumstances had forced him to confess. No one except maybe Elise had bought his story that he was just trying to avoid the hacking charge, though for a man like Hitoshi that could also have been reason enough. And that was what bothered Aaron. Fear is an old and potent survival instinct, and succumbing to it is not necessarily wrong. But there is a point beyond which self-preservation becomes a grievous sin; and Hitoshi had shown himself to be a sinner. He was so unlike his predecessor in fact, Aaron wondered whether Palmerton had transplanted the wrong twin's memories into him.

If this was what drove Hitoshi, so be it. Aaron still had Elise, and she was the better option at any rate. She was the one in direct communication with Manner; she was honest, fearless, and genuinely interested in the truth. Hopefully she'd also be strong enough to handle it. His imperative was to speak to her before

Manner next attempted to make contact, or else everything he'd worked for would come to nothing.

Only one question remained.

'Why you couldn't have told us this in the first place is beyond my ken,' Aaron said by way of asking, with only a petty interest in hearing Hitoshi's explanation.

Hitoshi looked him straight in the eye. His thin lips parted, but whether he actually had an answer for him or not, Aaron never got to know, as the deputy interposed.

'That's a nonissue,' he said. 'Even if he'd told us all of this yesterday, it wouldn't have changed the fact that our surveillance was either set up too late or in the wrong places. We wouldn't have caught Manner. We must focus now on working out what he wants; and in particular, what he wants with *David*.'

'Well,' said Elise slowly, 'everything he's done points to his obsession with the past. He's committed four murders in the name of vengeance. He's pulled out all the stops just to get himself here, and now he's obtained the disc ...'

'He must want to upload the data to the net, just as Omar planned to,' said Aaron. 'What else could it be?'

'Makes sense,' said Taylor. 'But the disc is very old. The data must have completely deteriorated by now.'

'Not necessarily,' said Hitoshi suddenly, to their collective surprise. 'If my memory serves me correctly, that data was saved on a mini DVD. They could last up to thirty years, or so the manufacturers claimed. There's a small chance that most of the data's still intact. Very small.'

At hearing this Aaron became worried. If there was the remotest chance that the data had survived, then he would have to act even more quickly.

'Whether or not it's intact,' he said, 'Manner couldn't test that disc without the relevant hardware.'

'And there's no way he'd find an old DVD-ROM drive in any of today's computer stores,' added Hitoshi.

'Then that's probably what he wants to talk to you about,' said Elise, 'since David was the technical expert.'

'I think you're right,' said Taylor thoughtfully. 'Perhaps we can take advantage of that. Manner's already indicated that he's going to make contact again, probably in the same way as he did last night. We can lay a trap for when he does. We can position a team at wherever he arranges the next rendezvous, and when he shows up we can apprehend him and get the disc back at the same time. But we'll only get one shot at it.'

Aaron had listened to Taylor's proposed strategy in quiet trepidation, all the while trying to resolve the issue of how he was going to stop the disc falling into the wrong hands.

'To get this to work then, we'll need both of you,' he said to Hitoshi, whilst in view of his own objectives he'd already made a decision along the lines of the opposite.

Hitoshi gazed at the undertaking he'd just signed. Aaron waited for him to say something suitably cynical, but for once, he didn't.

'Whatever you say, Agent.'

They left the spare office and went to a small meeting room, where they first worked through the finer details of Taylor's proposed strategy, and then finally held the original scheduled meeting. The GAILE officers took Elise and Hitoshi through what to expect at court in Washington. They would fly out on Sunday at the latest.

By the early afternoon all was done, and after taking a short lunch break in the meeting room they were ready to go to the Searle Lab. The lab was on-site at the GAILE Office complex. They left the Harper Building and took a two minute walk into a plain cube shaped building, situated at its rear.

In the waiting room Elise took a magazine from a rack. Aaron knew the testing would take a couple of hours. He had to stick around anyway, since he had to make a verbal report to the director. He would talk to Elise after they'd finished, under the pretext of accompanying her back to her apartment for her safety, and then return to make his report.

But he hadn't accounted for Hitoshi.

The hacker had just answered a text message on his cellphone and now he put it away. He leaned forward with his head tilted sideways, and his fringe came in front of his eyes.

'Lise, what are you doing later?'

She looked up from her magazine. 'I don't know,' she said. 'Nothing, I guess.'

'You want to hang out with me and the band after we're done here? We're rehearsing at one of our regular clubs this afternoon.'

Great, thought Aaron. Now Hitoshi would have her to himself for the rest of the day.

Something of his mood must have showed on his face. Elise glanced uneasily at him, and seemed unsure what to say.

'Or is it against security protocol for us to socialise?' said Hitoshi with a frown.

If only it was. 'Of course not,' said Aaron through gritted teeth.

The hacker returned with a little smirk.

Elise nodded. 'Okay.'

'Then it's a date.'

After a few more minutes, a lab assistant came in. 'Hitoshi Katayama,' he said. 'Please come with me.'

'I'll meet you here,' said Hitoshi.

He followed the assistant out.

Aaron finally had his chance to arrange a meeting with her. Otherwise he'd have to phone her later; and that was too risky.

Presently she sat to his right, engrossed in her magazine, and her left leg was crossed over so that she was essentially facing away from him. He coughed to try and get her to look his way. She turned the page.

'Elise?'

'Hmm?' was the nearest she offered to a reply.

'Listen, I need to –'

Then his cellphone rang. Now Elise looked up.

He pulled a face in despair and answered.

It was Kash, calling to inform him of a new development for which he was needed right away.

'Oh, you're at Harper?' said Aaron in reply. 'I'm next door at the lab. I'll be there in a minute.'

'Everything all right?' asked Elise, as he hung up.

'That was my colleague,' he said. 'There's been a robbery at the Morton residence.'

'Oh, no. Manner?'

'Possibly.'

'Do you want me to come with you, help you verify it with a psychometric check?'

He would have gladly answered in the affirmative, except that he'd been instructed to avoid taking the Project subjects to any *sensitive* locations.

'We've got it covered,' he said. 'And you've got to stay here.'

'Okay.'

At least he had her attention now. 'Anyway, before I go, I was going to ask –'

And again he was interrupted, this time by the lab assistant, who was back to collect Elise.

She put down the magazine and got up to join the assistant.

'What were you saying?' she asked.

Aaron smiled graciously and accepted defeat.

'Doesn't matter. We've both got to go anyway. It can wait.'

CHAPTER TWENTY-THREE
Memory Tests

The assistant led Elise through a set of double doors into an examination room brightly lit up under a fluorescent light. Shiny grey tiles covered the floor, and medical equipment cluttered the whole area. A doctor wearing a white lab coat was waiting for them. After getting Elise to sign an examination consent form and checking that she wore no earrings or other piercings, the doctor sat her down on a chair and put an aerosol injection to her neck. The syringe contained millions of nanospheres, tiny custom-built particles with multifunctional properties. The nanospheres were designed to help locate Joanna Sinclair's transplanted brain cells. Every sphere had a targeting molecule attached to its surface via a short DNA tether. This molecule was a bit like an antibody, binding to the surface of any neuron that belonged to Joanna, whilst ignoring Elise's own cell type.

The aerosol forced the nanospheres painlessly through Elise's skin into her bloodstream; and within a few minutes the spheres passed through the blood-brain barrier and reached her brain.

The doctors left her alone for around half an hour. They wanted to give the nanospheres ample time to locate and bind to the donor cells. They told her that hundreds of spheres should accumulate on the surface of each donor cell and form clumps.

Next the assistant directed Elise to a chair and asked her to remain as still as possible. He lowered a dome-shaped helmet device onto her head. It contained an ultra-low frequency magnetic resonance imaging machine, similar to the type found in regular hospitals. Since the nanospheres were coated with iron oxide, the MRI sensors scanned for clumps of iron oxide. If the sensors detected lots of clumps, this would give GAILE's prosecution the physical proof that Elise's brain contained Joanna's cells and that therefore she was a surviving Project subject.

The doctor switched on the MRI machine by remote control. Elise heard a slight whirring sound inside the helmet. After a few moments the doctor pressed more remote buttons in succession. Sensors in the helmet picked up information from inside her brain and wirelessly transmitted it to a tablet computer for processing. The doctor used a light pen to check over the information on the tablet screen. He looked at her and nodded to tell her that the machine had indeed detected some donor tissue.

Elise waited for him to come over and remove the helmet, but she soon discovered that they weren't finished with her yet.

* * * * * * * * *

Aaron went to an office on the first floor of the Harper Building. The Intelligence officers were visiting the house undercover. Kash was already in police uniform. The badge on each of his shoulders had a single gold bar, indicating the rank of a lieutenant.

'What did she say?' asked Aaron.

He was referring to Leon's sister, who had called that morning to report the robbery at her house. Charlotte had dialled the number on the card that Kash had left with her. She thought she'd called the police station, but in fact her call had been diverted to the Harper Building.

'She wanted to report a suspected robbery,' said Kash. 'She said it happened on Monday but she didn't find out until last night.'

GAILE hadn't set up their surveillance until Tuesday.

'If the robber was Manner, then we missed him by about twenty-four hours,' said Aaron. 'But don't call off the surveillance at the residence until we're sure.'

Kash nodded, and then he gave Aaron a uniform.

'Here you are, *Sergeant*. I'm your ranking officer,' he said in jest.

Aaron smiled uncomfortably. There was no malice in his colleague's tone, and indeed the man had a congenial nature, but Aaron was conscious of the fact that Kash had a good few years more experience in the field than he did, and really ought to have been given the lead in the investigation. Aaron had won the position only because of Robert Benedict's direct interference; and he had taken it only because it was essential to his objective. Kash of course didn't know any of this. He would be within his rights to harbour some resentment.

Once Aaron had changed his clothes he and Kash set off in a police patrol car that the Police Liaison Bureau had prearranged for them. They arrived at Preston Avenue just before three o'clock and met Charlotte Knight, Leon's younger sister. She was widowed and currently living with her elderly mother, Yvonne Morton.

Charlotte took them to the living room and Kash took notes as she gave her statement. They soon learned that she'd been out shopping on the morning of the alleged break-in and Yvonne was their only witness. The problem was that Yvonne had Alzheimer's disease, and she didn't recall anything about it.

'I try never to leave her on her own,' said Charlotte. 'My daughter helps me out as much as she can but she can't be here every single day. Sometimes I have no choice but to leave my mother for an hour or two.'

'But if you weren't home and your mother doesn't remember the incident, how did you find out about it?' asked Kash.

'Andrew told me,' she said. 'He's my grandson.'

She told them that on Monday her grandson had been skipping school. He'd come to the house in the morning, feeling fairly certain that his grandmother would be out shopping. Finding the gate open, he'd gone up to the house and found that the front door was also unlocked, his great-grandmother apparently having answered the door to a stranger. He went in and checked on

Yvonne. She was in a distressed state, though with her illness she frequently behaved irrationally. Nothing in the house seemed disturbed or out of place, so the boy thought everything was fine. After settling her down, he left and locked the door on his way out. He hadn't mentioned the incident to his grandmother, but only because he would have had to explain what he'd been doing there on a school day.

'I almost never found out,' said Charlotte. 'But yesterday I was clearing up the house and I noticed some money and a jewellery box were missing from my mother's bedroom cupboard. I was telling my daughter about it on the phone, and my grandson overheard and put two and two together. He came round this morning and told me everything. I remembered that missing man you were looking for and realised he might have come to the house. As my mother was on her own, she could have answered the door to him. So I called you.'

'You did the right thing, ma'am,' said Kash. 'Now I know you said your mother doesn't recall the robbery, but may we speak to her anyway, just for a minute?'

'All right, but I warn you, she's been quite bad this week.'

She took them upstairs to Yvonne's bedroom. The elderly lady was sitting on a chair by the bed, reading the Bible. She took off her reading glasses and looked at them with a smile. She was apparently totally alert.

'Good morning,' she said.

The officers returned the greeting.

'Mom,' said Charlotte, 'These policemen want to ask you about what happened on Monday.'

'Monday?'

'The robbery,' said Charlotte.

'Good Lord! Someone's been robbed?'

They looked at Charlotte. She shook her head at them.

Aaron gave Kash a furtive glance.

'My apologies ma'am,' said Kash. 'I think there's been a mistake. We won't trouble you any longer.'

Yvonne seemed unconcerned. She put on her glasses again.

'See what I mean?' said Charlotte, as they came downstairs.

'We'd like to speak to your grandson as well,' replied Kash. 'Where does he live?'

'You won't have to go to his house. He's out the back. I kept him from school this afternoon as I thought you might want to see him.'

She went and called Andrew in from the back yard. A boy of around ten or eleven years returned with her, with a basketball under his skinny arm. Charlotte took the ball off him and told him to sit down. He stared at them with wide eyes.

Aaron smiled at him reassuringly. 'Hi there, Andrew. We'd like to talk to you about what you saw when you came here on Monday. Okay?'

The kid nodded timidly.

'What time was it when you came here?'

'… Ten o'clock.'

'He was skipping school,' remarked Charlotte, with a rebuking emphasis directed at her grandchild.

The boy looked mortified.

'It's okay Andrew – you're not in any trouble,' said Kash. 'We just want to find the person who stole from your great-grandma. You want that too, don't you?'

Again Andrew nodded.

'Now, when you came here, what did you see?'

'The gate was open.'

'Anything else?'

The boy shrugged.

Charlotte folded her arms. 'What about that van, Andy?'

'What van?' asked Aaron.

'He saw a van come by the house.'

'No,' began Kash, 'our missing man doesn't have a –'

'Andrew saw the driver,' said Charlotte. 'And he sounds a lot like the man whose photo you showed me.'

Aaron and Kash looked at one another. Could Manner have obtained a vehicle? It was possible; after all it was an effective solution to two problems. With a van of his own he'd have both a means of transport and shelter.

Kash wanted to be sure about the validity of the statement. He produced the file photo from his pocket.

'Have a look at this photo, Andrew,' he said, 'and think carefully. Was this the man you saw in the van? If you're not sure, that's perfectly okay.'

The boy looked at the photograph and nodded. 'He had the same headband,' he said, drawing an imaginary line across his forehead with his finger.

Kash cast a doubtful glance in Charlotte's direction. 'Are you sure, Andrew?' he asked.

'Yeah,' replied the boy confidently.

'He told me about that headband too,' said Charlotte, 'without any encouragement from me.'

'I just had to make sure, ma'am. No offence meant.' Kash put the photo away. 'Now tell me, Andrew: What colour was the van?'

The kid didn't hesitate. 'Orange.'

That narrows it down, thought Aaron pessimistically. Orange was a fashionable colour in motor vehicles.

'Any idea of the make?' asked Kash.

'I ... don't know.'

'That's okay. You're doing very well.' Kash wrote everything down on a notepad. 'Now when you came inside, where was your great-grandma?'

'In the hall, at the bottom of the stairs. She was crying.'

'Did she tell you what had upset her?'

'No.'

'Did she say anything at all?'

'She kept saying *Leon*.'

'Leon?' asked Kash innocently.

'That's my brother,' said Charlotte. 'He went missing thirty years ago. We've never known what happened to him. My father died a few years later. Mom's never been the same since.'

'Sorry to hear that,' said Kash. Then he turned again to the kid. 'Thank you, Andrew. You've been very helpful.'

'Can I go now?' asked the boy.

'Yeah, go on.'

Andrew took the ball from his grandmother and ran out.

Charlotte frowned. 'How close are you to getting him?'

They were going to have to tell her a cover story. The regular police would be dealing with the robbery from now on. What it meant from her point of view – though she didn't know it yet – was that the perpetrator was never going to be caught.

'Your description may sound like that of our missing man,' said Kash, 'but it can't be him because he doesn't have a vehicle. Either someone else robbed you or you never had a robber.'

'Somebody took my mother's things,' said Charlotte. 'I looked everywhere for that money and that jewellery box. The box was locked in a cupboard in my mother's room, and now it's gone.'

'Could your mother have moved them?' suggested Aaron.

'No. She's kept the box in that cupboard for thirty years.'

'What's in it? I hope nothing too valuable.'

'I don't really know what was in it. Mom's never told any of us. But I think it was something that belonged to my brother.'

* * * * * * * * *

'*Joanna.*'

At hearing the name, Elise vaguely recalled a woman with long blonde hair, a button nose, and jade eyes.

'*Red.*'

Elise thought of strawberries, not quite consciously. She still had the MRI sensor on her head, but she also wore a blindfold and headphones to prevent any external stimuli from distracting her and affecting her brain activity. The doctor was subjecting her to a *keyword activation test*. His assistant sat nearby and read out a list of words into a microphone, which Elise heard through the headphones. Some of the words, as the doctor had just told her, were totally random whilst others were related to Joanna's past.

'*House.*'

She pictured her own home, and groaned inside at the thought of having to finish the decorating when she got back. The principle behind the test was to confirm – again – that Elise possessed Joanna's memories. This time they were going to try and make Joanna's donor neurons light up, since neurons emit electrical pulses in the process of thinking. Each nanosphere still in Elise's system had a tiny antenna – a carbon nanotube – attached to its surface. When Elise thought about something from her past life, a pulse from the donor neuron travelled along the nanosphere and to the nanotube. The nanotube acted as a complete radio with a transistor, and it turned the pulse into a radio signal. A radio receiver in the helmet listened for these radio signals and sent the information to the doctor's tablet.

'*Liberty.*'

Elise saw the statue of the same name in her mind, and simultaneously the word induced a feeling of puzzlement also. Where had she heard it recently?

'*Book.*'

And so, the list went on; colours, objects, people, and the occasional abstract noun.

'*Adam.*'

A momentary flash of him beside the fountain, ready to shoot. And a devilish smile.

'*GAILE.*'

A feeling that had haunted her all her life, and which still refused to leave her, overrode anything she might consciously have thought of in connection to it.

Elise had asked the doctor why the medical team needed to perform this second test. He'd replied that the clumps of nanospheres didn't necessarily prove beyond doubt that the donor cells were in there, and that they had to activate the neurons to confirm that they had bound to the donor cells. But Elise had found the explanation unsatisfactory. They had her statements to prove that she possessed Joanna's memories. That coupled with the first test should have been sufficient for their purposes.

The doctor's keyword list continued. '*Circle. ... Phone. ... Omar. ... Earth. ... Pen. ... Rain. ... Disc. ... Abdul Salaam. ... David. ... Car. ... Blue. ... System. ... Echo.*'

And just as she was starting to tire of the test, it was over.

'... *Three.*'

As a random number, it evoked nothing in particular, at least not to her conscious mind. But then she wasn't supposed to have been actively analysing what she was thinking anyway.

The assistant came over and lifted the helmet from her head. Elise looked to the doctor and waited for him to say something, but he seemed to have no interest in discussing the results with her. He perused the tablet in his hand.

Elise took the initiative. 'Have you got the results you wanted?'

'The preliminary results are positive,' replied the doctor.

He didn't elaborate.

'Meaning the donor cells lit up?'

'Yes, though we have yet to carry out a full analysis.'

She couldn't resist asking another question. 'I still don't understand the keyword test,' she said. 'Couldn't you have just asked me to visualise one of Joanna's memories and taken your readings that way?'

'This test is more scientifically valid,' he said inattentively. 'We needed to have a controlled and simple set of stimuli. A keyword-neuron activation test was an appropriate means to achieve this.'

'Oh,' said Elise, and left it at that.

Before she left the lab the doctor removed the nanospheres from her system. An electromagnetic pulse from the MRI was all that was needed to unbind the nanospheres from her neurons, exploiting the nanospheres' tendency to heat up when exposed to strong electromagnetic fields. The pulse did no harm to her body, but it heated the nanospheres enough to melt the DNA tethers binding them to the neurons, thereby releasing them. The doctors used an external magnetic field to direct the spheres to an artery in her arm, and retrieved them using a magnetised surgical needle.

Elise met with Hitoshi outside the entrance. They headed out of the complex and went to the taxi stop. They both got into the front of the car, Hitoshi taking the left side which would ordinarily seat the driver. As a self-service taxi that travelled on special self-drive lanes, the vehicle had no steering wheel. Hitoshi popped his credit card into a slot in the dashboard and typed in his pin number.

The computer responded in audio. '*Where to?*'

'Royce Place, Rock Moor.' said Hitoshi.

Elise frowned. 'Your apartment?'

'I need to shower and change.'

The computer charged the card and ejected it.

It was cold outside and the ground floor lobby wasn't much better. Elise wanted to get to the apartment quickly, but Hitoshi stopped at the lifts. He seemed agitated.

'What is it?' she asked.

He fished around in his breast pocket and took out a pack of cigarettes and a lighter.

'Tami's banned me from smoking in our apartment,' he said. 'She thinks she can get me to quit that way. Fat chance.'

He leaned against the wall and lit up, blithely disregarding the peeling *No Smoking* sticker right next to him, and took a couple of puffs. He closed his eyes satisfactorily as he blew the smoke out through his nostrils.

'Man, I needed that.' Then he looked at her. 'Is it just me, or were we just duped into taking a glorified lie detector test?'

So he'd had his misgivings as well.

'I did find the second keyword test a bit pointless,' she said.

'That's one way of putting it. That test had nothing to do with the court case. They just wanted to see what we remembered. Told you they couldn't be trusted.'

'Yes, but are you going to tell me why this time? Or have you just brought me back here just to socialise?'

A corner of his mouth lifted in the usual wicked way. 'Would that be such a bad thing?' he asked in a rumble.

She frowned reprovingly. 'Actually, it would. I honestly thought you were going to tell me what's really going on. But if not, then I'll just –'

'Relax. You're right. I did bring you here to talk.' He took another puff. 'And I do want to tell you everything I know, Lise. But there's a problem.'

'What's that?'

'I still think you're better off not knowing.'

'And what about what I think?'

Elise waited for his answer, but he didn't offer one.

She rolled her eyes. 'You know what? I can't be bothered.'

'Lise, wait –'

She went towards the lobby entrance, set on ignoring him.

'Do you know how much you remind me of Jo?'

Elise almost stumbled and came to a stop.

He was good. Had he simply asked her to wait again she would have kept on walking.

She turned round and folded her arms. 'What's that got to do with it?' she asked, trying to sound disinterested.

'Everything. You're just like her – smart and beautiful – but so stubborn! I don't want you to make the same mistake she did.'

She looked hard at him. Impervious to her scepticism, he had an earnest expression on his face. She sighed in exasperation and went back to him.

'I don't get it,' she said.

'I know.'

'So explain it to me.'

Hitoshi took another drag and let out the smoke slowly, his eyes fixed on her the whole time. Finally he nodded his assent.

'Okay. Let's talk. But you *must* keep this to yourself. I mean it, Lise. Because if you don't,' he said gravely, 'we're dead.'

CHAPTER TWENTY-FOUR
The Insiders

Hitoshi's eyes turned just then to the lobby entrance. A woman was at the door, apparently a resident, keying in the security pin. Half of Hitoshi's cigarette remained but he quickly pressed the stub against the painted wall and put it out, leaving a black mark.

'We shouldn't talk out here,' he said, discarding the stub, and he pushed the button for the lift. It opened immediately, and they got in before the woman had even entered the lobby. Hitoshi pushed the button for the sixth floor.

He let Elise into the apartment first and entered after her. He closed the door and stood with his back against it, as though he was afraid he'd been followed.

'This stays between you and me,' he reiterated. 'Okay?'

The angst was plain on his face. His coffee-black eyes had that same desperate, scared look that she'd seen the night she'd first met him. But this time he found the courage to say what he had been unable to say before.

'They were MWA officials.'

'What?'

'The people behind our deaths.'

They sat together on the edge of the sofa. Elise looked at him disconcertedly.

'There's no third party?' she said.

'That's a cover story.' His left leg bounced nervously on the ball of his foot. 'I don't remember it all. I just know that we took some information from them, and they wanted it back.'

Even Elise knew that much.

'What sort of information?'

'I can't remember, but it was pretty important. When we took the data we officially became a threat to international security. That justified the use of deadly force against us. Now up until that point, they'd done things by the book. The real problem started after they arrested us. They'd taken the disc from Leon – the disc they knew about, anyway – but Omar had gotten away and they wanted to find him. Enter Doctor Palmerton.'

'And his mind reading device.'

He nodded. 'We were expendable. They let him do what he liked to us, and they turned a blind eye. He was on their payroll when it all happened. That's why they're investigating all of this now. And you and I aren't just witnesses, Lise. We're the evidence. They're determined not to be implicated in the crime. They'll stop at nothing to safeguard their good reputation.'

Unease set her insides churning.

'Is that why you haven't been talking? You're worried that if they think we can identify them, they'll do something to us?'

'Got it in one.'

Elise pondered what he was telling her. If it really was an inside job, then what did that mean for the present investigation? And the upcoming court case?

Evidently Hitoshi had already made up his mind about that. He took out his lighter and began flicking it idly.

'Thing is,' he said, 'most of GAILE's personnel are puppets. The Civil Office is practically just a PR front. Intelligence, on the other hand … well, they're a different story. Intelligence is where the information's at. The heavy stuff. The stuff they won't even tell their sister department if it doesn't suit them.'

'Are you suggesting that Intelligence –?'

'It's obvious. You've seen how quickly Intelligence tied up the case at the public level. And to deal with us, they made up this story about a so-called *third party* in the hope that we wouldn't work out who actually funded Doctor Palmerton's sick little experiments. Don't you find it odd that no one ever found any sign of the men who captured us? They were *all* from Intelligence – including Adam. He wasn't a double agent. He was just doing his job. Thirty years ago Intelligence covered their tracks and threw our case in the back of the drawer.' He grimaced. 'They must have thought they'd gotten away scot-free, until the Palmerton scandal broke out. Whoever tipped off the press opened a can of worms.'

Come to think of it, to date the GAILE officers had hardly talked about the informant at all.

'Who was it, I wonder?' she said.

'If half the reports are true, it could have been anyone with a grudge. Palmerton experimented on a lot of people over the years. He ruined many lives.'

That didn't bear thinking about.

'Where does that leave us?' asked Elise. 'Were we really terrorists or not?'

He smiled dryly. 'We weren't terrorists by the standard definition. I don't remember us plotting to hijack a plane, take hostages, or blow anything up. But we were in cahoots with a radical, and that's almost as bad.'

'Omar?'

'Yeah.' Hitoshi held a steady flame and stared into it. 'He wasn't a so-called Islamist. He didn't even look the part. But Omar was something of a fanatic. He believed that an elite order rules the world, playing god, and that the World Democratic Revolution was a sham. He made it his life mission to expose them.' Hitoshi let go of the switch and the flame went out. 'He wanted to start a *new* global revolution. *Abdul Salaam* was his code word for it.'

'Abdul Salaam? I thought that was the name of his group.'

'What did I just tell you? There was no terror group. Omar was just a conspiracy theorist. He had no reason to blackmail the MWA. But it's true that he tried to make the data public.'

Elise waited for him to continue, but he didn't.

'… That's it?'

'That's it. Like every conspiracy theorist, Omar thought that once enough people knew the *truth* –' he said, gesturing quote marks with two fingers on each hand, '– there'd be an automatic uprising against the establishment. He wanted to make the data accessible to anyone and everyone, and to hell with the consequences. But that's sedition in the eyes of the law – worse, in fact, because it was a case of compromising international security. And when things turned ugly, he hightailed it and left us behind. We died in some lab, while he went off and made a new life for himself.' Hitoshi's face twisted again in disgust. 'He's spending his retirement on some tropical island for all we know, while we're still lumbered with his mess. You know what really gets me? We called Adam a traitor. But he'd actually warned me not to get mixed up with Omar. We should have listened to him.'

Elise paused to think.

'So why did we help Omar?'

'Beats me.'

'You must have some idea, if you remember everything else you just told me.'

'I don't remember it all, not really. I had to do some research to make up for some missing chunks in my memory. I looked up Omar a few years back. He was an academic from Cairo. There were also some journal articles about him and his conspiracy theories floating around on the net. Whacky stuff about elite world orders. He was totally demented.'

'And what you read about him – was any of it familiar?'

'Pretty much none of it.'

'*None* of it?' She was stumped for a second. '... Then how do you know that Omar wasn't really onto something? Not something security-related, but something bad?'

He looked at her sideways. 'Come on, Lise. The guy was obviously a nutcase.'

'But *we* weren't. What if we had a good reason for helping him?'

'Like what?'

'I don't know. But the disc is definitely the key to all of this. Jo called it the *biggie of all time*. Do you remember?'

He put down his lighter purposefully on the table.

'I don't like the sound of this. You're not getting any bright ideas now, are you?'

'Well ... if we could just find out what was on that disc –'

'You *are* getting ideas. This is why I didn't want to tell you anything! I knew you'd go into cop mode! These aren't your run-of-the-mill bad guys, Lise. You can't just put them away. Go after them and I promise you, it won't end well.'

She was undeterred. 'We'll be careful.'

'Hold it right there. In the first place, the disc is useless. As I said before, the odds of it being readable after all this time are phenomenally small. And even if it is readable, *they're* the ones who'll get it off Manner, not us. They'll probably destroy it without even checking it. We won't get so much as a peek at it.'

'Then maybe we could talk to someone.'

'Like who? We can't trust anyone – especially in Intelligence.'

'I was thinking of the Civil Office. Taylor.'

He shook his head. 'Even if we could trust Taylor, he doesn't have security clearance, and anyway, he'd probably feel obliged to let Intelligence know, since they're running the investigation. But even if we convinced him not to do that, he might talk to the wrong person in confidence. To get anything done, we'd have to play an insider game of our own. You and I both know that's out of the question. The only person we know in Intelligence is Agent Numbskull – and there's no way I'd trust that automaton. Whatever you ask him, you get the same answer: *It's classified.*' His eyes narrowed. 'I say: Bullshit!'

Elise bit her inner lip thoughtfully.

'There must be ... oh! We could try Nathalie Weston.'

He gave her a censorious look.

'Or maybe not,' she muttered, but never mind. She'd just had a better idea. They might find something useful on Manner's wall at Roseleigh Hospital. 'But there might be another –'

'For God's sake, Lise!' he exclaimed. 'Quit thinking like a cop for once and just listen! We don't stand a chance against them! We never did! I don't care what was on the disc. It was never worth dying for! Don't you get it? If we'd just stayed out of it, we'd both still be alive! You and I would still be together, married with kids by now – grandkids, even!'

Elise was taken aback. In his arresting gaze she saw not so much fury as forlornness. She suddenly remembered what he'd said in his statement just that morning; how he'd grown up alone, with nothing but memories of the people David had cared about most. She realised then how Hitoshi saw his predicament.

'Oh, Hitoshi,' she murmured, and instinctively reached over to hold his hand and comfort him.

But to her dismay, he shrunk away from her.

'Don't.'

She pulled her hand back.

Hitoshi stood up abruptly.

'I, uh … think I'll go take that shower.'

He left swiftly. She flopped back on the two-seater sofa, not quite sure what had just happened. Why was he so afraid of letting her get close to him? Perhaps it was because of Tami. *Oh, of course.* That had to be it.

Elise soon heard running water in the en suite. She sat and waited for a couple of minutes, but was fidgety. Feeling rather foolish, she got up and ambled over to the devil and angel painting that had caught her attention the last time she'd been in the apartment. She was idly studying the brushstrokes when she heard his bedroom door open.

Hitoshi now wore a white short-sleeved top, khakis and socks, carrying a pair of trainers by the laces. His wet hair was combed back, but the fringe was already drying out.

'Like the painting?' he said.

'It's … interesting.'

'It ought to be. I paid a lot of money for it.' He gave her a gentle smile. 'Sorry about before.'

'Oh, no, I'm sorry –'

'No, I shouldn't have gone off like that.' He sat on the sofa and put his trainers on. 'Fact of the matter is I'm not David anymore than you are Joanna. We're different people now. We have our own lives.' He finished tying his laces and looked up at her. 'You know what I'm saying?'

She nodded. Hitoshi sat forward and patted the empty spot next to him. She went across and sat beside him again.

'Don't get me wrong, Lise. It's not like I've never wondered about the past, because I have. I've thought about you – about *her* – every day. And I'm glad that we've met. When I look at you, I see her. That girl I was totally crazy about. If things were different ...' He closed his eyes momentarily. 'Like I said, we're different people now. I have my life here, and you have yours in England, right? Job, home, people who care about you?'

'I suppose so,' she said, sounding unintentionally despondent.

'Because that's what's really at stake here. David and Jo and Leon, they're gone. Nothing's going to bring them back. So let's not risk everything we have now as well. It's bad enough that they've found us and forced us to join this investigation. We have to stick it out, but we've got two choices. We either stay schtoom and hope they let us go, or we do something stupid and pay for it, like we did before.' He gave her an imploring look. 'We've got a second chance to get it right, Lise. I'm begging you, leave things as they are – for both our sakes.'

* * * * * * * * *

The Peace Man was parked on a street at the rear of a local and well-known saltworks. A high wall with barbed wire lining the top obstructed his view of the buildings on the site. On the front side of the saltworks, where he couldn't see, was a phone box.

He leaned down to the navigation system fitted beneath the radio, and touched the screen to activate the self-drive program. Using the onscreen map he picked the desired location. The navigator pinged and a dialogue box stating *OK* appeared to confirm he was ready to go. He left it where it was for the moment. He picked up the mobile phone lying on the passenger seat and held it tightly. As soon as he switched it on, he was certain they would know his location within seconds.

All day Peter had been thinking over and over about what had happened in Crescent Bay West, analysing every moment. He'd learned precious few things about his old comrade. Her present name was Elise Archer. From her accent he knew she was from England. She was Joanna's current incarnation, and she'd already met the new incarnation of David. Yet she hadn't brought him with her to the phone box. Most intriguing of all was what she'd said about Omar. What made her so certain that the professor hadn't been brought back like the others?

The Peace Man put the phone back on the passenger seat and got out of the van. He walked up the street and round the corner, turning right, and then followed the main avenue until he reached the intersection turning onto Piccolo Street, which ran down the other side of the block. He stopped and glanced down the intersection, and saw the phone box. Instead of turning right onto Piccolo Street, he turned left onto a much smaller street with rows of flat-roofed buildings, comprising offices and shops. As it was early evening, most people had left and gone home, and so there were only two vehicles parked on the street. One was a pick-up truck, and the other a coupé. Both vehicles probably belonged to business owners who were working late. But he needed to know how many people were inside the buildings. Fortunately his intuitive radar provided that information.

The coupé was parked on the left side of the street outside a print shop. A light was on in the window of the second floor. Peter detected two energy signatures inside. The pick-up meanwhile was parked a little further up on the right side of the street, outside a hardware store. If any lights were on, they were not visible at the front, but in any case he sensed one person inside.

Peter headed over, sticking to the left side of the street. He'd seen a small gap between two buildings just opposite the store. He slipped into the gap and kept his senses focused on the person inside. He expected to stay there for at least an hour, but he had to wait only around ten minutes. The energy signature soon moved from the rear of the building towards the front. His shoulders tensed up, and his heart began beating faster.

'Elise Archer,' said Peter, mentally picturing the woman. 'Elise, come to Piccolo Street, Murdock. I'm at the saltworks.'

He looked out, and finding that the road was clear he trotted back across the road and ducked down next to the pick-up at the driver's door. When he sensed that the owner was nearing his position from the other side of the truck, he pulled his dagger from his back pocket and skulked to the rear.

The owner came round from the front end of the vehicle and reached the driver's door. Peter surmised that the owner effectively had his back to him as he opened the door, and stood up to catch the man unawares.

He saw the owner and hesitated, as what he saw was only partially what he'd expected. The owner's back was indeed half turned to him, but the person in dark overalls had a slight build, long red hair in a plait and a leather handbag on one shoulder. She was patently a woman. Peter frowned. Why did it have to be a female? They could be such noisy creatures.

But he had no time to deliberate. Having realised that someone was standing behind her, she was beginning to turn round. Peter reacted in a reflex. He swooped in and swung his arm over her left shoulder, and clapped his hand over her mouth just as she was about to squeal. She writhed as though she'd touched a live wire and tried to scream regardless. He restrained her by putting his other arm round her and holding the blade close to her throat.

'Calm down,' he said. 'I'm not going to hurt you.'

The woman now stopped struggling, but breathed rapidly through flared nostrils.

* * * * * * * * *

Wearing a duffel coat, jeans, sneakers and a baseball cap, Aaron got off the bus on a street in Murdock, a district at the southwest end of Hadescape, almost at the edge of the city. Smaller than neighbouring Ashby, it was an industrial area inhabited mainly by working class families. Night had fallen, and though there was plenty of traffic, there were relatively few pedestrians on the streets. He went to the next block and to a public phone booth.

He dialled a phone number and his correspondent picked up without speaking. Aaron delivered his message.

'I'm making my move tonight.'

That was all he needed to say. No names or locations. Specificities always came from his correspondent.

He replaced the receiver and left.

Aaron went down a couple more blocks and took a different bus back to Verity Square. Due to heavy traffic it took over forty minutes to get back. It felt much longer than that due to the hammering in his temples. He wished he could have taken his own car, which was presently parked right outside his apartment.

Once back home he threw off his baseball cap and went straight towards the kitchen. He'd left both his cell and observer strap behind whilst he was out. After the unexpected visit to the Morton residence, Aaron and Kash had made a joint report to Kingswell, and then the pair had written up and filed some paperwork. Aaron had clocked off just after six and, thinking that he still had plenty of time, he'd returned to his apartment to change and eat before heading to Murdock. He was about to head back out again now, as soon as he'd taken yet another painkiller and picked up his observer strap. He needed to know where Elise was, mainly to ensure she wasn't still with Hitoshi. He hated the thought of getting back on the buses. Maybe he'd take a cab instead – though not a self-service one, which demanded a credit card.

Aaron heard the strap beeping before he reached the kitchen. He went over to the counter and picked it up. It displayed the coordinates of a signal from Manner's cellphone. The entire Intelligence search team had configured their observer straps earlier to automatically receive the information via a satellite data link as soon as Manner switched his phone on. Presently the strap showed him that Manner was in Murdock, of all places.

He grumbled and glanced at his wristwatch. It was 8:26 p.m., much earlier than expected for Manner's MO. He switched on his own cell and saw a flashing envelope icon at the top of the display.

He'd missed a mass text message that Elise had sent to Intelligence in the last ten minutes, and also a couple of calls from Kash. Aaron was supposed to have rung him the instant he received Elise's text.

He opened her message first. It read simply:

Piccolo Street Saltworks, Murdock

Aaron pinched the bridge of his nose with a finger and a thumb, and tried to think past his headache. What was he going to do now? He had to return Kash's call. He did so.

'*What are you doing, Lloyd?*' said Kash. '*I've been calling but you didn't pick up.*'

'My cell was switched off. Sorry. I didn't –'

'*I also tried your landline,*' said Kash, his tone suddenly flat. '*And your observer strap.*'

Aaron looked through the open kitchen door to the living room. The answering machine was in sight on the corner table, and the small red LED was flashing, indicating at least one missed call.

He had to think fast. 'I –' He winced as his brain jarred in his skull. Good timing, he thought, as it gave him his alibi. '– I didn't hear a thing. I left the observer in the living room by accident. I was sleeping off a bad headache.'

Kash sounded more concerned now. '*You're still getting headaches? Mine have pretty much worn off. You should go down to the infirmary and get yourself checked over.*'

'I will, later. What's your position?' asked Aaron, as he quietly picked up his observer strap again and pressed the right-hand button a couple of times.

'*There's a phone booth in front of the saltworks,*' replied Kash. '*Manner has been waiting three blocks away for the last fifteen minutes. We're on our way to intercept.*'

Kash and his team had already crossed Dean Bridge and they were almost at Ashby. They were four miles ahead of him. He pressed the strap button again to check on Elise and Hitoshi. They were together in Glensville but also moving west in the direction of Murdock, not more than two miles behind the Intelligence team.

'And you've confirmed with Elise?' said Aaron, just about sounding composed.

'*I told her and Hitoshi to head off.*'

'Right. I'll follow now.'

He rang off and hurriedly put his strap back on. GAILE's official objective was to capture Manner, hold him whilst they assessed him, and then return him to the British authorities. The Intelligence Office however had a different policy on dealing with the fugitive. The director of GAILE viewed him as an untenable threat. There was a strong possibility that if Intelligence found him tonight, they would kill him.

Aaron rushed out of the apartment and got into his car, with only one thing on his mind. Somehow he had to get to Manner before the search team did.

CHAPTER TWENTY-FIVE
Beacon

Traffic flow was significantly lighter on the way out of Verity Square than it was coming in, but still it moved far too slowly for Aaron. Once he'd crossed Dean Bridge, he took a slip road to the beltway that ran along Crescent Bay West, bypassing the outer limits of Glensville and Ashby. The Intelligence team had taken the direct route through the two districts. Technically the beltway route was a few miles longer but Aaron had the advantage of a higher speed limit.

He kept looking at the three green dots on his observer strap display. A single dot represented Kash and the two others in his team, since they were travelling together and their individual signals were merged. Elise and Hitoshi also registered as a single dot. They were on the same route as the Intelligence team but remained around two miles behind.

The third green dot representing the phone signal was three blocks west of the saltworks, just as Kash had said. Manner was probably inside his van, believing he was perfectly safe.

'Stay where you are, Manner,' muttered Aaron.

He sped down the beltway and within ten minutes he'd passed Glensville and Ashby. He overtook Elise and Hitoshi, and soon reached the end of the beltway near the outer side of Ashby, just as the Intelligence team were leaving the same district. He was almost neck and neck with them as they all entered Murdock.

Then he began to edge into the lead. Believing that he might just beat them to Manner's position, Aaron gave a little laugh of relief.

But the feeling was short-lived. At the next stoplights, a mile from the saltworks, he found himself slowing down as he came up behind a queue of seven or eight cars. They weren't moving.

'Don't do this to me.'

Aaron checked his observer strap. The Intelligence team were catching up again.

He looked down the queue anxiously, kneading his aching temple with his palm. The lights changed and the first few cars began passing through the lights. The queue inched forward.

'Come on, come on,' he mumbled impatiently, his nose almost touching the bumper of the car in front of him.

Six cars crossed the lights. The car in front also crossed just as the lights turned yellow, and then red. Aaron hit the brake and growled. He might have run a red light if traffic hadn't started rolling in from the left.

He waited an excruciating thirty seconds, his gaze flitting between the lights and the observer strap display. Every time he looked at the strap, the green dot representing Intelligence was closer to the dot representing Manner. Next the Intelligence dot split into two, indicating that the team had parked their vehicle and were now on the streets. They would be aiming to get onto Manner's block at both ends and trap him.

'Move!' Aaron yelled at the lights. 'Move it!'

At long last the lights changed. His car was on the crossing practically before the traffic had stopped on the other side. He came onto the path of a straggling station wagon on the left. The driver screeched to a halt to avoid him and honked angrily.

Aaron took no notice. His focus was on the road ahead of him. He zipped along at fifty miles per hour, going twenty over the limit. Within a minute he was on the main avenue of the industrial zone. Piccolo Street was five blocks away, and the cellphone signal three blocks beyond that.

He turned his eyes to the observer strap again. All the dots had fused again into one blip. Kash and his men were all within metres of Manner's signal now. Aaron eased his foot off the accelerator. He was only a quarter of a mile away, but he was too late.

Infuriated, he banged his fist on the steering wheel.

* * * * * * * *

Kash had parked his car one block away from the target and had instructed his men to get onto the target's block from both ends. All the officers were in plain clothes. He walked up the street and stood casually on the corner. He glanced round as though he was waiting for someone, but he was actually looking for a van. Down at the other end of the block, a hundred yards or so from his position, his two men had also arrived. One was loitering as Kash was, and the other strolled in his direction. By Kash's estimate, the latter officer was passing exactly opposite the source of the cell signal; yet there was no vehicle parked there.

Kash also proceeded with care in the direction of the signal source. As he got within twenty metres of it, the green dot on his observer strap began flashing. Still seeing nothing in front of him, he continued with more confidence. As he drew even nearer, the dot flashed at an increasing rate; and he became increasingly certain that either Manner was not in his van, or …

The green dot became stationary just as he passed a cylindrical trash can. He bent down and peered inside, but as it was dark, and the garbage wasn't full to the top, he couldn't see inside it. He didn't particularly want to put his hand in there.

He took out his own cellphone and called the telecoms officer at the Harper Building.

'Can you dial Manner's cell for me? I don't have the number on me. Just give it a couple of rings. Thanks.'

He hung up. A few moments later, the trash can began ringing.

Kash pressed the left-hand button on his observer strap.

* * * * * * * *

Aaron had just passed Piccolo Street when his observer strap beeped. It was Kash.

'*Alert. Manner has planted his phone in a trash can as a decoy. He's hiding elsewhere. Spread out.*'

Aaron was astounded. With hindsight it was obvious that at a distance of three blocks from the saltworks, Manner couldn't possibly have monitored the arrival of the project subjects, whether visually or psychically. Yet neither Aaron nor any member of the team had foreseen it.

'Yes!' he said jubilantly, and made a sharp U-turn.

Aaron went back the way that he'd come and instead of turning onto Piccolo Street he turned left and parked on the corner of the main avenue. He got out of the car and from his position he saw the phone booth clearly. His observer strap showed him that Elise and Hitoshi would arrive in a few minutes.

He jogged onto the main avenue and surveyed the area. The roads were wide, and a few vehicles were parked on them; but no orange vans. All the buildings on the main street were packed tightly together. The alleyways were too narrow to accommodate a vehicle. Where could Manner be hiding that simultaneously offered him a visual and a psychic advantage?

The answer came to him when he looked up. On the very next street, towering somewhat higher than most buildings in the immediate area, was a multistorey parking lot.

* * * * * * * *

The Peace Man had been hiding behind the concrete enclosure for the past three quarters of an hour, allowing only his crown to be raised above its edge. The car park was largely empty, but his radar detected lots of people in the area, and so he relied heavily on his sight. He looked at the streets below through his binoculars, watching vigilantly for suspicious activity.

A dark blue saloon arrived on the street opposite the saltworks and the brakes screeched as it ground to a halt. Peter was sure the same car had passed by only a couple of minutes earlier. A young man in a navy coat got out and ran light-footedly along the main avenue. His head turned in all directions as he looked for someone or something. If he was one of their scouts, then he was doing a poor job of being discreet.

The man stopped in the middle of the avenue for a few moments, looking lost. The Peace Man zoomed in to see the man's face, and recognised the GAILE officer who had accompanied Elise Archer both at the Harper Building and in Crescent Bay West.

Once again she had chosen to involve *them*.

Though Peter knew he ought to leave right away, he didn't move. Something about the GAILE officer had just come to his attention. He had practically no life force in him at all. Thinking back to Tuesday morning outside the Harper Building, Peter remembered that he'd noticed this aspect of the man then also. Perhaps, he thought, this was a mark of *their* kind.

The GAILE officer glanced at what appeared to be a large wristwatch. He pressed a button, and Peter realised it was some sort of communications device. But the officer didn't speak to anyone. Instead he raised his brow worriedly at whatever was on his display. Peter was intrigued.

Just then the GAILE officer looked up in his general direction. Peter's instinct was to duck down, but he knew that he was not visible, being nestled in the nook between the front tyre of his van and the wall. He remained as he was.

The officer gazed up for several seconds, and his expression told Peter that he'd had a realisation. Like a hound that had just got a scent he suddenly bounded towards the car park.

Peter moved back from the enclosure. He had enough time to get away if he wanted to; but the officer's behaviour was making him curious. He hadn't called his men to back him up.

The Peace Man decided to await the man's impending arrival on the roof. He ran to the side of the small entrance building leading to the stairs and the lifts, from where he knew the GAILE officer would soon arrive.

* * * * * * * * *

Aaron sprinted into the multistorey and took the stairs rather than the elevator. He ascended past the ground, first and second storeys as he knew they weren't high enough to get a bird's-eye view. He stopped at the third level to check it out. Of the dozen or so vehicles, only one was a van. It was parked at the west end of the level overlooking the wrong side of the zone, and it was white.

He hurried to the south side of the level. The parking lot was five storeys high – plus a roof level – and each was enclosed by a short wall. He looked out towards Piccolo Street. A small shop partially blocked his view. In order to get the clearest view Manner would have to be on the roof. He decided to go straight to the top and make his way down if he failed to find anyone there. He leapt up the stairs two or three at a time.

Aaron emerged from the landing onto the roof, and came to a standstill. A number of small floodlights and wall panels illuminated the level, making shapes and colours easy to discern. His attention turned straight to the south side, and the orange camper van on the corner was the first thing he saw. It was a mere ten metres from where he stood.

Was it really Manner's van? Aaron's heart told him it was. He was glad that his shield was protecting him. He didn't want to scare off Manner before he'd reached the vehicle.

He glanced once more at his observer strap. Kash and his men were out on the main avenue. One of them would soon see the parking lot and have the same idea as he'd just had.

Aaron's hands felt clammy all of a sudden. His gaze fixed firmly on the van, he stepped forward.

* * * * * * * * *

The officer had come up quietly, but Peter had heard his footsteps echoing inside the stairwell. He peeked out from behind the entrance building as the officer moved towards the van. Peter inspected the space about the officer's person, where he would expect to find colours. He literally saw nothing at first, as though his psychic eye was either blind to the man's aura or there was none to be found; but this could not be the case. An absence of energy usually appeared to Peter as a black shadow. His suspicions were soon confirmed, for suddenly he glimpsed a tiny spark of light. Then he saw another ... and another. Had he been standing more than ten metres from the officer, Peter would never have detected anything. But he could see tiny twinkling rays, rotating and disappearing like lighthouse beacons, and he realised that something was obscuring the officer's aura, perhaps an electromagnetic field. Underneath the invisible fog, the energy was strong and vibrant. The sparks were predominantly white and gold. Peter would have been less surprised had he found only blackness. What he observed was the exact opposite. The GAILE officer was not as he seemed.

The Peace Man drew his unsoiled blade from his back pocket and crept towards him.

* * * * * * * * *

Aaron approached the van and came to the rear first. He saw the license plate number and memorised it. He'd chosen to move in effectively unarmed, and whilst his handgun was in its holster beneath his coat, he didn't want to use it. Even with the silencer, it would make too much noise.

The back curtains were drawn. The same was true of the side windows. If this was the right vehicle then Manner was sitting at the front, positioned to look over the streets. Aaron glanced at the side mirror, which showed him a partial reflection of the interior on the driver's side. The seat appeared unoccupied.

Aaron's throat felt dry. He neared the driver's door and noticed that the latch was up. So was the latch on the passenger door. Someone had to be inside.

He put his back gently against the body of the van and peeped in over his shoulder.

It was empty.

The first thought that entered Aaron's head was that this wasn't actually Manner's vehicle.

He glanced again at the open latch, and his next thought was that this was the right vehicle, and Manner was simply not in it. But he had to be nearby. Aaron placed his hand on the door handle, in two minds about quickly checking out the interior. The prospect of finding the disc compelled him to take the risk.

Aaron checked to see if the coast was clear. Several cars were parked on the top level, but no one was about. He opened the door and quickly got in as though he was braving a dive into cold water. He closed the door and took a steadying breath. A musty smell came from the worn seats.

His eyes turned to the glove compartment. He had a feeling.

As he reached over to open it, he suddenly heard a soft whirr and click. He looked up in alarm at the door latch on the passenger side. It was locked.

Aaron turned the other way and stopped.

A tall man in a long green trench coat had appeared outside his window like a spectre. He had a thorn-shaped birthmark on his haggard face, and a red ribbon tangled in his unkempt hair. In his left hand he held out the remote key fob he'd just used to lock the van from the outside. The dagger in his right hand gleamed under the artificial lighting.

Aaron looked into Manner's glacial eyes, but couldn't gauge his mood. He thought of going for his handgun, but decided not to.

Manner pressed the remote button again and the doors unlocked. Without moving from his position, he beckoned Aaron with a motion of his dagger.

* * * * * * * * *

Elise waited inside the phone box whilst Hitoshi insisted on remaining outside. He had the collar of his beige raincoat turned up due to the chill in the air.

The pair had been at a Glensville nightclub watching the band rehearsal for most of the afternoon. With all the noise, the bickering, the bantering, and the raucous laughter distracting them, not once had they returned to the subject of their earlier conversation at Hitoshi's apartment.

Even now Hitoshi was quiet, but then she knew he had to watch his words. The GAILE officers had supplied Elise and Hitoshi with earpiece bugs in order to facilitate two-way communication, since the ES tags lacked the means. The bug fitted inside the ear like a hearing aid. The Intelligence team could hear everything she and Hitoshi said and at the same time they could send audio instructions via their observer straps. The pair had switched the bugs on shortly before they'd left Glensville, and so they'd heard Kash's alert about Manner's phone decoy just before they'd reached Piccolo Street.

'How long is he going to take?' said Hitoshi.

'He was quicker last time,' she acknowledged.

At that moment the phone began ringing. Hitoshi opened the door and leaned in so he could listen.

Elise picked up right away.

'Hello?'

'You didn't do as I asked. Now I will never call again.'

'What? No, don't –!'

The line went dead.

'What happened?' asked Hitoshi.

Elise looked in dismay at the receiver in her hand.

'He knew GAILE was here,' she said. 'We've blown it.'

* * * * * * * *

Aaron took the lift straight down to the ground level. He was on his way out of the parking lot when his observer strap beeped.

'Go ahead, Kash.'

'You're in the multistorey?'

'On my way out, actually.'

'Oh yeah, I see you.'

Aaron looked round. Kash was further up the street, near the turn onto the avenue. He waved and came over.

'How's the headache?'

'Gone,' replied Aaron.

'You heard what Manner said? He knew we were here.'

'Yeah, I heard. And I think he called from outside this zone.'

'Agreed.' Kash looked up at the multistorey. 'Good idea to look in there. But it's a big building. Why didn't you call for backup?'

'I only needed to check the higher levels, as you can't get a clear view of Piccolo Street on the lowers ones. I went to the third and worked my way up.'

'And the roof?'

'Checked. Nothing there.'

Kash looked thoughtful. Aaron held his breath.

'Right, you want to call it a day?'

Aaron nodded, keeping his cool. He didn't dare look back as they walked away from the parking lot.

He and Kash went to Piccolo Street together to tell Elise and Hitoshi that their attempt to catch Manner was a dismal failure.

'What are we going to do now?' asked Elise.

'We're going to Washington,' Aaron replied, 'as scheduled.'

'But Manner –'

'We fly out on Saturday morning. Agent Kash and his team will keep searching for him while we're gone.'

* * * * * * * * *

Lloyd offered Elise and Hitoshi a lift in his car. Neither was inclined to sit next to him, so they sat together in the back.

The agent looked at them via the rearview mirror.

'Straight home, is it?'

'Yeah – where else?' said Hitoshi.

'I just meant if you have a gig on tonight, I could take you wherever you need to go.'

'No gigs for me. I'm beat.'

'Yeah, we all could do with some sleep. And you, Elise?'

'I haven't got any gigs either.'

Lloyd seemed oblivious to her joke. He smiled like a sales rep who had just reeled in a customer. 'Good, good. Home it is, then.'

Hitoshi gave Elise a puzzled glance. She shrugged.

They arrived in Rock Moor first.

'Come to the Harper Building at one o'clock tomorrow,' said Lloyd as Hitoshi got out of the car. 'We'll be in the lab for a briefing about the Phoenix Project.'

'Sure,' said Hitoshi. 'I'll see you soon,' he said to Elise.

Lloyd drove on in silence until they reached her apartment building. He stopped around the corner from the entrance.

Elise was glad to get out of the car.

'I'll see you tomorrow,' she said quickly.

'Wait,' he said, also getting out, and came round to join her on the pavement, directly beneath a streetlamp. 'Have you eaten?'

'Huh?'

'It's still early, kind of.'

'It's nearly ten o'clock. Besides, I've already eaten. There was a cafeteria in the club where the band was rehearsing. I was there when I connected to Manner.'

'Then can we get a coffee?'

She couldn't believe the nerve of the man.

'What are you playing at?'

'Sorry?'

'Don't play dumb. This isn't appropriate and you know it!'

'This?'

'Yes, this! ... *Socialising* with a witness –'

He interrupted her with an incredulous laugh. 'Wait a minute! You think I was –? I wasn't!'

He sounded indignant. Convincingly so.

Elise wavered. But she had to double-check.

'Y-you weren't asking me out?'

'No! ... No.'

She wished she had the power to teleport herself away.

'... Oh. Sorry.'

'Forget about it. Can we please just go somewhere and talk?'

'Can't it wait until tomorrow?'

'This can't wait. It's important.' His tone was foreboding. 'You need to know the truth.'

Now she was worried. 'The truth? About what?'

'Your past life, the Wheeler Park disappearances. Everything.'

She stared at the agent. Hitoshi's earlier warning about GAILE Intelligence was still fresh in her mind.

'I don't understand,' she said.

'Everything you've been told is a lie.'

'... What ... Why are you telling me this?'

'I appreciate that you don't trust me. But hopefully you will, once you know who I really am.'

Fear gripped her so badly all of a sudden that she wanted to run. She coped by going off on a tirade.

'What is this, Mr Lloyd? First you won't give me any straight answers about the case, and now suddenly you want to talk one-to-one! Is this GAILE's way of finding out if I know more than I'm letting on? Do you hope to gain my confidence and trick me into making some sort of confession? Didn't those memory tests you ran today prove that I remember nothing?'

Lloyd was unaffected. 'I'm not doing this for GAILE.'

He held out his hand.

'What are you doing?'

'It'll all make sense if you connect to me.'

Baulking at the thought, she recoiled with a jerk. But before she even knew it he reached forward, took hold of her left wrist with his right hand and pulled her towards him.

Incensed more than frightened, she gave a small scream. 'Let me go!' she shouted, and tried in vain to pull herself free.

Elise considered herself to be quite strong, but Lloyd maintained a firm hold.

'Whoa! Stay still, will you?! Concentrate! Connect to me!'

Still clasping her wrist, he took her same hand in his left and pulled her closer. She was face to face with him now, and the pair became still. Stood as they were beneath the white light of the streetlamp, Elise had the peculiar thought that they must look like a pair of dancers on a stage set. Lloyd nodded at her reassuringly. Feeling self-conscious, Elise closed her eyes.

Immediately she became aware of a warm energy field rising up and around her. In a few moments it was so strong it was almost tangible, tingling on her skin. The energy thawed the chill in the night air; and the dread that had overtaken her just moments before evaporated with it. She felt at once calm and safe. She opened her eyes, and saw a hazy white and golden light radiating from Lloyd. Yet she knew she wasn't seeing his whole aura. It was diluted, due to interference from his implant.

Just then she broke through his shielding and established a brief psychometric connection. Two people appeared in succession. First she saw a man in a trench coat, with thin features, a goatee, and long curly hair: Manner. Then he was gone, and another face appeared for just a second: A man with bronze skin and black wavy hair. She didn't recognise his melancholy face, but she knew him from his tawny eyes.

Manner reappeared again without warning. His limbs were slack and to the side. His eyes were wide, staring at her in wonder. He opened his mouth and spoke.

The connection failed at that moment; but she'd heard what he'd said. Elise gasped and looked frenetically into Lloyd's eyes.

'It can't be true,' she whispered.

And yet she saw it there, clear as day.

Breathlessly, she repeated Manner's words.

'You! You're …'

Part 3

HONOUR

CHAPTER TWENTY-SIX
The Invitation

'… Omar!'

He smiled. 'Actually, my surname is Lloyd, after my mother. Omar was my father.'

'You're his son?'

'Yes.'

Elise lost her concentration completely now, and Lloyd's aura was gone as abruptly as the light from a snuffed candle.

'Then … is Omar still alive?'

'No. He died a long time ago.'

A rumbling voice suddenly came from the darkness. 'You can let go of her now.'

They turned their heads sharply. Hitoshi stood leaning against the car bonnet. He put a cigarette in his mouth and took out his lighter. Elise noticed that his nicotine aura, whilst not obstructed by any shielding, was notably dull compared with Lloyd's.

She and Lloyd turned to each other again now. Remembering that they were still holding hands, both hastily let go.

'What are you doing here?' asked Lloyd.

Hitoshi cupped his hands as he lit up, and his face glowed. 'I had a hunch,' he said, with the cigarette between his teeth, and then took it out. 'You were acting strangely in the car, so after you dropped me off I got a taxi and followed you here. She noticed it too – didn't you, Lise?'

She nodded.

Hitoshi's gaze was on Lloyd as he took a drag. 'So, when were you planning to tell *me* about your secret identity?'

'I wasn't.'

He smiled acerbically. 'What's going on here, Lloyd?'

'Nothing. Go home.' He turned to Elise. 'Can we go and talk somewhere indoors? It'd be best if we go somewhere public.'

Elise didn't move. 'You don't honestly expect him to just leave and forget what he's heard, do you?'

Lloyd looked at Hitoshi inimically. 'Do what you like,' he said, and began walking down the street.

They both followed.

Lloyd led them to a late night bistro on the next block. Before they went in he told them they couldn't stay for too long in case Intelligence found out from the observer strap logs.

The bistro was an intimate informal place, with soft jazz music playing on the radio, and low lighting. Half the tables were taken, mainly by couples. He led them to a table in the back corner where they could have some privacy, and waited for a menu. He said nothing until after they'd ordered some drinks, and the waiter had brought over a bottle of red wine and two coffees.

'I've seen Manner,' he said suddenly, as though he was referring to an old pal.

Hitoshi had just begun pouring himself some wine. He almost spilled it over the side of his glass.

'You what?'

It was now that Elise recalled the mental image of Manner from her connection to Lloyd. She'd practically forgotten all about it.

'Oh, my God ... you met him tonight! Are you –?' she began with a raised voice, but had to bear in mind the customers on the next table. 'Are you out of your mind?' she whispered. 'He could have killed you!'

'I know,' he said, 'but I had to take that chance.'

Hitoshi put down the wine bottle. 'How did you find him? The search team were crawling all over the place.'

'In a way he found me, which is just as well.'

'What did he say?' said Hitoshi. 'Did he give you the disc?'

'No. He asked me to meet him later and bring a compatible drive. He wants to be there when I upload the data to the net.'

Elise wasn't wholly attentive for the moment. 'What exactly is on that disc?' she asked for the second time that day, hoping to get a decent answer this time.

'Don't either of you remember?' said Lloyd.

The pair looked at him blankly.

Lloyd produced a battered old folded pamphlet from his pocket and handed it to Elise.

'Have a look at this,' he said. 'Tell me if it rings a bell.'

Hitoshi was seated next to her and so he leaned across to see the text on the front as she read it out loud.

'*The Cohesive Ethics Theorem, by Professor Hanif Omar.*'

'That's the handout from my father's presentation on his theorem at Hadescape University,' said Lloyd. 'The gist of his thinking was that universal ideals have a logical connection, and can be reduced to one. That was his theorem in a nutshell. He said that if humanity realised the inherent logic in ethics, then an intellectual revolution would occur. Nations and societies the world over would finally achieve both justice and liberty. In other words, he claimed that there would be world peace.'

There was a pause. Again Elise remembered Joanna's words: *The biggie of all time.* At least the line fit the bill.

'That's one heck of a claim,' she remarked. 'Even the MWA haven't managed that.'

Lloyd smiled. 'It gets better. He got SECOM and the STRO to fund an experiment that could prove it. Based on his proposals they created a simulation of some virtual countries on a supercomputer, each with a different political system, including one that represented his theorem put into practice. They called it the Systems Experiment. David and Leon were his colleagues. Do you remember?' he asked Hitoshi.

'Not especially.'

'David was the chief programmer. He designed everything from scratch: The simulation, the operating system, everything.'

Hitoshi was indifferent.

Elise saw scepticism in Lloyd's eyes; but as he had no grounds to challenge Hitoshi, he continued.

'Anyway, of all the different system types, my father's was the only theoretical model, so he coined the word *Libredux* for it, meaning to revive or return to liberty and justice.'

'Return to liberty ...' Hadn't she seen that line on the wall in Manner's old room? 'Liberty! That was one of the keywords in the test we had today!' She looked at Hitoshi in alarm. 'You were right. They were trying to find out what we remembered.' She turned back to Lloyd. 'What happened to the experiment?'

'Some powerful people opposed the theorem from the very beginning. They were used to being at the top and they wanted things to stay that way. But the Libredux model was promising real justice and liberty. Imagine what went through their minds when the preliminary output from the supercomputer came out, showing that Libredux looked to be the most stable model. They couldn't afford to let the simulation run its course, so they had the whole experiment shut down.'

Elise returned the pamphlet.

'But hundreds of people must have been involved,' she said. 'And it must have been publicised.'

'Actually, they deliberately never publicised it. As for the workers, the executive board told them to abort the experiment for reasons of international security. They gave the workers strict orders to never discuss the experiment, and warned that any action to the contrary would be looked upon as treachery against the MWA. But they couldn't silence my father or David, so they planned to kill them. They also targeted Joanna and Leon on account of their ties to David. Luckily a friend of my father found out about their plans and warned him in advance.'

She thought ahead quickly. 'So then we tried to save the data?'

'David was the only one with direct access to the supercomputer, so he had to retrieve it. My father went to a safe house ahead of the others, where they were supposed to meet up before they uploaded the data to the net. But he never heard from any of them again. He spent the rest of his life in hiding, and never knew what had happened to them. He never forgave himself.'

So, she thought, Omar hadn't left them behind on purpose after all. The guilt and the stress must have been unbearable for him.

'I'm sorry,' she said. 'When did he …?'

'When I was fifteen. Heart attack. After he died I swore that I'd find them and expose the truth. So I enrolled in GAILE. My father's old friend called in a couple of favours to fast-track me through the recruitment procedure and the background checks. It helped that my father had changed his identity before he married my mother. He'd even had his face surgically altered.'

'And what happened to his work? Did he ever try to make the theorem public some other way?'

'He couldn't. He would have endangered not only himself but also my mother. As I said, he was always running, always hiding. When I came along, he left us for our protection. I only got to see him during school vacations, and that too when he felt it was safe. He moved around a lot, so it was difficult.'

Lloyd stopped and took a sip of his coffee.

Elise wasn't ready to try her latte yet. She took the plastic stirrer next to her cup and gently turned the foam.

'How did you get this investigation started?' she asked.

'When you work for GAILE, you learn that expendable enemies of the MWA – like prisoners of war and terror suspects – are sometimes used as subjects in black military experiments. I heard a rumour about Intelligence having run a mind reading research programme in 2014, at around the time of the Wheeler Park disappearances. I did some digging and found some incriminating evidence linking Palmerton to the programme. Once I'd collected enough information, I tipped off the press.'

Elise frowned and took out the stirrer. 'That was you?'

'I had to kick-start an investigation somehow. I needed a legitimate query so I could ask questions and access classified files without rousing suspicions. I eventually learned that they'd run their mind reading experiment to try to learn my father's whereabouts. Originally I was going to give the evidence to my father's old friend, who is in a position of influence and has the means to raise a lot of publicity. At the time I thought the experiment data was lost, so I was just looking to clear my father's name. But the investigation turned up far more than anyone anticipated.' He smiled wryly. 'My superiors in Intelligence were more surprised to learn you were alive than I was.'

She glanced at Hitoshi. He'd just emptied his wineglass, and now held it to his lips with a frown on his face. Elise wondered if he was thinking about their earlier conversation. She certainly was. Despite his plea not to go after the MWA again, she hadn't given up on the idea. And in Lloyd she saw an opportunity.

'Who gave the nod to the Phoenix Project?' she asked. 'I know technically they were all MWA officials, but you can't take on the whole organisation at the end of the day. Do you have any names?'

'It's not as simple as that. We're not really talking about the MWA.' He scratched the back of his neck. 'How do I put this?'

Hitoshi spoke unexpectedly. 'Just say it,' he said. 'You're talking about a secret elite order, right?'

Elise looked his way obliquely. Was he referring to the same conspiracy theory he'd told her about that afternoon? *Surely not.*

She was taken aback when Lloyd answered.

'You remember!'

Hitoshi poured himself some more wine. 'Yeah, I remember all right ... the ones who have been running the world since time immemorial. What was it Omar called them?'

'The Triumvirate Committee,' said Lloyd. 'Also known as E3.'

Elise felt not so much a flutter as a twinge in her stomach.

'E3?'

'It means they have three elitist divisions working together: Economic, political and religious,' said Lloyd. 'It's a three-way control mechanism with which they programme us to believe that world peace is impossible; that we need them to rule us, to provide for us, and to protect us. But my father claimed the opposite was true, and what's more he proved it. The Systems Experiment was literally a threat to their existence. They tried to bury every last remnant of it, but *now* ... now that Manner has recovered the disc, we can finally expose them once and for all. And maybe we can also finish my father's work.'

Elise passed no comment. Her psychic sense was sounding the alarm, but the actual memory eluded her.

Hitoshi flashed a grin. 'Sound like conspiracy theory, much?'

'Except that it's not,' said Lloyd.

Hitoshi's eyes flicked to Elise and back to Lloyd again. 'Isn't it?'

'No, it isn't. I have my father's research as proof. I can –'

'Yeah, yeah, I know all about Omar's research. He was a revolutionary, a religious dissenter cum anarchist. He was anti-MWA and anti-democracy.'

'How do you know?'

'I've read articles about him.'

'Of course you have,' said Lloyd, with a blasé look. 'And what did these articles say about his theorem?'

'… There was nothing about that.'

'Exactly,' said Lloyd, 'because everything you'll find on him today is false. They made up so much trash about my father even when he was alive, there's a permanent stigma attached to his name. If you saw his literature, you'd know better. But I bet you've never come across any, because they've been systematically wiping it – especially what he wrote on his theorem.'

Hitoshi looked Lloyd in the eye. 'But for that to be true, they'd *all* have to be in on it – all the historians and journalists in the world. It's just not realistic, is it? Not very rational either. You know, Adam said that your old man was a lunatic –'

'Hey! Watch your mouth!' growled Lloyd, laying his palms on the table as though ready to jump over and attack.

Thankfully no one on the next table noticed.

Hitoshi put up his hands. 'Adam's words, not mine. He warned that Omar was trouble, but David chose not to listen. Big mistake. All the evidence I've found since backs up what he said.'

'Forget what you've read! Is that what you *remember*?'

Hitoshi picked up his wineglass and gazed musingly at the swirling red liquid. 'I guess not,' he admitted. 'I don't remember anything about the Systems Experiment. But that doesn't really change anything. So Omar might have come up with an interesting theory. And I can even believe the MWA might have shut the experiment down when the results didn't suit its interests. Politics is a dirty game, after all – nothing new. But there is no Committee, for God's sake. Everything that happened to us was down to Omar's vendetta against the MWA.'

'You're wrong.'

'I know you don't want to hear this, because he was your father.' Hitoshi gave Elise a meaningful glance. 'But Omar's sole ambition in life was to topple this so-called E3. He thought he'd start a world revolution and create a utopia afterwards. That's what operation *Abdul Salaam* was all about!'

'Come again? Operation *Abdul* –?!' Lloyd laughed weakly. 'And you think my father was crazy? I have news for you, Hitoshi. Your memory's warped! *Abdul Salaam* was just my father's nickname for David. *Servant of the Peace* just meant he was behind the *peaceful* revolution in the simulation. Have you forgotten?'

Hitoshi didn't reply; instead he turned to Elise. His expression communicated that he wasn't interested in anything Lloyd had to say, and that he expected her to take his side.

'Elise,' said Lloyd just then, 'you believe me, don't you?'

She looked at the two men in turn. Both sought her vote, but neither had won her over. In the end she went with what seemed the more sensible option.

'I have to agree with Hitoshi on this one,' she said. 'Systems Experiment aside, it does sound like a conspiracy theory.'

But Lloyd wasn't done yet. 'What if I introduce you to Nathalie Weston, Palmerton's former assistant? She has worked for the Committee, and she'll confirm that everything I've said is true.'

Elise was curious, even if she remained doubtful.

'Isn't she in custody?'

'She was, but she escaped at the end of last week.'

That was unexpected.

'You kept that quiet!' she said.

'GAILE always keeps things quiet. But they don't know that I found her. She's agreed to supply some information of her own.'

Elise looked at Hitoshi. He was unresponsive.

'And I can give you some instant proof as well,' Lloyd continued. 'It's a small thing, but maybe it'll help. Would you like me to show you?'

She nodded.

'Get out your ID cards.'

They did as he asked.

'Look at the front side. What's in the top right-hand corner?'

'The MWA insignia,' said Elise.

Lloyd watched them closely. 'Now turn your cards ninety degrees clockwise. What do you see?'

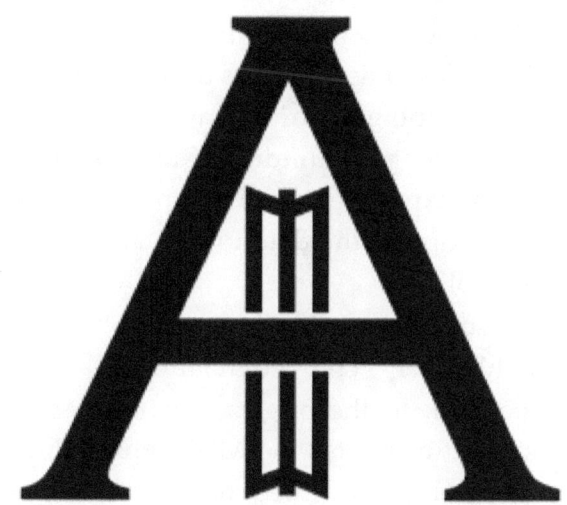

The alphanumeric characters *E3* jumped out at her as soon as she laid eyes on them. A vague memory entered her mind like a shadow, formless, but nevertheless it was there. Elise stared at the insignia and tried to remember. David might have shown the symbol to Joanna once before, long ago.

'Do you see it?'

Lloyd's voice shattered the memory before it had quite taken hold in her cognitive circuitry, but it didn't matter. Intuitively, she knew the truth now.

'Yes,' she said. 'And ... I believe you.'

She looked Hitoshi's way. He sighed and nodded to indicate that he too remembered.

Lloyd smiled approvingly. 'Funny thing is,' he said, 'they never wanted the MWA to come into being. They only wove their symbol into the insignia to try and stake their claim on it, when they were fighting a losing battle against the World Democratic Revolution. They knew that if the Systems Experiment results went public it would be the end of them. That's why they took such extreme measures to extract information from David, Leon and Joanna. They wanted to find and destroy everything and everyone connected with my father; his work, and anybody who helped him openly and in secret. In the end, they steered events in their favour. And with time they took control of the MWA as well.'

He sipped his coffee. Elise left hers untouched on the table.

'What are you planning to do?' she asked.

'I'm meeting Manner on Sunday. If all goes to plan, the data from the Systems Experiment will go public within forty-eight hours. I'll email a copy of the data to my father's friend, and he'll take care of the publicity.'

'What if the disc doesn't work?' she said.

'Which is highly likely,' chipped in Hitoshi.

'Then it'll be back to the original plan. We still have all the documentation that implicates the MWA and Palmerton. And we have you as the living proof of what they've done – that is, if you're willing to help us expose them.'

Elise was stunned for a second. As such, the request shouldn't have surprised her. It was probably dangerous to stay behind at this stage. Besides, she'd been looking to get justice for Joanna and her friends as well as for herself. But could she really drop everything and just go with Lloyd? She'd likely have to go into hiding. And what about everyone back at home? When would she get to see them again?

'It's a big ask,' she said.

'I don't want to pressure you. You don't have to get involved if you really don't want to.'

Hitoshi exhaled. 'Sure! I've heard that one before! You run off while we stay back and face the music! What do we tell GAILE once you're gone, and they start asking questions?'

'You can tell them that I asked you to come with me, but you wanted no part of it. They'll believe you.'

'Will they?'

'You forget that I've seen their assessment reports firsthand. They've got you down as *low risk*. If one or both of you were to stay back, it'd only confirm their assessment.'

They paused for a moment.

'What are you doing about Manner?' asked Elise. 'You can't just let him go free.'

'He's volunteered to hand himself in after giving us the data. I'll take him to a police station before I head off anywhere else.'

She looked at him agape. He was serious.

'And you believed him?'

'I think he meant what he said – but obviously I won't just take him at his word. I'll be armed anyway, and in case I lose him, I've already got his license plate number. I'll just give it to the police.'

'When are you leaving?'

'Saturday, before dawn.'

'Does your invitation extend to me?' said Hitoshi.

'I'm asking both of you.'

'But it's not like you planned it that way. If I hadn't followed you tonight I'd have been none the wiser.'

'You should be grateful,' said Lloyd sarcastically. 'I was trying to spare you from a moral dilemma.'

'What the hell does that mean?'

'You really have to ask?'

'Yeah, actually, I do. I had a right to know the truth too.'

'As if you ever *wanted* to know! Face it, Hitoshi. You haven't shown the slightest interest in this investigation. Elise has been asking questions – the right questions – but not you. In fact you've been doing your best to get away from them!'

'That's not fair,' said Hitoshi defensively. 'I didn't know the full story, that's all – especially about the Systems Experiment.'

'Well, you do now. Have you changed your mind?'

Hitoshi downed the rest of his wine.

'Maybe, maybe not.'

Lloyd gave a hollow laugh. 'See?! You don't care about the truth or doing the right thing. You look out for number one!'

'Up yours,' retorted Hitoshi. 'I died because of the *truth* before. So sue me if I want to make it to old age this time.'

Elise had heard enough. 'Hitoshi has a point,' she said. 'You're asking us to become fugitives and meet a serial killer for a disc that probably doesn't even work.'

Lloyd's face fell. 'That's a no from you, then?'

'I didn't say that. But there must be another way.'

'If you have a better alternative, I'd like to hear it.'

Elise had nothing constructive to offer. Involving the authorities was hardly a viable option.

The men finished their drinks quietly, and she finally picked up her untouched latte. It had cooled off, and she couldn't drink it all. Though Lloyd was undoubtedly genuine, and regardless of her instinctual feelings, she wished she could remember the facts for herself. Lloyd had merely supplied the missing information, and that wasn't nearly the same.

'I need some time to think about this,' she said after a while.

'Same here,' said Hitoshi.

Lloyd nodded. 'Fair enough. Meet me tomorrow night in The Chase. You have until then to make up your minds.'

CHAPTER TWENTY-SEVEN
Dissonance

Elise didn't awaken until eleven the next morning, which was probably the longest that she'd ever slept. No matter. The meeting with GAILE wasn't until early afternoon. Lloyd's invitation was in the back of her mind, but she felt that she owed herself a few more hours to *not* think. She had a decent mug of coffee, went for her morning run, and got ready in her own sweet time.

At the Harper Building just before one o'clock she poked her head round the meeting room door. The room had an elliptical table in its centre that could seat up to twenty people. A large interactive whiteboard was on the wall to the left, whilst the MWA and GAILE flags hung in prominence at the back.

Taylor had already arrived and he was seated beside Agent Kash on the right side of the table, where they were going through some documents. They looked up at the same time and nodded at her in greeting. She gave a small smile and sat opposite them.

Hitoshi arrived next. He walked in with his confident gait and took the seat next to her.

'Where's Lloyd?' he whispered.

'I've no idea.'

A doctor from the forensic team was last to join them. He was here to tell them about the mind reading device and the Phoenix Project, and to answer any medical questions or concerns they might have. He sat with the GAILE officers.

He began by describing Doctor Palmerton's electroencephalic transmitter. Unsurprisingly the device relied on nanotechnology. Nanoparticles captured electrical signals – that is, *thoughts* – from one brain and transmitted them to another. It sounded simple enough, except that it had meant drilling holes into the top of Joanna's head, inserting electrodes, and then sending an electric current into her brain – all while she was conscious. Elise was glad that she remembered none of it.

'For reasons that we're unable to ascertain,' said the doctor, 'the device not only failed, but also caused extensive brain damage.'

Hitoshi grinned scornfully. 'I'm no expert, but I'm guessing it had something to do with their brains being fried.'

The doctor ignored the comment and continued. The device had killed the captives. Determined to try again, Palmerton took some of their brain cells and inserted them into genetically modified embryos. But even this stage was riddled with problems.

'Several weeks were wasted due to difficulties in modifying the embryos,' he said. 'There were at least two failed attempts.'

'You mean some embryos died?' said Elise, with a gasp.

'Yes.'

The story didn't get much better from there. Elise, Hitoshi and Manner were the lucky ones to make it to the final stage. Just a few days after their birth, Palmerton subjected the genetically modified infants to the device. They came through the ordeal unharmed, but the device failed yet again. Palmerton wanted some more time to improve the nanoparticles, but his employers told him to terminate the project and dispose of all the evidence, including the infants.

'Fortunately, Ms Weston couldn't go through with it and so you were spared,' said the doctor. 'Have you any questions?'

He meant medical questions.

'I have just one,' said Elise. 'Who was Palmerton's employer?'

The doctor looked to the GAILE officers seated next to him.

Kash stepped in. 'I believe Agent Lloyd explained to you before that this is classified information,' he said.

'Why?' said Hitoshi.

'It's classified,' repeated Kash.

'But Ms Weston has told you?' said Elise.

'If you must know, she hasn't. She never knew the identities of anyone who hired Palmerton. She just did whatever he told her to do as an assistant, no questions asked.'

Elise stole a glance at Hitoshi.

'That's not what Lloyd told us,' he muttered, which was what she was also thinking.

'What was that?' said Kash.

'I said I've got a question too,' said Hitoshi.

'Go ahead.'

'What can you tell us about our parents?'

'Your parents?' repeated the doctor.

'Our biological parents. You told us that some embryos were implanted into surrogates,' added Hitoshi, 'but where did the embryos come from?'

'Ms Weston told us only that they were stolen from a fertility clinic. I doubt that we could find your biological parents.'

Elise was appalled, but not particularly surprised to hear the doctor's answer; and as she could see from the look on his face, neither was Hitoshi.

The briefing was over within the hour and all official business was finished for the day.

'What have you decided?' asked Hitoshi, as soon as they'd exited the complex.

When Elise had arrived at the GAILE Coordination Center, she still hadn't made up her mind about Lloyd's proposition. But now everything was clear. GAILE either could not or would not answer her questions. And contrary to what they'd just told her, Lloyd reckoned that Weston knew exactly who Doctor Palmerton's employers were. So as far as Elise was concerned, there was only one option available to her.

* * * * * * * * *

Aaron called in sick first thing in the morning to get out of the briefing at the Harper Building. Then he went to a public phone booth a few blocks from his apartment and went through the telephone directory. He called several computer shops in the region, starting with some local ones in town, but none of them had what he was looking for. One specialist in Philadelphia told him that he could probably get hold of one within a day, but he couldn't guarantee that it would be working. Aaron arranged to pick it up on Saturday afternoon, though it meant taking a detour that he would rather have avoided.

After having lunch at a local deli Aaron headed to the infirmary at the GAILE Office Complex. Besides the fact that he needed to substantiate his alibi, the headaches really had been much worse for the past few days. Having examined him, the doctor suggested that work-related stress was probably aggravating the headaches. He recommended that Aaron take time to rest, perhaps even take a vacation after his present case. Aaron assured him he'd take some time off very soon.

He left the infirmary just after two o'clock and went to Searle Lab to pick up the results of the keyword activation test, all the while thinking about getting home to pack and then heading to the nightclub. He'd cooled off from his altercation with Hitoshi, and was presently in a more forgiving mood. As much as he still felt that Hitoshi's influence was behind Elise's reluctance, he trusted that ultimately she would make the right decision. And whatever he thought of the hacker, he could hardly penalise him for having a defective memory.

He entered the lab where Doctor Fischer, who had performed the tests on the two subjects the day before, was expecting him. He gave Aaron an electronic file containing the analysis data.

'The subjects' brains developed as Doctor Palmerton predicted,' said the doctor. 'The pineal gland is eight percent larger than in normal brains, highly active in each case as expected, but to no obvious detrimental effect. The donor neurons in both subjects have been preserved at similar levels. However, there was a significant difference in the results of the keyword activation tests.'

'In what way?'

'With a similar level of donor tissue present in the two subjects, we predicted that their recall would also be similar,' he replied. 'But Mr Katayama's structural data does not correspond with his functional data. His donor neurons – particularly those in the amygdala – responded to the keywords at more than twice the frequency that we observed in Miss Archer's case.'

Aaron switched on the file and reviewed the data for himself, keeping his thumb down on the scroll button almost the whole time as he skimmed through it. Images of the scans and frequency distribution graphs confirmed what Doctor Fischer was saying.

So much, he thought, *for Hitoshi's defective memory.*

* * * * * * * * *

Elise and Hitoshi entered The Chase via the back entrance. It was still the middle of the afternoon and the club wasn't due to open its door for several hours. Hitoshi knew the manager well, and he was allowed to come and go as he pleased. Elise was just glad she didn't have to conform to the club's dress code this time. They went backstage and to the dressing room.

She was startled when Lloyd arrived right behind them. He came through the door almost immediately after they'd sat down, and after closing it behind him, he just stood where he was. His arms were by his sides, but his fists were partly clenched. His lips were pressed together, stretching the skin on his face.

Elise thought that he was just anxious to hear their answer.

'I've made my decision,' she said. 'I want to join you.'

Lloyd glanced cursorily at her. His focus was on Hitoshi.

'Me too,' said Hitoshi now.

'You've changed your tune,' said Lloyd.

'After what you told us, I got thinking. David was murdered, no matter what. I figured I'd do the right thing for once.'

'How very noble.'

Lloyd still hadn't moved. Elise became concerned.

'Is something wrong?' she asked.

He was oblivious. 'Remind me Hitoshi, how much about the Systems Experiment did you say you remembered?'

'Nothing.'

'Really? Want to try again? And tell the truth this time.'

'I told you. I remember nothing.'

Lloyd sauntered up to Hitoshi, who was seated to Elise's left, and held up a datafile in front of Hitoshi's face.

'Know what this is?' he said. 'This is the results file of yesterday's keyword test.'

Hitoshi's brow twitched ever so slightly.

'And guess what? It shows that you remember a *lot* more than you say you do. The cells in the emotional centre of your brain responded to every significant keyword on GAILE's official list, as well as one or two supposedly random ones that E3 must have thrown in – including the word *system*. It's all on there. What have you got to say for yourself now?'

Hitoshi stared at the file, and said not a word.

Elise was perplexed. He'd obviously lied to them again but she failed to see what had made him do it.

'Why?' she asked. 'Why didn't you tell us what you knew last night?' But he didn't even have the decency to look at her, let alone answer. 'Say something!' she said hotly.

Lloyd put the datafile back in his pocket. 'It's all right, Elise,' he said. 'We can settle this right now – if you connect to him.'

Hitoshi started.

'Go on. Let's find out what he really remembers!'

Hitoshi shook his head at Elise. 'No,' he said, pleading with his eyes, 'you can't. No.'

Something in Lloyd snapped. He seized Hitoshi by the collar and practically lifted him off his stool.

'You don't get a say in this!' he hissed.

Before Elise could react, Lloyd shoved him with the force of dynamite. Hitoshi tumbled back over his stool and crashed against the dressing table, knocking bottles and spray cans onto the floor. He yowled and rolled off to the side, rubbing his lower back.

Elise had seen enough brawls and skirmishes in her time not to be intimidated. She got up and stood between the two men.

'Lloyd,' she said firmly.

He smoothed his tie calmly. 'I'm done.'

'Good.' She turned to Hitoshi as he was getting up. 'And as for you,' she said, with considerable restraint, 'I think you'd better let me connect to you now.'

Hitoshi stepped aside. 'Sorry Lise,' he said. 'I can't let you do that. I ... I have too many demons.'

'What's that supposed to mean?'

'Lise, I don't want you to –'

'Just explain yourself!'

'Okay! But just give me a second.'

Hitoshi sighed and undid his tie. Elise and Lloyd watched in puzzlement as he also unfastened the top two buttons of his shirt. He pulled his collar apart to reveal a red birthmark on the middle-left of his chest. It was almost perfectly round, and about a centimetre in diameter.

'I've had it since I was born,' he said. 'It's where I was shot.'

Elise only partly understood. She'd heard of birthmarks corresponding to fatal wounds in some reincarnation cases. *But ...*

'... I thought David was shot in the abdomen.'

'He was. And anyway, as you know it wasn't a fatal shot. He died in a lab.' Hitoshi paused. 'This is where Leon shot Adam.'

She jolted at the utterance of his name. 'Adam?' she repeated, with a shallow breath.

'I ... I have his memories. I know, I should've –'

'You're Adam?!' She thought of the last few days; the little things he'd said; the looks he'd given her. That gentle smile. *His* smile. How could he be *Adam*? 'What about David?' she said, her voice low and trembling.

'I have his memories too. ... It's a twin thing, I think.'

Elise was rendered speechless. Joanna's feelings for the two brothers could not have been further apart. Love and hate were absolutely separated in watertight compartments, and they could never be reconciled.

So far Lloyd hadn't voiced his reaction to Hitoshi's latest disclosure. He rubbed his left temple with his thumb.

'This explains a lot,' he said.

Hitoshi buttoned up his shirt. 'Neither David nor Adam's memories give me the full picture. I did the best with what I got from both of them.'

'I'm sure that's true,' said Lloyd. 'But if you remember anything about Adam at all, then you know that he was an assassin who answered directly to the Committee – codename *G-Force*.'

'He –'

'– And yet last night, you denied that the Committee even exists. You called my father a lunatic, when all along you knew he was telling the truth!'

'Until last night Agent Numbskull, I thought you were a GAILE officer! And as I told Elise yesterday, this isn't about E3. E3 doesn't exist. This is about some corrupt MWA insiders who already see the Project subjects as a liability. If it ever got back to them that I have Adam's memories – and that I could name the superiors who gave him his orders – they'd want me dead for sure.'

'You're a fast talker, Shaman! But I told you who I really am last night. You should have come clean then.'

'You also tried to freeze me out! How could I open up to you about Adam when you made it so obvious that you don't trust me as it is? I knew how you'd react!' He looked at Elise. 'See? I can see it in your eyes now. You hate me, because of him.' He turned to Lloyd. 'It's all black-and-white for you, isn't it? Adam's the traitor. David and Jo and Omar and Leon, they're the victims. But it's not so simple for me. I know something of *both* sides. For one thing, you're wrong about Adam. He wasn't an E3 assassin. I remember nothing like that. He didn't set out to kill anyone.'

'That's a moot point,' remarked Lloyd.

'He was just an Intelligence officer doing his job. He really thought David had fallen in with the wrong people, and that Omar was trouble. When his superiors told him that *Abdul Salaam* meant something sinister, he had no reason to doubt it. He never wanted to hurt his brother or his friends. But they left him with no choice.'

'You're defending him now?!' exclaimed Elise.

'No! I didn't mean –'

'It sounds like it!'

'I'm not defending him! … But I can't help what I remember.' He gazed ruefully at her. 'I was going to tell you, Lise – I swear it. … I just didn't know how. Forgive me?'

Elise looked back at him with a rigid frown. He'd driven her half-crazy with his mind games, but now that she knew the reason for his behaviour, could she really hold it against him? It was challenging enough living just with Joanna's memories. She couldn't imagine how Hitoshi had been managing with both twins' memories in his head. *But still …*

Her eyes grew moist in anger. 'I want to, Hitoshi. I *really* want to. It's just … I *believed* you. I believed you over Lloyd, because of your link to David. You knew this, and you took full advantage! And for some reason, I didn't even notice … oh-ho, of course!' she said with a grimace, as she suddenly worked it out. 'That's why you haven't let me anywhere near you! I thought you were being chivalrous! But *you* … you were just trying to stop me from finding out your dirty little secret!'

'Lise, I –'

'I don't want to hear it! You disgust me!'

Hitoshi exhaled as though he'd been winded. 'Lise!'

'Oh! – I can't be around you right now!'

He came towards her. She brushed past him and ran out.

* * * * * * * * *

Hitoshi moved to give chase. Aaron caught hold of his arm.

'Let her go.'

Hitoshi yanked his arm free. 'No! I've got to explain!'

Aaron stopped him again. 'You heard her! She doesn't want to talk to you. I'll go.'

Hitoshi's face was one of pure condemnation. 'You're just loving this, aren't you? You've wanted me out of the way ever since she joined the investigation – and we both know why. I've seen the way you look at her.'

The accusation took Aaron completely by surprise. He snorted, but didn't rise to the bait.

'Hey. You've brought this all on yourself. Now you wait here. We'll finish this when I get back.'

Guessing that Elise had probably gone outside for some air, Aaron headed to the back end of the hallway. To the right was the back entrance, but as he reached the turn, he happened to glance to the left, and halted. At the far end of the corridor he saw Elise sitting on some stairs next to the fire exit. She had tucked her feet beneath her on the bottom step, letting her black and green patterned skirt cover her boots and drape over the bottom two steps. Her hands were clasped loosely round her right knee. Her cheeks were a little flushed, and her eyes were cast down.

He walked slowly over to her. She didn't stir.

'Are you okay?' he asked.

She looked up and dabbed the corner of one eye with her little finger, as she tried to discreetly dry a tear.

'I feel a bit stupid, that's all,' she said.

He wanted to put a sympathetic hand on her shoulder, but figured she'd probably scream at him if he did.

'You must think that I'm overreacting,' she said just then. 'I mean, I hardly even know the guy.'

Aaron smiled softly. 'No, not at all,' he said. 'You just had high expectations. I can understand that. I did too.'

'You did?'

He sat down at the foot of the stairs. 'Of course. I heard so much about David when I was growing up. My Dad told me that he was a courageous and honourable man who gave his life for the truth. I came to really admire him – all of them in fact – David, Joanna, and Leon. So yeah, though I knew perfectly well that I wasn't meeting the real David, I still expected a lot from the man who had his memories. Unfortunately, Hitoshi was a bit of a letdown.'

Elise was looking at him attentively. *Not you though*, he felt like telling her. *You're amazing.*

He suddenly realised he was staring, and checked himself. 'But it must have been worse for you,' he said, rubbing the back of his neck, 'since you're more … personally involved.'

'That's no excuse,' she said emphatically. 'If anything, my personal knowledge of being a Project subject should have better prepared me – not to mention my training. But I failed to distinguish between David and Hitoshi. I didn't handle myself professionally. That's why you saw through him, and I didn't.'

'Give yourself a break. You're only human. And, much as I hate to say it, so is Hitoshi. His conflicting memories have obviously been clouding his judgment. At least it's all out in the open now.'

Elise turned her head to the side. 'You surprise me, Lloyd. I don't think I could be so forgiving if someone talked about my father like that … if I had a father.'

'It's not really about forgiveness,' he replied candidly. 'I'm just trying to be objective.'

In the dressing room Aaron and Elise found Hitoshi back on his stool, smoking a cigarette.

'Elise,' he said, standing up, 'I'm really –'

'No need for that,' she interjected. 'I understand. I still think you should have been upfront about this, but … I understand.'

'Thanks, Lise.'

'Don't thank me. Lloyd was the one who convinced me to give you another chance.'

Hitoshi stiffened up, unable to contain his discomfort.

Aaron smiled inwardly.

A strong crease suddenly appeared in Elise's brow. 'But if you *ever* lie to me again –'

'I know. I won't let you down.' Hitoshi turned uneasily to Aaron now, and gave him a nod in grudging gratitude. 'So … does this mean I can come with you?'

'Not necessarily. You need to explain a couple of things first.'

Hitoshi expelled the smoke in his lungs through his nostrils.

Aaron sat down and gave Hitoshi his interrogator's stare. 'After everything you said last night, I don't even understand why you want to join us. First you say my father was a madman. Then I find out you remembered the Systems Experiment all along.'

The hacker took a deep drag. 'I thought Omar was dangerous.'

'So you keep saying. But –'

'– Any man who says he can solve all of the world's problems is dangerous, whether he calls himself a prophet or a philosopher. The trouble with Omar was that he connected his theorem to his religious beliefs. He thought it was divinely inspired ... perfect. And he had David, Jo and Leon on his side. But Adam's superiors told him that the Experiment results were actually inconclusive.'

Aaron bristled with indignation. 'That's not –!'

'Let me finish,' said Hitoshi unabatedly. 'They said the theorem wasn't as perfect as Omar thought, but that didn't make it any less dangerous. Intelligence feared that some politico-religious groups in the Middle East could use the results to justify their resistance against democracy in that part of the world. They might even have waged a holy war against the MWA, because all of its member nations are democratic – that is, irreligious.'

'Did it *never* occur to you that the MWA was really just trying to suppress the findings of the Systems Experiment to protect their vested interests,' said Aaron, 'and that they murdered innocent people in the process?'

'I genuinely thought they were trying to prevent a world war, and the ends justified the means. When GAILE told Elise that Adam worked for some third party, I knew that something stank, but I didn't dare say anything to anyone. I couldn't, not without explaining where I was getting my information from. And I still believed the Systems Experiment was a failure, and that E3 didn't exist.' He paused to take a drag. 'But after last night, I realised that if everything you said was true – if there really is an E3, and they only suppressed the data to protect themselves – then they should pay for what they've done. And like Elise said to me earlier, we'll only know the truth if we meet Nathalie Weston, and if we see the data on that disc. That's why I want to come with you.'

'And it's not because you'll be a sitting duck if you stay back?'

'If it was just about that I'd go into hiding on my own – in fact, I'd be better off doing that to avoid being associated with you. But I want to know whose truth is the real truth – Adam's, or David's.' He flattened the stub on an ashtray. 'Besides, you need me.'

Aaron squinted at him. 'Really? What makes you say that?'

'Manner. He asked specifically for *David*, remember? And I do have the technical know-how.'

'We can manage without you, and in case we can't, I'll take the disc to my father's old friend. He'll have the means to retrieve the data and make it public.'

'Don't you already have your own DVD-ROM drive?'

'I can't find one – not locally.'

'Only I have a friend who's into vintage computers. His house is a techie museum. He's got a working laptop with a DVD-ROM drive on it – which is rare. As he owes me money, I can get him to sell it to me cheap and we'll call it quits … if you're interested.'

Aaron was admittedly intrigued. 'You really have been thinking about this, haven't you?'

'Ideally it's better to have a complete machine rather than just a drive,' Hitoshi went on, 'but you still need to transfer the data onto a modern computer, because the old one won't connect to the net. Then you need a custom cable to hook up the machines, because they're probably not wirelessly compatible, and that's before you get them to interface.' He took a new packet of cigarettes and a silver lighter from his breast pocket. 'It takes time to set up. You really need someone who knows what they're doing.'

Aaron looked to Elise for her opinion. She'd hardly spoken at all in the last few minutes. Now she raised her brow to express her scepticism, but she also shrugged apathetically, to tell him it was his call. Of course he scarcely trusted Hitoshi himself, but in good conscience he couldn't leave the man behind – not if he really wanted to join them; not if he genuinely wanted to know the truth.

'Fine. Go and get the machine,' he said, in a measured tone. 'We leave early tomorrow.'

Hitoshi lit up with a contented grin.

* * * * * * * * *

Gregory was sitting up in bed and reading when the phone rang. The call was coming through on his special line. He'd been waiting for it all evening.

He picked up the handset lying on his pillow.

'Report.'

Kash reported that their traitor had left his apartment earlier that evening without his observer strap. He had gone to a nightclub in Glensville, where he'd met with the Project subjects.

Gregory knew what this meant, but they were ready for it.

'Proceed as planned.'

CHAPTER TWENTY-EIGHT
Passage

The image of a beaming Stella appeared on the laptop screen.

'Hello Elise! To what do I owe the pleasure?' she said chirpily.

'Happy anniversary!' said Elise.

'Thank you! Look at what Mike bought me!' She pointed to the gold earrings she was wearing. 'Just the ones I wanted! Thanks for telling him about them,' she added, with a wink.

'You're welcome. Is he about?'

'Oh, you just missed him.'

'Where is he?'

Mike was supposed to have prearranged his time off to coincide with his anniversary. Elise had assumed he would be home.

'He's gone to get a few groceries. He's cooking tonight.'

Elise looked at her in feigned dismay. 'You're letting him cook?'

'I know, but he insisted. I've pre-booked the ambulance.'

They laughed.

'But never mind him!' said Stella. What's happening with you? How are things in Hadescape?'

'Erm ... okay.'

'... And? What have GAILE told you about your past life? Any news on that serial killer?'

Elise smiled apologetically. 'I can't really talk about the case.'

'Oh, right! I understand. Say no more. ... Where are you right now?' asked Stella, trying to look behind Elise through her screen.

Elise lifted the laptop and turned it slowly 180 degrees in order to give Stella a proper look.

'I'm in my apartment in Verity Square. This is the kitchen.'

'Ooh, very posh! *And* tidy! Puts your house to shame – but then, so would the average student's flat!'

'Ha-ha, very funny!' said Elise with a smile.

It was nice to talk to a normal person for a change.

Stella looked at her watch. 'What time is it over there?'

Elise knew it was 9:30 a.m. British time.

'About half past four.'

'Why aren't you asleep?'

'Still a bit jet-lagged, I guess.'

'You can't be jet-lagged. Technically you only gained an hour.'

'You forgot the three hours I spent on the plane.'

'That's neither here nor there. You've been there long enough to get over it!' Then Stella frowned. 'Is everything all right, Elise?'

'Of course! Why wouldn't it be?' she said cheerfully.

But her oldest friend knew her too well to be fooled.

'Are you sure?'

'I'm fine!' insisted Elise, a little too keenly.

Stella looked at her doubtfully. 'Uh-huh.'

Elise thought she'd better get off the computer before Stella gave her the third degree.

'Anyway, I'd better get some sleep now,' she said hastily.

'Hang on a minute! When are you coming home?'

'… I don't know. We've had some unexpected developments.'

'Well, call again when you can, okay?'

'I – I'll try,' said Elise, suddenly feeling emotional, but she hid it. 'Take care – and give my love to Michael.'

After switching off the laptop Elise packed a few things into an overnight bag: Her notepad, hairbrush, toothbrush, compact, and a fresh change of clothes. She'd just changed into jeans, flat shoes and a lavender cotton top. She was leaving her other clothes behind, and also her mobile phone, at Lloyd's request. She left it on the kitchen top along with her ES tag. Lloyd had safely removed her and Hitoshi's tags at the nightclub, but without deactivating them. He'd told them to leave the tags in their apartments in the morning to buy them some time.

Lloyd's itinerary was straightforward. First they were going to meet Nathalie Weston in a remote location, and then they would return to Hadescape and rest for the night before meeting Manner at René Raison Dam. Elise thought that returning to the city once they'd left was a huge risk, but Lloyd believed that they would actually be quite safe, since GAILE wouldn't logically expect them to have come back.

An hour later Elise slipped into her everyday jacket. She took the gun which Lloyd had given to her at the nightclub and put it in her jacket pocket. Though she'd had some firearms training back in England, she wasn't comfortable with the thing. The safety was on, and she wanted it to stay that way.

Elise wrapped a russet scarf round her neck and went outside. It was still dark, and bitterly cold. Parked across the road was a white coupé convertible car. Hitoshi was inside. He'd borrowed the car from one of his many friends rather than risk bringing his own. He turned the engine and the headlights came on. He leaned over and lifted the latch as she approached. She got in.

The two greeted each other awkwardly.

He turned to his dashboard and pressed the self-drive button, followed by another button to input a preset destination. The car automatically pulled onto the road.

Then he turned to her. 'Lise, you and me – are we okay?'

She didn't quite look him in the eye. 'Yes. Mm-hmm.'

'I know I hurt you last night, and we didn't really have the chance to clear the air.'

Elise winced. 'Look, I was ... I was a little shocked, that's all. But I shouldn't have overreacted like that. I mean, it's like you've said before – I'm not Joanna, and you're not David.'

'I'm not Adam either,' he added solemnly.

'... I know. It's not your fault that you have his memories. I can't hold that against you.'

'No you can't. But I don't blame you for being mad at me.'
His piercing eyes sought confirmation that all was forgiven.
'Well, I'm over it,' she said. 'Just … no more surprises, okay?'
He gave her a small smile in reply.

* * * * * * * *

Aaron got out of bed just before five and put on a white shirt and
dark trousers. He picked up his wristwatch instead of his observer
strap. He wasn't bothering with luggage. All the things he needed
were in his reefer jacket: cash, handgun, spare bullets, painkillers
and a new unused cellphone that Intelligence didn't know he had.
He had a few phone numbers saved on it strictly for emergency
use. He also took a pair of handcuffs and a stun gun. He wanted to
avoid seriously injuring Manner in the event of a struggle.

He left the apartment and looked down the block. A white two-
door coupé convertible came round the corner. Hitoshi got out and
slid the driver's seat forward. He climbed into the back, letting
Aaron take the driver's seat.

They headed out towards Rock Moor and began following the
signs for Peninsula Drive, the highway out of Hadescape. Hitoshi
asked where they were going, and Aaron gave the brief reply that
they were going to a town in Pennsylvania.

No one felt like talking after that. After around forty minutes
they passed Hadescape Airport and the city exit. Peninsula Drive
was the only highway on the narrow land strip connecting
Hadescape to New Jersey State. It ended at an intersection onto
Joline Avenue, soon becoming Route 36, in the city of Long Branch.
They continued west and took a looping ramp onto Route 18.

After another few miles they came to the turnpike at the Garden
State Parkway. Everyone in the car became tense as they queued
behind three other vehicles. Aaron paid the toll and they passed
through without incident. They made it safely through the town
areas and came onto the open highway as dawn approached. The
sky turned gradually from black to chalky grey, but it didn't

improve much beyond that. The road, lined sporadically with spindly trees, rolled on ceaselessly.

After another hour they reached the US 22, and then headed to Philipsburg. They remained on the city outskirts, but they moved along relatively slowly with the Saturday morning traffic. They soon reached the Easton-Philipsburg Toll Bridge and paid another toll before crossing the bridge over Delaware River, marking the boundary between New Jersey and Pennsylvania.

As they entered rural areas, the landscape changed markedly. The highway passed along increasingly hilly terrain covered in evergreens. For the longest part of the trip they traversed 200 miles along the Interstate 80. Sloping banks covered in thick green, brown and red vegetation spilled off the road. The highway was fairly worn and bumpy, as it had to accommodate large volumes of traffic, especially heavy goods vehicles. In the last ten miles of the journey, they had to slow again to a limit of 45 miles per hour, as the highway had become precariously narrow, winding through the steep hills with almost no guardrails.

They got off the I-80 and followed the signs to Stockwell, a small town 15 miles east of Du Bois. Aaron headed along a dusty county route until he got to a truck stop. He finally stopped the car on a muddy patch of ground outside a grey building with corrugated walls and a flat roof. A sign above the front door simply read *Diner*. To the right of the diner was a fuelling station.

They went inside. Of the eight booths, only two were occupied. A middle-aged man and a young couple were the only customers.

The smell of fried food made Aaron's empty stomach growl. He glanced at his watch. It was just after 11 o'clock.

'I told Nathalie we'd be here by half eleven,' he said.

'Then we're early,' said Hitoshi. 'Lunch is on you, yeah?'

Aaron ordered some food, and then went outside and had the car refilled whilst they waited for the food to arrive.

They were finishing up, and Aaron had just counted out the cash he needed to pay the bill, when a woman came through the door, wearing a powder-blue blouse, caramel pencil skirt and heels. Her hair was greying ash-blonde and cut in a layered bob.

The woman saw Aaron and came over to them. She sat down next to Elise inside the enclosure of the booth, directly opposite Aaron, who sat at Hitoshi's left.

'Elise, Hitoshi,' said Aaron, 'meet Nathalie Weston.'

Elise managed a civil nod. Hitoshi wasn't inclined even for that.

Nathalie stared at Hitoshi for several seconds. Her mouth opened and she inhaled as if about to speak, but then she seemed to change her mind. She averted her gaze and turned to Aaron.

'I didn't think you'd bring them with you,' she said quietly.

'I'm sorry,' said Hitoshi. 'Are we making you uncomfortable?'

'It's not that.' She took a piece of paper and put it on the table in front of Hitoshi. 'It's just that you may need to be in Hadescape to act on the information I have for you. I hear you've inherited David Cohen's computer skills?'

'What of it?'

She moved her head as a gesture that he should read the note. He tentatively picked it up and looked at it.

'What does it say?' asked Elise.

'It's information about a computer network,' Hitoshi replied slowly. 'At Creux Island.'

'The power plant?' said Aaron.

'Not the plant,' replied Nathalie. 'This network is connected to the Meteorology Research Center. It's hidden inside the island's hollow section. A friend who works there gave me this information and said you'd know what to do with it.'

Hitoshi's eyes narrowed. 'What do you expect me to find?'

Nathalie half cupped a hand over her mouth. 'The source of their unrivalled power,' she muttered. 'The reason why no one has given them an effective challenge for decades.'

Now she had Aaron's attention. It was true that no one had challenged E3 for a long time, and that was down to the overwhelming success of the MWA. There was no *material* reason to challenge the status quo – at least, not for anyone living in a member state of the MWA. Under the circumstances it was easy to forget that they'd merely changed tack, and hadn't really given up their power. But Aaron couldn't forget. Nor could he forgive them for what they'd done to his father and his friends. But never had Aaron thought that he could do anything beyond merely exposing them. So what was Nathalie offering him?

'What do you know?' he asked.

'Go there and you'll find out.'

Hitoshi glanced sideways at Nathalie. 'I hacked Creux Island as a kid,' he said. 'Lots of newbie hackers do it to test their skills. I've never heard anything about an extra network.'

She snorted. 'Do you think they'd make it easy for *anyone* to just stumble across it, let alone some snot-nosed kid? It's very well hidden and difficult even to detect. Most of the time it's not even online, and when it is, it's only for a short time.'

'Then how do I even get in?'

'You should start with the island's weather analysis server. It sends the network a one-way communication every night. You probably won't have the time to access the network – but you might be able to pick up the communication itself.'

'The weather analysis server? There's nothing particularly interesting there – unless you like looking at holograms of clouds. Is this communication or whatever encrypted?'

'That would be too obvious. Encryption is like a red rag and they know it. They'd never use it.' Nathalie lowered her head but kept her eyes on Hitoshi. 'They prefer to hide – in plain sight.'

'You keep saying *them*,' said Elise. 'Who are we talking about? Who do you work for?'

Nathalie frowned. 'You know who. And that's *did*, young lady, not *do*. Past tense.'

'... E3?'

'Keep your voice down!'

'E3, yes or no?'

'For goodness sake, yes! Why is she asking me this?' she said to Aaron. 'Didn't you tell them?'

'Of course I did, but they wanted to hear it from you, since they don't remember much.'

'Oh, wonderful!' she said despairingly.

Elise looked Hitoshi's way, but he didn't seem to notice.

'Just tell me what I'm meant to be looking for,' he said.

'I've told you everything I can already.'

'That's fine. We understand,' said Aaron. 'Hitoshi, do you think you can find this network?'

Hitoshi stared at Nathalie. '… Sure.'

'Good,' she said. 'Now, we never had this conversation. Got it? If anyone asks, you say *nothing*.'

She got up.

'Not so fast,' said Hitoshi, also rising. 'We haven't finished yet.'

He'd been seated on the external part of the enclosure, so he only needed to move over to her side to block her in.

Nathalie sighed. 'What else is there to talk about?' she said.

'Our mothers.'

She paused.

'This is neither the time nor the place.'

'We won't get another chance.' Hitoshi tapped the table with a finger a few times, to indicate she ought to sit back down. 'So you'd better start talking.'

Having no choice, she resumed her seat, as did he.

'They don't want to be found,' she said matter-of-factly.

'I don't mean the surrogates. Who are our biological mothers?'

'I don't know.'

'Then how did my surrogate know I was Japanese? She visited a confessional just after I was born and gave the priest my full name, right before she dumped me there.'

'Oh, I see.' Nathalie took a slow breath. 'There's a simple explanation for that. The names of your biological mothers were printed on the Petri dishes containing the embryos from the fertility clinic. That's how your surrogate mother knew your ethnicity. She named you – that is to say, I assume she named you after your biological mother.'

'So you *do* know who our real mothers are?' said Elise.

'No. We had just their names – nothing else.'

'Well then, give them to us,' said Hitoshi.

'It was so long ago. I don't remember them now.'

'Where was the fertility clinic, then?' he said.

'I don't know. I wasn't responsible for obtaining the embryos. Now if that's all, I'd really like to leave.' She got up again. 'For what it's worth,' she said, 'I'm sorry – and the mothers are too.'

She stepped sideways to leave the booth. Hitoshi obstructed her for a second time.

'Wait.' He cocked his head to the side and looked at her intently. 'You're not ... one of the surrogates, are you?'

She looked him long in the face.

'Dear me, no,' she said flatly.

With that she moved past him and walked out.

Hitoshi looked to Aaron.

'She told me the same thing when I asked her,' said Aaron, anticipating his question.

'Yeah? Well I don't believe her,' said Hitoshi.

He strode out after her.

'Hitoshi!' said Aaron.

He and Elise quickly followed, leaving the cash on the table.

Their car was parked several yards to the right, facing the road. Nathalie hurried towards a small red sports car parked a few spaces to the left and against traffic, near the fuel pumps. Hitoshi was a few yards behind her.

Just as the pair went after them, Aaron suddenly saw what looked like a single black metallic object appear on the road to their right, the direction from which they had come. He soon realised that in fact two cars were fast on the approach; both black sedans with dark tinted windows.

Aaron looked at Nathalie. She was distracted with getting her keys out of her purse and hadn't noticed anything.

'Elise! Hitoshi!' he said, and pointed up the road.

They both stopped. Nathalie looked up. They saw all the cars.

'They've found us!' said Hitoshi.

Aaron pointed the remote fob at their coupé to unlock it.

'Go, go, go!' he shouted, and began running.

Hitoshi sprinted ahead of them, nimble as a thief, and reached the car first. He flung open the passenger door and jumped into the back. Elise reached the car next and got into the passenger seat. Aaron got in right after her and started up.

The vehicles were almost upon them.

Nathalie too was in her car now. She turned round and took off to the right. One of the cars skidded halfway to a halt, then turned 180 degrees and went in pursuit.

Aaron turned left onto the road. The other car charged from the rear and attempted to overtake and block them, or perhaps knock them off the road. Aaron scraped his car against it and managed to push in front. The hit slowed the sedan long enough for Aaron to get the coupé up to speed.

Hitoshi was watching the black cars through the back window.

'Guys, we've got trouble!' he said.

Aaron glanced in the rearview mirror. The sedan was perhaps fifteen metres behind them. The agent in the passenger seat rolled down his window, and stuck his head and arm out. He had a gun in his hand. It was Kash.

'Down!' yelled Aaron.

Hitoshi and Elise ducked. Aaron slid down in his seat and swerved the car side to side. Just then they heard a report, and a bullet ricocheted off the roof. Elise gave a short scream.

Although hollow point bullets were standard issue in GAILE, Aaron worried that Kash might be using hardball ammo. He hit the accelerator harder to try and put more distance between them. The sedan also increased its speed.

'Faster!' said Elise.

'I'm going as fast as I can! Just stay down!'

Two more bullets hit the coupé in the next minute. Neither of them appeared to penetrate the bodywork, though one might have taken out a tail light.

They soon approached the last intersection on the town's edge. Straight on from there was a county route that would eventually rejoin the interstate highway. Going left or right would take them back into other areas of the town.

'Turn! Turn! We won't lose them on a straight road!' said Elise, peeping just above the dashboard to see what lay ahead of them.

Aaron disregarded her advice. He ran a red light and went straight ahead. Unfortunately the sedan came right after them, encountering no trouble, as both lanes happened to be clear.

It was time for another tactic. Aaron suddenly let go of the accelerator. The car slowed rapidly.

'What the hell are you doing?!' shouted Hitoshi.

Aaron hit the cruise control button on the dash.

'Elise, take the wheel.'

'Huh?!'

'Take the wheel!'

He had to let go of the steering wheel before she finally took it. Aaron rolled down his window and took out his handgun. The sedan was soon within five metres behind them and it too slowed down. Aaron saw the front left tyre and tried to take aim. He actually had a better view of the driver, but it was futile to shoot at a bulletproof windscreen.

Aaron let off a round. He missed.

Being on the driver's side, he couldn't quite see Kash. At this distance Kash could easily succeed in hitting them, especially since he wasn't confining himself to shooting the tyres of their car.

Aaron prayed for a sure aim.

He suddenly heard Hitoshi shouting at Elise in the car. 'He's going to shoot!'

In response Elise veered sharply to the left. Aaron's finger was on the trigger and the sudden movement of the car caused him to accidentally fire.

'Whoa!'

Kash also fired, and missed.

'Ha!' exclaimed Hitoshi.

Aaron hastily readjusted himself and took aim for a third time.

'Again!' hollered Hitoshi.

In the microsecond between Hitoshi's warning and Elise's reaction, Aaron took another shot.

Elise swung the car again.

Behind them, they heard a loud pop. The sedan lurched, almost spinning right round, and crashed into the right-hand barrier.

Aaron pulled himself back into the car. The three cheered and whooped jubilantly. They pulled away easily now, and the sedan soon disappeared on the horizon.

They continued west on the county route for a few miles and at the first opportunity Aaron took a state route going back east. But he wasn't returning to Hadescape just yet.

'I wonder how they found us?' said Elise.

'They must have been following Nathalie,' said Hitoshi.

Aaron however was thinking differently. 'If they were behind her they would have ambushed us in the diner right away, not arrived ten minutes later. Anyway, Kash was in one of the cars.'

'So?' said Hitoshi.

'He should have been in Hadescape today, but he was less than an hour behind us. Intelligence shouldn't have realised we were missing for at least an hour or two. Somehow Kash knew right away that we were gone.'

'But how?' said Elise. 'Unless they already know about you? But if they do, why would they let us leave town?'

'Because they want us to lead them to the disc,' said Aaron.

'I don't think so,' said Hitoshi, staring at the back of Aaron's head. 'If they just wanted to tail us, they wouldn't have shown themselves just now.'

Aaron frowned. 'True. How did they find us, then?'

'Your mobile?' suggested Elise.

'It's a brand new phone. They don't know about it.'

Hitoshi was still staring at Aaron, and now he smiled shrewdly. He sat forward and leaned one arm against Elise's headrest.

'I've got it,' he said. 'It's your cranial chip. It must also double as a tracking device.'

'No way,' said Aaron.

'It's the only explanation.'

'Is there any way to disable it?' asked Elise.

'I'm not sure,' said Aaron.

But even as he said so, he had an idea.

CHAPTER TWENTY-NINE
Gambit

The sedan collided with the barrier and came to a rest. Kash and the driver were dazed for a minute. As he recovered Kash saw the fugitives getting away, but he wasn't overly concerned for the time being. Fortunately neither he nor his colleague was hurt.

The front end of the car faced the road at an angle, so Kash was able to open the door on his side. The two agents got out and assessed the damage. Thanks to its sturdy bumper the rear had just a minor dent on it. A tyre change was all they needed to get the vehicle back on the road.

The driver opened the boot and took out a car jack and a toolbox. Kash helped him lift the heavy spare tyre, and then waited by the side of the car as the driver slid the jack beneath it.

Kash checked a special channel on his observer strap, which was set to receive signals from Lloyd's cranial implant. To his surprise, it showed that their defector was just a few miles away – and that he wasn't moving.

* * * * * * * * *

After another four or five miles Lloyd stopped the coupé on the hard shoulder and asked Elise and Hitoshi to get out. He led them off the side of the road and behind a tree, where no one could see them, and then produced a black chunky rectangular device from his coat pocket. It was when she saw the two metal prongs at its top end that Elise realised what he was carrying.

'Is that a stun gun?' she asked nervously, as she also guessed what he might be planning to do.

'Yes.'

'You're not thinking …?'

'I want you to give me a shock – and hold on long enough to knock me out.'

She looked at him aghast. 'Please tell me you're joking!'

'I can't do it myself. The only other way to get rid of the chip would be to surgically remove it – and it's very small.'

He handed her the stun gun. It had a small innocuous button on the side, and that was all.

'Ever use one of these before?' he asked.

'… I think I can work it out. Where's the chip? It's not implanted in your brain, is it?'

'It's behind my ear. But you won't need to put the stunner to my head! Just hit me in the shoulder. The excess electricity should short the chip – as long as you hold the button for long enough.'

He stood with his back against the tree and closed his eyes.

She hesitated. 'Are – are you ready?'

'Just hit me. I want this over and done with.'

Feeling more than a little apprehensive, she pressed the button to test it first. A bright blue arc appeared and danced between the two prongs, and the device made a rhythmic crackling sound like a Geiger counter. She released the button and the arc vanished.

'You know Lise, if you're not up to it I'm happy to give it a shot,' said Hitoshi, with an impish grin.

'Shut up, Hitoshi,' said Lloyd. 'Go for it, Elise.'

'Okay … here goes.'

She bit her lip and pressed the button, then lunged like a fencer and jabbed him in the right shoulder.

Lloyd flinched. 'Yeow!'

She gasped and dropped the device. 'Sorry, sorry, sorry!'

'I don't see your aura,' said Hitoshi, looking at the space around Aaron's head. 'The shield's intact.'

'You shouldn't have let go!' said Lloyd, rubbing his shoulder.

'I'll try again,' said Elise.

She picked up the stun gun and Lloyd resumed his position against the tree. Elise steeled herself and stabbed him again.

Lloyd squawked and doubled up. She held out for about two seconds before the stun gun ended up on the ground again.

He was still standing – just. He stumbled around and howled.

'Oh, God!' she said. 'I'm so sorry!'

'Still hasn't worked,' remarked Hitoshi unhelpfully.

'Argh! Elise!' said Lloyd. 'You've got to hold on!'

She looked at the poor man apologetically. 'I know! I just panicked! Just give me one more go – I'll get it right this time, I promise. I – I'm getting used to it now!'

'*You're* getting used to it?!'

Hitoshi laughed.

Lloyd grimaced and stood against the tree once more.

'Five seconds!'

She gulped. 'Okay! Hitoshi, I want you to count for me!'

Then she went all out. Lloyd's face contorted and he gave out a horrible, choked scream as he became completely paralysed. She held on for dear life.

Hitoshi counted loudly. He got to four before Lloyd fainted.

* * * * * * * *

Whilst the driver was changing the wheel, Kash kept a close eye on his observer strap. The defector's coordinates remained the same, but Kash knew that could change at any moment.

The car was ready to go within ten minutes. Kash got back into the car and waited for the driver to put the jack in the boot. He put his seatbelt on and looked at the observer strap again. He was just in time to see the signal from the implant suddenly disappear.

* * * * * * * *

As Aaron gained consciousness, he heard a mumbling voice far off in the distance. A warm hand lightly tapped his face.

'Lloyd? Are you okay?' said the same fluty voice, sounding clearer to him now.

He opened his eyes. He was lying on the ground under the tree, and Elise was kneeling over him, looking at him anxiously.

'How do you feel?' asked Hitoshi, who stood next to her.

'Like I've been electrocuted. How long was I out?'

'About a minute,' said Elise.

She helped him up and offered him some bottled water that she'd fetched from the car. He took a swig.

'Did it work?'

She nodded.

'Then let's do something about the car. Hitoshi, you're driving.'

* * * * * * * *

Kash knelt down on the shoulder of the highway. He'd just reached the defector's last known coordinates. Tyre tracks in the dirt indicated that a car had recently been and gone.

The white coupé convertible in which they'd last seen the fugitives was nowhere to be found. Kash looked down the highway in the only direction that they could have gone. He assumed they would get rid of the car sooner or later. Up ahead were signs for an upcoming intersection. He had no idea which route they had taken from there.

They'd lost the fugitives, for now.

* * * * * * * *

'You got engine trouble?'

The man was quite short, probably in his late sixties, with a chequered shirt and old boots. He'd pulled over in front of the coupé as soon as he'd seen Elise waving.

'I don't know what's happened,' she said. 'And my phone's dead. Can you help?'

'I'll certainly try.'

He had a kind, grandfatherly face. Elise smiled at him, guilty inside about what she was doing.

'Pop the hood for me.'

She got back into the car briefly and released the bonnet latch from the inside. Had he been able to see the back of the car, he might have spotted the abrasions on the bodywork and the smashed rear light. Lloyd had deliberately positioned the coupé to face oncoming traffic, in order to hide the damage.

'How long have you been out here?' asked the man.

'Oh, about twenty-five minutes,' she said.

'Doesn't surprise me. Hardly anyone comes down this route.'

She knew that already, for Lloyd had chosen this particular road for the very reason. But they'd actually been waiting for nearly an hour and a half. Elise had deliberately ignored the first couple of cars that had come by, as they'd wanted to catch a lone driver. She'd also ignored a heavy goods lorry which would have been too big and slow for their purposes.

'So what's wrong with it?'

The man pouted in puzzlement. 'Nothing that I can see. Could be an electrical fault.'

He was so busy checking the engine that he didn't notice Hitoshi and Lloyd as they stepped out from behind a tree.

'The car's fine,' said Hitoshi.

The man stood upright hastily, and almost bumped into him.

'What in the world ...?'

He saw the handgun in Lloyd's hand and froze where he was.

'Hands up sir,' said Lloyd.

Elise and Hitoshi also drew their weapons.

The man raised his hands.

'We need to borrow your minivan,' said Lloyd. 'Please hand over your keys.'

The man reluctantly did so.

Lloyd passed the keys to Hitoshi.

'Get everything from the car.'

Hitoshi and Elise quickly retrieved their belongings from the coupé. Hitoshi fetched the two carry cases containing the computer equipment and Elise picked up a bag containing the other bits and pieces. Hitoshi unlocked the sliding door on the passenger side of the old man's dark blue minivan. It had three rows of double seats. He climbed in, opened out the third set at the back and put the equipment inside. Then he climbed back out and closed the door.

'You have our car,' said Lloyd to the old man.

'And let me have your cellphone,' added Hitoshi. 'Don't want you making any phone calls.'

The old man gave him a black look, and tossed the phone over. Hitoshi threw it to the ground and stamped on it a couple of times to smash it. He still had the keys to the coupé, and so he took them from his pocket. But instead of giving them to the man, he pitched them over the grassy knoll behind the barrier, where they disappeared into the yellowing shrubbery.

'You rotten scoundrels!' said the man.

'We can't have you following us either,' said Lloyd. He directed the man into the back of the coupé. 'Wait there until we're gone.'

The man nodded from inside the car.

'Sorry,' mouthed Elise sheepishly.

Lloyd closed the door and kept the gun pointed at him. Hitoshi went to the minivan and clambered into the back, and Elise got into the passenger side at the front. Lloyd walked backwards, gun still pointed at the coupé, all the while ensuring the man stayed inside the car, until he reached the minivan on the driver's side. Then he quickly got into the driver's seat and started the engine.

Watching from the rear window as they pulled out onto the motorway, Elise saw the man getting back out of the coupé.

'I feel awful,' she said.

'Don't worry,' said Lloyd. 'He'll find the keys.'

'Who cares about him?' said Hitoshi. 'My friend's going to kill me when he finds out we just gave away his car.'

CHAPTER THIRTY
Three Minutes to Midnight

The three arrived back in Hadescape just before sundown. The roads were busy, as they'd caught the tail end of the rush-hour traffic. An amber fog had descended over the darkening valley and turned the city into a smouldering cauldron. Saffron light saturated the whole sky right down to the ground. At a distance all structures and objects were burned-out silhouettes. Black shadow puppets walked the streets.

Though Hitoshi could theoretically get onto Creux Island's network from anywhere in the world, he'd just told Aaron that this would take too long. They were better off getting direct wireless access to the island's own local area network, or LAN. The snag was that Creux Island was around three hundred metres off the shore. To get within the LAN's wi-fi range, Hitoshi would have to boost the reception of his tablet computer with a makeshift reflector, as he doubted that the integrated antenna in his laptop would be sufficient. Luckily he was able to get just what he needed from any twenty-four hour superstore. To avoid passing through the city centre, they turned off the main road shortly before Dean Bridge and headed northeast into Rock Moor. Hitoshi directed Aaron to a store a few blocks away. Aaron parked on the main street outside the store instead of the parking lot.

'Don't use a credit card,' he warned, as Hitoshi got out.

'Sure,' replied Hitoshi. 'I'm a bit short on cash though. Could you lend me fifty bucks?'

Aaron gave him a few notes.

Hitoshi got out with the cash and put it in his trouser pocket. He turned up the collar of his beige raincoat and went alone into the grocery store. A short while later he emerged with a small plastic bag in one hand and a packet of cigarettes in the other. He put the cigarettes in his coat pocket, and then came and got in.

Aaron heard something heavy clunking in the bag.

'What did you get?' he asked.

Hitoshi partly pulled out a parabolic vegetable strainer from the bag with a cryptic smile.

'Essentials.'

'Does that include the cigarettes?'

The hacker looked at him unashamedly. 'I was all out.'

At twilight they reached a popular public campsite at the west side of Soren Forest. As it was the weekend there were some caravans and cars parked in an open area at the wayside, but the campers themselves were nowhere to be seen. Aaron assumed they'd gone further into the forest to set up camp. He parked the minivan, switched on the interior lights and looked behind him.

Presently Hitoshi was seated right behind him, studying the note Nathalie had given him, and making marks with a red pen. Next to him was the bag of items he'd bought from the superstore.

'How long will it take to get into the network?' asked Aaron.

'Not too long,' said the hacker, looking up. 'I'll have to get past the encryption protecting their connection first. I have the tools for that anyway, and if I need anything else I can always download it from my personal server. I should get in within half an hour.'

'That quick?' said Aaron, a little sceptically. He'd done a short course on computer security and cybercrime during his GAILE training, so he knew a little about the process.

'You're talking to the best. I'll be on their network in thirty minutes – thirty-one, tops. The hard part will be the hidden network. The note says that the hidden server goes online just after midnight, but not how long for.'

They stayed at the campsite until nightfall, giving them the chance to take a rest. Aaron passed round some cold sandwiches that they'd bought at a service station on one of the state highways, and bottled water. It wasn't much of a meal, but after a long day of almost nonstop driving, it was more than welcome. Unfortunately that also left them with nothing for breakfast except maybe water.

Hitoshi began his work whilst the others were still eating. He turned to his bag and emptied it onto his seat, revealing his purchases: A wireless adaptor plus extension cable, the vegetable strainer, tin snips and a roll of black tape. He used the tin snips to cut a small hole in the centre of the strainer. He squeezed the wireless adaptor into the hole, and held it together with black tape.

'Voila,' said Hitoshi. 'We have wok-fi.'

An hour later it had grown dark, and so they moved on. Beyond the forest and after Wheeler Park, they turned onto Hegel Boulevard. Aaron saw St Mary's Cathedral, illuminated with large floodlights. He noticed Elise was staring at the fountain in the cathedral grounds. Looking in the rear mirror, he found that Hitoshi too was staring at the fountain. He wondered whose version of events was passing through the hacker's mind.

'You pass this way often, Hitoshi?' he asked.

Hitoshi turned away from the window. He glanced at Elise.

'Not if I can help it.'

Cape's End was a breathtaking corner of the peninsula. Jagged cliffs ran along much of the shore, enclosed by a narrow silver bay and a small dockyard at the northeast. Creux Island was offshore at the northeast tip, and was accessible from the peninsula via a road bridge built straight off one of the cliff tops. The bridge was open to permit holders only.

Aaron drove down to the bay and along the road by the beach. Hitoshi wanted to get as close to the island as possible in order to scan for the weather analysis network. Aaron had to consider where to stop the minivan, a job fortunately made easier by the fact that it was dark. He parked near the dock amongst other vehicles belonging to fishermen and tourists, placing them under the left side of the bridge. The lights on the island were visible from the shoreline. Aaron left the minivan's interior lights off.

Hitoshi took out a wafer-thin item from his pocket, the size of a playing card. It opened out into a 15 inch computer laptop made of a foldable yet tough nanomaterial, with a touch keyboard and touchpad. He placed the machine on a seat-rear flip down tray in front of him before switching it on. The laptop booted up within a couple of seconds, and the glow of the screen filled the minivan interior. A fine layer of miniscule solar cells coated the laptop and powered it, but without sunlight the batteries lasted only a couple of hours. Hitoshi flicked a switch on the side of the laptop and asked Aaron to press a button on the minivan's dashboard. The laptop now took wireless power from the minivan's battery.

He connected to the net using a free public wi-fi access point supplied at the campsite, and routed his connection through the minivan's inbuilt modem to make it that much more difficult to trace his attack back to him – 'Not that anyone will even know that there's been an attack,' he added, with a self-assured grin.

Next Hitoshi connected the extension cable of his wok-fi to the laptop. He propped the handle of the strainer into his passenger window and wound it up to hold it in place. The minivan had warmed up considerably during their journey, but the temperature soon dropped as the heat escaped through the window gap. Aaron heard the tide whooshing from outside.

Hitoshi looked at Aaron and Elise.

'Let's do this.'

He ran his left thumb over the laptop touchpad and then tapped it to open up a program. Aaron figured that he was scanning the airwaves for a network.

'I'm getting a signal from the island,' said Hitoshi. 'And quite a few machines are active. This should be pretty straightforward.'

He began humming tunelessly. Aaron turned round after a few minutes, as did Elise, and left him to it. Elise tuned into a local radio station to pass the time.

'I'm in,' announced Hitoshi less than half an hour later, as promised. 'But there's a problem.'

Aaron turned back to him. 'What is it?'

'I can't find any signs of the hidden network. I've run a port scanner and located the port that connects the weather server to the hidden network. It's closed – which is what I expected, because the system on the other side is offline – but otherwise there's no way to tell if the network even exists. There's no unusual network profile anywhere on this side. I can't find anything in the server's network lists or the log files.'

'Then how is the server connecting to the network?' asked Elise.

'I guess we'll have to wait until midnight to find out. And while we wait we can look for the *communication* that Nathalie was talking about. She implied that the server is a conduit for sending messages to the hidden network.'

'But the message won't just be sitting here on the server waiting to be found,' said Aaron. 'It must come in from someplace else.'

'Yeah, but it still comes here at some point,' said Hitoshi, his left thumbnail skating idly on the touchpad. 'We just need to know when it arrives, and how long it stays on the server.'

'And what it looks like,' said Elise.

Hitoshi nodded while still watching his screen. 'The only thing I know for sure – from what Nathalie said – is that the message is unencrypted. So it's in disguise. The analysis system's pretty much stuffed with this weather data, but it could be anything – an operating system file, or a text document, or an image. And I don't have the time or the space on my machine to download the whole system and go over it with a fine-toothed comb.'

'Then we must be selective in what we download – and we'd better be quick,' said Aaron, looking at the clock on the dashboard, 'as we only have two more hours before the system's taken offline.'

'Okay,' said Hitoshi thoughtfully, 'We know that this message can't be sitting in the system for too long, or anyone could find it.'

'I'd say no more than twenty-four hours,' said Aaron, 'since they connect the two systems every night.'

'Yep. And we can rule out email as the source of the message, since the server doesn't have email set up on it.'

'Unless we're talking webmail,' said Elise.

'But to access webmail,' said Hitoshi, 'the admin would have to stay connected to the net *after* midnight. Besides, that's not a secure way to send anything in secret.'

All brains ticked away for a minute or two.

'What about the weather data?' said Elise suddenly. 'Could they conceal a message inside the cloud holograms?'

Hitoshi seemed struck by the idea. 'Yeah, they could. And new holographic data comes in precisely every ten minutes. They could easily slip a message into that data mass.' He moved his cursor and began typing a few commands with his left hand. 'Think of the message as a digital watermark – masked and hidden inside the hologram. Who'd even think to look for something like that? Especially when the weather holograms are freely available to view on Creux Island's website? It's the perfect place to hide a message – and like Nathalie said, it's in plain sight.'

'Then you'd better download all the holograms that have come in over the last twenty-four hours,' said Aaron.

'That's still too much to download. The holograms come in from various meteorological servers across the States.'

'How many sites?' asked Elise.

Hitoshi blew through closed lips. 'I don't know … dozens. It'd take maybe six or seven hours to download them all. We don't have that kind of time.'

Aaron sighed. 'Then what do you suggest we do?'

'Look, it doesn't matter *where* the message is coming from. We can intercept it when they transfer it from the server to the network. Let me take a look at their database.'

Hitoshi's attention went back on his screen, and his long fingers hopped between the keys and the touchpad. Elise closed her eyes after a while and appeared to be nodding off. Aaron was too restless to do the same. He watched the dashboard clock faithfully count the minutes, far too quickly for his liking. Yet aside from the occasional movement of his fingers, Hitoshi was a statue.

The hacker came to life some fifty minutes later.

'That's interesting.'

Finally!

Aaron turned round, and Elise too was alert right away.

'What have you got?' said Aaron.

'The holograms arrive in compressed packets,' said Hitoshi. 'As I said before, they come in once every ten minutes – but there's one exception. The midnight packet comes through a few minutes early, at exactly eleven fifty-seven every single night. So I've checked the file properties of all the eleven fifty-seven packets from the past week. And in every single packet, there is one hologram that is slightly different from the rest. This hologram is modified a minute or two *after* midnight, when the server's offline.'

'Then these must be the watermarked holograms,' said Elise.

Hitoshi nodded. 'My guess is that they decode the holograms to separate the plain text of the messages, and then they send the text on its own to save upload time. They leave the stripped holograms behind in the weather server, so nobody's any the wiser. And if I'm right about that, then the steganalysis program they use to decode the holograms has to be somewhere on the system. If I can find it, I can copy it to my machine or get myself a copy from the net, and use it to retrieve the message for myself when it arrives.'

'Sounds like a plan,' said Aaron. 'Do it.'

Hitoshi spent another half hour in front of the screen, and was in a world of his own.

'I can't find it,' he said, just after the dashboard clock turned 11:14 p.m. 'Maybe there's nothing to find.'

Aaron overlooked the cynicism in Hitoshi's tone. 'Then let's see what they do when they go offline,' he said patiently. 'What are your chances of getting onto the hidden network itself?'

'Low,' said the hacker. 'The server reconnects to the net by ten past twelve, so it's only connected to the hidden network for a maximum of maybe seven minutes. I'll only have enough time to pick up the eleven fifty-seven packet.'

Hitoshi turned back again to his screen.

'What are you doing now?' asked Aaron.

'I'm installing a rootkit. It'll force the connection to stay open without the admin realising it.'

The packet came through at 11:57 p.m. on the dot, and took a full two and a half minutes to fully download onto the weather server. Hitoshi acted right away to copy the packet to his machine. It was still downloading when the dashboard clock struck midnight.

'The admin's taking the server offline,' he said.

At this point Hitoshi didn't have to do anything. His rootkit had overwritten the internet logon daemon, so that when the admin clicked the *disconnect* button the computer falsely displayed the message that the server had disconnected, whilst it actually remained online. Hitoshi was now a fly on the firewall, and more. He could watch everything that the admin was doing, and was free to sneak around and do as he wished at the same time.

Aaron half lifted himself off his seat, peering down over the top of the headrest at the laptop, but couldn't see the screen properly.

'What's happening?' he asked.

Hitoshi glanced at the right-hand side of his screen. 'Nothing yet. The port to our hidden server is still closed.' Then he frowned. 'The admin's opening the recycling bin – and the folder containing the eleven fifty-seven packet.'

'Have you completed your download of that packet?'

Hitoshi was distracted. 'That's weird … he's just dragged a hologram into the bin.'

Aaron tried looking over the top of his seat again, and got an upside-down view of the screen. The recycling bin window was open, and it had one file in it.

He frowned. Was that the watermarked hologram?

'He's going to delete it!' said Hitoshi.

The white cursor arrow appeared to float around its own. In fact the admin was controlling it and they were watching. The admin moved the cursor over the *restore* button and clicked it. The file now vanished from the bin.

Aaron sat back down, flummoxed by what he'd just seen.

'What happened?' asked Elise, who couldn't see anything at all from where she sat.

'The hologram's back in the eleven fifty-seven folder,' said Hitoshi. 'And the admin's reconnecting the server to the net. It's done! And ...' He gave a hopeless laugh. 'The port's closed! It *was* open, but it's closed now. You know what that means?'

'No, not really,' said Aaron.

Hitoshi's tone rose in excitement. 'The recycling bin is two programs in one! It's both the steganalysis program and the gateway to the hidden network! The restore button processed the hologram and uploaded the message – all in just one second!'

'But you managed to copy the watermarked hologram to your machine?' said Aaron.

Hitoshi was working again. 'You bet! And now I'll copy the recycling bin as well.'

'You can do that?' said Elise.

'We hackers have a saying,' he said with a grin, taking his eyes off the screen to look at her. 'If you can think of it, you can do it.'

The laptop beeped at that moment.

Hitoshi's face dropped. 'Crap! Downloading the bin has set off the security system!' he cried.

He moved his cursor and began typing fast.

'Get out of there!' said Aaron.

'What do you think I'm doing?!'

'Just disconnect!' said Elise.

'I can't! Not until I clear the log files!'

Aaron and Elise now had to wait. They watched Hitoshi agitatedly for a few minutes, powerless to do anything to help.

Finally he turned to them with a relieved expression.

'It's okay. I got out. Luckily the admin had already logged off, and I cleaned up, so no one will know that I tripped the alarm.'

'Did you get the recycling bin?'

'Sure did. Good news is that Creux's regular server uses the same operating system as I have on my machine. So we'll be able to test our eleven fifty-seven hologram right after I make a couple of changes to the bin.'

Hitoshi unplugged the cable from the wok-fi, took the dish down and rolled up his window.

They drove back towards the campsite in Soren Forest, and on the way Hitoshi got to work dismantling the recycling bin's program code. He explained that he wanted to rewrite it so that instead of trying to send the message to the hidden network, the bin would simply send it to his laptop's desktop.

The hacker became quietly absorbed in his task. There was an air of calm in the minivan, and Aaron relaxed for the first time that whole day. But then all of a sudden –

'Bastards!'

Thanks to the glow of the laptop screen Aaron clearly saw Hitoshi's expression through the rearview mirror. His mouth was turned down like that of a pike, and his cheeks were sucked in.

'What's wrong?' said Aaron.

Hitoshi looked at him, and shifted his eyes back to his screen.

'Nothing,' he said quietly.

'Doesn't sound like nothing,' said Elise.

Hitoshi waved brusquely at her. 'Quiet. I'm thinking.'

He continued with whatever he was doing, and didn't speak.

Hitoshi made Aaron and Elise wait until they were back at the campsite before he shared his news.

'The bin has nothing in it,' he said, once Aaron had switched off the engine. 'There's no customisation of any kind. No file transfer protocol, and no steganography subroutine. *Nothing.*'

'What?!' said Aaron.

'But we saw the admin upload that hologram!' said Elise.

'No, we didn't,' said Hitoshi. All we saw was somebody putting a hologram in the bin and then restoring it.'

'That's just what it looked like!' said Aaron. 'They do the same thing every night! You said as much yourself!'

'I know. And I don't like it any more than you do. But this is an ordinary recycling bin. I even created a second copy of the hologram and ran that through the bin as well. I compared the two copies for changes, and they were still identical.'

Aaron was unwilling to accept it. 'Something's not right here. Nathalie was adamant. She said –'

'Who cares what she said?! God, I knew the moment I met her that there was something off about her. I wouldn't be surprised if she was still in cahoots with GAILE.'

'She's not in cahoots with GAILE.'

'Then she's crazy.'

'No. We just missed something back there. You said the port to the network went on for a second. We have to go back.'

Hitoshi pulled a face. 'We can't. Not tonight, anyway. Our next window isn't until eleven fifty-seven tomorrow night.'

Aaron was growing weary of Hitoshi's pessimism. 'Then we'll return there at that time,' he said through his teeth.

Hitoshi's tone also changed. 'Don't you ever let up? I told you there's nothing there. I checked the whole damned system.'

'The port opened, didn't it?'

'But I never saw what it was for. It was probably a printer!'

'You don't know that!'

Elise tried to ease the tension. 'All right boys,' she said, 'take it easy. We've all had a very long day.'

'Haven't we just!' snapped Hitoshi. 'We've been driving around like idiots all day, we've been shot at, we've lost my friend's car, and we've hacked a weather lab looking for secret messages that weren't even there! Everything's gone wrong! And to top it off, we're about to go and meet a psychopath for a defunct disc! This is nuts! What are we doing this all for?'

'The truth,' said Aaron.

'Bull crap! You're just chasing your old man's ghost. You're so hung up on trying to prove him right, you don't care if we get killed in the process.' His eyes narrowed. 'Like father, like son.'

Aaron was ready to shout back, but Elise put a hand on his arm.

'Hitoshi, that's totally uncalled for!' she said. 'We're both here of our own free will. Lloyd has never made us do anything – and neither did Omar.'

Hitoshi was finally silenced; or so it seemed for a moment. He powered off his laptop, and the minivan became completely dark.

'Look ... I say we forget the dam,' he said matter-of-factly, folding and pocketing the laptop. 'It's a bad idea. I can feel it.'

'You have a bad feeling?' Aaron sniggered at the absurdity of the suggestion. 'Well, that's just great, Hitoshi! But where do you want us to go from here, huh? Because there's nowhere to go!'

'Lloyd's right,' said Elise. 'We can't go –'

'– I know,' he interrupted. 'I know. I was just ... Forget it.'

He unlocked his door.

'Where are you going?' she said.

'I need a smoke,' he said, and got out.

He slammed the door.

Aaron looked out of the window on Elise's side. Though it was almost pitch black outside, he saw that Hitoshi had gone round to the back end of the vehicle. His lighter sparked as he lit a cigarette.

The two sat in the darkness for a few minutes.

'I think he's just frustrated about Creux Island,' said Elise.

Aaron sighed. 'No, he's spooked. And he has every right to be.'

He couldn't see her face, but saw her eyes glisten as they widened in surprise.

'Everything *has* gone wrong today,' he added.

'Not everything,' she said. 'GAILE haven't caught us yet.'

CHAPTER THIRTY-ONE
The Colour of Duplicity

Elise awoke at dawn and found herself lying on the middle row seats. Hitoshi was on the back row, and Lloyd had slept in the most uncomfortable place – in the driver's seat. He was already up and had switched the interior light on.

He looked at her now. 'I was about to wake you,' he said.

She saw the dashboard clock and sat up with a frown. It was just after half past six, but she should have been up much sooner. They'd agreed to take turns keeping watch during the night. Hitoshi had volunteered for the first shift, probably as an apology for his earlier tantrum. Lloyd had taken over by a quarter to three.

'You were supposed to wake me two hours ago,' she said.

'I thought one of us should get some proper sleep,' he replied.

René Raison Dam was built across Silver River, and was used to divert some of river flow away from Crescent Bay East to a nearby canal to the west, as well as for hydroelectric power generation.

When they arrived the sun was already rising. They'd come from the highway through Soren Forest and had moved south via the Coppice Gate area. Presently they were on a downhill stretch of road that ran parallel to the river on their right. The road ended abruptly before they even reached the vicinity of the dam. Lloyd took the minivan to a small empty parking area a quarter of a kilometre from the site. He stopped, but left the engine running.

Beyond some trees and shrubs on the slopes they saw the wall of the dam below. Woody thickets covered the short steep hills on both sides of the dam. Some white hydroelectric power plant buildings were just visible behind the thickets on the left side. The sky above the wall was greyish blue with an orange band at the horizon. At the far right-hand side of the wall, with the sun coming up exactly behind it, was the silhouette of an oblong vehicle.

'Is that what I think it is?' said Elise.

'That's a camper van all right,' said Hitoshi.

'How did he get down there?' said Lloyd. 'The road ends here.'

Manner had evidently arrived on the dam wall by coming in from the west, but there were no obvious signs of vehicle access through those unruly thickets, especially for a van.

'The top of the wall is a disused road,' said Hitoshi. 'It was meant to be part of a route between Penrose Fjord and Verity Square but they never finished it. He must have found a way through the woods.'

'Then we'll do the same,' said Lloyd.

He drove through the parking area onto the undeveloped land, and downhill into the thicket on the right side. It was a bumpy ride but they soon emerged on the wall opposite the camper van. The sky became lighter with each passing minute.

The dam wall was only a couple of hundred metres across. Four spillways were spread along its length, and a waist-high brick ledge lined the road. Over the left side, frothy spray crashed through the spillway and into the watercourse below, noisily enough that they heard it inside the van. They trawled along the narrow road until they were within five or seven metres from the camper van. Now Lloyd switched off the engine.

Elise felt a strong flutter in her stomach, but this wasn't down to her psychic alarm. From a psychic perspective in fact, she was going blind. She looked nervously at Lloyd's aura, scarcely able to make out its golden glow. Hitoshi's signature was no more than a wisp of mustard smoke.

'Why did he pick a place surrounded by water?' she said. 'If anyone else turns up here we won't get any warning.'

'I don't think we'll be ambushed out here,' said Hitoshi.

She smiled mirthlessly. Wasn't he the one who had tried to talk them out of coming to the dam last night?

The figure sitting in the camper van nodded at them, and made a move to get out of his vehicle. The trio did likewise.

Elise was astonished at the sight in front of her. Though the air was cold and moist, Manner wore no coat over his blue T-shirt. He was leaner than in his file photo, and he seemed somewhat taller than his actual height of six foot one. A blue vein pulsed from beneath the ribbon round his head, and he had a stony expression on his unshaven face. Yet his eyes were … peaceful.

Despite the dampening effect of the water, Elise could also see the hushed inferno that raged about Manner's person. Dark streaks of soot and dried blood dented his aura at sharp angles and gave it a skewed tornado shape. This was hardly atypical for a murderer, but something golden-orange burned brighter underneath like molten rock, accompanied with violet electrical sparks. Elise had never seen anything quite like it. Perhaps his aura was the reason he'd brought them here, to a place that would cloak it.

'Geez!' said Hitoshi, and an unlit cigarette fell out of his mouth. 'He's in … tatters!'

Lloyd didn't reply, but then, Elise thought, he was the only one who couldn't see Manner's aura.

Manner was looking at Hitoshi now. 'David?' he said, above the noise of the water.

'… Yes,' replied Hitoshi, with a squeak in his voice.

'Have you got the equipment?'

'It's all in the minivan.'

Manner pulled out an item from his back trouser pocket and held it out to him.

'Come here,' he said.

'Me?'

'Just you.'

Hitoshi glanced at Lloyd. Elise knew he was fretting about coming in close proximity to Manner, in case the man picked up on his twin problem.

Lloyd urged him on with a nod.

Hitoshi had his back to them, but Elise could see the small box in Manner's hand. Hitoshi cautiously reached forward, placed his hand on the box, and lifted it like a deck of cards.

'Show them,' said Manner.

Hitoshi turned partially towards them and opened the lid. He took out the purple DVD inside and held it up carefully by the circumference edge so as not to touch its surface. Then he raised it to his face, supposedly inspecting it for imperfections. But Elise noticed that his eyes were darting round, almost as though he was watching out for something.

'Hold it right there!'

It was a new voice.

Elise looked behind her. Five armed GAILE officers wearing protective gear were within twenty feet of them. Two more appeared from behind the minivan. She saw no vehicles, which meant they'd all arrived on the dam wall by foot. They'd probably parked nearby, but the sound of the water had drowned out the noise of their vehicles.

Even now Elise was unable to detect them, not only because of the water but also because they all had shielding implants. They'd even escaped the notice of the hypersensitive Peter Manner.

Leading the agents were two men in black ribbed pullovers with plated bulletproof vests. One was Kash. The other man had a heavy square build, and was in his late forties or early fifties.

'... Kingswell?!' said a flabbergasted Lloyd.

Kingswell ... Did he mean the director of GAILE? Elise took a closer look at his broad face and small hawk-like eyes, and recognised him from TV. Seeing that the men carried military style carbine rifles, she had the chilling realisation that they weren't GAILE officers, but were from E3's assassination unit, G-Force.

'Hands up!' said Kingswell.

Elise, Manner and Hitoshi raised their hands. One of the men marched over to Elise's side and pointed a rifle at her. Another pointed a rifle at Lloyd, forcing him to drop his weapon and also put up his hands. A third pointed his rifle at Manner.

The director of GAILE nodded just then, and the gesture was directed at Hitoshi. Everyone turned their heads to Hitoshi, only to find him looking right back the G-Force agents. Not one of them held a weapon against him.

Hitoshi lowered his hands with a smile on his face.

A familiar smile. But not David's.

Hitoshi produced his own gun from his breast pocket and pointed it at Manner. Then he took the disc between his index and middle finger and flicked it away. The disc flew straight over the top of the wall, catching the early sunlight and glinting before it vanished into the foamy water below.

'Hitoshi!' yelled Lloyd.

Manner looked at Hitoshi with murderous intent. His entire body tensed up and his knuckles cracked as he clenched his fists. But since at least three guns were aiming at him, he couldn't move.

'Why?' he growled.

He still had no idea. No one answered him.

'Excellent work, Mr Katayama,' said Kingswell. 'You always were our finest agent. Unlike Agent Lloyd. Or is that Agent Omar?'

Elise's mind was awhirl with Hitoshi's elaborate lies, the different versions of those lies, changing his lines so fast and so easily that she'd lost track of what he'd said and when. Was anything he'd told her true at all? And how long he had been talking to *them* for? Had he been with them from the start?

Lloyd put similar thoughts of his own into words, but he expressed himself succinctly.

'Hitoshi! You two-faced snake! You told them who I am!'

'Not quite,' said Kash. 'We were suspicious for some time. We ascertained your identity when we exhumed your father's grave.'

Poor Lloyd was visibly shaken. 'You ... what?'

'Don't worry,' said Kingswell. 'We left it as we found it – though we had to take the skull. Hope you don't mind. I'll make sure Kash gives you a full report covering every detail at HQ ... right before your interrogation. We want to know who, other than the late Robert Benedict, you've been working with.'

'... *Late?*'

'Oh, did I forget to tell you? We realised that he'd been helping you and your father for years. So he had to die. We've been intercepting all the messages you've sent him since. You only got this far because we let you, Mr Lloyd. We even supplied the vintage technology you so desperately needed.'

Elise frowned, but not at what Kingswell was saying. Through the dampening field she was becoming aware of several energy signatures behind the G-Force men. She assumed they must be GAILE proper, for they were not mentally shielded. They felt distant, but that only meant they had to be very close by. Just out of sight, coming up behind the minivan in fact, or she wouldn't have sensed them at all.

She stealthily looked at Hitoshi and Manner in turn. Manner was to her left. He caught her eye and gave her a signal with a subtle nod. He'd sensed them too. Hitoshi on the other hand didn't seem to have noticed anything. His focus was entirely was on the director of GAILE.

'In case you don't feel like talking,' said Kingswell at that moment, 'do bear in mind that your friends here are under arrest for conspiring to commit a terrorist act. They might get sent to better prisons if you cooperate.'

Elise looked helplessly at Lloyd.

'Freeze!'

It was the distinctive raven-like voice of Brent Taylor.

Kingswell and Kash turned round this time, to see Taylor and five men emerging from behind the camper van. They too wore protective gear. Two men flanking Taylor came from the driver's side; three came from the other and stood behind Kingswell.

'Stand down!' ordered Taylor.

No one budged. A dozen weapons pointed in every direction in the short space between the two vehicles, threatening a deadly shower if anyone dared to pull a trigger.

But someone had to break the deadlock.

Kingswell had his gun pointed at Taylor's trio. He abruptly fired three rounds at blank range. Bits of brain and blood exploded. They didn't stand a chance.

In the same instant Kash turned his weapon towards Taylor and his two flanking officers. One man went down.

Elise didn't wait to see what happened next. She had to deal with the G-Force agent holding his carbine to her head. She hit the nozzle with her palm and grabbed hold of it. Seizing the butt with her other hand, she yanked the rifle from the agent's hands and kicked him in the torso, sending him backwards.

A gurgling cry a few feet away temporarily distracted her. Manner had somehow knocked down his would-be guard, and had just thrust a dagger into his neck. Dark blood oozed onto the tarmac. Manner took the agent's rifle and threw it into the dam.

Where was Hitoshi?

Elise looked to where he'd stood. He was moving towards the camper van. And he was shooting at … Kash.

'Elise!' shouted Lloyd.

She spun to her right. Too late. Another G-Force agent opened fire at her from just two metres away.

He would surely have killed her, had Lloyd not tackled him sideways. Bullets sprayed into the air. Lloyd shoved the agent with enough momentum to hurl him over the right edge of the wall.

The man screamed as he plummeted into the water below.

Oh, my God.

Lloyd had just saved her life.

But there was no time to think about that. No time even to give him a look of gratitude. Lloyd was swinging an arm like an oar at her, by way of ordering her to take cover.

She ran to the passenger side of the minivan with Lloyd at her heels. Peripherally she saw Manner dive on top of the man whom she'd tackled just moments before. There was no scream, only a grunt. Elise guessed a broken neck.

The pair scurried to the rear. As they knelt down against the hatch door, the gunfire suddenly ceased. Everyone at the scene was either down or hiding. At least Elise and Lloyd knew no one had gone into the thicket behind them.

Lloyd looked at the carbine Elise had taken from the G-Force agent. 'Be careful,' he whispered. 'Those things can shoot through cars, but not through car engines. They can't penetrate hard vests either. Do you understand?'

Elise nodded and quietly handed the rifle to him. It was better if he took it, since she wasn't a good enough shot to aim for the head, and she didn't have the nerve for it either. Lloyd bent down and moved past her to look back round the other corner. Finding it safe, he beckoned her to follow.

She almost jumped out of her skin to find Manner on his haunches below the front passenger window. He gave her only a passing glance, and turned his gaze to the camper van standing opposite them. Taylor and his one remaining officer were positioned parallel to them, crouching behind the camper van below the window line. Hitoshi was also with them.

'What's he doing over there?' said Lloyd.

Elise remembered what she'd seen just before the G-Force agent had almost shot her. Hitoshi shooting at Kash.

'He's changed sides again,' she murmured.

She had the cynical thought that he'd probably only done so after realising he was outnumbered.

'Hitoshi!' yelled Kash at that moment from the other side of the camper. 'You're a dead man!'

'What's wrong with him?' asked Manner.

He posed the question with clinical coolness, like a psychiatrist.

'He has the memories of both twins,' she said.

Manner squinted thoughtfully.

Taylor held up two fingers to signal that two enemy men remained on the other side of the camper. Lloyd nodded at him and pointed to his left. Taylor returned the nod. Lloyd gestured to Manner and Elise that they should stay back.

Lloyd knelt on both knees to stabilise himself, and faced the camper van. He lifted the rifle and put his eye to the sight, his finger on the trigger. He took a couple of short breaths, then swiftly turned and fired a short burst diagonally across the bonnet. The noise was frightful.

Rapid gunfire greeted him from the other side.

Lloyd withdrew. Thankfully he was all right.

He paused, turned and fired again. Kash reciprocated.

Both missed. Both pulled back.

Both paused, turned, fired. But Lloyd had changed his rhythm and turned a split second sooner.

'Argh!' cried Kash, and they heard him tumble.

Lloyd patted his own left arm and chest to inform the deputy where he'd hit Kash.

'Give up, Kingswell!' shouted Taylor. 'Your last man is down!'

Kash was certainly injured. Bulletproof vests were really only bullet resistant, and couldn't fully protect against the punch of a high-speed projectile. Elise was sure he was hit in the thigh from when Hitoshi had shot at him. And with Lloyd having just unloaded a good number of bullets with an automatic weapon, Kash could have anything from severe bruising to cracked ribs in addition to heavy blood loss. Kingswell really was the last man.

Everyone waited. All was now silent except for the perpetual thunder from the spillways. Taylor couldn't check on the situation on the other side without leaving his position. The windows of the camper were small, and in addition the curtains were drawn. Nor did anyone take the risk of peering beneath the vehicles. Taylor and Kingswell both hid behind the camper van's front tyres.

Lloyd snorted impatiently.

He signalled again at Taylor.

The deputy nodded.

Lloyd put down the rifle as it was out of ammunition. Taking a handgun from his shoulder holster, he stood up.

'Stay down here,' he instructed her and Manner.

Elise realised he was moving in, and at that moment she had a rotten feeling in the core of her being.

'Lloyd –' she began.

But he'd already stepped past her.

Taylor and his man likewise stood up. Hitoshi stayed down. Taylor waved his man to move towards the rear of the camper, whilst he went towards the front.

'Kingswell!' said Lloyd again. He was out in the open space now, so his voice resonated freely. 'Come out with your hands up!'

This time a hand threw a rifle low to the ground. It slid across the tarmac and appeared in front of the camper van. Kash was surrendering his weapon.

'It's over,' said Lloyd.

'Imbecile,' said Kingswell. 'It's never over.'

A sudden loud bang – a shot from a handgun – shattered the camper van's front windows. Everyone recoiled, and hands flew up in front of faces to defend from flying shards.

Kingswell rose fast from behind the campervan like a shark from the deep, wielding a pistol. His face was all hard lines and teeth. He aimed straight at Lloyd.

'No!' screamed Elise.

All opened fire in unison: Lloyd, Taylor, his officer. Bullets hit Kingswell in the neck and head.

He dropped back behind the van.

All was quiet again, except for the echo of gunfire fading into the distance, and the ringing in Elise's ears.

But neither she nor anyone else had noticed Kash crawling out on his belly from the front of the van. He too had a spare handgun. He aimed it at an awkward angle, upward at forty-five degrees.

Elise was heaving a sigh of relief when she sighted him among the dead bodies. Her sigh cut short and became a gasp – just as he squeezed the trigger.

CHAPTER THIRTY-TWO
René Raison

A single shot was all it took.

Lloyd looked down at Kash, then at his chest.

He staggered to the side.

'Oh,' he said, and collapsed.

Elise's heart stopped. And so did time.

Taylor hurriedly hopped over the bodies and wrested the gun from Kash, who was in any case too weak from blood loss to resist. The other GAILE officer meanwhile went round the rear to see to Kingswell, for what it was worth.

Elise moved towards Lloyd, stumbling to get to him as she'd lost the power in her legs. Shaking, she checked him over. The bullet had passed through his shirt and into his lower left ribcage. A small patch of blood had appeared, and it was spreading.

'... Need an ambulance.' Taylor was on a mobile. 'Two officers with gunshot wounds ...'

Lloyd was motionless and his eyes were shut.

Surely, surely, he couldn't be dead? Not just like that?

'Lloyd, stay with me! ... Please, God ...'

She lifted his head onto her lap and put her ear near his mouth. He was still breathing. She raised him up a little to try and find the exit wound. Finding nothing, Elise touched his face with the back of her fingers. She wanted to find his pulse. Not of his heartbeat, but of his aura. With the river's veil thrown over the scene, it was impossible for her to know how accurate her reading was. But what little she could feel of his life force seemed to be ebbing away.

Not again. It can't happen again.

Elise acted automatically on her knowledge of first aid and tore his shirt open. A stab wound and a bullet wound to the chest had similar rules of treatment. Though she'd never dealt with a gunshot wound before, she saw that the blood in the hole had bubbles in it, which meant that she was looking at a sucking chest wound. It needed a seal to stop air getting into his pleural cavity. Having nothing else immediately to hand, she clamped her right palm over it and applied pressure to try and stem the bleeding.

Manner's reedy voice startled her. 'Tell me.'

He was right behind her. In her panic she'd left him alone beside the camper van.

Elise didn't move. She turned her eyes up first to Hitoshi, who sat on the ground a few feet from her. He stared over her shoulder at Manner, in an almost catatonic state. To her right she saw Taylor's colleague. He was back from the other side of the camper van, and he was pointing his handgun at Manner. To her left Taylor was off the mobile and still kneeling beside Kash. He had just armed himself again.

'Put the gun down, Peter,' said the deputy sternly.

Gun? But Manner hated guns.

Or was she confusing him with Leon?

Elise turned her head. Manner had a rifle in just one hand. Not the best way to hold a weapon with that kind of firepower. The nozzle swayed precariously in Hitoshi's direction.

None of this fazed her. Right now she hated Hitoshi so much she didn't care what happened to him.

Really she didn't care about anything.

Manner tried to move past her towards Hitoshi.

'Freeze!' said Taylor at top volume.

Manner halted. His sinewy arms were stiff and quavering, as though charged with electricity.

'I have to know.' He was addressing Hitoshi. 'Why did you destroy the proof?'

Hitoshi took his time before he replied. He rubbed his index finger and thumb together as if that might conjure up a cigarette.

'It was the right thing to do under the circumstances.'

He said it so candidly.

Manner mouthed something silently to himself. Then he asked the inevitable question.

'Which one are you? David? Or Adam?'

Hitoshi looked at him without fear. 'Both. ... And neither.'

Whatever that was supposed to mean, Manner at least was impressed. His eyebrows rose as though the answer made perfect sense, and he gazed back at Hitoshi, checking for some sort of confirmation – though of what, Elise couldn't imagine. Then he nodded, apparently satisfied.

Rifle still in hand, Manner vaulted onto the foot-wide brick ledge. He released the gun and it fell onto the road beside Elise. Only then did it occur to her that this was Lloyd's empty carbine. Manner had never intended to hurt Hitoshi, because of David. And Hitoshi had known it too.

'Hold it, Peter!' said Taylor. His tone was still assertive, but not aggressive. He lowered his weapon. 'Don't do anything hasty.'

'You promised to hand yourself in,' said Hitoshi.

'But the disc is gone, friend,' replied Manner.

He stretched out his arms and looked up to the sky. The wind tugged his scraggly mane. He looked over his shoulder into the deadly torrent as though it was welcoming him in. He smiled.

'Peace, man,' he said.

'Stop!' said Taylor.

But he was unable to do anything.

Manner closed his eyes and let himself go.

Taylor's colleague ran to the ledge and looked down into the foam. He turned to the deputy and shook his head.

'That's a hundred foot drop,' he said. 'No one could survive it.'

Elise scarcely heard him. Her attention was back on Lloyd. His breathing was unsteady, and his face clammy and pallid. Thick blood seeped through the gaps between her fingers onto his shirt and his reefer jacket. The metallic odour caught her nostrils as it mingled with the gunpowder in the air, which in turn smelled exactly like the end of a fireworks display.

Taylor came over.

'Ambulance is on its way, Elise. ETA ten minutes. How is he?'

'He's still breathing, but –'

'We need to seal that wound properly. Preferably with plastic. Have you got any plastic bags, anything like that?'

She found the minivan keys in Lloyd's coat pocket. 'Try the glove compartment. There's some black tape in there too.'

Taylor went to the minivan.

She glanced to her right. Hitoshi was just watching everything like an innocent bystander. She hoped they'd lock him away and throw away the key.

'He's awake,' said Hitoshi.

'What?'

'Lloyd.'

Elise looked at Lloyd. His eyes were open.

She forgot all about Hitoshi.

'Lloyd! Can you hear me?'

He mumbled something.

'Lloyd?'

His voice was hoarse and faint. He struggled with each breath, and with each word. 'Ng ... N-name ... is ... Aa-Aaron!'

Hearing him speak was enough to break her. 'Oh, Lloyd!' she whispered, and began to cry. 'I thought you were gone!'

He smiled weakly.

'Lloyd ...' Her salty tears suddenly gave way to a more peppery emotion. 'Lloyd! You little git!' Elise almost grabbed his collar, until she remembered that her hand was covering his wound. 'Don't you *ever* scare me like that again!'

Lloyd started to laugh, and then spluttered in pain. At least his humour was intact.

She chuckled nervously and stroked his hair. 'Don't you dare give up,' she murmured. 'Everything's going to be just fine.'

Because of the access problem, the emergency services sent an air ambulance. Taylor ensured that the two vehicles on the wall were moved out of the way (fortunately Manner had left his keys in the camper van) before the helicopter's arrival. The ambulance arrived within ten minutes and landed gracefully as a dragonfly at the west side of the wall. Its whirring roar wound down somewhat like a jet engine, and though it wasn't nearly as loud as one, it nevertheless kicked up a strong air current, creating ripples on the river surface and a lot of spray.

Three crewmen quickly tended to the injured. Taylor had done his best to make both Lloyd and Kash more comfortable before their arrival. But the paramedics couldn't do anything for Kash. They soon pronounced him dead.

Lloyd meanwhile lay on his injured side so that blood wouldn't affect his other lung. Taylor and Elise had cut out a square from a plastic bag and taped it up on three sides across his chest wound, leaving the bottom side free to allow excess air to escape. The crewmen in orange uniforms now took over, placing an oxygen mask on his face, checking the makeshift seal to see that it was doing its job, listening to Lloyd's breathing, and asking him how he felt. One of the paramedics declared it an open pneumothorax – the technical term for a sucking chest wound. As they strapped him onto a stretcher, another paramedic assured Taylor and Elise that Lloyd's condition seemed fair under the circumstances, though obviously he needed urgent surgical intervention.

Within a minute, they began lifting him into the helicopter.

The dead – nine in all, and not counting Manner and the G-Force agent who had wound up in the dam – had to be left as they were. A GAILE team from the CO were coming down to collect information on the scene. They were also going to search for the two missing bodies. The road ambulances would take the rest of them to the morgue. As the helicopter prepared to take off again, Elise and the others moved towards the thicket where the minivan and the camper were now parked.

She checked the time. It was 7:40 a.m. The watch face had a bright dot of blood on it. That was when she noticed how red and sticky her hands and clothes had become. She gulped.

'On second thoughts,' she heard Hitoshi say suddenly, 'I'm glad we left my friend's car in Pennsylvania.'

He was stood to her left, and was touching a bullet hole in the side of the minivan.

Elise rolled her eyes and snubbed him.

Taylor had been talking on his mobile again a short distance away. Now he approached them, holding a pair of handcuffs. He was taking Hitoshi into custody.

'Give me a minute,' said Hitoshi. 'Please.'

Elise pulled a face at Taylor. But he nodded so as to indicate she should hear him out.

She sighed. Taylor went back to his colleague.

Hitoshi looked at her wistfully. 'Lise ...' he began.

Elise forced herself to look directly at him.

'Lise, I didn't want to –'

'Save it.'

'They worked out I was Adam. I didn't want to help them, but they threatened me. I had no choice.'

'There's *always* a choice!' she hissed.

He took a slow breath. 'You're right.'

His face betrayed both remorse and hurt. If he expected her to feel sorry for him, she didn't.

To her annoyance, he just stood there.

She scowled. 'Is that it?'

He shook his head. 'Listen,' he said quietly, 'They'll want to talk to you sooner or later.'

Now he was getting to the point. He wanted something from her – probably a plea to Taylor for leniency on his behalf.

'So?'

'Don't give them your statement,' he said. 'Not until you've spoken to Lloyd, anyway.'

She hesitated. Why did he say it like that, as though he knew something that she didn't?

'Why?'

'Someone called the cavalry. And it sure as hell wasn't me. If I were you, I'd want to know how come Lloyd knew we were headed into a trap.'

Fair point, but she couldn't decide whether or not he was up to something. As usual his eyes gave nothing away.

'Just think about it,' he muttered, before she could answer. At normal volume he added: 'Tell him I'm sorry. I didn't know about his father's grave.' He gave her a final strong look. 'Anyway, uh ... that's it. Bye, Lise.'

Hitoshi passed behind her to go to Taylor, and suddenly her stomach fluttered ... the first psychic feeling she'd had in an hour.

What was that?

Elise turned to him, but he was already out of reach. Taylor's colleague cuffed him and led him away.

She went across to Taylor with a mind to ask who had called him to the dam. But then he'd know that she was in the dark, and that might bring up some awkward questions from his side.

'It's a good thing Lloyd contacted me,' said the deputy. 'I doubt any of you would have come out of this alive otherwise.'

She selected her words. 'When did you get his message?'

'Three in the morning, as soon as he sent his text.'

Now she had confirmation of who had called Taylor. He and his men would not have come so heavily armed had they been planning to deal just with Peter Manner.

But how did Lloyd know?

CHAPTER THIRTY-THREE
The Spider's House

The bullet had entered Lloyd's chest below his heart. It had travelled up into the right side, puncturing his right lung near the top, and had become lodged behind a rib. He was in theatre for almost three hours, not only to remove the bullet and splinters, but also to repair tissue damage. The doctors used nanoparticles first to staunch the bleeding, and then to deliver a large dose of growth factor to his lung cells. This substance (usually present in cells in much smaller amounts) would boost lung cell reproduction and so speed his recovery. Elise remained in the waiting room the whole time and so was first to learn that his condition was serious but stable, and that he was in the recovery room on a ventilator as a precaution. The surgeon told her that Lloyd was very lucky. The bullet was a point forty calibre and yet aside from his lung, it had missed all his other vital organs and major blood vessels. By midafternoon, the doctors moved him into a private room in the intensive care unit where they kept him sedated.

Elise dodged Taylor's attempts to get her down to the Harper Building for her statement. She told him she couldn't think about anything until she knew Lloyd was all right – even though the doctors wouldn't let anyone see him until morning. She returned to her apartment briefly to change out of her bloodstained clothes and freshen up, and then to Lloyd's to pick up a few things for him. Thereafter she returned and stayed at the hospital overnight.

She finally got to go in and see Lloyd at 9 a.m., and that too because she pestered the nurses. Formal visiting hours didn't start until 11 a.m., so Taylor wasn't back yet.

Elise opened the door to his room. He had a drip in his arm and a heart monitor next to his bed. A tube stuck out of the right side of his chest, presumably to drain blood. He was sitting up on the electric bed, and though he still looked pale, he was wide awake. The best indicator of his improving health however was his aura, which was honey and sunshine.

'Hi, there,' she said. 'How are you feeling?'

Lloyd gave her a vague half-smile in response. He was off the ventilator, so he was able to speak.

'Not bad,' he said croakily. 'But I'll be happier when they take this tube out of my side.'

Elise closed the door and took a chair at his bedside.

'I never thanked you for saving my life,' she said.

'Nah ... it's all part of the job.'

She didn't know what else to say to him. 'You were very lucky not to have been killed,' she blurted out.

Lloyd looked at the door, and for a second she thought she might have upset him, or perhaps he didn't want her there.

'I've been trying to work out what happened,' he said.

Elise imagined his memory was foggy from the shooting.

'What do you remember?' she asked.

'Well ... everything up until I was shot. But one thing is bugging me. How did Taylor know where to find us?'

Of all the things to forget!

'You sent him an SOS, remember?'

'No, I didn't,' he said resolutely.

'He said you texted him!'

'What? Where's my cell?'

Elise opened a drawer behind her. Lloyd's clothes were inside. She reached for his bloodied reefer jacket and soon found his mobile phone in the breast pocket.

She switched it on and checked the *sent messages* box.

'Here it is. See?' She read it out for him. '*Urgent: Need backup at René Raison Dam, sunrise. Manner is meeting us. Suspect we may encounter enemy agents working inside Intel. Kingswell, Kash, Katayama are involved. – Lloyd.*'

'I never sent that.'

'Are you sure?'

'Positive. I never knew that Hitoshi was on their side.'

She frowned. 'Then ... then it must have been Hitoshi! He's the only one who could possibly have known that Kingswell was going to ambush us.'

'Where is he now?'

'In custody,' she replied slowly. 'You know, before they took him away yesterday he asked me not to give a statement to GAILE until I'd spoken to you.'

'Huh! We've been had!'

'Just what I was thinking. But why try to make it look like you sent the SOS to Taylor?'

'I guess he's covering his tracks. He double-crossed them but he doesn't want them to know.'

'Looking after himself as usual.'

'He called for help, Elise. He didn't have to do that.'

'He didn't have to destroy the disc either.'

They paused.

'We have to talk to him,' said Lloyd.

'How can we, if he's in custody?'

Lloyd was contemplative. 'He must have given GAILE a statement by now,' he said. 'I can get a report on that and see what he said. I'm still the leading officer in this case.'

'You're also in hospital. You're in no condition to work.'

'We have to try,' he said. 'At the very least I can ask Taylor to update me in person.'

'But he'll be expecting you to explain how you knew Kingswell was coming to the dam.'

'We'll worry about that if and when it comes up. Let's just call Taylor now, and see what he has to tell us.'

Elise wasn't happy about it, but she acquiesced with a nod.

Mobile phone use was forbidden in case of interference with the heart monitor and other sensitive equipment, so she had to leave the room. Once in the corridor, she put her hand in her pocket to reach for her own mobile phone. Her fingers grazed a piece of paper, and a couple of foreign square objects, one of them metal.

Elise gasped. Her stomach fluttered in exactly the same way as it had the last time she'd seen Hitoshi. She took out the items and found a datafile and a silver lighter. The third item was the note that Nathalie Weston had given to them. On the back was a message in another hand. She read it and her jaw dropped.

Oh, my God.

Elise turned back and burst into Lloyd's room.

'Lloyd, I just found these in my pocket!'

She sat down beside him again and showed him the note. On the back was a message. She read it out.

'*Tell them I emailed Kingswell from my laptop at 2 a.m. Sunday about the meeting at the dam, and that you found it and called Taylor for backup. But don't tell them where else we've been!*'

'Check the datafile,' said Lloyd.

Elise switched it on and found two text files. She opened the one named *read me*, and read out the short message.

'*Even Agent Numbskull should get what this is, but check my comments enclosed in hash marks.*'

She opened the other file.

It contained rows of numbers. Scrolling through, they saw the names of the world's major cities, population statistics, public revenue, corporate finance information, crime rates, employment rates and even weather patterns. All in all it read like a huge table of figures from the stock exchange.

They stared at one another.

'Is this what I think it is?' said Elise eventually. 'A readout from the Systems Experiment?'

'… I think so. Except …'

He lifted his arm slowly and pointed at the comments Hitoshi had added at the top of the file.

 # Operating System: Myriadder (© 2012 D Cohen); Input for Paragon3 retrieved on 10 04 2042 at 23:57 hrs #

'Look at the time log,' he said. 'The data was retrieved from the server dated just two nights ago.'

'That makes it Saturday.'

'Yes. At Creux Island.'

'I don't get it. Hitoshi said there was nothing … oh.'

'– He was lying,' they finished together.

Elise grumbled in amazement. The recycling bin *was* the gateway to the secret network after all. Hitoshi *had* found something inside the watermarked hologram. And far from a mere *message*, he'd actually found all this *data* … the readout that they were looking at right now.

Yet she was unsure as to what it all signified.

'So … the experiment's still running, thirty years on?'

Lloyd's eyes shone with excitement. 'It is indeed,' he said, 'but with some major differences. Firstly, they aren't using simulated or theoretical population data anymore. They're collecting real data from every country. Secondly, they're running only one system type, whereas in the original Systems Experiment the STRO tested five system types, if you count Libredux. And this single system has a new name: Not monarchy, or theocracy, or communism, or even capitalist democracy, but … see that in the comment line?'

'Paragon3 … the *three* meaning E3?'

'Looks like it,' he replied, and coughed. 'But what we're seeing here is Libredux reinstated as an E3 self-preservation program. Remember that Libredux was just an algorithm, a problem-solving program designed to process population data in line with the Cohesive Ethics Theorem. But since the theorem conflicted with their interests, they overwrote it. Paragon3 works much like Libredux – but instead of calculating for the good, their version works on ways to help them retain total control, and prevent people from even realising that they're trapped. Convince people they're free when they're really slaves. Give them what they need to live – food, homes, maybe money and security too. But they're still caught in the same old meaningless cycle of survival. They're miserable and unfulfilled all their lives. And they never quite figure out why.'

So this was what Nathalie had meant by the source of their *unrivalled power*. A chill ran through Elise, not unlike her lifelong feeling of dread.

'Hitoshi saw the data and twigged what was going on,' she said.

'Actually,' said Lloyd, 'I think he had some idea before we even got to Creux Island. Look.'

He'd just turned the note over. Nathalie's list was on the other side, and one of the items read: *OS: Myriadder*. It was circled aggressively in red ink.

'See that? It's the operating system David wrote specially for the System Experiment's supercomputer. He probably recognised it and decided to check out Creux Island for himself. God knows he had ample opportunity to let Kingswell know we were going there. He had a net-ready laptop in the back of the car and neither you nor I could see what he was doing with it. Luckily for us, his curiosity got the better of him.'

'And later, so did his conscience,' added Elise, 'otherwise we wouldn't be here now. So what's our next move?'

'I'm not sure just yet. But we mustn't tell anyone about this. Let Hitoshi do the talking. We'll play along and let everyone think I sent Taylor that SOS message. I owe Hitoshi that much,' he said, holding up the datafile, 'for the ace card he's given us. We just have to wait for the right opportunity to use it. Shame he was only able to get the input data. If only we had the output, or maybe even the program itself.'

'We didn't have much time,' said Elise.

'Not this time. But we can always go back.'

Now there was a scary thought. But first things first. Elise gazed at the note and the lighter in her hand, and realised why Hitoshi had left the lighter with her.

CHAPTER THIRTY-FOUR
Know the Truth

On Sunday evening Taylor phoned the Chairman of the MWA Security Council in Washington, who in turn phoned the MWA Secretary-General in Paris, who in turn called the entire MWA Secretariat for an urgent meeting. At some point along the chain of phone calls, the news also reached Shafiq Al Badri.

The President of Egypt was in his office when he received word from his personal assistant that the attempt to destroy the enemy had failed, and that his nephew and Gregory Kingswell were dead.

Shafiq looked down and gave a long mournful sigh for the loss of his blood, his sister's son.

Then he looked up again at his assistant. 'What of Katayama?'

'He's in custody, and has agreed to testify for the prosecution.'

Shafiq was livid. Did this vermin really think he could just switch allegiance and get away with it?

'He will pay for this! Has he named names?'

'He has named Mr Kingswell,' she replied. 'And no one else.'

This was reassuring. If the Civil Office believed at worst that Gregory was one of a few individuals, the Committee would easily manage damage control. Katayama had some sense after all.

'And what has Lloyd said?'

'Nothing yet. We're awaiting his statement.'

* * * * * * * * *

On Monday afternoon Lloyd gave GAILE his statement from his hospital bed. He followed Hitoshi's instruction to tell a half-truth about the events leading up to the shooting, and to make one or two omissions as well. He told the full story about the Systems Experiment but without mentioning *them*. Instead he made a point of mentioning that as long as the courts cleared his father's name, he would be satisfied that justice had been done and that he'd accomplished all that he'd set out to do. He had no intention of pursuing the matter any further, and since the case was still classified, he wouldn't try to make it public. Elise knew these remarks were tacked on for E3's benefit, since they would likely scour his statement for anything that might implicate them. At the Harper Building she too provided a carefully crafted statement of her own, corroborating all that Lloyd had said.

Back at the hospital Lloyd requested Taylor to give him the reports on the investigation. Taylor complied, despite the fact that Lloyd was in hospital, despite the fact that the Civil Office had just officially taken over the case from Intelligence, and despite the fact that he was now acting Director of GAILE.

Elise and Lloyd read the reports together once Taylor had left. The crime scene report from René Raison Dam revealed that GAILE had found Hitoshi's laptop in the stolen minivan. It had little of interest on it except for an email to Gregory Kingswell, informing him where Lloyd was meeting Manner.

Hitoshi's confession was a masterpiece of half-truths and full lies. Gregory Kingswell had forced him to assist in a plan to eliminate Lloyd and bury the truth about the Systems Experiment once and for all. That bit at least was true. Hitoshi admitted that he'd informed Kingswell of Nathalie Weston's intention to testify against Dr Palmerton, her former boss and the brains behind the Phoenix Project. This was a half-truth omitting the part about Creux Island. As to the identity of the *third party*, Hitoshi said (as he had once told Elise) that the whole conspiracy was the work of one or two corrupt MWA officials. Conveniently he didn't know the names, but Kingswell's involvement in the cover-up soon led the CO to one of the culprits. It was surely no accident that his father, General Frank Kingswell, was a member of the MWA Security Council during the time of the Systems Experiment. Unfortunately neither father nor son was alive to be questioned, let alone be tried for the crimes; and so Hitoshi's biggest lie wrapped up the whole thing rather neatly. Even E3 would be pleased with that particular outcome.

The following morning Taylor told Elise that she was free to go home whenever she wished. If the prosecution needed her testimony at Hitoshi's trial, they would set up a video link to Alterham. But she'd already decided to extend her stay another week in the United States. DCI Johnson wouldn't mind. He'd been trying to get her to take a holiday for years.

That same morning doctors removed Lloyd's cranial implant and moved him into a regular private room. He needed a couple of nanosurgeries to help repair the tissue in his lungs and prevent scarring. These were noninvasive procedures, but at any rate he had to stay in hospital for another week. The doctors said his prognosis was excellent, and he would likely make a full recovery.

After Monday neither Elise nor Lloyd spoke much about the investigation or about Creux Island. Elise was at the hospital every single day, whiling away the hours listening to Lloyd virtually uninterrupted. She soon began to look forward to her daily visits, in part because she learned some trivial things about Joanna from him. But Elise was far more interested in hearing about the little boy born on a small island off Vancouver, who visited his fugitive father in far-off and exotic locations during school holidays. The boy grew up on his father's stories, especially the legend of the Original Conspiracy. The legend goes that human history is the record of an eternal battle between the Order of the Selfish Ones, and the Order of the Truth Seekers. Through the ages many Truth Seekers have embarked on the quest to unlock humanity's true potential. But the Selfish Ones have slandered them, murdered them, and rewritten history, all to make humanity forget and stop believing. The boy was torn between a father who expected him one day to take on the Triumvirate Committee, and a mother who was so bitter about the effects of her husband's choices on their family that she forbade her son from chasing his father's legacy. His parents had come together in trying circumstances: Farah Lloyd was the plastic surgeon who had given Omar the first and most dramatic change in removing his old identity. They'd fallen in love and married in six weeks. Their only child had come along less than a year later, and unbeknown to them this was just a few months before the surrogate mothers from the Phoenix Project also gave birth. But they'd agreed to separate whilst she was still pregnant. Though the young man respected his mother's wishes whilst she was alive, he never forgot what his father had taught him. Both his parents were gone before he was sixteen, one of heart failure, the other from leukaemia. He made his choice and joined GAILE. Elise was glad that he had, and not only because it had given her the chance to learn the truth about herself.

Each day Elise sat at his bedside and observed the little traits: The warmth of his voice, and the subtle inflexions when he spoke about those whom he loved, especially his father; the groove in his jaw that appeared only when he laughed; the spark in his faraway eyes; and the twinkling stars in his aura. Elise simply liked being around him. She also opened up to him about her own life, talking about her days in the children's home, her first days on the force, and how she introduced her two best friends who were now married. Elise found she was able to talk to Lloyd about anything. She could tell him things about herself that she'd never shared with anyone; things she'd never even confided to Stella. Once upon a time she would have kept her secrets to herself. Now she didn't think twice about it.

Her only regret was the fact that she couldn't stay.

Elise walked up the driveway to her house and unlocked the front door. She stepped inside and pulled her suitcase into the hallway. As the house was cold, she didn't take off her coat right away. She got a whiff of wallpaper stripper and old wood, and screwed up her nose. Gone for two over weeks, and the dratted smell was still in the house!

But that wasn't all.

Her stomach fluttered.

Her psychic sense had just detected some energy signatures. She couldn't be sure how many. And they were in the living room.

Elise stood still, wondering if she'd had a break-in. It was so very quiet. She took the only thing that came to hand – an umbrella in the hallway – and tiptoed towards the living room. The door was ajar. She peeked inside.

'Surprise!' shouted a roomful of voices.

The living room was transformed. The walls were painted lavender with white coving lining the top along the ceiling. The floor had a brand new deep maroon carpet, and the windows had matching curtains. Her coffee table was freshly varnished. The old lamp was still there in the middle of the ceiling, but it was now a glittering centrepiece of glass. Above her TV on the far wall was a banner reading: *Welcome Home.*

Elise dropped her brolly and looked in bewilderment to her friends, who all laughed and started clapping. Half of Alterham Police Force stood in the room – including Martin, DI Paige and even DCI Johnson. Martin handed Elise a slice of cake on a plate. The two senior officers raised a glass to her.

Stella and Mike stood immediately to her left. She smiled, put an arm around each of them and hugged them together.

'Whose idea was this?' she asked.

Mike grinned and pointed at his wife. 'Hers. She did most of it too – with a little help from yours truly.'

'It was only fair, since we made you mess up your house for that bet,' said Stella. 'You like?'

'I love it. And thank you so much. Truly. But ...' Elise sighed. 'But I do wish you'd told me before you started!'

Stella snorted. 'Well that would've spoiled the surprise!'

'Yes, but you wouldn't have wasted your time.'

'What?'

The whole room suddenly lost its zing. Smiles faded all round.

Elise blinked hard to hold back her tears. 'Oh, Stella,' she said. 'There's something I have to tell you. All of you.'

* * * * * * * * *

Tuesday, 2 December 2042: Washington, D.C.

The secret trial of Hitoshi Katayama had taken six weeks, and today he was due to be sentenced in the GAILE Coordination Center. Few people outside of GAILE knew about the secret courtroom here, which held hearings for crimes connected with international security. For Brent Taylor, this was the first time in his career of twenty plus years that he was seeing it.

In November a jury had found Hitoshi guilty of aiding and abetting in a cover-up of the truth surrounding the Wheeler Park disappearances. The sentencing might have been over and done with sooner, but the case was extremely complicated. The Wheeler Park disappearances and the Phoenix Project were still under independent judicial review, and there were several ongoing investigations into other experiments that Palmerton may have worked on. These investigations were themselves moving slowly, as the Civil Office was having trouble getting hold of reliable witnesses, in particular Nathalie Weston. She was still missing.

As Brent was heading the investigation since its transfer to the Civil Office, he was also providing the tribunal with much of the information for their inquiry. He sat among just a handful of people in the gallery at the back, and was the only GAILE officer from the CO in the courtroom. The new director of GAILE sat a few places from him with another Intelligence agent. Aaron Lloyd hadn't attended any of the proceedings. He'd testified for the prosecution by video link in the previous weeks.

'Hitoshi Katayama, please stand,' said the black-robed judge.

Hitoshi wore a well-fitted suit with a black tie, and his hair was slicked back. He stood up in the dock and faced the bench. His lawyer also rose from his seat at the counsel table, directly opposite to the bench.

Brent had heard that the best Hitoshi could hope for was a year. The maximum was likely to be nearer five.

The judge folded her arms on the polished oak desk and gave Katayama a scrutinising look.

'Mr Katayama,' she said, 'your claim that you were coerced into trapping your friends, and even your admission that it was the wrong thing to do, does not alter the fact that you chose to be an accomplice in a conspiracy involving the blatant obstruction of justice and potentially even murder. However, I have taken into account the difficulty of your position, having no less than the director of GAILE putting pressure on you, and the fact that you have shown remorse and taken full responsibility for your actions. Nevertheless, due to the seriousness of the crime I'm obliged to make an example of you. So you are hereby sentenced to five years in the state penitentiary, with no possibility of parole.'

Hitoshi stared forward with an expression of acceptance.

But the judge hadn't yet finished. 'This sentence is suspended for three years.'

Hitoshi's eyes turned to his lawyer in subdued astonishment.

The judge went on. 'If you commit another federal, state or local crime within this time, you will serve this term in full. Make sure that you stay out of trouble Mr Katayama.' Then she added: 'Because we're always watching.'

CHAPTER THIRTY-FIVE
Until Tomorrow

The couple arrived at The Chase on the first Saturday of the new year. He wore a crisp midnight shirt and dark pants. She wore an ivory flowing dress cut at the knee, and holographic hummingbird earrings. He led her by the hand through the crowd on the dance floor, where strobe lighting intermittently snapped over the scores of people in time to the beat of the blaring music, and the bass vibrated through the floor. But they weren't here to dance.

They headed straight to the bar, where she was the first to see the man in a yellow leisure suit and a loose red tie. He was gazing into his drink. Everything about him was the same, except for his hair, which was jet black.

He had his back to them, but he became aware of their presence before they'd quite reached him. He looked up and lifted his glass to them in acknowledgment. Without saying anything he rose from his stool. They followed him backstage, where the walls buffered the sound of the music, and the air was cooler. A radio chattered in the hallway.

They went into the dressing room.

As Aaron and Elise each took a stool, Hitoshi closed the door and stood against the dressing table.

'Well, if it isn't Elise Archer and Agent Numbskull,' he said.

'Hey, you can't call me that anymore,' said Aaron. 'I had my chip removed a long time ago.'

'Who ever said I was talking about your chip?'

Aaron laughed dryly.

'How are you, Hitoshi?' asked Elise. 'We went to your apartment today and Tami said you'd moved out.'

'Yeah, we split up a couple of months back.' Hitoshi glanced at the diamond ring on Elise's left finger as he took a cigarette from his shirt pocket. 'She wanted more than I could give her. No big deal. But we're still working together. And the band's doing well.' He lit up. 'So … when's the big day?'

'End of the month,' said Elise with a smile.

'Congratulations. Both of you.'

For once he actually sounded sincere.

'You're invited, of course,' said Aaron.

'Great. Now are we going to talk domestics all night, or are we going to get to the point?'

Aaron and Elise looked at one another.

He took the lead. 'All right,' he said, 'we wanted to talk to you about the data from Creux Island.'

'No kidding.'

'You gave us just the input data. I know you had no time for anything else, but still, it's pretty useless on its own. A copy of the program would be far more useful.'

'Sure,' said Hitoshi. 'But even if I'd had the time to get onto that network, I couldn't have given you the program in a useful form. It would have been just the source code, which would be no good to you. Only someone who knows how to compile and execute the program could do anything useful with it.'

'Like a hacker?' said Aaron.

'Like a hacker,' he replied innocently.

Aaron looked at him suspiciously. 'Tell me something. Have you still got access to the system?'

Hitoshi blew out some smoke.

'… Or have you already been back there?'

Hitoshi was about to put his cigarette to his lips. His hand stopped midair, as though he was thinking twice about sharing whatever was on his mind.

'Well, have you?' asked Elise anxiously.

The Shaman indulged himself in the draw. He peered at them from behind his dark fringe.

And he gave them a devilish smile.

Radio Hadescape!

CHAZ
Good evening folks and welcome back to the Late Night Show live with Chaz and Danny! We've got a great lineup for you in the next hour – but first, here's an odd bit of news for you. I caught this in the papers yesterday – some of our listeners out there might have seen it too – you remember a few months ago, when Hadescape was hit by the "ATM robber"?

DANNY
Oh yeah, I remember that story! You're talking about that guy who went round mugging people at ATM machines?

CHAZ
That's the one. And then he disappeared, urban myth style!

DANNY
Ah, you should have seen Chaz's face just then, folks. It was something spooky!

CHAZ
Do you know the latest?

DANNY
Nah, I missed it.

CHAZ
Well, he's back!

DANNY
Oh no!

CHAZ
But not to rob anyone! Don't worry! Instead – get this - he's been giving people their money back!

DANNY
What? You're having me on!

CHAZ
I'm not! This is absolutely true! A man in a trench coat and a baseball cap has been to three different banks this week and handed in the money, along with the credit cards he stole. A total of over a thousand dollars!

DANNY
He's really given them their money back?

CHAZ
He has! And now ... he's disappeared again!

DANNY
Whoa! Wonder where he went?

CHAZ
What I want to know is: Where did he get the money?

DANNY
Good question! Hmm ... maybe he won the lottery! Or he went to another town – some place with richer people to rob!

CHAZ
Uh, Danny, that's just silly. He probably just got himself a job.

DANNY
Ha ha! Now that'd be something! If you're listening, ATM robber dude, drop us a line and let us know what you're doing these days! We won't tell anyone! And while we wait for him to call, we've got a song for you – we've had a number of requests for this one – by an up and coming band from right here in Hadescape ... Here's The Glitch, with "My Fate" ...

* * * * * * * *

MY FATE

I should live just for today
But I can't forget last night
I'm unsure of what I want
Let alone of how to fight

And in the silence I hear
'This is my fate'
Conflicted voices in my ear
Tell me, tell me, 'this is my fate'

So you promised me the dawn
But I never saw the light
Let's pretend there's nothing wrong
It's too late to make things right

The odds are stacked against me
This is my fate
No one can see what I can see
I know this is my fate

I'm torn in two
No matter what I do
The outcome will be the same
A hell of a choice
Like a double-headed coin
So I lose the game
Either way
This is my fate
This is my fate

Like a loaded die
And only I know
Just what is at stake
How much is at stake

I'm torn in two
No matter what I do
The outcome will be the same
A hell of a choice
Like a double-headed coin
So I lose the game
Either way

I'm torn in two
No matter what I do
The outcome will be the same
A hell of a choice
Like a double-headed coin
So I lose the game
Either way
This is my fate
This is my fate
This is my fate

Is this my fate?

* * * * * * * *

LIBREDUX.COM

www.ingramcontent.com/pod-product-compliance
Lightning Source LLC
Chambersburg PA
CBHW031056260626
47172CB00001B/103